Cathedrals of Venom

RENNEY SENN

Cathedrals of Venom

Acknowledgments

While the Cathedrals of Venom story is my own creation, my better part, Susie, was invaluable in both copyediting and proofreading modes. Invariably, she would have cogent reasons why a character would not react the way I had written it, or how an important element should occur at a different point in the story. Simultaneously, she would spot errant commas and grammatical problems. I found her ability to detect minute logical and as well as plot sequential errors very impressive. I am also profoundly grateful to our son, Christian, who has created another masterful cover design. Throughout, this has been a true family affair, something that has been deeply satisfying for each of us.

Also by Renney Senn

The Turncoat
Hidden Insight

1

1865 - Chicago

Fritz's mother kept a nervous eye on her ten-year-old son as they walked past the ramshackle box frame houses lining the street of a long-depressed Chicago neighborhood. As usual, Martha found these outings a way to briefly escape a terrorizing marital relationship that had failed years before. She had spent unending hours poring over what had gone wrong with her fairy tale marriage to Ernst Graff and what the future held for her and her son.

When she and Ernst met a dozen years before, she was mesmerized by his good looks, his gifted, if unorthodox, intellect, and the excitement gushing from his outsized personality that could swing wildly from one extreme to another. He also lived in a lavish home that gave him the appearance of wealth, an impression he was desperate to maintain.

The way Ernst first told her his story, his family founded the prosperous Chicago Overland Transport Company that hauled merchandise back and forth by wagon between Chicago and St. Louis in the early 1830s. Concurrently, they were speculators in Chicago real estate, plowing their company's profits into land ventures that had increased in value a thousandfold by the middle of the decade. This high point was where he always ended his story.

Before meeting Ernst, Martha and her family had suffered during the periodic financial panics of the mid-1800s. They were painfully aware of how even wealthy people could end up in the poorhouse quickly. This experience made her wonder how the Graffs had seemed to glide through the period unfazed. When asked, Ernst always found a way to make it sound as if the secret to his family's success was shrewd business acumen that required an advanced level of financial sophistication to comprehend. The first hints that there might be more to the Graff story than Martha knew arose within months of their meeting when the family canceled its annual trip to Europe. When asked about it, Ernst attributed the decision to urgent business needs that required his family's presence. A few months later, Martha noticed that the Graff's butler was no longer anywhere to be seen. When she inquired, Fritz told her that the man had family health challenges that forced him to quit.

Both of these events occurred during a recession when Martha and Ernst were courting. The abrupt changes left her curious but not concerned enough to call off their engagement, something she would later regret. Only after they were married would Martha come face-to-face with a reality that was devastating and revealed a deep fissure in Ernst's character. She eventually learned that the family's financial decline had begun seventeen years earlier when a severe downturn obliterated its Chicago real estate holdings. This loss led to a series of failed ventures that further drained the family's resources. To complete the tragedy, all of this had occurred as the Graffs' Chicago Overland Transport Company was suffering a slow and painful death caused by the mid-century opening of the Illinois and Michigan canal, making their company's failure inevitable.

By 1855, Ernst and Martha had been married over a year, and he was unable to sustain the illusion of wealth any longer. Martha was on the verge of delivering her first baby, Fritz, when Ernst admitted his long-maintained fraud. By the end of the Civil War, Ernst's family had been living in poverty for a decade.

These were some of Martha's thoughts as she walked home with her son. She had taken Fritz to a nearby park in the early afternoon to escape the stifling temperatures inside, give the boy a chance to work off some energy, and then stop by the grocery store on the way home. Having commiserated with other mothers about the challenges of raising a child, Martha was well aware that many kids have tantrums now and then. Much to her dismay, however, it was just after Fritz's second birthday that she became convinced that her son was different. His predisposition to fly off the handle into an uncontrollable rage after the most trivial provocation inevitably led to his inability to subdue his fury for extended periods. Her son's mercurial nature kept her apprehensive as she struggled to fulfill her daily parental chores.

"Come along, Fritz, please keep up. You know we have to get home before it's completely dark or your father'll be angry," she said when her son stopped to kick some leaves into the street. A few minutes later, they were standing on a corner while Martha waited impatiently for a horse and carriage to pass before crossing the street and getting home. She would always feel relieved when Fritz was finally inside their house, where the boy's unpredictable and uncontrollable temper could erupt out of the shocked view of strangers.

As they came to the narrow stairs that rose to the front door, Fritz's mother looked into one of the house's front windows. She had expected her husband to have returned home from work before they arrived and found it odd that the downstairs was still dark. As she forced open the front door that had been sticking for months, she felt annoyed that her husband had ignored lighting the candles when he got home. She had forced herself to get used to the awful smell of the burning fat, which was a constant, irritating reminder that they were unable to afford the slightly more expensive paraffin candles with their far less offensive odor. Shaking her head, she announced their return as she lit a couple of hall candles and then entered the kitchen to light more of them before putting away some groceries. "We're back," she shouted again. Ignoring the absence of a reply, she began putting away the food.

Trudging upstairs to his room, Fritz was looking forward to playing with several toy Union soldiers and a miniature cannon that his mother had given him as a secret present. He had never received such extravagant gifts in his life and was thrilled when his mother gave them to him. She knew that they would help calm his temper, providing hours of diversion for both her and her son, a break in an otherwise bleak existence.

He also knew that his father had nothing to do with the sliver of happiness the toys afforded him. The young boy had no memory of kindness or even an encouraging word from him. His only recollections were of his father's ceaseless taunting and criticism with an occasional slap to punctuate his verbal abuse. He had always been puzzled by his father's resentment of his existence from the moment he was born. Convinced that his father hated him, he believed that what he felt in return was something similar.

At the moment, however, his father was furthest from the young boy's mind as he entered his converted-attic bedroom. Instead, he was preoccupied with the new toys he knew were sitting on his bed. Most of the long room was barely visible from the last vestiges of dusk entering through its one open window. As he plopped down on his bed, eager to play with his soldiers, he suddenly had a vague awareness of something unusual nearby. Struggling to see down the length of his dark room, he heard an unfamiliar, faint creaking sound that seemed to be coming from the exposed wooden rafters that crossed the room overhead. As his eyes slowly adapted to the dimly-lit room, the source of the sound took shape. He began screaming.

Instantly panicked by her son's shrieking, Martha dropped several cans of soup as she dashed out of the kitchen and raced upstairs. Looking into the room, she could barely make out the shape of her son sitting on his bed just inside the open door. He was still screaming, transfixed by what his mother was not yet able to see.

Despite her frantic effort to calm him, Fritz continued to wail. Unable to quell her son's hysteria, she struggled to look down the dark oblong room at what was terrifying him. Desperate to penetrate the semidarkness, she squinted and froze.

About fifteen feet away, she was barely able to make out the shape of her husband suspended over an overturned chair with a leather belt cinched around his neck, twisting very slowly in the warm breeze wafting in through the window. An overpowering morbid fascination glued her eyes to her husband's body while beckoning to her to slowly approach the hanging corpse. She could see that his neck was ravaged with claw marks, his tongue protruding from jaws that had slammed shut, nearly severing it.

Badly shaken with her knees barely able to support her, Martha finally recovered her senses enough to turn to her son as he continued to shriek. Leaning over unsteadily, she grabbed him by the shoulders, averted his gaze from the horrific image, and stammered. "Settle down, Fritz.... Now just settle down. Come with me.... Come away.... Come on now," she said, trying vainly to use the soothing words to calm them both while they slowly walked out of the room.

It was nearly forty-five minutes before several police officers arrived at the Graff residence and began inspecting the house for signs of foul play. In the kitchen, Fritz was already sitting with one officer, a warm and friendly middle-aged man, who was doing his best to distract the young boy with some amateur magic tricks and stories. After Chief Detective Garner introduced himself to Martha, they sat down in the small living room as he took out his notepad to record her version of events.

"I'm very sorry for your and your son's loss, Mrs. Graff. It's a tragedy when something like this happens, especially when it's a family member who discovers the deceased. We'll do our best to determine as quickly as possible if there's anything more to this than meets the eye. In the meantime, please feel free to call on me or Sergeant Mallory if you need anything or you think of something that you believe can help us with our investigation." Looking over his shoulder at Sergeant Mallory and Fritz, who were both still engaged in conversation, he observed, "One good thing, the sergeant appears to have been successful at calming your son a bit. I hope there's a friend or relative you can stay with until things settle down."

"Yes, detective, there is. My sister lives only a mile or so away. We'll be moving in with her for the time being."

Detective Garner had been through this situation too many times to be unsettled by the stunned soul sitting in front of him. He also knew that before the book closed on this apparent suicide, he would be speaking with the Graffs' neighbors to learn what he could about the entire family.

The first thing the following morning, he was interviewing both next-door neighbors. "It's real shocking news, officer! I just can't believe it. My God, right next door! What a horrible thing for Mrs. Graff and Fritz to have to witness. I never knew the Graffs real well, though. They pretty much kept to themselves. Mrs. Graff seemed nice enough the few times I seen her, but Mr. Graff, well, he was always real cold, real distant—seemed real unfriendly. You didn't want to be around him, so I can't tell you much about the man. I actually saw the kid more than his parents. If you ask me, his father's the reason the kid's so mixed up."

"What makes you say he's mixed up, ma'am?" inquired the detective.

"Oh, everybody knows it, officer. Even when Fritz was real little, everybody saw there was somethin' real wrong with him. Me, I always thought he had a wild appearance with those light, starey eyes and that wild head o' straight blond hair. He always looks like he's gonna do somethin' bad. But the worst thing's that violent temper o' his whenever he thinks someone's crossed him. My God, he's always bruised 'n bloodied up from school or neighborhood fights."

"Anything else you can think of, ma'am?"

"Ah no...no, that's all that comes t'mind fer now, officer."

"Thank you for your time. You've been very helpful," said the detective as he headed for the door to speak with the other neighbor.

After he knocked and introduced himself, the neighbor invited him into her living room. "So, you've known the Graff family as long as they've lived here?"

"That's right, officer."

"Can you tell me what Mr. Graff did for a living?" inquired the detective as he took out his notepad.

"My, oh my, now that's a real story. I ain't thought 'bout these things in a long time 'n don't know all the details 'n stuff, but I remember somebody tellin' me that once the Graffs was real rich. If I r'member right, I think his company was called the Chicago Overland Transport Company, or somethin' like that. That's till it went in the crapper. I think it's gotta be almost twenty years ago or so when that big canal got put in that let barges reach the Mississippi from here. From that day on, I guess their company's days was numbered.

"I heard tell they used to live in some big mansion or somethin'. After they had to step way down 'n move in here, I r'member hearin' the ol' man blamin' everything on—well I r'member just how he put it—he'd shout real loud 'bout 'the goddamned Jews who gave the goddamned money for the goddamned canal to be built in the first place.' God, I musta heard that comin' outta his mouth ten times a day. Then it got real bad, but it wasn't 'bout just the Jews—he was even blamin' poor Martha and Fritz. I'd hear him shoutin' somethin' horrible 'n then I'd hear crashes 'n…well, anyway, it ain't somethin' nobody wants t' hear.

"Oh yeah, the kid went through some kinda hell with that father o' his. I guess we shouldn't had to wonder 'bout where he got his dark, well, his real bad temper. Some of us thought maybe it was from growin' up in Chicago with the Civil War 'n all. Or maybe just somethin' real dark that'd been growin' inside him from when he was born. The more I saw 'n heard, though, the more it seemed real clear t'me that it came from his father."

"After his business failed, was Mr. Graff able to provide for his family?" probed the detective.

"I think they was real stretched all the time, to tell ya the truth. I do r'member him tryin' some other businesses, but nothin' worked. Now you tell me he done himself in. To me, it ain't no secret why. With everythin' havin' gone bad for s'long, I think he had one thing left he could do to show jus' how much he hated this world 'n everybody in it. He knew he could hurt both Martha and Fritz if he hung himself in the boy's bedroom where it'd be the kid who'd find him first. Yeah, he really seemed t'have it in for that kid o' his. He knew Fritz'd be terrified and Martha'd be ruined by what it done to her.…Real evil if you ask me. Just pure evil, that's what it was."

2

1871

Over the next several years, Martha struggled to keep her little family afloat. As Fritz entered his teens, he showed no sign of outgrowing his chronically fragile, violent emotional condition. Despite this, Martha took solace in watching him become a clever and extremely ambitious young man and felt hopeful when he began obsessing over stories of the meteoric rise of the powerful men who would later become known as Robber Barons. "Perhaps," she thought, "he's going to make something of himself after all."

Driven by these tales of real and imagined success and a steely determination to repudiate his father's final violent rejection of him, Fritz was sixteen when he thrust himself into his first enterprise. It was late 1871 when his chance arose out of the ashes of his hometown's infamous 2,000-acre blazing maelstrom that quickly became known as the Great Chicago Fire. In one day, Fritz witnessed the inferno devour virtually the entire city. The sudden and vast devastation promptly gave rise to widespread legends of horror and heroism.

Fritz saw neither. Instead, he saw a great opportunity. With so many established construction businesses suddenly in ruins, he used the overwhelming chaos and desperation to persuade a few remaining lumber yards and hardware stores to permit him to deliver their construction materials all over the destroyed city. Despite his hatred for his father, Fritz hearkened back to the family's once-successful transport business and borrowed a horse and wagon to get his new endeavor off the ground. Almost immediately, his reliability and speed of response earned him a reputation that, in the reckless and ruthless opportunism of the moment, made his fledgling business explode. Within weeks he had several young people working for him while his little venture started earning a respectable profit.

One year later, Fritz had accumulated enough money to open a business he had been mulling over ever since his delivery business had started to show a glimmer of success. Now seventeen, Fritz had not completed high school, but his innate curiosity and passion for reading had aroused in him a love of science and business. To pursue his dream, he approached a neighbor, Michael Rudman, who was a charming, young, newly-minted chemist he had befriended before the great fire. Rudman had impressed him with his knowledge of advanced chemistry and his ambitious nature. Using Fritz's capital, his friend's scientific knowledge, and the driven characters of both, the two young men laid the cornerstone of Graff Chemical with an initial product line of agricultural pesticides.

It was only two years after the company opened its doors that Michael first witnessed signs of future trouble with his partner. In rapid succession, Graff Chemical lost two potentially lucrative contracts to develop pesticide compounds to other, well-established firms outside of Chicago. While Michael was depressed by the loss, Fritz became obsessed, unable to either control or dissipate his anger. Once they learned of the second missed contract, Fritz flew into a rage, destroying his desk and chair and then throwing a small library of technical manuals across the room. Regardless of what he did to try to calm the storm, Michael was unable to defuse his partner's fury. After Fritz bashed his fist into a wall creating a dent with radiating cracks that would forever act as an omen for Michael, he flew out of the office, his rage unabated. Michael now saw his partner as someone whose shrewdness could be trumped by his inability to cope emotionally with the inevitable setbacks of business.

The following day, Fritz entered Graff Chemical's front door, and Michael looked up to welcome him. "Good morning, Fritz. I hope that you're feeling in a better frame of mind than when I last saw you," he said, unable to hide his leeriness.

"Those sons-of-bitches'll regret not giving us that business, Rudman! Mark my words," replied Fritz as his eyes flashed once again. Michael had always been struck by his partner's consistent use of his last name in conversation. The young chemist took it as Fritz's way of distancing himself from any intimacy as if he were hiding something. Had their business not been growing so dramatically, Michael knew he would have little interest in sticking around long enough to see what other dark recesses there could be inside his partner. It took several months of Graff Chemical's success before Fritz was finally able to get past his rage. Michael became convinced that such a readily-provoked, deep-seated fury was an ominous warning for their mushrooming business.

Graff Chemical's growth over the next several years enabled the two young men to penetrate social circles that earlier would have been unthinkable. It was at a spectacular birthday celebration for the scion of one of the city's industrialists where Fritz became smitten with Anne Gottfried, the enchanting daughter of a highly successful local merchant. Despite his tendency to fly into rages, Fritz could also exhibit considerable charm. His charisma and his burgeoning success were a potion for the young lady, and they began dating a few days later. After two months, they were married. Eight months later, they found themselves in the maternity ward of Chicago's recently opened German Hospital.

The first time Fritz and Anne were to meet their newborn son, Maximilian, she was smiling with wondrous anticipation despite having endured a prolonged and agonizing labor. In contrast to Anne's eager demeanor, the nurse approached the hospital bed soberly and handed Anne her baby wrapped in swaddling blankets. After removing them to examine her child, Anne reacted with a mixture of love, shock, and horror as Fritz quickly backed away stiffly as if to avoid being afflicted. The nurse also stepped backward when Anne reared her head and wailed, "What's happened to my baby?! What's wrong with him?! What's wrong with him?!"

The second he heard the ruckus, the delivery doctor ran into the specially outfitted hospital room, scolding the nurse for disobeying his instructions that he was to present the mother with her baby. With her eyes overflowing with tears, Anne appeared to be in a mild state of shock as the doctor explained, "I'm so sorry, Mr. And Mrs. Graff, but your child has been born with what is called a club foot. Unfortunately, this is a fairly common condition and does not mean that your child will necessarily suffer any other health problems. We may be able to take some limited corrective action, but I'm afraid that his right foot and his ability to walk will never be normal."

"Goddamn this! Goddamn him! Goddamn you all! This abomination will never be my Maximilian Graff!" shouted Fritz suddenly as the doctor, his nurse, and Anne winced in shocked silence. Fritz stormed out of the room, as the other three adults looked at one another, perplexed by what could be going through the man's mind.

By the time Maximilian was three years old, his awkward hobbling had receded in Anne's mind, but Fritz had never forgiven her or their son for his deformity. The only saving grace for the little boy was that his intelligence counterbalanced his disfiguring physical impairment. Since Anne's tortured labor had left her unable to have more children, Fritz saw his son's intellect as little more than a better-than-nothing attribute that would one day be important for Graff Chemical. Despite his physical deformity, Fritz knew it was inevitable that young Maximilian would one day inherit and head one of the most successful chemical companies in the Midwest.

3

1893

Graff Chemical's twenty-first year opened with severe snow and ice storms that made Chicago's roads often impassable. Regardless of the cold outside, Fritz Graff and his partner, Michael Rudman, were basking in the warmth of five blockbuster years for their company. Pesticides for farmers throughout the Central and Midwestern US had been Graff Chemical's golden goose, catapulting it into the ranks of some of the fastest-growing companies in the country. As the business and scientific heads of a company that now employed nearly three hundred people, both Fritz and Michael had become very wealthy men. To enhance the company's profits, Fritz had steadily invested the firm's returns into a large number of high-yield bonds held by a variety of Chicago financial institutions.

It was not long before the first signs of trouble appeared. "Have you seen this, Fritz?" asked Michael as he looked across the front page of the Chicago Tribune at the beginning of the workweek. "The Philadelphia and Reading Railroad has gone into receivership. I remember some of our banking friends telling me that they were badly overextended, but can you believe it?"

"Now that's just bad management, Rudman. Nothing but poor leadership. I'd never let us get into such a state of weakness. You just keep tending to the chemistry. I'll handle the business side, and we'll never get into such a mess."

By midyear, it was clear that the Philadelphia and Reading Railroad had been the nation's warning of impending calamity. Virtually no industry was unaffected by what became known as the Panic of 1893, with thousands of businesses and banks failing at a dizzying rate. In contrast to the self-satisfaction that Fritz had felt when the year had begun, his worse fears exploded when the vast majority of the company's bonds vanished, having been issued by many banks that had ceased to exist overnight. Just as bad was the hatred of his father that was suddenly washing over him as he saw history repeating itself, proving himself undeniably worthy of his father's rejection.

As winter approached, the Panic had devastated the nation, wiping out the savings of much of the middle-class. Graff Chemical's business plunged as its domestic golden goose farming industry fell into insolvency, aggravated by the collapse of the international wheat market.

The Graff Chemical bonds that had not been lost enabled it to hang on, but if their dormant market did not recover soon, Fritz and Michael were now in jeopardy of the company collapsing. As Michael had feared so many years before, his partner's lurking inner monster soon unleashed itself on him and their enterprise.

A fateful conversation between the two men began innocently enough as they wrestled with alternatives to the ever-tightening vice now squeezing their company's prospects. The exchange descended rapidly after Michael suggested a possible new market opportunity.

"Well, of course, goddamnit, Rudman!" shouted Fritz, "We can't just open up new markets overnight! Trust you to think you could actually come up with any real business solutions. Perhaps if your so-called scientific talent had been stronger, we wouldn't be in this mess!"

Still able to control his anger, Michael responded. "How can you say that, Fritz?! Our problems have nothing to do with science! Our business has dried up in a matter of weeks, and our reserves are almost gone!"

It was only a few more seconds before Fritz crossed a fatal line. "Well, goddamnit, that's another thing, Rudman! If you'd used just a little bit of that huge Jew brain of yours and looked into what other places we could be putting our money, we'd be in a hell of a lot better shape! Isn't that what you kikes are supposed to be so goddamned good at, money?! What the hell happened with you?! Are you really even a Jew, Rudman! I didn't know Jews could be so goddamned dumb! No wonder the world hates you goddamned people so much! You're a fucking worthless piece of shit and always have been! You've done nothing but suck off of me and my money for years, you parasitic fuck!"

The dark beast Michael Rudman had feared ever since he saw it smash its fist into the office wall so many years before was now standing before him, shaking with rage. Seeing the inevitable end to this conversation that he would never forget, Michael stared into the wild eyes of his seething verbal assailant. He issued a decree that had been lying dormant in his mind for years.

"Enough, Graff! Enough! I've had it! No more! You're a monster! I quit! I'm no longer part of Graff Chemical, a company that you never could've built without me! How dare you condemn someone who's been so faithful and protective of you, even when you were so often at your most ridiculous! I'm no longer your partner, and I won't ever have to see you, speak to you, or listen to your wretched insults again as long as I live! For years I've known there is evil inside you and that someday I'd have to confront it. Well, that day is today! Now that the hideous and evil, slithering creature that lurks inside you has come out in the open in all of its ugliness, I won't have anything more to do with you anymore! You're a monumental disgrace to the human race!" Michael then turned and stalked out of the office, slamming the door shut.

Fritz's fury now had no place to go except into the destruction of everything within reach. With spit and invectives shooting out of his mouth, the crazed animal of a man picked up and threw everything in the office against the walls before taking the remaining vestiges of the furniture and crashing them on the ground leaving the entire room a shambles with large dents and holes in every wall.

Beyond any ability to control himself, he fumbled feverishly with the doorknob until he finally clutched it and slammed the door open. Stomping out of the office, he yelled through the executive offices, several of which were still occupied by men who were cowering behind their desks, "You fucking bastard! You never were worth a damn! You're the cause of all this, and I'll see you burn in Hell! That's right! Burn in Hell! You're nothing, Rudman! You're worse than nothing! You goddamned kike!"

Spinning around, in one last gesture of violent futility, he bashed both arms into the office door's obscured glass, sending shards flying before kicking his foot through the door and ripping it from its hinges. After several seconds of hearing nothing but Fritz's labored breathing, the other executives instinctively ducked when the office's top door hinge crashed to the ground shattering the only sizeable piece of door glass left. His employees frozen, the wild man dashed out of the shambles of his office and through the corridor of the executive offices before racing down three flights of stairs and charging out the front door of Graff Chemical's executive building.

4

1914

Fritz's son was just nine years old on that watershed day when Michael Rudman rid himself of Fritz and Graff Chemical forever. Maximilian's physical anomaly had already barred him from playing sports of any kind at school and instead had made him the object of his classmates' endless ridicule.

Now at thirty, Maximilian was an imposing figure, despite his deformed right foot. He was a tall, imperious man with a violent disposition even worse than his father's. As a visible warning to everyone, Maximilian shared Fritz's incessant frown. Unlike his starkly blond father, however, Maximilian had a head of thick black hair that he always combed straight back in slick dark grooves. To make his appearance even more daunting, he had grown a large, black mustache that covered the width of his entire upper lip and crested over it like a wave.

Unfortunately, the two decades since Michael Rudman's departure from Graff Chemical had not been long enough for Maximilian to get past that day, much less forgive its central characters. "Goddamnit! I'll never get over it! It still makes me blind with rage just thinking about it," he said as he hobbled around his office, barely aware that his new senior executive, Karl Stampf, was even in the room. Karl knew his boss well and what to expect when he saw Maximilian periodically release his extreme, irrepressible fury whenever he recalled the day so many years before that had nearly destroyed Graff Chemical. Maximilian's experience and memory of the event had poisoned his relationship with his father and, by association, his father's partner forever.

"How that shit-stinking Jew could allow my father—my goddamned father—to be so goddamned dumb to put all that money into bonds that nearly sank the company and then walk out on him! It makes me want to kill them both, that's what it does!… That's enough! I have to think of something else before I explode! Get out, Stampf! Just leave and get some work done."

As he rose to leave Maximilian's office, Karl immediately recalled how the uncontrollable rage of his boss's father had finally destroyed the Graff family. He remembered how Maximilian had once told him how his father had been so blind with fury at Michael Rudman's sudden departure that he could barely walk home without almost hurling himself to the ground several times. Then how he stormed through his front door and before his wife, Anne, could get out of the way, threw her against the wall. His assault was so violent that she caromed off the wall and went headlong into a massive newel post at the bottom of their main stairway. After repeated, unsuccessful attempts to revive her, Fritz yelled for his butler to summon a doctor who lived three properties away.

Nine-year-old Maximilian had been in a different part of the mansion when he heard echoes of the ruckus. Karl recalled how Maximilian described his desperate hobbling to the entrance and seeing the open front door with his mother lying lifelessly, her head resting in a large red pool, while his father, kneeling by her, yelled for the doctor. In the end, the arrival of the physician was in vain. Maximilian's mother remained in a coma for a year before finally succumbing. Her loss destroyed the Graff family and scarred Maximilian with a more severe version of the same emotional defect that had afflicted his father—a volcanic, unquenchable rage.

Karl also recalled how, after Michael Rudman's abrupt departure, Maximilian's father had immediately descended into an emotionally lethal morass of self-pity and violent anger as time proved him unable to recover his company's prior success. Instead, over the next two decades, Fritz entered into a long series of marginal chemical contracts that kept Graff Chemical alive but only as a skeleton of its former self. Even when his son was an adult and bright, Fritz summarily ignored all his son's pleas to have any role at the company. Then in 1914, just as Maximilian turned thirty and Europe was nearing the threshold of war, Fritz was hit with a massive, paralyzing stroke. At long last, Maximilian was able to turn his back on years of frustration at being denied any role at all and seize the reins of Graff Chemical.

Shortly after taking the helm, Maximilian hired Karl Stampf, a stellar young manager, to oversee operations as he threw himself into rebuilding Graff Chemical. Within months of the European war's onset, Graff Chemical had won many contracts to develop toxic products for the US Government's recently formed Chemical Warfare Service, or CWS. By the following year, Graff Chemical became one of the primary beneficiaries of CWS's plan to stockpile chemical weapons as it became clear that the US would likely not be able to avoid entering the war. The financial future for Maximilian and his company was beginning to look promising.

The US government had saved the company, and as the Great War reached its conclusion, Graff Chemical continued its growth with a rapidly increasing number of commercial products. Instead of steadily building on his success and taking the occasional downturn in stride, however, Maximilian became increasingly obsessed with dominating the US chemical industry. Since Maximilian was facing other, much larger competitors, Karl knew that his boss's new fixation meant that it would not be long before he would witness the same kind of mindless rage that had made Michael Rudman a casualty of Graff Chemical so many years before. Unlike his predecessor, however, Karl was strong enough to withstand his boss's fury, having long ago made the decision never to resist the demands of the steadily darkening Maximilian Graff.

Karl saw his boss's descent steepen long after the Great War when an odd opportunity presented itself to the increasingly domination-obsessed Maximilian. Well into the Roaring Twenties, it was clear that Prohibition had been dramatically unsuccessful at imposing itself on a culture that was not about to stifle its love for alcohol. Maximilian was part of this "wet" culture. When asked if he could create an additive for a non-prescription, high-alcohol medicine called Jamaica ginger, or Jake, to make it more palatable, he wasted no time seizing the opportunity. The chemical that Maximilian introduced was designed to overcome the federal government's attempt to make the non-prescription Jake taste so awful that people would avoid it, despite its seventy to eighty percent alcohol content. In short order, Graff Chemical was selling vast amounts of its additive to profit-hungry Jamaica ginger distributors. Always suspicious of the toxicity of his additive, Maximilian had heeded Karl's advice from the outset and sold the chemical compound through several layers of carefully selected intermediaries to insulate Graff Chemical from potential liability. This decision proved to be critical when the additive was later discovered to cause severe neurological damage. Afflicting tens of thousands of mostly immigrants and poor people desperate to use anything they could afford to escape their wretched lives even fleetingly, Jake eventually became a public symbol of the powerful once again destroying the lives of the helpless for profit.

After an extensive investigation, the federal government finally announced it was coming after all Jake distributors for the countless lives they had destroyed. Maximilian had no illusions that if Graff Chemical's involvement were ever uncovered, it could kill the company. It would be one more catastrophic failure for the Graff name, one that he knew his constitution would never permit him to survive. Unaware that it was infecting him, Maximilian's growing obsession with his company's survival ushered in a dark transformation that would soon overtake him. On the other hand, Karl was confident that the arrangements he had set up with so many intermediaries would successfully hide the company's involvement. The awareness also haunted him that something awful was growing inside his boss.

5

1935 - Long Island, New York

The Long Island Railroad constantly lurched as it made one of its summer weekend journeys from Penn Station in Manhattan to the farthest stretches of the island. Years later, it would be said that an evil destiny had placed two very different men together on this train. At least on the outside, they appeared as if they were almost two separate species. Oscar Hahn was a blond twenty-nine-year-old with piercing, light-blue eyes that seemed to radiate from under his robust, golden eyebrows. The angular features of his face and the carefully-manicured mustache made him a handsome man. Many took his slender frame and extremities and agile manner as an indication that he was probably a professional athlete. The man's grace and ease were perfect complements to the polished way he expressed himself.

Sitting across from him was a man whose sole similarity was having the same age. Gus Erstad constantly fidgeted with hands that terminated in fingernails bitten back to the quick. A large, bulbous, closely-cropped head was punctuated by two dark eyes that were disconcertingly close to one another and darted back and forth ceaselessly. His oversized skull sat squarely on a bull neck that strained the limits of the top button of his slightly soiled white shirt but was in keeping with the rest of his hardened bulk. Ill at ease with others, he found chatting challenging and rarely desirable. Despite Gus's hesitation, the two ended up shortening their two-hour train trip with a conversation that both assumed would be forgotten the minute they disembarked.

"It's a coincidence that we're both going to Yaphank," observed Oscar pleasantly. "I'm visiting a new camp that my organization has recently opened there. We're calling it Camp Siegfried, after the legendary German hero."

After a prolonged pause, Gus responded, "Ah, I'm goin' to see some friends o' mine. Ain't never been there b'fore."

"You'll like it. It's a pleasant little community," said Oscar as he extended his hand. "By the way, my name's Oscar Hahn."

"Oscar," replied Gus with an awkward nod that displayed his unease as he extended a meaty hand that engulfed Oscar's slender fingers. "Erstad, Gus Erstad." The heavy physicality of the handshake made Oscar feel slightly unsettled.

Oscar spoke from the beginning with polished ease while it took Gus considerably more time before he was comfortable enough to reveal the true nature of his visit.

"So, you're part o'…what'd'ya say's the name of your group again?" asked Gus.

"We're called Friends of the New Germany," explained Oscar. "We've gone through several names over the years, but with Herr Hitler having become the Führer of Germany two years ago, he's the strength and brilliance of a revitalized Germany. He is truly superhuman. To me, he's nothing less than godlike."

As Oscar expanded on what his organization stood for, Gus was intrigued by the man's gushing enthusiasm and hard-edged points of view. It was not long before they discovered that, despite their vastly different backgrounds, their deepest, most virulent passions were remarkably similar.

"You from Germany? Sounds t'me like ya are," observed Gus.

"My parents emigrated from there, but I was born in Chicago," replied Oscar. "One thing I'll say about my family, we all love this country, but we also have an unshakable belief in Germany's destiny and who's responsible for all the problems that the Führer's now solving so successfully."

"Who's that?" asked Gus as a frown quickly formed on Oscar's face.

"The goddamned Jews, that's who!" exclaimed Oscar, whose sudden vehemence startled Gus.

"Din't know that. Sure sounds like you hate 'em plenty!"

"They're vermin who're trying to take over the world and should be eliminated!"

Gus's ears immediately perked up. "Well ain't that somethin'. We ain't so diff'rent after all," he said. "Ya see, my organization's dedicated to gettin' rid 'o the niggers, 'n even though I don't run into 'em that much, we ain't so happy with the Jews neither."

"Where'd you say you live?" asked Oscar with heightened interest.

"I live in Steubenville, Ohio. It's in the eastern part o' the state."

"Yes, I've heard of Steubenville, but I thought there was a sizable Jewish population there."

"There're a lot of 'em, all right, but they're real clannish and stick to themselves, so I don't see 'em that often."

"So you're going to see some friends of yours, Gus. Where do your friends live?"

"Right in Yaphank."

"Do you know if by any chance they're members of the Friends of New Germany or know of it?" asked Oscar eagerly. "It's a big organization and growing quickly. There're quite a few supporters in Yaphank, and they could be members."

"I ain't sure. I kinda doubt it, though. Ya see, Oscar, ta tell the truth, they ain't really friends o' mine, they're just former Klan. I hear tell there're quite a few in Yaphank. I'm meetin' 'em to try 'n recruit 'em for my organization."

"What organization's that?"

"We're called the Black Legion, and we use'ta be the strong arm that protected the big Klansmen. After the Klan started havin' problems in the late twenties, we sorta went off on our own."

"So, what's the purpose of your group now? The Klan's been largely inactive for years, hasn't it?"

Despite there being only one other couple seated at the far end of the railroad car, Gus leaned forward and spoke in a low voice. "The Klan's been sorta underground for years, but the Black Legion's been cleanin' up Ohio by gettin' rid o' the niggers. All our guys are real heroes an' ain't nobody 'fraid of doin' what needs to get done. But we got some problems, though. The word's out that some o' our guys are bein' looked at by the law and, if they're picked up, that could be big trouble fer me."

"What kind of trouble, Gus?"

"I was involved in gettin' rid of a few o' the niggers, an' I'm real proud o' what we done. Ain't many people got the stomach for the kinda stuff we done. We're a class outfit."

"I see," said Oscar in a preoccupied way. "Yes, that's interesting. Very interesting, indeed. Say, Gus, since we're both going to be in the same place, there's something I think you'd be very interested in seeing. Are you up for it?"

"Since I may be needin' to get outta Steubenville pretty fast anyway, sure. What d'ya got?"

"I'm a territory leader for the Friends, and I'm helping to open Camp Siegfried. We're teaching Aryan youth about camping, hunting, and shooting."

"I ain't sure I got the time fer all that, Oscar, but we'll see."

"I think you'd find what we're doing very interesting, Gus. You see, we're about to solve all our problems with the Jews and the niggers once and for all."

6

After thinking about Oscar's invitation, Gus decided to visit the new Camp Siegfried. It was close to where he was staying, and Oscar's tantalizing promise of eradicating their hated enemies drove him to his decision. Arriving a few minutes before he was to meet up with Oscar, Gus looked at the entrance to Camp Siegfried and the surrounding rugged, natural, forested setting. After hearing Oscar's description of the place, he was not surprised by a discrete sign nearby that added essential qualifications required for entrance— "German American Settlement League. Private community. Members and guests only."

"Good morning, Gus. Thanks for coming. Welcome to Camp Siegfried," said Oscar enthusiastically as he bounded up to shake Gus's hand. "Tomorrow, the population here'll swell to thousands of young Aryans and their parents who're eager to learn more about the miraculous Nazi movement. It'll be quiet today, however, so it'll be easy for me to show you around. There'll be great facilities here including an archery range, swimming pool, miles of hiking paths through the woods and, of course, Oktoberfest, which should be quite a show with bands, costumes, and lots of great German beer. Maybe you'd like to join us?"

In response, Gus gave a noncommittal grunt.

"Let's go in. Adolf Hitler Road is the main road through the facility. It immediately sets the tone for everyone entering. Just down the way ahead of us are Goebbels and Göring Streets. It makes me intensely proud just to know I'm part of this. Notice the American and Nazi flags flying next to one another. Everyone here's very proud of both America and Germany. You see, along here, we plan to have…" As the two strolled, Oscar went on while Gus only half listened. After finishing their walking tour, the two men sat down at a picnic bench under the canopy of an immense tree.

Oscar continued praising Germany's astounding accomplishments under Hitler as Gus became unable to control his impatience. "So what's this big solution to the nigger and Jew problem gonna be, Oscar?"

"I can't really talk about it yet, but it's in the next phase of development. A special facility'll be located near the far end of the grounds, set off by itself. I haven't heard what it'll consist of exactly, but I've heard it's going to be a scientific marvel. In fact, the rumor is that Hitler himself is paying close attention to what we'll be doing here."

"Where's the money comin' from fer all this?" inquired Gus.

"You wouldn't believe me if I told you, Gus. Some very powerful people are on board. There won't be any need we have that won't have ample funding."

"Ya mean ya got some rich Germans behind all this?"

"No. It's rumored that we have some very wealthy Americans, Gus. Big money with big names."

7

1936 - Chicago

Gus Erstad had been right when he told Oscar Hahn on the Long Island train about the jeopardy his beloved Black Legion was facing. He had stayed in contact with Oscar, and less than a year after their fateful summer train ride, he needed to reach out to his new friend.

"R'member what I told ya last summer 'bout the Legion's problems, Oscar. Well, things've got a lot hotter, and the Detroit lawyers're gearin' up to kill us, all right. When I was in Yaphank, I met some people who was visitin' from Chattanooga who're now good friends. They said they'd put me up as long as I needed. I wanted to let ya know that I'm leavin' Steubenville, and when I get settled, I'll get in touch."

"Then, I'll look forward to hearing from you, Gus. It so happens that there're some big changes coming my way as well. A new and greatly expanded version of the Friends of the New Germany has been established in Buffalo, New York. We're changing our name to the German American Bund, and it's being headed by a German-born American who fought for the Kingdom of Bavaria in the Great War. I'm very excited about our plans, Gus. We're patterning the organization after the German Nazi Party and dividing the US into three territories, New York, West, and Midwest, with headquarters in New York City. We're also using German words for the three territories, which will be called 'gaus.' I think I'm going to be asked to head one, and my title will be 'gauleiter.' In English, it means regional leader. I can't tell you how thrilled I am about all this. I'll look forward to hearing from you. Good luck!"

Oscar Hahn had always been popular with his Nazi compatriots and was the embodiment of the Aryan ideal being idolized in

Germany. His blond hair, light blue eyes, and angular features were the perfect book jacket for his radical racial views, making him appear to be the ideal American Nazi. His seniority in what was now the German American Bund also increased the respect of his peers.

Born in 1906 in Chicago, Oscar was part of a family that had emigrated from Prussia to pursue the great opportunities they had heard existed in America. Intensely proud of their German heritage, the Hahns soon witnessed the remarkable chances to excel in America that had been unthinkable in Prussia. In a relatively short time, their hard-working ethic soon bore fruit and embedded in them a profoundly patriotic attachment to their adopted country. This devotion became painful after America entered the Great War when domestic German families experienced widespread ridicule, even for people like Oscar, who had been born here. At school, he was constantly bullied, his classmates often running after him shouting, "Filthy Hun!" His English was superior to his German, but that meant nothing to his young schoolmates who were acting out what they had learned at home.

The relentless attacks left the young Oscar feeling deeply scarred, something he frequently shared with his family. His parents comforted him with a cultural bromide of anti-Semitism, attributing his treatment to the evil effects of a vast Jewish conspiracy. With its large Jewish population, Chicago was evidence to his parents of this ever-expanding threat. Under his parent's tutelage, their young son unconsciously intertwined his pride in his heritage and his love for America with the conviction that the Jewish conspiracy was behind his torment at school. Oscar knew his parents were right—they had brought him up to believe that they were his superiors, and superiors were never questioned.

It was no surprise that years later, in the mid-1920s, he became mesmerized by the alluring message of a new American Pan-

Germany movement that intended to unite America and Germany. At nineteen, he joined the Free Society of Teutonia. The Great War had been over for seven years, and people's harsh behavior towards German Americans had softened considerably. At the same time, Oscar was furious that his beloved Germany was reeling under the crushing economic dictates of the 1919 Treaty of Versailles and the humiliation of losing the "war to end all wars." As a member of the Free Society, he was surrounded by many other people who felt the same way. His membership fortified Oscar's and his family's pride in being both American and German.

As 1933 opened its doors, the Great Depression had blanketed much of the world in misery and financial desperation for over two years. It promised to be a particularly dismal year for many millions of Americans and Germans. The Hahn family was among them.

Oscar had now been deeply entrenched in the cultural cocoon of his Teutonic society for eight years. Despite his devotion to his family's former homeland, like so many others, he was unaware of a sudden and profound shift in global power then taking place. Forty-five hundred miles away, Adolf Hitler bowed slightly as he shook the hand of a doddering President Hindenburg, who, at six and one-half feet tall, towered over the Austrian. This seemingly respectful gesture was deceptive for everyone except those closest to the ceremony and its main participants. Behind the cameras, both men detested one another, but to a vast, admiring German public, the ceremony appeared to demonstrate a progressive step that promised a new, vital Germany.

Barely eighteen months later, the old president was facing his final moments on earth. Unwilling to wait for Hindenburg to gasp his last breath, Hitler had already used his dominance to launch a massive investment in a new and unparalleled German war machine. The enormous influx of capital lifted the economy out of its doldrums and catapulted his popular image into the pantheon of great Germanic leaders. With Hindenburg now hours away from surrendering his life to lung cancer, Hitler had the German cabinet agree that upon the old president's demise, Hitler would become both president and chancellor, thereby controlling the government and the state. Everything he was doing was devoted to methodically perfecting his possession of absolute power and securing his position as dictator.

Thrilled with Germany's remarkable success under its new leader, Oscar's Free Society of Teutonia decided to cash in on the Nazi revolution by changing its name to Friends of the New Germany. As months passed, Oscar and his fellow Friends felt exhilaration with each new revelation of Germany's continuing meteoric rise. Before Hitler, the organization's pride had been nourished only with the dogma surrounding Germany's past victories. Now, everyone in the organization was thrilled by what they saw as a triumphant future. Oscar was elated with the blossoming of his ancestral nation. He felt an ever stronger allegiance to it and the man who appeared to be crafting its brilliant rebirth out of the wasteland left by the Great War.

While the Friends' confidence in Germany's continued ascendancy was growing, its leadership also became more insistent on bullying and cowering a growing number of anti-Nazi protesters at its increasingly grand assemblies. Oscar saw it becoming commonplace for large groups of anti-Nazi protesters to attempt to disrupt the proceedings. As violence grew to involve nearly all Friends events, it was spurred on by the increased brutality exhibited by the Nazis overseas.

However, with his organization's growing savagery, Oscar was finding it increasingly difficult to hide a debilitating weakness of his. Despite his ideal Aryan appearance, as pressure continued to mount on him as a leader to participate in increasingly frequent brutality, he knew that he lacked the visceral fortitude to be violent. Oscar was well aware that his reticence to fight had first shown itself when, as a young child in school, it was easier for him to absorb physical abuse than to strike back. Recognizing the need to overcome this handicap to his future in the Friends, he had developed a way around his personal pacifism by quickly delegating the violence required of him to subordinates who appeared to be overjoyed to knock heads and pummel guts. Oscar learned that while he was incapable of violence himself, he had no qualms about demanding it of others acting in his stead. The strategy worked and enabled him to maintain his standing in an increasingly violent organization, at least for the time being.

Shortly after the Friends of the New Germany once again changed its name, this time to the German American Bund, Oscar was promoted to the senior position of gauleiter, which was accompanied by the strict responsibility for assuring more extreme violence. While his subordinates were up to rally skirmishes and occasional beatings, he feared that at some point in the not-too-distant future, he would need a right arm that would gladly embrace any kind of brutality, including murder.

Months went by, and as pressure increased on Oscar to exhibit a brutal nature he had never possessed, his strategy of violence delegation was beginning to draw him ever closer to exposure. He knew the time was upon him to recruit a super-loyal enforcer, a violent alter ego, or else become a victim of vicious retribution. In Chattanooga, several hundred miles to the south of him, forces were stirring that would end up delivering his ideal candidate.

8

1936 - Wilmington, Delaware

The attorney entered the room and simply could not help but stop to admire once again the splendor of the ivory inlaid occasional table and, in its precise center, two immaculate Fabergé eggs placed carefully on two gold filigree stands. Ahead of him, two Louis XIV chairs sat in front of a large ornate desk resting on a glistening 17th-century parquet floor. Bernard Haskins thought of the many times he had been in his sole client's lofty, expansive office and how he never failed to be impressed with its abundant opulence. Ironically, the extravagant delicacy of it would also prompt Bernard to envision what underlay this magnificence—tens of thousands of mass-production-line workers toiling to churn out millions of industrial products several hundred miles away in the Midwest. Once the largest stakeholder in this colossus, Howard Magnum's family had been the greatest beneficiary of one of the world's largest industrial enterprises.

The butler quietly closed the massive, carved door as the attorney advanced into the room, carefully acknowledging with a smile and a nod his fastidiously-dressed boss sitting behind the desk. The frames of his boss's polished glasses were so slight that the lenses seemed to float on the bridge of his nose. His flatly-combed hair, with its carefully carved part, demonstrated the same fastidiousness as the precise placement of the discreet gold watch chain resting across his dark vest.

Bernard Haskins began to sit as his boss inquired, "What's this I hear about the Black Legion running into trouble, Haskins?"

"I'm afraid that's correct, sir," explained the man's chief personal counsel. "Once the police discovered the Legion's role in the murder of that federal organizer for FDR's Works Progress Administration, it opened the way for the Wayne County prosecutor to investigate the organization. Now there's talk of the prosecutor's uncovering a significant number of murders committed by the Black Legion. It's become a real mess, sir."

"Whatever happens here, I don't need to tell you that my family's and the Magnum Corporation's name must be kept out of this at all costs. The publicity would be extremely damaging for us, our companies, and the country, not to mention the rest of the collaborators in our alliance. You understand all this, I know, but this makes me very disturbed considering the important initiatives our alliance has underway."

"Yes, I understand completely, sir. I have already taken the appropriate steps to ensure that the family's involvement and the identity of your companies will never be revealed."

After he paused and reflected on his predicament, the man behind the desk continued. "This is all very troubling, Haskins. I thought we had a reliable strong arm against the unions with the Legion. With the money we've poured into it, I'm astounded that the leaders weren't more capable of being discrete. What do you recommend we do now? What will take its place so that we'll be able to meet our objectives?"

"After some investigation, I found what I believe could be a workable solution. However, unlike the financial support we provided to the Black Legion, this time around, we'll ensure that we protect ourselves even more rigorously from any highly-publicized excesses by keeping the organization walled off from you."

"This ideal solution you speak of, tell me about it."

"It's a particularly violent offshoot of the Black Legion that's assumed the name of the Silver Swords. It's presently in Chattanooga and is small but growing and is headed by a reputedly fearless person by the name of Gustav Erstad. I'm told that, despite his violent nature, he can be controlled in service of a mandated objective. If we tie Erstad's Silver Swords together with the Bund, it could be formidable. As you know, our friendly competitor is supporting the Bund financially. If we underwrite the Silver Swords, together we'll have a powerful force to stifle the unions as well as help support our alliance to achieve its primary objectives."

"This all sounds encouraging, Haskins. We should inform the rest of the group immediately. It appears as if, properly controlled and motivated, this combination could, as they say, kill many flies with one blow."

9

1936 - Chattanooga, Tennessee

It was late in the evening when Gus Erstad shut his front door after initiating two more members into his Silver Swords organization. He always found proselytizing exciting and as he headed to his bedroom, he was still too fired up to sleep.

As he lay down on his rumpled bed, he looked into the darkness and recalled simpler times a dozen years before when he was a fresh recruit. A great deal had happened since that day just after his eighteenth birthday when the eastern Ohio where he had grown up was teeming with speakeasies and flappers, loud, fast music, and liquor—lots of liquor—but always behind closed doors.

While he enjoyed beer, the chance to get drunk was not what filled Gus's mind, however. Instead, he recalled his delight at being a new member of an extremely violent arm of the Ku Klux Klan tasked with protecting its regional officers. He recalled how proud he was to wear his uniform with its skull and crossbones on his black hood and robe. He was part of what he saw as an elite paramilitary organization. It also took him millions of miles away from a brutal father who had killed his mother and older brother before vanishing forever.

Despite his bitterness at his father's violent nature that had destroyed his family, he was well aware that this same rage also sat deep within himself, always eager to be released at the flimsiest opportunity. His fellow vigilantes became his family and were young men like him, overfilled with fury and eagerly awaiting their next orders to either bludgeon someone into line or make them disappear.

In the mid-1920s, young Gus and his comrades were all existing in a world covered in the transparent, moralistic veneer of

Prohibition. The times were as hot as the economy, which was being propelled by the universal conviction that a new age of "Anything Goes" had finally arrived and had relegated to the trash heap any piper who would ever need to be paid. In such a freewheeling world, Gus was free to unleash his darkest instincts with enough regularity to nourish the belief that he was fulfilling his destiny.

Like everything else in the mid-twenties, the Klan and its violent enforcement arm were growing. As a result, Gus's organization assumed the name of Black Legion to tout its size. He knew that the virulence of his racial hatred and his talents for extreme violence were impressing his senior Black Legionnaires. They even shared with him that they saw him as the kind of leader who could one day ascend to head the Legion, if not the Klan itself. For the first time in his life, Gus was becoming confident that his future would be bright.

He then recalled seeing his dreams unravel as the Roaring Twenties drew to a close while the Klan began to rot from the head down with many of the Klan leaders thrown into prison for sensational crimes involving money, sex, and murder. In this chaotic environment, Gus had developed a reputation as a fearsomely violent leader of unusually brutal men.

As the new decade's financial panic descended into widespread desperation, Gus's dreams of becoming a ferocious tyrant blossomed. Despite the death of the Klan, his Black Legion had lived on, able to survive on an irregular diet of hangings and stabbings that were financially supported by strike-breaking companies. By 1936 his dominance in the Legion had become unquestioned throughout Michigan, Ohio, and Pennsylvania. He was riding higher than he ever had and was especially thrilled by the fear he inspired in others, especially his Legion's competing commanders.

In the darkness of his bedroom, Gus turned on his side and let out a low growl as he recalled how history then repeated itself, once again throwing his future into an abyss. Like the Klan, the Black Legion also became a victim of its own brutal excesses when over three dozen of its leaders were convicted of murders and other violent crimes against blacks, Jews, Catholics, and eastern Europeans. He smiled as he remembered his involvement in several killings and how proud he was to have escaped the dragnets that had surrounded him. While he deeply resented having to flee his native Ohio, he felt better knowing he was headed with several of his Klan friends to the "Dynamo of Dixie," as Chattanooga was affectionately known. Although he had never been there, Gus felt comfort in knowing that he would be only a couple of hours away from a place he revered as hallowed ground—Pulaski, the Tennessee birthplace of the original Ku Klux Klan.

Shortly after renting a house outside of Chattanooga, he invited some of his Klan friends over for a get-together. After drinks had liberated them all, Gus remembered how excited he became when a friend offered a solution to his desperate need for revenge for the collapse of his beloved Black Legion. He urged Gus to create something no one could ever take away from him, his own elite paramilitary unit.

Momentarily returning to the present, Gus turned onto his back once again and looked at the ceiling, which became an empty canvas onto which he projected the memories of his happier, more recent past. He smiled when he recalled the moment he thought of fusing the symbols of his two great passions, money and violence, into the name of his new force—the Silver Swords. He had been revitalized by the endless recruiting and whipping up of his new warriors into a frenzy. Unlike the zealous building of his Silver Swords, however, he found the occasional lynching of hapless blacks and random violence unfulfilling, and certainly not befitting a leader of America's white supremacy movement.

Gus's success with the evening's recruiting efforts reminded him once more that his ever-growing band of Silver Swords zealots was growing impatient for some lofty, violent purpose. He also needed money. He started to drift asleep fearing that if he couldn't solve these two key issues, he could lose control of his rabid minions, which would obliterate his image as a brutal tyrant that had taken so many years to construct.

It was only two days later when Gus picked up the phone and answered with his customary, suspicious demand, "Who's this?"

"Hello, Gus. It's Oscar. Do you have a minute? I have a proposal to make to you that I believe you'll find interesting."

10

1938 - Boston

Despite being located in Boston, the revered Tilner and Associates law firm had long dominated the practice of civil rights throughout Washington D.C.'s halls of power. During his long tenure as his firm's senior managing partner, Fess Tilner was always considered by most Washington legislators and cabinet members to be as much a senior statesman as he was the leader of his venerated firm. Planning to spend his remaining years with his wife, Beth, Fess had announced his decision to retire from practicing civil rights law at the national level in 1926. Immediately after that, the Tilners had moved back to his ancestral home in Gilbert, Alabama. Their son, Malcolm, had joined his parents in moving to Alabama until he returned to Boston four years later to head Tilner and Associates. Since then, Malcolm had been managing the firm successfully and had brought it to new heights of influence and prestige.

As Fess sat in the luxurious vestibule of his old firm, he found himself reflecting on the twelve years since his departure from Tilner and Associates. The last ten years, in particular, had been golden for him. He had been spending his days with Beth traveling abroad or in their home in Gilbert.

Widely respected in the Boston-Washington DC corridor for his integrity, legal astuteness, and wisdom, Fess found it ironic that he felt so uneasy with the meeting he was about to have. It would mark a milestone in his life. For the first time, he would be acknowledging that his formidable, lifelong influence and political power were showing the first signs of frailty. He wondered if the proximity of his seventieth birthday, now just months away, was accentuating his sense of obsolescence and amplifying his anxiety. He was curious about his conflicting feelings.

"How odd. Here I am at the firm I headed for so long, where I did battle with some of Washington's most formidable forces, and now I'm actually nervous about seeing one of the dearest people in my life. My, how things change."

While reflecting on this turn of circumstances, Fess exhaled slowly just as he heard footsteps he knew very well. Mustering his warm but patrician manner, he immediately felt a measure of relief when his daughter-in-law turned the corner to greet him.

"Hi, Dad," said Anna Tilner as he stood and gave her a warm embrace. The second he heard her voice, Fess felt a disquieting combination of affection and apprehension. "What brings you all the way here to the house that Fess built?"

As he greeted her warmly and they began walking arm in arm to her office, he was transported back a decade when he was introduced to Anna and had the first of many conversations with her that he had never forgotten. He recalled how staggered he was by her perceptiveness, intellect, and cool-under-pressure gifts. It was these remarkable qualities and a warm and caring nature that had then catapulted her into the Tilner family. Now working for Tilner and Associates, even Malcolm had been overwhelmed when Anna completed her undergraduate degree and became a distinguished Yale-educated attorney in under five years before joining his family's firm.

As the former patriarch of Tilner and Associates accompanied Anna through the familiar corridors, the pair was stopped by several partners who came up to express how happy they were to see him and to inquire how he was enjoying retirement. When the inevitable question arose as to why he was there, he deflected it with, "Just some family business to take care of."

Continuing down a long hallway, Fess imagined how Anna would instantly recognize what a profound personal admission he was about to make as well as the ominous significance of his revelation. He felt blessed to be so close to such a gifted person but was still uneasy about relinquishing an executive role that in years past, he would have assumed without question. He also knew that she was alone in being able to comprehend and deal with what he was about to tell her.

Approaching Anna's office, Fess said warmly, "I trust you and Malcolm are both well. Oh yes, and Beth sends her love."

"Thanks, Dad. Yes, we're both just fine. How's Beth holding up with her now constant companion?" replied Anna as she ushered Fess into her well-appointed office.

"She's doing her best to make me believe that I should've done this a long time ago," he replied as they both took a seat on the sofa in the office's sitting area. After another minute of family small talk, Fess's demeanor suddenly stiffened as he turned to the purpose of the meeting.

"With all this retirement time on my hands, I've stumbled onto something I find odd and extremely troubling. While years ago I would've pursued this, I'm confident that of all the people I know, you're now the one to uncover what it means."

"How intriguing. Of course, Dad, if you believe that whatever this is could be so significant, I'm sure Malcolm can redistribute my caseload. Malcolm's in court, or I'd have asked him to join us."

"You and I both know Malcolm finds any new adventure of yours extremely disturbing, and for good reason. So, I wanted to speak with you privately first. To be frank, I was concerned that, knowing and fearing your boldness, he would forbid me to say anything at all to you. In that event, of course, I wouldn't have gone around him. Having said all this, were I not so deeply concerned with the danger to our nation that I see, I would certainly not be burdening you with this information. I believe that once you've heard my concerns and if you're willing to take this on, there's no one better able to explain why to Malcolm."

"I see," replied Anna, needing no reminder of how her past exploits had unnerved her husband. "Well then, what's on your mind?"

"In conversations over the past year with legal friends of mine around the country, I've been hearing a groundswell of disturbing conspiracy theories cropping up. While this is nothing new in the South, there appears to be a far more widespread growing fear of blacks and Jews by whites all around the country. In response, there are homegrown fascist and Nazi-sympathizer groups that have been increasing in numbers and violence. This could mean even darker days ahead for minorities here.

"It seems that in the five years since Hitler's 1933 assumption of power, his actions've given rise to some alarming consequences in this country. His remilitarization of the Rhineland, the imposition of the ruthlessly repressive Nuremberg laws, rounding up of thousands of Jews, gypsies, and homosexuals, and his annexation of Austria, have caused an explosion in the number of American Nazi organizations. These Americans are blindly loyal to Hitler and his Nazi movement. They attribute the miracle of Germany's economic explosion to his brilliant leadership rather than Hitler's obsession with pouring massive amounts of capital into an immense new German war machine that was dismantled after the Great War.

"As if all this weren't concerning enough," Fess continued, "shortly after Hitler became Germany's dictator, the Congressional Committee on Un-American Activities was learning of a serious American fascist plot that aimed to overthrow President Roosevelt. It had some powerful, well-known people behind it, people associated with such companies as JP Morgan, GM, and DuPont. If you can believe it, it took until last month, a full four years, before the committee was willing to publish its findings. While the plot fizzled, it's still surprising that such a coup attempt could get as far as it did with the support of so many influential people."

"As terrible as all this is, I suppose we shouldn't find it too surprising, Dad," responded Anna. "Anything like this profound financial depression we're still going through terrifies people, and their fear causes all sorts of strange and extreme organizations to surface."

"Of course, you're right, Anna, but this growing paranoia seems to me to be different now."

"How so?"

"You know how many leading political and government figures I've come to know over the years. In the past, they'd happily give me an inside track on what's been taking place in DC's power salons, but not this time. Even the cabinet members and ex-cabinet members I've spoken with are keeping their mouths tightly shut about some of these fascist and Nazi outfits and what the government knows about them. Some of the senior Department of Justice and FBI officials I know won't say a word. Even one of my closest friends, someone you know, former US Attorney General Walter Hofstedler, has been unable to penetrate this wall of silence. In my experience, this is unprecedented. Our leaders seem to be taking great pains to hide something, and I find it very troubling."

"So you want me to see if I can determine what these powerful government people are withholding about these extremist groups and why they're not doing anything about them," responded Anna. "How can you be sure that any of the people you've spoken with actually know what's going on inside these organizations that would make them a real concern for national security? After all, most of them are fringe groups run by fanatics who rarely have shown the ability to sustain and grow an organization over time."

"The thing is, Anna, I've noticed that this strange silence pertains to only a few such organizations. Some of them have even ceased to exist. However, I believe that such reticence could grow to be a serious threat to this country and our way of life."

"Would examples be the now-dead Black Legion and the German American Bund?" inquired Anna.

"Why, yes, you're right. How do you know about these outfits?"

"We have several powerful Long Island clients who've recently expressed a similar apprehension to some of our partners. These people were alarmed by the widespread racial hatred and violence of the former Black Legion and found it disgusting, divisive, and destructive to our national unity. While the Black Legion was dissolved two years ago in a flurry of capital indictments of its leaders, such outfits inspire and spawn other such violent, disruptive, and dangerous organizations. Such groups are especially disturbing when our national solidarity may be facing a severe test considering what's happening in Europe.

"Regarding the Bund, our clients are less concerned with what it is than what it could become the closer we get to war. As I understand it, the Bund appears to be a band of white nationalists in lockstep with the Nazis to promote some vague alignment of this country with Germany. Surely the FBI is looking into these groups."

"If I knew for certain that they were, I wouldn't find all this so mysterious and frustrating. This odd, close-mouthed, almost aggressively silent attitude of senior people in the federal government, people who have always been candid with me about things that concern them, I find completely baffling. It seems that the more senior the person, the more reluctant they are to say anything. A good friend of mine, an FBI executive, made it very clear that this entire topic was taboo. In all my years of working with him, I've never heard such a thing before. To me, this's all very strange and ominous. I fear something must be done and quickly."

"So why come to me?"

"Well, Anna, considering that you have repeatedly demonstrated a mixture of sleuthing, resourcefulness, and courage beyond anything I've known to exist in any other person, you seem to fit this task perfectly. Getting to the bottom of this could be of profound significance to us all, and since the government appears hesitant, unable, or unwilling to deal with it, I felt compelled to talk to you."

"Of course, I'm very flattered you think of me this way, Dad, but penetrating what sounds like a unified federal stance, if not a conspiracy, is a little out of my bailiwick."

"You may believe that if you wish, but I just learned of something that made me realize that this may be a much more insidious situation than I had originally thought, and I can't just sit by and watch whatever this is play out. Anna, you know how very dear you are to me, Beth, and Malcolm. You must also know that I realize how dangerous getting involved in something like this could be. All that being said, having seen you face extraordinary danger so many times before, your unique gifts are essential for this challenge. What's more, since you're not part of the government apparatus, you're ideally suited for it. I hope you can see this the same way."

"So, what did you learn that caused your sudden call to action?"

"Hard as it may be to believe, Germany's Grand Cross of the Supreme Order of the German Eagle, the highest Nazi honor for a foreigner, was just awarded by Hitler to Henry Ford."

11

Malcolm was making no effort to hide his exasperation with the conversation he was having with his wife. His mind raced through the near-calamities he and Anna had experienced together in Alabama. He still marveled at how, shortly after they had met, this winsome, diminutive woman had stood up to the most ferocious Klansman in Alabama. This stunning confrontation was followed a decade later by another, even more-harrowing adventure. They had been married for nearly eight years when she returned to Alabama and uncovered and thwarted a massive, diabolical operation to commit mass murder near Montgomery. He was still recovering from her having had so many close brushes with death in the process.

From the moment Malcolm met Anna in 1928, he was mesmerized by her combination of extraordinary gifts—among these was her boldness. Since then, he had seen enough to know that his wife's courage was remarkable, although for him, it was also a burden that both he and she were helpless to control, much less thwart. In the end, he knew he would always end up surrendering to whatever she was determined to do.

Setting his drink on their coffee table, he leaned forward and stared at his wife before pleading his case one last time. "Anna, I simply can't understand. You've been nearly killed several times. After all we went through, that you're even thinking about this new escapade absolutely baffles me, even if it did start with my father! Do you have any idea how crippling it'll be for me to worry about you and your safety on top of managing the firm?!"

"I know, Malcolm, but this isn't the first time we've had to face a potentially dangerous situation that just couldn't be ignored, and I'm still here—a little worse for wear, maybe, but still very much intact.

If your father weren't so deeply disturbed by all this, I wouldn't be giving it a second thought. Why your father, of all people, is confronting such odd, stonewalling behavior by our government concerns me, too, especially considering what's happening in Europe. You spoke with him after I did and you know how careful and deliberate he is. He wouldn't have called me if he didn't feel this was imperative."

"I know that, Anna, but it still doesn't make it one whit easier for me to believe, much less accept, that you're the only person or even the best person who can deal with this! Where's our FBI and other national security agencies? Surely, these are the people who should be handling this," said Malcolm with marked desperation.

"I certainly won't deny that many other people and agencies should be able to deal with this far more effectively. However, whatever's driving this bizarre situation, there's some compelling and hidden reason behind why the agencies in the best position to look into the Bund, and who knows what other white nationalist outfits, are looking the other way. Federal law enforcement and security agencies all appear to be mysteriously resisting doing anything. In your father's words, it's 'all very strange and ominous.' He fears something must be done and quickly. I'm afraid that after thinking about it, I couldn't agree more."

"Have you even thought about how to tackle something so immense and ill-defined."

"I'm developing a plan that'll take some time, but I'm confident I can get to the bottom of this."

"Of course you are. Based on what I've seen you do so many times before, I don't doubt that you'll succeed," Malcolm responded. "But that's not my point, is it? You'd be able to pull this off, all right, but that assumes that whatever powerful monster is behind all this doesn't murder you first!"

12

The secluded mansion was dark except for one end of the massive structure where two men were sitting in Queen Anne chairs in front of a roaring fire. "When did I hire you, Stampf?" asked Maximilian Graff of his loyal lieutenant as they both settled in with a glass of grand cru fine champagne cognac. Before Karl could respond, Maximilian followed up with another recollection, "If it hadn't been for that damn Jew Roosevelt and his goons, we'd still have the Graff Chemical I inherited. Well, it's been a long time since we went underground, hasn't it?"

Knowing that Roosevelt was not Jewish but always eager to avoid confrontation with Maximilian, Karl let that part of the remark slide. Instead, he chose to respond to the more innocuous question. "I've been with you since the year the Great War started in 1914, so that would make it twenty-four years. Since we came back as Graff Industries in 1930, it's been only eight years, so not that long, really."

Suddenly, the senior man flashed with anger, "When I say it's a long time, goddamnit, it's a long time, Stampf! Don't ever, ever dispute what I say!"

"I'm very sorry, Mr. Graff. It won't happen again." His own words grated on Karl's ear, but, as had happened so many times before, he would go along. Well paid for putting up with his boss's hypersensitivity to the slightest hint of dissent or criticism, he knew his position with Graff had been his salvation, especially during eight years of the Great Depression.

Karl knew he could tolerate his boss's frequent tongue-lashing— he also knew that he could never endure poverty again. Having grown up in a poor immigrant family, he had long promised himself that in a country so filled with opportunity he would succeed and would never suffer poverty again. In the years before he met Maximilian, Karl was able to become the vice-president of operations for a prosperous Chicago pharmaceutical company. Enjoying a reputation as an exceptionally talented manager, Karl met his future boss shortly after Maximilian assumed his role as head of Graff Chemical. Lured away to became second-in-command of the struggling company, Karl soon saw his opportunity to cash in on a promising enterprise while protecting it from the volatile, uncontrollable emotions of its owner. He had resolved to do whatever was necessary to meet both goals and would suffer the verbal abuse of Maximilian, no matter what.

The two men's uneasy relationship had been buttressed eight years earlier when Karl's foresight had saved the company by ensuring that Graff Chemical's fingerprints were never found anywhere near the toxic chemical called Jake that his company had devised, manufactured, and sold. When a federal dragnet snagged the largest Jake distributor, it fell victim to the government's desperate need to find a culprit and ended up taking the fall for Graff Chemical's creation. Avoiding the government's wrath, Karl always found it ironic that twenty-four years earlier Graff Chemical had been the darling of the federal government's Chemical Warfare Service.

It was also thanks mainly to Karl that both men's wealth had continued to grow. Although the days of the sprawling Graff Chemical were gone, Graff Industries was a somewhat smaller but even more profitable operation thanks to Karl's operational skills. By the end of 1934, it appeared that Graff Industries could again be on the threshold of significant new success in the agriculture market. After several failed attempts at creating new chemical products in the most severe early troughs of the Depression, Maximilian had again turned to creating pesticides when he saw the agriculture market starting to return in 1933. By 1935, his company was positioned to enjoy its most prosperous year since Graff Industries had emerged five years earlier.

Other players were eyeing the same opportunity, however. Agriculture was reviving, and a burgeoning need for insecticides arose in 1935 as both Maximilian and Karl had foreseen. At this point, the Magnum Corporation, a much larger company than Maximilian's, announced it was flooding the market with a new pesticide it had been developing that was more effective and less dangerous than the arsenic-based products from Graff Industries. In less than a year, Maximilian was once again facing a formidable threat to his business, something he was helpless to stop and even less able to tolerate.

The chance for another failure once more raised the specter of a growing Maximilian monster that had been held at bay by his latest venture's encouraging prospects in the insecticide industry. Magnum's overwhelming market entry that had destroyed this potential overnight put him into an emotional tailspin, one so severe that Karl feared for his boss's sanity.

Despite his familiarity with his boss's ferocious temperament, Karl was still unprepared for what he saw when he entered Maximilian's office the day after Magnum's announcement—it was in shambles with his boss hobbling frantically in circles and shouting. "I will kill those fucking Jew Magnums and every one of their goddamned Jewish offspring," Maximilian screamed as he continued to kick the remnants of what had been his office furniture. At one point, Karl jumped away to avoid a flying piece of picture frame that Maximilian had launched with his left foot as his club foot lost its traction on a large shard of glass, bringing him crashing to the ground. Now exploding with uncontrolled rage that produced flailing body movements, Maximilian's legs kept shooting out from under him as he continued to shriek and struggle to stand in his destroyed office.

Finally, Maximilian managed to stand and remain stationary, although rocking back and forth from one foot to the other. Karl was surprised by the sudden silence, although the menacing presence before him was still clearly seething. Finally, the man who had been berserk just one minute before stood utterly still and spoke in a shallow, aspirated voice filled with malice. "I'll strike back.... I'll strike back at all the Magnums and their fellow-Jew scum. I'll use my wealth to devastate them, destroy them, and rid the earth of them! They're worse than vermin. I've suffered my last defeat! Never again will I be the victim—NEVER!"

In the entire twenty-one years of their fractured association, Karl had often endured Maximilian's fits of rage and his vile curses. This pronouncement, however, was something he had not seen before—Maximilian's icy, slow, and deliberate delivery of a deeply vindictive pledge made his skin tingle. Momentarily devoid of any outward sign of his customary fury and physical violence, Maximilian appeared to Karl to be particularly menacing and ominous. For the first time in his employ, Karl found himself fearing his future.

All this had occurred three years earlier, and now, drawn back to the present with a pleasant whiff of his cognac, Karl knew that he would not have to wait long before enduring Maximilian's next assault. Until then, he decided to enjoy his boss's expensive liquor and a brief period of silence as a pinch of compensation for having to endure his boss's often acerbic company.

It was not long before Maximilian interrupted the peace, "Tomorrow I'll be taking a trip to a small place on Long Island called Yaphank. Have you heard of it, Stampf?" Before waiting for an answer, Maximilian concluded his thought. "There's an event being planned there at something called Camp Siegfried by the German American Bund, and I'd like to learn more about the group. It sounds like something I could use."

Mercifully, Karl was extraneous to his master's monologue, so he sat quietly and enjoyed his exquisite cognac, wondering how this Bund organization fit into Maximilian's no doubt demonic plans for revenge.

13

1938 - Camp Siegfried, Long Island

"We are now just one month away from a great Bund festival, a glorious German Day, at Camp Siegfried!" announced Gauleiter Oscar Hahn to the rest of the fifty-person Bund planning committee. "The Nazi and Hitler youth flags will be flying everywhere to commemorate our Führer's great victory in the Sudetenland and once again reuniting so many of our Austrian family with the Reich! We have invited young Bund members from all over the nation to celebrate our unity with our Führer and, through us, the glory he's bringing to America, our other national home. It is our job to prove to Berlin that we are nothing less than Germany's loyal western outpost. Accordingly, we are expecting 40,000 of our people to attend the festivities, so we must do everything to show our dedication to the Reich and the fatherland so that our leaders in Germany will be proud when they hear of this great celebration of triumph."

Gus Erstad looked around the room and felt considerable satisfaction with having become an integral part of the German American Bund two years before. As Oscar's speech began building to its crescendo, a technique he had developed after seeing newsreels of Hitler's tirades, Gus's mind wandered. He remembered the thrill he felt from the telephone call from Oscar inviting him and his Silver Swords to join the Bund as its strong right arm. This memory led him to recall a shock he experienced two weeks later when he received a peculiar call from a stranger.

"Who's this?" demanded Gus gruffly.

"That's not important, Mr. Erstad. What is significant is what I have been authorized to offer you so that your work with your Silver

Swords organization can continue and grow," announced the unknown caller.

"What d'ya mean? What d'ya got that I'd be interested in? Who's this anyway?"

"I have been authorized to provide you sufficient funding to carry out your objectives, so long as they meet the needs of the German American Bund and Gauleiter Oscar Hahn. This offer is also conditioned upon this conversation not being shared with anyone but Gauleiter Hahn and that you make absolutely no effort whatsoever to discover the source of this support. Do you understand?"

Gus then recalled how, despite his utter disbelief, he followed the mysterious caller's instructions and agreed to coordinate the receipt of his payments with Oscar. In light of what Gus saw as an immense amount of money, he recalled how calm, almost eerily serene, the stranger sounded as he dictated the terms of the agreement and what the next steps would be. As the call drew to a close, he was almost overwhelmed by the extreme courtesy of the caller, something that Gus was not used to hearing.

"Unless you have further questions, these matters will be coming to you in the form of two copies of a letter agreement in the next few days," advised the caller. "Please read it carefully and affix your signature. Until then, please contact Gauleiter Hahn and advise him, and only him, of our conversation. You will then leave a signed copy of the agreement with him. We will not be speaking again. It has been a profound pleasure discussing this with you, Mr. Erstad. Heil Hitler!"

Until that conversation, Silver Swords income had been entirely dependent on tasks assigned by Oscar for the Bund. The mysterious caller had changed everything. Gus remembered how his skin tingled with the thrill that there would now be no limits on what the Silver Swords and he could become.

With Oscar's increasingly strident voice in the background of his attention, Gus remembered the past two years as thrilling. His unending discussions with Oscar and the occasional "persuasion" of people who would occasionally attempt to damage the Bund gave him confidence that he was where he needed to be. His need for ruthlessness was well fed by the increasingly violent Bund meetings where he demonstrated his talents for commanding his brutal Silver Swords. He was particularly proud when Oscar would refer to the Silver Swords as his own, personal SS.

As Oscar's harangue continued in the background, Gus continued to feel his indifference to the rants about such things as "Lebensraum" and "Herrenvolk," that had been explained to him by Oscar as Germany's need to ruthlessly expand its borders to make way for the coming of a super race. By contrast, he remembered becoming intensely interested when Oscar described his plans for how to accomplish this by doing away with Jews, blacks, the mentally retarded, and other assorted "undesirables." Every skill Gus had so carefully cultivated as a killer, and then a feared leader of murderers was now a grisly toolbox to fulfill Oscar's and his most extreme objectives.

Just then, Gus was suddenly returned to the present when Oscar snagged his attention with some of his favorite, most virulent words that always arose when his hate-ridden speeches were approaching their climax. All logic and reason had vanished, and the audience had become a frantic froth of seething hatred as the speaker declaimed, "We will never stop eradicating this vermin, this Jew and black infestation in our midst! The Jews are responsible for the deaths of countless numbers of our brothers and sisters in the fatherland, and they are hell-bent on replacing us. But it is WE who shall replace them and the Negroes and take their pestilential bodies and burn them wherever we find them! Wherever they continue to breathe! Wherever they continue to breed! Their offspring are curses on the planet! It is up to us and our Aryan brethren to wipe this mighty scourge from the face of the earth!"

At long last, Gus Erstad had found his home.

14

Another person present who focused on Oscar Hahn's speech was Maximilian Graff. He found himself impressed with the passion and content of the last fifteen minutes of the speaker's furious rant. As soon as it ended, the Bund organizers stood and shouted "Heil Hitler" while jutting out their arms in the Nazi salute. As the audience members began splitting up into their event planning sessions, Maximilian wasted no time hobbling up to Oscar to introduce himself. Oscar had just been congratulated on his speech by several people and was speaking with Gus when Maximilian tapped him on the shoulder.

"Gauleiter Hahn?" inquired Maximilian.

"Hang on, Gus," said Oscar as he turned to face the stranger. "Yes, my name is Oscar Hahn. It is a pleasure to meet you, Mr...." he said as he discretely eyed the man's deformed foot.

"Graff...Maximilian Graff. I believe Heinrich Mann informed you that I might be attending. Is there somewhere we may be able to talk privately?"

"Of course, Mr. Graff. I'm glad you were able to make it today. Before we go, I would like to introduce you to my strong right arm. His name is Gustav Erstad, and he runs the Silver Swords, our security and enforcement group," said Oscar as he motioned for Gus to join them. When Gus shook his hand, Maximilian was surprised by the intensity of the man's grip in the same way that Oscar had been when he and Gus had first met on the Long Island Express. Oscar explained to his subordinate how his special guest had come to attend the meeting and then informed Maximilian that he would like Gus to join the discussions. While Maximilian was taken aback at Gus's imposing presence, he was indifferent to his addition to the conversation and nodded his assent.

"Then, gentlemen, please follow me," said Oscar as he motioned the two men to walk with him into a small room in a nearby building that contained a few tables and chairs scattered haphazardly around the small space. Shutting the door, Oscar spoke first as the three men took their chairs and sat facing one another.

"Thank you for coming," said Oscar. "So, we have a mutual friend in Herr Mann. He has been an ardent supporter of our organization from the beginning."

"I've known Heinrich for many years, and he spoke to me often about what is now the Bund," responded Maximilian. "He was a good customer of mine in the twenties when I owned a chemical company, and he's been a friend ever since. What did he tell you about why I would be here?"

"He said that you wanted to learn more about the Bund to determine if you might be interested in associating with us. Is this accurate?" asked Oscar.

"First and foremost, I insist on discretion. No one can know I would be involved. Is that clear, Mr. Hahn?

"Of course. A number of our members require such discretion. So, Mr. Graff, what exactly is your interest in the Bund?"

"I wish to support your organization with ample funds to carry out your and my objectives."

"I see, and may I inquire as to what your objectives are?"

"I will divulge that only after we have made an arrangement. That is something I insist upon."

"Well, Mr. Graff, I very much appreciate your interest in providing financial support, but without knowing your intentions, I'm afraid I must say no. We have a constitution that was adopted last year, and it clearly outlines our objectives. I wouldn't be able to commit the Bund to some other objectives that could conflict with our own. Surely you can understand."

"You're actually going to turn down my money?!" replied Maximilian with disgust as he stood to leave.

"Only for the moment, Mr. Graff. I am confident you will understand after you see and hear a special Bund rally that I would like to invite you to attend at Madison Square Garden next February. Would you be available?" Maximilian's anger had already flared up enough for both of the others to see it in his flushed face, but Oscar's invitation mollified him enough where he was able to sit down again.

"It will be a spectacular affair!" gushed Oscar. "We expect over twenty thousand members to attend to hear our leader, Bundesführer Fritz Kuhn, describe our movement and our plans. If what you hear pleases you, I will be delighted to explore our relationship further. It's only six months away, and in the meantime, I would also like to invite you to German Day next month. You will be able to see perhaps forty or fifty thousand of our supporters in attendance. Are you interested?"

"I will make arrangements to attend both events, and then we can talk. I do not expect to be disappointed."

"I can assure you that you will never see more dramatic support for our movement and the highest Nazi ideals outside of Berlin. Let me share with you some of the details of these events," said Oscar excitedly. As Maximilian listened, he was still fighting his urge to explode on the spot after having had his offer of financial support rejected. However, there was something he detected in the beefier man sitting next to Oscar—his overpowering dimension, dark, small eyes, and oversized head with closely-cropped hair—that bridled his temper, a new experience for Maximilian.

15

1939 - New York City

As he shuffled along through the snow and the New York crowds, Maximilian was reflecting on the vast hordes of Bund members and their enthusiasm at the German Day festivities the prior October at Long Island's Camp Siegfried in Yaphank. All the Nazi flag waving and fervent, jutting salutes left no doubt in his mind who their supreme hero was. Despite the passion, however, the speeches by various local leaders failed to reassure him that the Bund was an organization that he could bend to his will.

That was five months ago. Tonight, as Maximilian approached Madison Square Garden, he had to navigate around the mounted New York police while muscling his way through the throng of frenzied protesters facing off against Bund members dressed as stormtroopers. Nearing the entrance, he looked up to see the marquee advertising "Pro American Rally" with hockey and basketball games taking second billing. Invited as Oscar's special guest, he was permitted to enter the immense facility early. The only people to be seen were maintenance men putting the final touches on what was designed to be an awe-inspiring event. Walking into the great hall, Maximilian was struck by the grandiosity of what stood before him. A thirty-foot wide stage with a two-foot-tall white barrier extending along its entire front was at the far end of the hall. A six-foot-tall podium dominated the front and center of the stage. Behind it by some eighteen feet were four narrow, vertical versions of American flags that towered over the stage, stretching nearly forty feet to the ceiling. Two specially designed flags highlighted with swastikas were interspersed with the stylized American flags. As Maximilian continued to make his way to the stage, he found it odd that the centerpiece of this immense panel of banners was a thirty-foot rendition of George Washington standing erect in full military regalia.

Just then, Oscar came from behind the stage with his henchman, Gus, to welcome their important guest. "Good evening, Mr. Graff. It's a great pleasure to see that you have joined us for this momentous event. Welcome."

"Mr. Hahn, Mr. Erstad," Maximilian replied as he shook their hands, again somewhat startled by Gus's vice-like grip. "As you promised me at Yaphank, I'm here to learn if the Bund's objectives are consistent with my own. To be clear, that's my purpose in being here."

"I can assure you that you will not be disappointed. All of your questions will be answered before the night is over…. Ah, yes. Here we are," said Oscar as he spotted a slightly portly man in thin-rimmed glasses dressed in black trousers and a brown tunic approaching them. The man's uniform was complete with black epaulets, a broad, black collar accent, and a John Browne belt crossing his chest. His features were heavy and his oversized brow so low that his upper eyelids seemed almost nonexistent. Maximilian noticed that the man's hair was slicked back in the same manner as his but was finer.

"Before we do anything else, permit me to introduce you to Bundesführer Fritz Kuhn," said Oscar as he bowed slightly.

"Heil Hitler!" said the man as he stopped, steeled his expression, and shot his arm out to fulfill the required Nazi flourish. A distinctly German accent dressed his fluent English prompting Maximilian to think that Kuhn had probably been born in Germany but was a longtime resident of America.

"I am Bundesführer Kuhn, Mr. Graff. It's a pleasure to finally meet you." After some preliminary remarks intended to establish rapport, Kuhn said, "You know, Mr. Graff. I understand that you owned a large chemical company at one time, is this correct?"

"Yes, that's right."

"You probably did not know this, but until the Bund began demanding all of my efforts, I was a chemist for the Ford Motor Company."

"Is that so? Good for you."

"But that is not all we share, Mr. Graff. You may be closer and have more in common with the Bund and Nazi Germany than you realize."

"How's that, Mr. Kuhn?" responded Maximilian while looking at the ground and deliberately avoiding the man's official title lest he inflate further the bundesführer's estimation of his and his movement's importance to him. Maximilian had pledged to himself that once he recaptured success from his father's failure, he would never again surrender the spotlight to anyone, especially such a pompous pretender like Fritz Kuhn.

"You see," Kuhn continued with evident delight, "you share a rumored distinguishing characteristic with Germany's Reich Minister of Propaganda, the famous Dr. Goebbels. It is said that he, too, has a deformed right foot that is very similar to yours, Mr. Graff. Heil Hitler!" he announced as his right arm once again shot forward.

Taken aback by the suddenness of what Maximilian immediately saw as an intolerable insult from someone who could never hope to earn his respect, he took several moments to respond. "Listen carefully, Kuhn! I am not going to stand for having anything about me pointed out or highlighted by anyone, and especially someone like you!" Maximilian's temper was instantly out of the bottle for all to see. As the others abruptly took a step backward, Gus shot toward Maximilian and grabbed his arm with his armored grip.

"Mr. Graff. You'll calm down now," said Gus quietly but with a perceptible menace. "The bundesführer din't mean no disrespect. He was givin' you a compliment." As had happened before with Gus, Maximilian's temper was immediately checked when he felt the imminent, tangible threat of severe bodily harm, which was made especially disturbing by its chilling contrast with the icy calm with which Gus had delivered his warning. Gradually, Gus released his grip while nodding slowly at Maximilian and keeping his eyes fixed on him. Maximilian quickly shrugged his shoulders and straightened his sleeve in an unconscious attempt to shed his anger as he struggled to recover an even temper. Satisfied that an altercation had been avoided, Oscar recommended that they take their seats in the dignitaries' section to the side of the stage as people started entering the hall.

Forty-five minutes later, there was an aggressive stirring of the vast, multi-tiered audience that had filled Madison Square Garden. The crowd was so large that it sounded to Maximilian like a massive surge of ocean surf continuously assaulting an endless beach. Having returned to a more settled frame of mind, he was impatient to hear what Bundesführer Fritz Kuhn would say about the German American Bund's objectives and intentions that Oscar had promised him months before when they had first met. While they awaited the opening ceremonies, Oscar spent his time preparing his visitor for what the gauleiter knew would be a stirring and fiery performance.

A large drum corps signaled the commencement of the event by entering the hall with drums beating loudly. A long column of men brandishing American and swastika flags and banners followed. The entire troop mounted the stage in several rows that spanned its entire width. Gus's security detail positioned itself at strategic points on the stage's perimeter. Maximilian then saw a river of young male and female Bund members wearing short-sleeved dress shirts and neckties flowing into the hall from the rear, marching to the incessant beat of the drum corps on stage. This seemingly endless procession broadcast the future power of the Bund. Several times, Maximilian turned his eyes away from the spectacle and scanned the immense crowd, imagining the best of them obeying him and fulfilling the grand plan he had devised.

Once the stage was filled, the drumming halted. For a few moments, the mishmash of American flags, swastikas, and the colossal effigy of George Washington looked down on the proceeding in silence. The American Pledge of Allegiance was then led by a man who delivered it in a Hitleresque accent as if to prepare the audience for the main event. When the Pledge came to its conclusion, Fritz Kuhn strutted onto the stage. Maximilian was astounded to see the entire congregation rise as a unit and thrust out their right arms as if they were saluting the Führer himself. As Kuhn stepped up to the platformed lectern, he motioned for everyone to sit before he launched into brief attacks against the "Jewish" press and then descended into what Maximilian came to hear.

"If you ask what we are actively fighting for under our charter, first and foremost, a socially just, white, Gentile-ruled United States. Second, Gentile-controlled labor unions, free from Jewish Moscow-directed domination." Just then, Kuhn turned his head to see a protester dash onto the stage only to be immediately buried by Gus's Silver Swords grabbing and beating the invader before New York police entered the fray and dragged the man away. After the brief fracas, Maximilian looked again at the speaker who appeared to be smirking at such a feeble attempt to disrupt the proceedings. He then continued with a harangue that was peppered with references to FDR as "Frank D. Rosenfeld" and his "Jew Deal." Kuhn's speech grew in intensity with each minute and stirred Maximilian's deepest hatred of Jews and blacks.

As he listened, Maximilian had no illusions that, for him, the Bund represented an opportunity as well as a threat. While his plans could be fulfilled by such blind loyalty on the parts of such people, he knew that the bitterness in his soul demanded a level of satisfaction that only his total control of the Bund could satisfy. He also knew that, despite his being intimidated by Gus's apparent tendency toward violence, he could use such a person and his Silver Swords for what he had in mind. This challenge of how to control the Bund and its Silver Swords now pushed Kuhn's rant to the back of his mind as he weighed his options to fulfill what had long been an obsession. As Madison Square Garden retreated to an ever more distant corner of his mind, Maximilian immersed himself in his dark and vindictive vision.

16

Sitting on two chairs outside his house, Oscar Hahn was sharing a beer with Gus Erstad one balmy evening several months after the Madison Square Garden event. They were experiencing a quiet moment recalling what serendipity had brought them together. Despite being opposites in temperament, demeanor, and sophistication of thought and expression, they had become a perfect team in the four years since they shared the train to Yaphank. Gus was the hard fist and Oscar the tactical leader side of the duo, enabling Oscar to conceal his resistance to violence from his superiors. Both men felt a debt of gratitude for having been the yin to the other's yang and were basking in the warm thoughts of a rewarding future together.

"You know, Gus, we've been very fortunate that we found one another. Wouldn't you say?"

"Sure thing, Oscar. I ain't shy t'say that I was about to have real trouble when you called me with yer offer to join the Bund. It's been real good. Real good. All those jobs you had me and my men do, I ain't ever felt so good about doin' such things. The Bund takes no shit, Oscar, 'n I ain't 'bout to start takin' none neither. You been a good boss, and the Bund feels like just the right place fer me, that's fer shore."

Oscar was not used to hearing such sentimentality from his right-hand man, but three beers and their earlier conversation about the spectacle of Madison Square Garden had made them both slide into a state of maudlin nostalgia. At the moment, Oscar was enjoying to the fullest having such a fearless yet obedient friend.

After Oscar stood up and went inside the house for another couple of beers, he turned on the kitchen light just as he heard a sudden pounding at the front door and went to answer it. "Relax! I'm coming! I'm coming!" he shouted. His protests did nothing to halt the loud pounding that he knew would stop only after he opened the door.

"What in hell's this banging all about, Stengle?" Oscar said to his young adjutant, whose look of desperation immediately put him on edge.

Gasping for breath from his dash to Oscar's house, the young man paused before delivering news that he knew his boss would immediately regret hearing. "Have...have you heard...the...the news, Gauleiter Hahn?"

"News? What news, Stengle?"

"It's...it's Bundesführer Kuhn,...gauleiter."

"What on earth are you talking about? What about Bundesführer Kuhn?"

"He's been...well...he's been arrested."

"He's been WHAT?! WHERE?! Arrested for what?... Who arrested him, for God's sake?!"

"I think...I think it happened in...in Pennsylvania, gauleiter."

"Pennsylvania?! Why in hell was he arrested in Pennsylvania?!"

"I don't...I don't know the...I don't know the details, gauleiter, but...apparently it was...it was federal officers."

"You're telling me that federal officers arrested Bundesführer Kuhn?!"

"Yes, sir...Gauleiter Hahn."

After a few seconds of struggling to make sense of the information that had just assailed him, Oscar dismissed the young man and, in a daze, slowly shut the door. Entering the darkened living room that was lit only by the light from the adjacent kitchen, he sat down slowly on his living room sofa, his eyes transfixed on an indeterminate point straight ahead of him. His outward appearance betrayed no internal turmoil as he sat perfectly still. "Where does this leave the Bund?! Is it over?! Where does it leave me?! What happens next?!" he thought, still grappling with the ultimate significance of such a potentially disastrous event.

Moments later, Gus entered the house. "Oscar? Oscar? Where're you?" he said as he caught sight of his friend sitting like a stone figure in the dimly-lit room. "What happened?! What was all that bangin'? Who the hell was at the door?! Oscar?! Oscar!" Oscar's lack of response to his attempts to shake him from his stupor left Gus unnerved as he sat down slowly next to his friend. "What the hell's goin' on, Oscar?"

Finally, Oscar faced him, but Gus saw that his mind was in another place, his eyes empty.

"I still don't believe this, Gus.… I was just informed by Stengle that Bundesführer Kuhn was just arrested…by federal officers," he said as he turned his face forward again. This was followed by Gus's repeating the questions Oscar had asked Stengle. After Oscar told Gus what little he knew, both men were now plagued with the same doubts as they sat back and silently pondered what was ahead.

17

"Excuse me, Mr. Graff," said Karl Stampf as he stuck his head inside his boss's office.

"Yes, Stampf, what is it?" replied Maximilian as he looked up from some papers.

"Wasn't the German American Bund the outfit that put on that big rally at the Madison Square Garden that you attended a few months ago?"

"Yes, it was. Why do you ask?"

"Here, look at this newspaper article," said the executive as he handed his boss the morning paper.

Maximilian took the publication and glanced at the front page. "What?! How in the hell did this happen?!" he exclaimed.

"I have no idea, Mr. Graff, but it looks like this Bund group is in for trouble," said Karl as he watched his boss barely able to wait for one sentence of the lead article to end before devouring the next. As Maximilian hunched over the New York Herald Tribune dated May 26, 1939, the headline proclaimed that the day before, detectives, under the direction of Manhattan District Attorney Thomas A. Dewey, had seized Fritz Kuhn. Only hours earlier, a New York County Grand Jury had indicted him on twelve counts of grand larceny and forgery.

Sitting slowly back in his chair while staring at the headline, Maximilian could see that a possible solution to the problem he had been wrestling with—how to take charge of the Bund—had just been delivered to him. Seeing his boss riveted on the story, Karl wondered why this news was so important to him.

"This is good news, then, Mr. Graff?"

After a pause, his boss answered, "It could be, Stampf. It could be. I want you to contact two men—Hahn, Oscar Hahn, and Gus

Erstad—summon them here immediately. Do not take no for an answer. Do you understand?"

"Yes sir, of course," replied Maximilian's senior executive as he quickly left the room to begin the search for the two men.

It was two days later that Oscar and Gus were sitting in front of Maximilian's imposing desk at the Graff estate—a fateful discussion was in the offing. Karl stood at the back of the room next to a huge, intimidating person, Gunther Gunshau. Dispensing with any pleasantries, Maximilian made his intentions clear.

"It appears that the German American Bund is in quite a bind. Would you agree, Hahn?"

"I'm not sure where this terrible blow leaves us, Mr. Graff, but there are other leaders who will come forward."

"And where do you stand, Erstad? How has this affected your Silver Swords?" probed Maximilian.

"Uh, I dunno, Mr. Graff. Yesterday our funding was stopped, so I dunno where we go from here."

"What was the source of your funding, Mr. Erstad?"

"I ain't real sure. Ya see, I'd get the money as long's I never asked."

"Do you know, Hahn?"

"Since that funding's now gone, I suppose I can shed some light on this, Mr. Graff," said the gauleiter hesitatingly.

"And?…" prompted Maximilian.

"Well, my understanding is that it was established by an attorney."

"An attorney no doubt acting on behalf of someone else?" replied Maximilian.

"I believe so, yes."

"Well, then, who was this someone else?!" demanded Maximilian with a flash of anger.

"A Mr. Magnum. Mr. Howard Magnum."

"What?!" shouted Maximilian. "Are you telling me the Magnums funded the German American Bund?!"

"It would appear so, sir."

Maximilian was thunderstruck. The people who had done such damage to his insecticide operation four years earlier and had given birth to his chilling oath of mortal revenge had been helping to fund the very organization that he now sought to control. Contemplating this revelation in silence, a smile slowly spread over his face.

"Both of you listen to me very carefully. Nazi Germany has taken over the Rhineland, Austria, the Sudetenland, and Czechoslovakia. It won't end there, and I am convinced that Europe will be at war within months. This'll cause considerable pressure on the US to enter the war, although this is still a very unpopular idea here, so it won't happen quickly. Nevertheless, the minute this country goes to war, the Bund as you have known it is as good as dead."

"This is nothing short of treasonous, Herr Graff! Heil Hitler!" shouted Oscar as he jumped out of his chair and gave the Nazi salute.

"Sit down and shut up, you fool!" erupted Maximilian while keeping his eyes on Gus, who remained motionless. Without any indication of protection from Gus and remembering the presence of the mountainous person standing at the back of the room, Oscar, visibly upset, settled back in his chair.

"I said that you were to listen, not speak, Hahn! Do you or do you not understand this simple instruction?!" Oscar looked down and slowly nodded.

"Listen to me, both of you," commanded Maximilian, who was still wrestling with aftershocks from his emotional reprimand. "I've decided to extend an offer whereby you can maintain your status as a regional leader, or gauleiter if you prefer, with your current level of funding, and you, Erstad, will have all the money you need for your Silver Swords. However, considering the problems that are now facing the Bund, you'll bring only your most faithful members along and make them swear their allegiance to me, Hahn, and denounce their allegiance to the Bund. You both will be reporting directly to me and must do exactly as I say and never, ever question any commands I give. Is this clear to both of you?"

"You must understand, Herr Graff," said Oscar, more sheepishly this time, "I cannot go back on my oath to the Bund—I've sworn to uphold its ideals."

"Your oath, Hahn?! Ideals?! What in the hell do they mean if the Bund ceases to exist?!" said Maximilian, his voice rising as he glanced at Gus. "What's more, I'm warning you both that I've just made this offer for the first and the last time! If you leave this room and haven't accepted my terms, I won't be your savior, and you'll go down with the rest of your sorry brigade! Then what'll your oath be worth, Hahn?! And you, Erstad, how'll you keep those guards of yours under control?! Neither of you has a choice, and you know it!"

Maximilian was still trembling when he sat back in his chair stiffly and waited for the two men to consider their fates as they quietly spoke with one another. Finally, Oscar turned away from Gus and looked back at Maximilian.

"All right, Herr Graff. After consideration of your offer, you have both my and Herr Erstad's complete loyalty."

"How many members of your organization will you be bringing along with you, Hahn?" asked Maximilian.

"Let me think for a moment, Herr Graff."

"Well, hurry up! This shouldn't be a difficult question to answer!"

"To the contrary, Herr Graff. Many members will be reluctant to leave the Bund. They will still be very loyal to Bundesführer Kuhn."

"I don't give a shit about Kuhn or anyone who thinks the sun rises and sets on the fool! Now answer my question! How many can you depend on coming with you?!"

"I would estimate something like twenty or twenty-five members."

After thinking for a few seconds, Maximilian replied, "Mmm. Yes, I believe that'll be sufficient for my purposes."

"Now that we've come to an agreement, what is this plan of yours?" asked Oscar.

Maximilian paused before responding in an unusually low tone of voice. "In time, I'll inform you of only what you need to know to fulfill my objectives. Your first task, Hahn, will be to oversee a special project that I have planned for an area along Oyster Bay on Long Island. I'll have the land development plans delivered to you when they are completed, which should be just a matter of days. Erstad, you'll be working for Hahn and will be responsible for the project's security. Until the project is ready to commence, I'll say only one more thing: you are both fortunate to have chosen more wisely than you know."

18

The summer of 1939 was a year after Anna's difficult discussion with Malcolm concerning her intention to follow up on his father's concerns with the government's puzzling reluctance to control various domestic terror organizations. Pursuing her inquiry, Anna found herself knocking on the front door of the expansive but warm and charming home owned by Dr. Eric Franzen.

"Thanks so much for seeing me, Dr. Franzen," said Anna after the door opened and she looked into the professor's eyes. She thought they conveyed a certain sadness, but his calm, welcoming voice fit comfortably with his benevolent, patrician demeanor. He put Anna in mind of her father-in-law, making her feel immediately at home despite the two never having met before. Once inside, she was taken by the home's bright and airy feel and the breathtaking views of Long Island Sound through the large bay windows on the far side of the living room.

The two moved towards one of the brightly patterned living room sofas near the bay windows. As they sat down, Anna raised a topic that had been preoccupying the entire northeastern United States for months.

"Remember when I first called you last fall, I had no idea how seriously September's hurricane had devastated Long Island and your neighborhood here. Even that long ago, I still saw signs of the terrible damage on my way here today. I now certainly understand why you wanted to put off our meeting until things could get back to normal. Where my husband and I live in Boston, we're only ten miles away from Blue Hill Observatory, where they registered the worst wind gust ever recorded in the United States. I believe it was over 185 miles per hour, if you can imagine such a thing. While we didn't have to contend with the savage wind and water surges that you did, we still lost about a hundred people."

Nodding his understanding, he responded, "Well, it was certainly terrifying here, Mrs. Tilner. There was simply no warning before we seemed to be facing the end of days. In all, I read that we lost some 600 people in the storm. The damage throughout the region was unbelievable. Harvard, where I went to school, owns a 3,000-acre forest for their forestry program about seventy miles east of the campus, and it was destroyed. I seem to remember that New York and New England lost some 2 billion trees. How terrible, just terrible."

"Well, I'm relieved you're all right, and I just want you to know how much I appreciate the time you're giving me. May I ask how long you've been one of my firm's clients?"

"Why, of course," replied the man in his soft, pleasing tone of voice. "But before I answer, I understand that Fess's your father-in-law. Isn't that right?"

"Yes, he is. He, his wife, Beth, and my husband, Malcolm, of course, are all very dear to me. They truly are my mentors as well as being wonderful human beings."

"I can assure you that you made an excellent choice when you joined this family, my dear."

"I agree and want nothing more than to be a credit to the Tilner name."

"Now, there, Mrs. Tilner. You're being overly modest," replied Eric as he took the opportunity to reveal his reaction to his engaging guest. "Fess's made it very clear to me that as both an attorney and an intrepid sleuth, he sees you as truly extraordinary. I'd be remiss if I failed to say that you're the only person I know whose talents he holds in such awe."

"That's very humbling to hear, Dr. Franzen. Would you please call me Anna?"

"Thank you, Anna. It will be a pleasure. Please call me Eric. Now, concerning how long I've been a client of your firm. Let's see, I've known Fess for…well, since 1922, so it's going on seventeen years. For a long time before I met Fess, I'd heard that Tilner and Associates was widely recognized as the finest civil rights firm in the country. What led me to seek your father-in-law's services was his reputation for fair-minded objectivity, his concentration on civil rights issues, and his legal competence. The matter was so important that I couldn't afford to take a chance on anyone I couldn't trust absolutely."

"Why exactly did you want to see him, Eric?"

"That requires a bit of a story. I received my doctor of science degree in biochemistry from Harvard in 1892. Years later, my wife…my wife was awarded a prestigious position at Princeton, and so we moved to New Jersey. A year after that, I was fortunate enough to join their teaching staff. As a new assistant professor, everything went along pretty much the way you'd expect for a good long time. Eventually, I became a full professor, and, on occasion, the position involved being a part of a doctoral dissertation team. There was nothing out of the ordinary here either. That is until 1916, when I was overseeing the dissertation of someone I came to see as anything but ordinary.

"His name was Harry Laughlin, and he was barely ten years younger than I. He was smart, all right, and appeared to be focused on cell biology, about which he knew a great deal. I was still unaware of what I was dealing with when he told me he intended to write his dissertation on the mitosis of onion root tips, of all things. This was all very erudite and respectable until one evening when we were discussing his dissertation over some wine, and the conversation took a very dark turn. I'll never forget it."

"Did it involve cytology or something else?" said Anna eager to get to the point.

"Ah, you know the term for cell biology. Good for you, Anna. No, no. It involved something else, something that could be catastrophic if it's allowed free rein. Are you familiar with the term eugenics?"

"Isn't this the study of controlling human reproduction to increase the frequency of people's superior attributes and decrease their negative ones?"

"Correct. But I fear there may be more to this that you don't understand with implications that I find terrifying."

"But Eric, it's my understanding that the scientific community widely accepts eugenics. It's been part of the curriculum at several prestigious universities here and abroad, especially at your alma mater. Isn't that right?"

"Regrettably, that's largely true. In its early days, it attracted funding from several wealthy people. At present, however, its acceptance as a legitimate science is under attack by an increasing number of respected scientists. Its reputation is declining rapidly, but it's still being used for horrific purposes. You see, there's a very dark side to all of this that's being used in this country to justify discriminatory immigration control, marriage restrictions, segregation, and, even worse, forced sterilization and abortion for all sorts of people who are arbitrarily being deemed 'unfit.'"

"That's very troubling. I simply had no idea, but what exactly did Laughlin say that spooked you so?"

"Remember, this is over twenty years ago, back in 1916 or 17, while he was still becoming Dr. Laughlin. As I said, after a glass or two of wine, he gradually became quite intense—a different person actually. He began talking to me about wanting to develop a socially-sanctioned system of sterilization of all sorts of people— Jews, the feebleminded, southern and eastern Europeans, blacks, criminals…well, you get the idea—gradually getting rid of any group that those in power deem 'inferior.'

"At the time, of course, I was well aware of eugenics, considering that I live just a few miles from Cold Spring Harbor, which has been its epicenter for a long time. Since 1910 it's been the home of the Eugenics Record Office, or ERO. Backed over the years by the Carnegie Institution, Rockefeller Foundation, and the Harriman railroad fortune, in the twenties it was considered by many to be the leading eugenics organization in America. However, I was preoccupied with my academic work and was unaware of just how pervasive and unhinged the eugenics movement had become. When I learned of the backlash coming from many distinguished and widely-respected scientific authorities, I dismissed Laughlin's ramblings as meaningless. Now it appears that this was a terrible mistake."

"How so?" inquired Anna.

"To begin with, after our bizarre conversation, I was shocked when I saw that in 1922 he published a horrifying book entitled *Eugenical Sterilization in the United States*. In it, he included something he called his 'Model Eugenical Sterilization Law,' which was a legal framework for compulsory sterilization. His apparent obsession with such things is what had startled me years before. With the publication of his book, and then the reported eagerness of so many states to adopt its so-called 'model,' I felt compelled to seek out your father-in-law."

"How could all this be taken seriously by intelligent people?"

"Oh my, Anna. Encouraged by numerous well-credentialed scientists, promoters, and racially-motivated organizations, eugenics became the foundation for state laws that permitted the forced sterilization of women in mental institutions. If you can believe it, the greatest catalyst to the involuntary sterilization of thousands of women was the United States Supreme Court! In a 1927 ruling, it upheld Laughlin's legal model in a case involving a Virginia home for the mentally retarded. This paved the way for his legal roadmap for forced sterilizations of all sorts of people to spread to dozens of states, California having the longest list of victims!"

"California? How horrible! Was this widely known?"

"Some of it became news here as well as in Europe."

"Wouldn't this discourage people from even wanting to come to this country?!"

"Actually, Anna, it's worse. This eugenics movement is a cover for a super-racist group of powerful people who wish to redefine and strangle our entire immigration system. Just look at the evidence. In 1924, two years after Laughlin's book came out, a group called the Immigration Restriction League used eugenics to terrify people into believing that hordes of vermin-infested, pestilential, feebleminded, and dangerous foreign criminals were invading our country and would eventually wipe out the white race."

"This must be the same Immigration Restriction League that I read about when I was studying immigration law," responded Anna. "As I recall, the League was lobbying for a literacy test for immigrants since they believed that literacy rates were lower in 'inferior races' and that this would keep them out of the country. Is this the same organization?"

"The same. After years of fighting to all but eliminate immigration from Asia and eastern and southern Europe, the IRL, as it's known, succeeded in intimidating the US Congress into passing the Immigration Act of 1924. The results? To give you just one example, a little over a year later, the number of people emigrating from Italy dropped from an average of over something like 200,000 to just 4,000. In fact, more immigrants were leaving than being allowed to enter the US. Naturally, the Act was enthusiastically supported by the Ku Klux Klan."

"I had no idea! My studies dealt with the Act itself and not its results. You're right, this's very disturbing!… You know, this makes me wonder if eugenics has had any impact on Adolf Hitler's constant rants about his 'master race' and his repression of the Jews in Germany."

"You have just hit on something that I find particularly devastating, Anna. Have you read Hitler's *Mein Kampf*?"

"I'm afraid not, Eric."

"Well, the book is his manifesto for Nazism that he wrote when he was in prison after a failed coup attempt in the mid-twenties. In it, he praises the eugenics developed here in America, especially to justify its darker path to create a super race. What's more, he copied America's eugenics legislative blueprint to create his own Nazi version after he came to power in 1933. No doubt, under his dictatorship, this has led to horrific abuse in Germany and its occupied territories, leaving virtually everyone except his 'Aryan master race' vulnerable to incarceration, sterilization, and, I fear, even murder. Have you heard what happened throughout Germany last November, about two months after our hurricane?"

"No, I haven't. I must say, this seems to be particularly disturbing for you."

"Oh, but it is Anna! Throughout Germany, stormtroopers destroyed thousands of synagogues. Jewish-owned buildings, hospitals, schools, and businesses were ransacked and destroyed with sledgehammers! It also appears that they murdered nearly one hundred Jews and arrested tens of thousands of Jewish men while the police looked on and did nothing. Now it's called Kristallnacht, or the Night of Broken Glass, after the shattered windows from Jewish buildings that covered the streets all over Germany. I can't tell you how upsetting this is to me!"

"I'm still wondering why Fess thought I should speak with you, Eric. Did he say what you knew that could be of help?"

"Yes, Anna…yes, he did," said Eric as he struggled to gain his composure. "Fess shared with me his conversation with you and how troubled he is at our government's official nonresponse to the rise in this country of some organizations sympathetic with the Nazis and their brutally repressive behavior and ideas. He's most puzzled and disturbed by the tight-lipped reactions of some of his most highly-placed, closest friends in the government who are in a position to do something about such groups.

"He wanted me to tell you what I knew about Harry Laughlin and eugenics and who had been behind the Eugenics Record Office. He also wanted me to tell you whatever else I knew about the behavior of domestic Nazi organizations. However, I'm afraid that, at present, I can't be of as much help in that area as I'd like. It's all very troubling, especially considering the increasingly frequent and violent events overseas."

"Eric, I hope you can forgive me, but there's one thing that I find especially disturbing about our conversation and must ask," said Anna as she leaned toward her host.

"And what's that, my dear?"

"Is there something that you haven't told me about this whole matter that's made you immerse yourself in this horrible topic. If so, it seemed just below the surface when you mentioned your wife. Again, I apologize for being so direct. Still, I sense extreme anguish in your descriptions of Kristallnacht, and I believe it goes beyond any intellectual curiosity or a desire to protect our country. To you, all this seems to be intensely personal. Please tell me if I'm overstepping my bounds here."

Anna could see Eric's emotions quickly welling up inside him until he burst into tears. It was a minute before he could even speak.

"You…you're correct, Anna," said Eric between sobs. "I'm sorry, but I know I must face this, I simply must," he added before exhaling a deep breath. "My dear wife, Sarah…her maiden name was Menz…she's Jewish," he said before breaking down again. "She…she's ten years younger than I and was born here as were her two older brothers. She'd always been extremely close to both of them. When the Menz family heard about Kristallnacht last November, both of her brothers saw the danger ahead and immediately took a ship to Germany hoping to rescue their relatives who were still in Germany."

"But Sarah stayed here with you?" added Anna.

"Yes, but you have no idea how difficult it was for her parents and me to get her to remain here. She was absolutely beside herself when both of her brothers left without her. She fought me tooth and nail to go, but I just couldn't face losing her. It was all I could do to comfort her that they would soon be back home, and all would be fine."

Anna was moved by seeing how much difficulty Eric was having to get through his story. Hoping to offer whatever comfort she could, she broke the silence, "But at least, she remained here safely with you."

All of a sudden, Eric broke down once more and was unable to speak for several minutes. Finally, he was able to say, "That's what I thought, Anna. That's exactly what I thought."

"My God, Eric. What happened? Were Sarah's brothers able to bring back their relatives?" asked Anna becoming increasingly apprehensive.

After several moments of considerable effort to collect himself, Eric came to what appeared to be a different part of his saga. "Anna, please bear with me. This is profoundly challenging...you have probably not heard of the MS *St. Louis*." Anna acknowledged that she had not.

"It was a ship filled with over 900 European emigrants, mostly Jewish people desperate to escape the widespread and deadly brutality of the Nazis. They were seeking asylum in Cuba, the United States, or Canada. When the ship arrived in Havana, only twenty-eight passengers were allowed off. Not having valid visas due to the suddenness of their departure, Sarah's family was barred from getting off the ship. As it was, Cuba wasn't pleased taking even this tiny number of Jewish refugees.

"Then the *St. Louis* headed for Florida. Sarah's brothers must have been confident that their US citizenship would enable them to disembark. However, by this time, the Immigration Act of 1924 had become far more restrictive, and the US Secretary of State, Cordel Hull, strongly urged FDR to deny entrance to all of the refugees. Sarah's brothers were lumped in with everyone else, and not a single person was let off the ship. To make matters worse, the Coast Guard was ordered to shadow the *St. Louis* to ensure that no one jumped ship." At this point, Eric took a deep breath before finishing his story.

"By this time, Sarah was frantic that not only would her relatives be banned from entering the United States, but that her brothers would also be sent back to Germany and face certain death. Once Canada also refused the ship, the captain reluctantly set sail back to Europe. This shattered Sarah." With these last words, Eric put his head in his hands and began to sob once more, his shoulders heaving as Anna reached out to touch him. It was several minutes before he could go on.

"You don't need to continue, Eric. This's obviously too much for you to bear, and I now understand why you've been so obsessed with looking into all of this eugenics and immigration business considering how it's devastated Sarah's family. Please comfort yourself however you can. There's no need to continue crucifying yourself, Eric, it won't bring them back."

With this, Eric abruptly stopped sobbing and sat up, facing straight ahead. The muscles in his face and neck stiffened as the tears still washed down his face, as he said in a low, monotone voice with his jaws clenched, "There's more. You're correct that my grief will not bring back Sarah's brothers and the rest of her family.... Oh, God! Oh, God!... It will also not bring my Sarah back to me!"

"What?! Oh my God, Eric, what's happened to her?! What happened to Sarah?!"

"With her brothers trapped, she was suffering, helpless with agony.... She was tortured with grief." Staring straight ahead and sitting completely still before releasing a long, slow breath, he added, "She's dead. She took her own life." Then Eric turned, leaned forward, and looked into Anna's eyes. Looking deeply into his, she saw only a dead, lifeless soul sitting beside her.

Sitting up and once again looking down, his voice lowered as he said, "Today...today is the one month anniversary of...of when Sarah shot herself."

19

Most of those driving on the private drive through the heavily wooded, 3,000-acre estate were stunned the first time they came into the vast clearing and laid eyes on the mansion. Its late-eighteenth-century French architecture enhanced the massive appearance of the three-storied structure with its immense wings. It brandished the power of its owner by also being perfectly situated in the large clearing to reveal its endless manicured gardens, maximizing the impact of someone's first glimpse. Guests were supposed to be overwhelmed.

The men whose limousines were being parked along the large circular entrance and who were now walking up the eighty-foot-wide portico were not. Nearly every one of these industrialists and financiers occupied residences of comparable ostentation and grandeur, designed to declare their exceptional power as well as their lifetime membership in the pantheon of America's and the world's elite.

As the group assembled in the massive and ornate library, it was a collection of faces that often appeared on newspaper front pages with names that arose periodically on the radio, usually to the chagrin of the man involved. Standing unobtrusively near the door to the high-ceilinged room, Bernard Haskins thought to himself, "Outside of the White House, I'm not sure anyone could assemble such an impressive collection of notables." He had worked for an alliance of these people under the direction of his boss long enough to witness how deftly they surreptitiously manipulated the massive levers that made America, its government, and the rest of the industrialized world run.

Urged on by Howard Magnum, Bernard's boss, the illustrious group began taking their places at the long, rosewood table, pulling out their chairs that had been placed at the table with precision. With everyone seated, the man at the head remained standing and calmly began to speak in a tone that belied his influence.

"The meeting will please come to order," said the immaculately-dressed gentleman. Despite his soft-spoken manner, a rather slight build, and the stature of the legendary group of people he was addressing, it was clear to all that Howard was in command. "By way of a reminder," he began, "as a security measure, we've agreed not to use any of our personal or corporate names when we're together. While we're all well aware of the sensitive nature of our planning, it's also important that I repeat that nothing said within these walls can be heard by another human being. Now, let us proceed. As you all know, we have an ambitious schedule if we're to meet our objectives. First, we'll hear from our esteemed colleague representing the chemical industry, which, as you all know, is affiliated with its sister company in Germany. Would you please start us off?"

"Thank you. As you all know, thanks to the bond issues handled by American banks and our cartel agreements with the oil, automobile, chemical, and metal industries also represented in this meeting, I'm pleased to announce that Germany is finally preparing to enter the active phase of its major expansion. Most recently, the Führer has communicated to me that he is deeply indebted to our petroleum partner, in which you know we own a sizable stake. He's profoundly grateful for their having provided him with its process for the creation of iso-octane, without which the Luftwaffe and the Wehrmacht would have trouble getting off the ground!" A subtle murmur with barely disguised smirks followed the remark.

"Once Germany takes the next step, which I'm assured will be very shortly, all of us will begin to realize the profits I envisioned when I founded my company in 1925. It seems a century ago, but, be that as it may, we're very mindful of our American friends' roles in bringing us and, as a result, Nazi Germany, into existence so that all of our business interests could be so greatly enhanced. Our cooperative efforts and, of course, those of the Führer, have made it possible for our industries to envision unparalleled growth."

"Thank you. This is very encouraging," replied the group's leader, who then turned to another person seated at the table. "Where do we stand on vehicle manufacturing?" he inquired.

"Thank you," responded the domestic automobile executive as he surveyed the people sitting around the large table. "I'm pleased to report that the steps both we and our friendly competitor made earlier this year have been successful. We are enabling our German operations to retool to provide heavy trucks, armored cars, and tanks to Germany for its impending military operations. We have converted our Russelsheim plant to building aircraft engines, and our German subsidiary is progressing well in building warplanes for the Luftwaffe."

While the various status reports continued, Bernard once again found himself deeply impressed by how his boss and the other luminaries in the room were successfully navigating their vast and profitable businesses despite the upheaval caused by Hitler's seizure of the Rhineland, Austria, and Czechoslovakia. As the administrator for the group, Bernard was familiar with most of what he was hearing. So far, however, he had been excluded from discussions concerning the organization's ultimate objectives.

After several more reports on Germany's vital long-term needs for large quantities of strategic raw materials, including rubber, various chemicals, and fuel additives, the meeting came to a close. As the people broke into small groups of friends, Bernard took the opportunity to approach his boss and said, "Well, that was a very encouraging meeting, Mr. Magnum. We're making real progress."

"Yes, Haskins, I believe we are. I believe we are on the verge of one of the most significant wealth-generating collaborations in the history of the world."

20

"Hello, Sal? This is Anna. How've you been, my dear friend?"

"Anna Tilner. My God, I haven't heard your voice in over a year. I'm fine, just fine. How is one of my favorite people on the planet?"

"I'm doing just as well as one of my favorite people is doing, Sal."

And so began a warm telephone conversation between two unlikely allies who had risked their lives fighting side-by-side to uncover and foil a vast, horrific conspiracy the year before in Alabama. Sal Puma was born in Sicily and, when Anna first met him, he quickly impressed her with his absolute fearlessness and devotion to seeing evil people brought to justice, especially powerful ones, characteristics they both shared. Anna was diminutive and attractive, which, for some, tended to obscure her formidable intellect and physical boldness. He, on the other hand, was what he appeared to be. A determined and shrewd man, Sal's charm extended from his wavy black hair, past his ruggedly handsome face, all the way down his stocky frame to his custom-made Italian shoes.

Anna enjoyed her colorful friend who, during Prohibition, had lived an outsized existence. He had told her of his having been a successful bootlegger in a business culture that by the late 1920s had become unsustainably violent and self-devouring. Appalled at the wanton brutality of these people and not wanting to fall victim to it, Sal decided to hedge his bets by becoming a Bureau of Investigation informant before the Bureau caught him. The deal he cut allowed him to continue his lucrative bootlegging operation in exchange for his identifying and testifying against the decade's worst criminals. Ultimately, he became one of the Bureau's and the Department of Justice's favorite inside men, highly respected by even the US attorney general.

Anna also recalled how Sal had decided to take his considerable pile of chips off the table and live the life of a retired gentleman farmer outside of Montgomery, Alabama. She found this amusing considering the extraordinary "farm" this fugitive from organized crime had fashioned for himself. It was an elaborate armed fortress in the countryside to ensure that he would never fall victim to any of his former bootlegging associates seeking revenge.

Sal's first impression of Anna was that she was exceptionally bright, even brilliant, but that she was still "just a woman." It was not long before he began revising his position. He saw her detect a vast number of virtually imperceptible details of physical evidence and then mesh them with signs of subtle human motivations into a clear legal case of criminality. Then Sal saw her confront and take down people who he knew to be ruthless and brutal Klan leaders.

His assessment was further revised when he learned that she had been one of the few women to become a US Marine reservist in World War I. Despite being in what was supposed to be a non-combative role, she had somehow acquired a remarkable knowledge of armaments, fortifications, and logistics. Within a few weeks, all of Sal's lifelong ideas about the limitations of the female sex had been challenged and then utterly destroyed. From then on, he was a devoted admirer of a person whose formidable talents he would never again doubt.

"Well, I'm glad that you and Malcolm are doing so well at Tilner and Associates, although it's hardly a surprise to me. So, apart from the pleasure of speaking with you, what brings us together on the phone, Anna?"

"This'll be different from last year, Sal. I'll be eternally grateful that the federal government underwrote your efforts then. Very much has changed. It now seems that the same government is, for some as yet unknown reason, paralyzed from taking the protective action I thought it would've a long time ago. In short, they won't be paying you this time to help me with an unusual investigation that could take us into some dark corners filled with some pretty ugly characters. Would you be willing to help me, or do you want to think about this before committing yourself?"

"I'm surprised at you, Anna! Considering what we've been through together, has the brilliant Anna Tilner already forgotten everything about me? Of course, I'm in. Tell me more."

"Surely the wily Sal Puma knows that an attorney never asks a question to which she doesn't already know the answer."

"How could I be so stupid as to forget that you're always several steps ahead! Okay, Anna. What's this all about?"

"In light of our last project, I'm well aware of how much you know about the KKK. In this case, it could be helpful. That being said, for starters, how much do you know about the current white supremacy movement, American Nazism, eugenics and the Eugenics Record Office at Cold Spring Harbor, Harry Laughlin, and the German American Bund?"

"My God, Anna. What in the hell have you gotten yourself into this time?"

"I have some suspicions, but there's something vast, powerful, and dark that has put sand in the gears of our American institutions that are supposed to shield us from such things. It's our job to find out what this is all about and why, and do whatever we can to put sand in its gears before it's too late."

"You sound quite concerned about all this."

"If you knew even the limited amount I've discovered, you'd have the same reaction I have."

"And what's that, Anna?"

Knowing her to be unshakable, Sal was shocked by Anna's response. "It's horrific, Sal. I believe that whoever or whatever's behind this, it's truly evil and a threat to this country and our way of life."

"You think it's that serious?"

"Yes, I do. This may sound odd to you, but I believe that it's a big enough threat that before long, we'll need to seek the help of one of your more powerful prior associations that I recall you saying you hadn't alienated."

"Really? Surely you're not suggesting what I think you are, Anna? No goddamned way!"

"Yes, Sal. The Mafia. Specifically, the Jewish Mafia."

"Hell! You don't mean that, Anna?!" said Sal frowning, reflexively pulling back both sides of his mouth, hoping for Anna to say she was just kidding. After a few seconds of hearing just crackling on the line, he exclaimed, "Jesus! You're serious!"

21

Both men sat amid the luxury of the walnut-paneled Italian Terrace Room with its overarching sculpted ceilings at Pittsburgh's posh William Penn Hotel. They always looked forward to their quarterly dinner at this elegant midpoint between their two far-flung offices. It had been their favorite meeting place ever since the hotel had opened in 1916. For over two decades, Bernard Haskins and Forrest Ledbetter had enjoyed one another's company as they became a vital private bridge between America's two largest auto makers. Sheer coincidence had brought these two distant cousins to the edge of the inner circle of the powers controlling both industrial giants. They had also become mirror images of the hearts and souls of their famous bosses, making them critical for their companies' coordinated support of Germany's plan of domination.

Not long after their cocktails were served, Bernard was the first to delve into the topics now preoccupying both men, their patrons, and the western world. "Our people tell me that the time's very close now when we'll have to maintain the strictest confidentiality. Regarding our German operations, you and I must remain tied at the hip. As I think you're aware, our company started a new plant near Berlin several years ago to build what the Germans are calling their "Blitz" truck to be part of a lightning invasion capability. I trust your German operations are prepared for the massive production output that'll be required shortly?"

"Yes, indeed," responded Forrest. "Our German subsidiary's building the same trucks that your Opel unit's producing. Also, we've been setting up arrangements to give Germany access to large quantities of strategic raw materials, especially rubber. Another thing, I think you told me that your company's been supplying synthetic fuel technology to Hitler, isn't that right?"

"That's correct, Forrest. Without this fuel technology, I believe the invasion would be out of the question. By the way, I've heard that Hitler's developing his timetable to coincide with a belated celebration of his fiftieth birthday. "

"Could be. Speaking of his birthday reminds me, our German operation made a personal birthday present to Hitler of 35,000 Reichsmarks four months ago. Did I tell you that?"

"No, you didn't. So far, our company's invested $100 million in Germany, and we're fully expecting a handsome return on that investment, so if your birthday gift helps to solidify our relationship with Hitler, it'll have been money very well spent.

"The truth is, though, I'm not very worried about protecting our interests in Germany," continued Bernard. "Our Russelsheim facility is making engines and other key parts of the German "Wunderbomber" that'll play a central role in Germany's coming assault.

"I understand that our plant is so significant to Göring that he's planning a visit to see it sometime early next year. We all have to play this carefully, though. We're playing in Hitler's sandbox. For this to work for us, we'll have to play by his rules.

"One other thing. How're you coming along with your German labor issues?"

"Well, for the time being, we're using German domestic labor, but somewhere down the line, we've been assured by the Germans that soon there'll be an unlimited pool of slave labor available. Mostly Jews, I guess."

"We've been told the same thing, so it seems that our enterprises can look forward to a generous payday," agreed Bernard.

"It's more than likely that the US is going to be dragged into this war sooner or later," added Forrest, "and then things'll get tricky.

We've got to keep a lid on our golden goose relationship here once we're in the fight. Agreed?"

"Of course. I understand my boss has already made several subtle hints to our political friends that any rocking of our boats would be very ill advised. He's always been confident that they'll play ball. After all, what choice do they have?"

22

Four hundred miles due east of The Italian Terrace in the famous William Penn Hotel, Maximilian's secret project along Oyster Bay, Long Island, was well underway. For nearly three months, Oscar Hahn, Gus Erstad, and about twenty of their former Bund faithfuls had been hard at work transforming their boss's obsession into reality. In keeping with their prior roles in the Bund, Oscar was in charge of the land development and construction with Gus and the others providing manual construction labor before becoming Oscar's security force.

After dinner, Oscar was enjoying a conversation with Gus outside as they had done when both were still members of the Bund. Tonight the breeze was balmy, which enhanced the refreshing taste of the frothy German brew that Oscar always had refrigerated in abundance.

The two unlikely friends had not seen one another outside of work in the three months they had been in Maximilian's employ and were enjoying one another's company. Such occasions were now rare because Maximilian demanded their total loyalty and secrecy. As part of their contract, they had agreed not to see one another after hours. Contract or no contract, Maximilian's ceaseless pressure and his frequent, belligerent outbursts were starting to get to Oscar. Despite this restriction on his personal time, he needed some emotional support from his former henchman and decided to break the rules. For his part, Gus felt more loyalty to his friend than to their boss. Unlike Oscar, he had no fear of Maximilian.

"Graff is showing up at the construction site, tomorrow, Gus," said Oscar as he began sipping his third beer. He was now feeling free enough to share some of his inner thoughts with his former right-hand-man, who now also appeared to be Maximilian's hammer of choice.

"Whenever he comes around to inspect our progress, it makes me very uneasy. It's as if he's looking for me to make some fatal mistake. Somehow he expects me to keep his timeline for this large project while he keeps me in the dark about why it's being built at all. Haven't you been doing some work for him on the plans? Do you know what this's all about?"

"Yeah, Oscar, I know what ya mean 'bout Graff. He sure goes off over nothin', don't he? Sorry, but I don't know nothin' 'bout this stuff. Ya know I'm more on the buildin' 'n security side so I don't know much 'bout what's goin' on with the project plannin' and such. But, ya know, come t'think of it, a couple months ago he took me to someplace in Dover where there were lots o' designers, arch'techs, or somethin' like that. I din't even know why I was there with him. But, then I heard him say to this one guy—he looked like the head guy—that if he knew what was good fer him, he'd remember to keep his mouth shut about some work he was doin' fer Graff—it was a whole bunch o' plans 'n papers 'n stuff. Then he pointed to me—I was 'bout ten feet away—an' he said somethin' like, 'Or I'll have Erstad here pay ya a little visit.' Then I knew why I was there. I r'member Bundesführer Kuhn doin' the same thing when I worked for the Bund, but this was the first time with Graff."

"I've become very curious about what we're really building out there, so if you hear anything, you let me know, okay?"

"Sure thing, Oscar."

"I've got a suspicion that he's going to be keeping you very busy, Gus. Just be careful whose heads he asks you to crack," said Oscar as paused to stretch and yawn. "Well, I suppose it's time for me to get some sleep. I have a busy day ahead of me."

"Fair enough, Oscar. I'll get along, then," said Gus as they stood, shook hands, and went their separate ways.

The next day was sunny as Maximilian surveyed the large project with Oscar, occasionally having to shout to be heard over the roar of the tractors driving by. "This's promising," he said, offering what was for him a rare morsel of praise.

"Oblique," thought Oscar, "but still a compliment."

"You've been very exacting in following my blueprint, Hahn. Now that the land development is nearly complete, point out where the special facilities'll be," he asked as the roar of the tractors was momentarily diverted by an offshore breeze.

"Very well, Herr Graff," said Oscar with a barely discernible smile. "You see where the edge of the woods've been cleared about two hundred yards in that direction," he said while extending his arm and moving it back and forth.

"You mean next to that other forested area?"

"Yes, just to the left, where the tractors have cleared the brush."

"I'm presuming the facilities will be sheltered by the trees and not visible from the road as I dictated, correct?"

"That's correct....Herr Graff, I haven't yet seen the plans for the buildings. Have they been completed?"

"It's not yet time for you to see them, Hahn. The beginning of construction appears to be very soon, though. Am I correct?"

"No more than a few days. The land is fairly flat and sandy, so much of the earth moving has been completed quickly, considerably ahead of schedule. They're now finishing grading the building pads. I will need to see those construction plans to make sure that the building sites are properly positioned and so we can get busy scheduling the delivery of building materials."

"I just told you, Hahn! You'll see those plans when I'm good and ready for you to see them! Not until then! This is highly confidential, and it will stay that way until I say otherwise! Do you understand this, or am I speaking too quickly for you?!"

"Of course, Herr Graff, of course.... Please understand that I only wish to meet your requirements and your deadlines exactly."

"Then shut up about the building plans until I decide to make them available to you! Understand?!"

In the months Oscar had worked for Maximilian, he had witnessed the short fuse of his boss's violent temper many times. Almost from the beginning, it seemed to him that any question concerning the special facility and its function was particularly likely to set his boss off. Unsure of the overall plan of the large project, he was left to guess what its purpose was. He had seen enough hints from his boss's behavior, however, to know that whatever was being constructed was critically important to him and, above all else, was to be hidden from everyone else's eyes. He was finding himself increasingly concerned about what appeared to be Maximilian Graff's grand obsession.

23

"All right, all right, gentleman. Please take your seats," pronounced Howard Magnum as he moved to bring the summit meeting to order. "I know we're all very excited about what's happening overseas, but we must get down to business. Now that Poland is already collapsing and Britain and France will surely declare war on Germany in a matter of days, we are entering an exciting but perilous phase of our business opportunity. First, in light of the impending demand for war materials, let's receive updates on our production levels and preparedness for their escalation. As in the past, we will use no personal or corporate names. I would now like to call on our representative from the chemical industry to speak first. Please give us an update."

The man who headed the chemical and pharmaceutical giant rose with the slow, deliberate pace and carriage of someone acutely aware of his position of power and privilege throughout the entire industrialized world. He was also aware of a secret that he was not yet prepared to share with his fellow industrialists. The time was approaching when a German subsidiary of his company would be shipping lethal cyanide-based pellets of Zyklon B to a large complex of former Polish army barracks called Auschwitz. Not yet aware that before the end of the Nazi regime that he so generously supported, he would be swimming in the blood of a million human beings, he gave his production statistics with the dispassionate delivery of an executive delivering his annual report to shareholders. For the moment, his future victims were still unaware of their fates, very much alive, working, playing, going to school, tending their homes, and feeding their families. In little more than eighteen months their ghosts would begin rising out of their ashes. As he surveyed his powerful audience, he relished knowing that this secret was all business, very big business that he would not be sharing with his comrades any time soon.

While the group's progress reports continued through the late afternoon, their industrial empires had already been nourishing the wholesale slaughter then underway thousands of miles away in Eastern Europe. The itemization of vast quantities of machines, chemicals, and materials mesmerized these people with its promise of immense riches that successfully obscured for them the mass slaughter that was part of the bargain. How these men in their posh surroundings were so impeccably dressed, coiffed, and manicured, and the calm, self-satisfied manner they used to recite their endless inventories served to insulate them from the wasteland of doomed legions that their industries were helping to destroy.

Not so far away, the sun was also setting near Oyster Bay on Long Island with Maximilian again admiring the realization of his grand plan. The development had turned a heavily forested area near the north shore into a collection of building frames and a carefully-constructed roadway that led directly to the beach. As he stood triumphantly in the light of dusk, he bore no relationship to the elegant men who were completing their reports at the Magnum mansion. Instead, he wore rugged khaki trousers, brown leather boots covered with dust, and a plaid working shirt under a leather jacket. Oscar had never seen his boss so casually dressed before and hoped that his work was satisfying his patron.

The elite remnants of Gus's Silver Swords were the ones usually guarding the entrance to the facility while, for the time being, the perimeter was protected by an immense embankment. Wherever possible, the buildings had been carefully nestled in amongst the trees to block them from being detected from the air, the Long Island Sound, or the only public road that skirted the property several hundred feet away.

One small building complex, in particular, was more extensively camouflaged than the others and had been Maximilian's primary interest two months earlier when Oscar was pointing out the layout of the entire facility to him. Despite being in charge of the project, Oscar knew virtually nothing about the complex apart from it being some kind of specialized facility that was strictly off-limits to virtually everybody not involved with its construction. What he did know was that Maximilian was particularly edgy about it.

Other numerous buildings were outfitted with bunks, kitchens, bath, and storage areas. Like the heavily-camouflaged complex, the function of these structures was also a mystery to Oscar, who was growing more curious about the entire project as it approached completion. He had learned early on, however, that when his boss ordered no intrusion into the particulars, he would quickly become violent if there was the slightest hint of persistence—a question, a curious glance, a cocked head, or a furrowed brow.

Not long after the project had started, Maximilian introduced Oscar to his long-time executive assistant, Karl Stampf. Oscar found Karl pleasant enough and wondered what his job was that kept him busy. The two had gotten along fairly well from the start.

Not long after meeting one another, Karl invited Oscar for dinner. To Oscar's dismay and surprise, he discovered quickly that Karl did not share his and his boss's hatred of 'undesirables.' Oscar was curious how Karl had been able to keep his heretical racial sentiments from ending his association with Maximilian long ago. He also remembered being surprised how Karl had so readily revealed his beliefs to him, knowing that he shared Maximilian's racial worldview.

"Karl, how is it even possible that you don't share our ideas of the superior place that the master race deserves and that it must be preserved at all costs?!"

"I must say, I can't begin to understand how you think this way, Oscar. I have no hesitancy whatever to say that, at least on this matter, we have no common ground. I've always found these ideas to be absurd, repugnant, and completely alien to my way of thinking."

"You're certainly blunt! I just don't see how you've managed to continue being Mr. Graff's trusted executive for so many years. His racial beliefs are so enlightened and so contrary to your own!" pressed Oscar, who Karl could see was becoming visibly upset.

"Enlightened? That's not how I'd characterize such thinking. In any event, I've been with Mr. Graff for over twenty-five years, so we share a considerable history. When I first joined him—it was the same year that The Great War began—he had long been filled with hatred, a fury that I believe arose from his father's extreme racial attitudes and his father's having been responsible for his mother's death. This was made worse by his father's total rejection of him at birth due to his hideous deformity.

"A paralyzing financial fear amplified all of this anger. When I first met him, the company that had been the source of his family's wealth was about to collapse completely. This fear fed his rage towards his father's Jewish business associate, who many years ago left Graff Chemical after a devastating confrontation with his father. Maximilian never forgave the man for deserting his father and, as he sees it, causing the family's subsequent prolonged decline. After a string of bitter business disappointments spanning two decades, his father had a severe stroke that left him paralyzed. Suddenly it was up to Maximilian to step up and do what his father had failed to do— somehow save the company.

"That was when he hired me and, despite his strong intellect, it was my assistance that became critical in helping to right the company, preserve his fortune, and also protect Graff's business from being persecuted out of existence by the federal government. I suppose you could say that I've been his silent benefactor."

Oscar now found himself calmed by his interest in hearing some of the history behind the man he worked for. He turned to another question that had been preoccupying him. "That's all very fascinating. I'm also curious about something else, Karl. In the several months I've been an employee of his, I've been the target of Mr. Graff's wrath on too many occasions. I've nearly quit once or twice. Having been with him for so long, you must have experienced the same. What on earth makes you stay on?"

This question prompted Karl to realize that, in addition to answering Oscar's curiosity, his divulging of Maximilian's private past was a subtle act of rebellion against his boss. It was satisfying a slowly growing sense of frustration with the steady abuse he had taken for so long.

"It's not complicated. He's paid me extremely well over the years, given me a share of the profits, and, though he doesn't seem to know how to express it, I know he's well aware of how important I've been to him. This's why we've stayed together so long, despite our very different views. Now then, I trust our relationship is no longer such a mystery to you."

"I'll say one thing, Karl. You've certainly been frank about your thoughts and your relationship with Mr. Graff. While you and I disagree on many things, I'm pleasantly surprised at your candor and respect your forthrightness. So what else have you been doing for Mr. Graff? Are your other duties related in some way to this project that I've been overseeing?"

"They're pretty straightforward, really. I run Graff Industries, which provides the capital for whatever it is that you're building along Oyster Bay."

24

September 2, 1939 - Berlin

Walking down the dimly lit, empty strasse, Dr. Georg Loh kept thinking over and over again, "And to think that barely forty-eight hours ago I was feeling so carefree and happy. How naïve I am! How could I have failed to see this coming?!"

Looking both ways before making his way to a front door he had knocked on many times, the thought crossed his mind that anyone spotting him would immediately think of some shadowy figure in a cheap mystery novel. Knocking quietly while still surveying the empty street, it was only a few moments before the door opened. A muted light briefly flooded the front entrance as Georg entered hurriedly and motioned for his host to close the door quickly behind him.

"Thanks so much for agreeing to see me under these frightening circumstances, Aldus," said Georg as he removed his coat and laid it on a chair near the entrance. He was desperate to get into his conversation with the man standing next to him, Aldus Stromberg, a man he saw as having one of the world's greatest minds. "I'm aware that I'm taking you away from your limited piano practice time," said Georg to his host as both entered the modest living room while the host closed the shades. "I know how fiercely you guard it, but this simply can't wait. With yesterday's invasion of Poland, we have to talk. I trust you agree?"

"Of course I agree," replied Aldus. "Everything's changed, so we must be on our guard more than ever."

"I haven't been in on all the discussions you have, but do you think such a device is possible? The consequences would be staggering for all of us. You're convinced it could work?"

"Yes, I do think, at least theoretically, that it could work. The paper submitted last December by Hahn, Meitner, and Frisch clearly shows that the first experimental steps've already been taken successfully, although a great deal remains to be done to know for sure. I still find it hard to believe that Meitner had to leave Berlin before the paper's submission to seek refuge in Stockholm before the Nazis arrested her as a Jew. Even the great Kaiser Wilhelm Institute couldn't protect its own head of the physics department! Imagine!"

Georg was painfully aware that, despite Aldus's having been awarded the Nobel Prize for Physics seven years earlier, he had been called a "white Jew." He invited persecution and worse when his university lectures did not attempt to hide his esteem for Einstein's work. While Aldus was not Jewish, his high regard for one, especially one as brilliant as Einstein, had resulted in his being threatened with violence many times. Georg was aware that were it not for his friend's scientific importance and personal connections, he would have already been packed off to a concentration camp.

"Make no mistake, Georg. We're facing immense danger here, even in our just talking about this," said Aldus as he raked his fingers slowly through his straight, unruly, dark brown hair in a hand gesture Georg had seen only once before when Aldus was reading a written death threat for the first time. For such a fearless man, Georg was sure that this hand movement revealed significant emotional stress, stress that he knew this conversation was prompting.

"How much time do you think it'll take before it could be demonstrated?" asked Georg.

"It will take several years, certainly no less than 'five, and that's where the greatest danger for us exists."

"Wouldn't it be worse for us not to raise the prospect at all?"

"I believe not. I've spoken to the others, and they agree with me. Considering the barbarians who'd be overseeing our work, if we tried and failed, which would be a great possibility, we'd never live to see another sunrise. This, I believe, is the most dangerous thing we could do," declared Aldus.

"But what about the Americans?"

"My recent trip there convinced me that they're starting to work on this also, but it'll be years away if they succeed at all. I believe our best course is to downplay the possibility that such a device could exist, drag our feet on its development, and wait for the whole idea to die before we're forced to suffer the same fate."

"But what if the Americans enter the war, something I believe's inevitable? If they develop such a weapon and we haven't, won't we be held responsible?"

"Then we won't have escaped an early visit by the Grim Reaper after all, will we? Let's cross that bridge when we come to it. Perhaps a short war'll save our necks!" observed Aldus mordantly.

25

"I don't want to overemphasize it, but, as I said earlier, Mrs. Tilner, the assistant attorney general is very eager to speak with you," said the young Department of Justice staffer as the two waited for his boss to get off the phone.

"He made it very clear that, depending upon the outcome of your conversation with him today, we're to clear the decks and provide any service you require. He shared with me the esteem in which you are held by former Attorney General Hofstedler. That's quite an accomplishment."

Anna admired the gushing enthusiasm of the young man and his desire to help, something she had not expected. It was at odds with her father-in-law's concern over the federal government's recent curious stonewalling behavior about anything having to do with several fascist and white supremacist organizations. His apprehensions had prompted her to set up the meeting she was now awaiting. Her trust in Fess Tilner was so deep that she was now more eager than ever to meet Assistant Attorney General Eric Gorman to see if this cooperative attitude could survive their conversation. In the meantime, she found herself quite taken with the young man sitting next to her.

"How long've you worked for the assistant AG, Mr. Cohen?"

"I joined his team right after the midterm elections a little less than a year ago. I've enjoyed the experience immensely and greatly prefer the high-energy environment here to the more academic, studious atmosphere of law school, even with all the exciting arguments that go on."

"Congratulations on your appointment! This's quite a feather in your cap for someone so young."

"Well, to be perfectly honest, Mrs. Tilner, my family pulled some strings."

"They were able to pull some pretty big strings."

"Yes, indeed. One of my relatives and the attorney general are both members of The Order—although you probably haven't heard of it."

"So, you're a Yalie also."

"How'd you know?"

"Well, of course, as a woman, I could never have been a member of Skull and Bones as an undergrad, but I'm a Yale Law grad. So, now we have two things in common."

"What's the second thing we have in common?"

"You're a Yale Law grad, and, no doubt, you were also excluded from Skull and Bones, but in your case, because you're Jewish." The last word was not out of her mouth before she saw the young man tense and then quickly relax.

"Pretty quick there, Mrs. Tilner. I'm afraid you're right. I guess I'd forgotten, or more likely, repressed that until you raised it. I've just learned to roll with the punches, no matter where they come from."

"I'm afraid my being a woman puts me in a similar, although usually less dangerous, position. I've always been glossed over by other men and pigeonholed as 'just a woman.' While at times it's been frustrating, I've also found it to be invaluable to have powerful men consistently underestimate me—I'm able to fly under their radar and witness things they might otherwise not have revealed."

"I wish I could say that I've had some similar, counterbalancing experience, Mrs. Tilner. Unfortunately, apart from my faith and my family, it's been a terrible burden to be Jewish in these times. My grandparents lived in Germany until less than a year ago when they were tortured and killed by the Nazis during the November pogroms. People are calling it Kristallnacht because of all of the broken glass left from the violence. I don't believe I've ever felt so depressed and furious as when I got the word that they'd been murdered. I'd always been very close to them and that dreadful news…well, it destroyed me."

Just then, the woman seated at the desk at the other end of the waiting room put the telephone receiver back in its cradle.

"The assistant attorney general will see you now, Mrs. Tilner," intoned the secretary, revealing the profundity of her respect for the office she served. "Thank you very much," replied Anna as she stood and turned towards the now sullen young man and shook his hand.

"I'm so very sorry for your having had such an unthinkably horrible experience. I'm very moved that you shared it with me. Thank you for making me feel so at home, Mr. Cohen."

"I suppose I should apologize for burdening you with my personal story, Mrs. Tilner, but somehow I felt comforted sharing it with you. Please, call me Richard."

"Very well, Richard, as long as you call me Anna."

"Thank you, Anna. It was a great pleasure to meet you," replied the young man. "I hope our paths cross again."

"Oh, Richard, I have a feeling they will," she said with a smile before she turned towards the imposing office door near the secretary's desk.

"I do hope so," thought Richard.

The door was opened by the secretary to reveal a large, walnut-paneled office. The tall, middle-aged man sitting behind the desk rose quickly, walked around his desk, and offered his hand to his guest. "Richard didn't exaggerate," thought Anna. The man made it apparent that he had indeed been looking forward to this visit as he warmly urged her to have a seat near the coffee table at the far end of the room. Unable to wait until they both sat down, the assistant attorney general launched into an extended welcome.

"Mrs. Tilner, I must say that ever since my mentor, former US Attorney General Hofstedler, called me, I've been looking forward to meeting you. As you know, he retired some time ago and regards your father-in-law as one of the finest legal minds to ever inhabit a person of such integrity. And you, well, he sees you almost as a daughter. I must say that he could not speak highly enough of you on the phone. He told me about some of your exploits—I confess that I find them too fantastic to believe. Anyway, it's a great pleasure to meet you finally. With the sudden horrible turmoil in Europe, just having you here has already brightened an otherwise pretty dreary day."

"You're more than kind, Mr. Gorman. I feel very flattered. General Hofstedler has been an extremely close friend of my husband's family ever since my father-in-law and he attended law school together nearly fifty years ago. I believe this close tie is largely responsible for how he regards me."

"To the contrary, Mrs. Tilner. Although I haven't spent time with Walter in quite some time now, I've known him for many years. After we first met, he was responsible for persuading me to go to Yale rather than Harvard Law—no trivial task—and then, as I mentioned, he became the most remarkable mentor anyone could hope to have. My point is that more than all the other people I've known, Walter deals in logic and facts, perhaps facts that he's brilliantly deduced, but facts nonetheless. If he's as impressed with you as he's indicated to me, I have no doubt whatever that his assessment's accurate. So then, how may I be of service to you, Mrs. Tilner?"

"Thank you once again for your kind words, Mr. Gorman. Unfortunately, what brings me here is that I've learned of several troubling organizations that I'm hoping you may be able to shed light on, as well as something Walter asked me about in particular. Before I go into that, however, I'd like to understand how much you know about various domestic Nazi and fascist movements?"

"Well, as you know, my responsibility encompasses domestic threats, and we've been following a wide range of domestic fascist groups closely for years."

"So, you're familiar with the German American Bund?"

"That's on its way out, but yes, I'm very familiar with it."

"The Commoner Party?"

"Yes."

"The Christian Front?"

"Yes."

"The Silver Shirts and the Khaki Shirts?"

"Well, yes, but these two were very small and weak and died out several years ago. They were far too disorganized to be a serious threat to America."

"I see," said Anna as she entered the critical part of her interview. "Then what can you tell me about the American Liberty League?"

"Who? I'm afraid we're not following this group."

"Then how about the Sentinels of the Republic?"

"Sorry, haven't heard of them."

"The Southern Committee to Uphold the Constitution?"

"No."

"The Silver Swords?"

"Never heard of them."

"Then what about the Eugenics Record Office at Cold Spring Harbor on Long Island?"

"No."

"Dr. Harry Laughlin?"

"No, no, no! I know absolutely nothing about any of these! Now, come along, Mrs. Tilner...why're you asking all these questions?!"

"Well, Mr. Gorman, I'm responding to the concerns of some of my firm's most powerful and patriotic clients. They've told me that these and other white supremacists or homegrown fascist factions are apparently spreading violence and hatred and often disparaging America and its government when the country could be on the verge of war. They want some assurance that our government is doing all it can to protect the country from such destructive people."

"You can reassure them, Mrs. Tilner, that if there is any possibility of any of these groups harming an American citizen, we will preempt it." Just then, Gorman looked down at his watch. "Oh, I see that it's about time for my next appointment to arrive. Is there any other way I may be of service to you?"

"Not at present, Mr. Gorman. I do appreciate your time. You've been extremely helpful. Thank you again." Rising to shake his hand, she added, "I can see my way out."

After Anna turned away from her host and walked through the office entrance, her smile suddenly dissolved into a barely perceptible frown as she closed the door quietly. Turning around, she approached the desk of the assistant attorney general's secretary one last time before leaving.

The assistant attorney general hurriedly walked around his desk and fidgeted for a full minute before picking up his phone. "Is she gone?!"

"Yes, sir. She just left," replied his secretary.

"Get me the attorney general, immediately!"

26

As Anna walked across the street towards Boston's South Station main entrance, she did what she usually did whenever she approached the massive train station—she looked up to admire the great clockface that crowned the main building of the largest train terminal in New England. She saw that she still had fifteen minutes before her guest from Alabama would be arriving and, once inside, decided to sit in the main terminal before going out to meet him on the platform.

As she sat waiting for the train to arrive and watched the train passengers going in every direction, she was struck by the contrast with the circumstances of her first meeting Sal Puma at his formidable home outside of Montgomery. She recalled when she and her husband, Malcolm, had first approached the heavily-guarded entrance to Sal's estate by car. It reminded her of a smaller version of the immense gate protecting the native islanders from King Kong. Malcolm and Anna had seen the film not long after it had been released in 1933, and the image still came to her mind whenever she thought of Sal.

With a grin, she recalled her introduction to him, and how she was immediately taken by his disarming charm that camouflaged his past as a successful bootlegger turned even more successful government informer. In the next several weeks of their relationship, he measured up to all of her expectations of being resourceful, shrewd, and fearless.

They became close friends quickly as they worked together to unearth an evil conspiracy that had killed thousands of people in a mysterious facility on the outskirts of Montgomery. In this baptism by fire, the two had survived extreme danger together, and she was looking forward to seeing her colorful comrade once again.

Hearing an announcement of the arrival of the train, Anna rose and walked out to the platform to see the iron horse lumbering into the station a few hundred feet away. It took no time at all for the great vehicle to finally come to rest after its long journey. Moments later, the two saw one another, and Anna began waving before Sal hopped down onto the platform and walked briskly towards her. Although she was eager to see Sal, she was just as interested to hear what he had learned since they had talked on the phone the month before.

The steam from the engine partially enveloped them as they gave one another a hug. Sal immediately got down to business while they walked towards the main building. "It was just as you suspected, Anna. I found out some fascinating information from Dave Gottlieb, one of my contacts who'd been with the Jewish Mafia years ago. He also became a government informant, so we've always had a special bond from that common experience."

"What did he say?"

"Well, when I was still in the game back in '33, the Jewish Mafia was still largely focused on increasing its share of the Sicilian mob's business in major cities. Since then, they've been cooperating more with the Sicilians to build a nationwide organized crime syndicate. This means that their attention's been freed up to increase their business rather than eliminate their competition. It also means something else, Anna."

"What's that?"

"They've been paying more attention to what's been going on outside of their rackets. How the Nazis've been treating the German Jews has some of 'em very fired up. So much so that David assured me there were a good number of these guys who'd be willing to help us if there's even the smallest possibility that the same crap could happen here.... Hold on, Anna. I got so caught up in telling you this that we passed the entrance to the luggage area, we've gotta go back."

"Turnabout's fair play, Sal," Anna responded whimsically as they turned on their heels to retrace their steps and retrieve Sal's bags. "That's excellent news about your…well, your friends, Sal. We may well end up needing their help. I can certainly understand their being so upset. Now, I have some news of my own."

"Okay, Anna, let's have it."

"It's not conclusive, mind you, but it's certainly intriguing. Yesterday I had a rather peculiar five-minute meeting with US Assistant Attorney General Eric Gorman."

"Peculiar?"

"Yes, quite. The meeting was arranged through our old friend, former Attorney General Walter Hofstedler. Gorman said that years ago, Walter had been his mentor and that he was eager to help in any way after being asked by a person he held in such high esteem. I hadn't been in the office for more than a couple of minutes when I asked him if he knew anything about several suspected fascist and domestic Nazi groups. He responded that domestic terror organizations were under his jurisdiction and so he'd be very familiar with them."

"So, what was unusual about that?"

"Nothing. Nothing, that is, until I mentioned the sixth group, the American Liberty League, which's been around for about five years and is notoriously powerful and brutal. It's a highly anti-progressive, anti-semitic, racist organization."

"Anna, I can assure you that this wouldn't be the first time the federal government was behind the investigative curve," replied Sal as they approached the platform that was still awaiting the arrival of Sal's luggage.

"There's more, Sal."

"How did I know that was coming?" said Sal under his breath.

"There were three other smaller organizations that he professed to know nothing about. One promotes anti-Semitism, another, white supremacy, and the last one, American Nazism. The first is the Sentinels of the Republic, the second is the Southern Committee to Uphold the Constitution, and the last is the Silver Swords."

"Perhaps they were too disorganized or not big enough to represent a real threat in the Fed's eyes."

"Not exactly, Sal. I also asked him about the Eugenics Record Office on Long Island."

"So?"

"I chose these last few organizations because they all had one critical ingredient in common."

"They all hated blacks and Jews?"

"No, they were all financed at one time or another by powerful people such as the DuPonts of General Motors, Henry Ford, the Rockefeller family, the Carnegie Institution, executives at Standard Oil and Alcoa, as well as leaders of an assortment of the nation's largest banks."

"This sounds outrageous, Anna! What's their motive? Why would they put money, which they seem to value above everything, behind such organizations?"

"I'm sure the motive is also money, Sal. A number of these groups are also violently anti-labor, something that would maximize the money pouring into the pockets of these industrialists by intimidating workers from joining unions or organizing in any way. This sounds like the most reasonable explanation to me."

"I agree that it sounds plausible, Anna, but then again, everything you say always seems to make abundant sense. I just don't know that you can draw some vast conclusion like this from a single meeting with…what's his name again?"

"Gorman. Eric Gorman."

"Yes, Gorman…. Well, anyway, I don't think your five-minute meeting with him warrants jumping to the extreme conclusion that the federal government is involved in some treasonous conspiracy to support big business."

"There's one final curiosity, Sal."

"Oh yeah? What's that?"

"I very much wanted to spend more time with Mr. Gorman."

"Well, why didn't you, and what did you expect to learn if you had?"

"I wanted to know what he was so afraid of."

"Afraid of?! Why'd you think he was afraid of something?"

"As soon as I inquired about the last few groups in rapid succession, to which he professed complete ignorance each time, he suddenly asked why I was asking all these questions and then looked at his watch. Suddenly, he stood up and announced he had to meet his next appointment."

"I'm not surprised, Anna. You know as well as I do that these high-level government officers have extremely tight schedules. Five minutes with you sounds about right to me. But you still haven't told me why you thought he was afraid of something."

"He appeared to be uneasy the second I mentioned the Liberty League, and after the following rapid-fire questions, he appeared to be increasingly agitated before cutting me off for his next appointment."

"That's it?! You just thought he was uncomfortable with your prying?! Anna, I have to say this just doesn't sound like you!"

"No, Sal. He was flummoxed. He didn't even attempt to ask about something else I'd deliberately raised at the outset that should've been very significant to him. I'd told him that his revered mentor, Walter Hofstedler, was very concerned about something that he hoped Gorman could shed some light on. Instead, he cut the meeting short before we even got to it. As a result, after going out the door to his office and closing it, I asked his secretary how much time he had allotted for me."

"And…what'd she say?"

"Her calendar showed that rather than a few minutes, an hour had been set aside for our meeting. Now wouldn't that make you suspect that he was afraid of something? Tomorrow, you and I have an appointment with someone who may be able to shed some light on what it is."

27

"You must have left very early. Here are some refreshments after your long drive," said Eric Franzen warmly as he carefully set the large tray with coffee and pastries down on his coffee table in front of Anna and Sal.

"Thank you very much, Eric," said Anna. "We did leave as the sun was coming up so this is very welcome, as is your home. It's like a breath of fresh air, truly a lovely place. You must treasure that view of Long Island Sound."

"I heartily agree," added Sal. "It almost seems like it's a beautiful painting."

"You're both absolutely right. I never tire of it," said Eric as he poured three cups of coffee.

"I'm very pleased you called," said Anna as she looked up to accept the coffee from her host. "The timing is fortuitous since Sal arrived just yesterday. Whatever you have to say can be shared with him. He's working with me on this. What little you told me was certainly intriguing, and, of course, I understand why you wanted to meet face to face before getting into it."

"I apologize for all of this being so mysterious and you having to drive all the way here, but since our meeting last month, Anna, I've been particularly aware of what we discussed and, I'm not sure, but what I've learned may be of some help to you."

Franzen then turned to Sal. "Did she tell you the details of our conversation, Mr. Puma?"

"She did, Dr. Franzen."

"Please call me Eric. Is it all right if I call you Sal?"

"Of course, Eric. I was very sorry to hear from Anna about the tragic loss of your wife."

"Thank you, Sal. It's been challenging, as you can well imagine.... Well, anyway, let me tell you why you're here. I'm not sure if you know this area at all, but my home here is not too far from Cold Spring Harbor, where a place called the Eugenics Record Office, or ERO, is located. I'm not sure if you're familiar with eugenics, but the ERO has been its nerve center for many years."

"Anna knew that this topic would come up and was good enough to give me a primer on the entire subject," responded Sal.

"Very well. Did she also tell you about Dr. Harry Laughlin?"

"I've come to depend on Anna's absolute thoroughness, so yes, she's described him and your relationship with him."

"Excellent. Well, as you're no doubt aware, the Nazis are getting escalating amounts of negative publicity in this country. This's due not only to their invasion of Poland but their alarming treatment of Jews and their use of eugenics to justify their outrageous behavior. This has damaged eugenics' credibility in American scientific circles significantly in a very short time."

"I can well imagine," added Anna as Sal nodded in agreement.

"As I explained to Anna at our last meeting, years ago I did some research into the Eugenics Record Office when Dr. Laughlin had taken charge of it and was very disturbed by what I uncovered. All of this is just to give you a background to what I've been hearing most recently. The Eugenics Record Office is often a topic of conversation amongst my scientific colleagues, especially now considering what's going on in Germany. A couple of them live close to the facility and, after many years of very little outward sign of activity, they've been noticing some recently. Trucks have been seen entering and leaving the facility, but only in the wee hours of the morning."

"Do any of your friends have any idea what they're carrying or where they're going, Eric?" asked Anna.

"Unfortunately, no. But there's been talk of…I don't know if you could call it a rumor or if there's more to it…of some secret project walled off by a giant berm that's been under construction for some time now located near Oyster Bay. It's not far from here. My understanding is that a week or so ago, just before Germany invaded Poland, the trucks began their nighttime trips into and out of the Eugenics Record Office. According to my friends, they always drove in the direction of this Oyster Bay project. To my knowledge, there's nothing else down that road. What does all this mean, and who's behind it? I'm afraid I don't know those answers. However, your concern with the rising number of Nazi and fascist movements in this country, Anna, and their links with eugenics made me think that, in light of Germany's sudden military aggression, I should let you know about this without delay."

"Excellent, Eric. Thank you. I must say, for being so far outside of your scientific discipline, you're certainly proving yourself to be a good detective," said Anna with a smile before she turned to Sal.

"I'd say our next steps've just been laid out for us. I also think some of your prior associates would be more than interested in helping us pursue this. Wouldn't you agree, Sal?"

"Yes, I would."

"Might I inquire how these past relationships figure into getting to the bottom of all this, Sal?" inquired Eric innocently.

"Rather than get into that too deeply, Eric," responded Sal, "I can safely say that these people are naturally highly motivated to uncover the truth behind what you've been describing and have little fear of what they might encounter."

"They sound as if they're perfectly suited for such an assignment then," responded Eric.

"They certainly are, my dear friend," replied Anna.

28

Anna's husband, Malcolm, was walking over to his bar at home when she and Sal opened the front door after returning from seeing Eric Franzen. "Well, come on in, you two. Your timing is excellent—I thought I'd have a French 75, and now that you're both here, I can mix us all one. Sound good?"

"That sounds just great, Honey," responded Anna. "Thanks for being the bartender. After such a long drive and what we heard today, I could sure use one," said Anna.

"I must be from the other side of the tracks," admitted Sal. "I don't believe I've ever had one. You called it a French 75. What's in it?" he inquired as he and Anna walked into the living room.

"It's very popular in Boston," volunteered Malcolm over his shoulder. "It's pretty simple, really, just champagne, gin, a little lemon juice, and a little less simple sugar syrup. It's light and very refreshing. Anna loves them. They'll be ready in a couple of minutes, and you can tell us how you like it."

After serving the drinks and sitting down in his favorite living room chair, Malcolm maintained his role as host. "I'm so glad you could stay with us, Sal. It's been too long since we've had the pleasure of your company."

"As I said yesterday," Sal replied, "Anna's call came out of the blue, but her request for help was simply too tempting to pass up. I must say, you have a magnificent home here, and while this is my introduction to the Boston area, your Weston neighborhood looks like it's pretty much at the top of the heap."

"Actually," said Malcolm, "this is a family property that was originally built by my great-grandfather, Cornwall Tilner, when he moved his family here in 1851 from Alabama. My grandfather and father were both born here, as was I. Over the years, it's been upgraded and modernized, of course, but its soul holds many wonderful memories for me and now Anna…" Malcolm's voice trailed off as he said under his breath, "and then some not-so-wonderful ones."

Malcolm paused abruptly as he appeared to be looking far away. Anna knew his nostalgia had revived the memory of his first wife and unborn daughter, both of whom he had lost when his wife gave birth. Despite the twenty-three years separating him from the most tragic event of his life, his reference to his ancestral home had been enough to rekindle the awful memory. His sudden silence also reminded Anna that this was why he became so disturbed whenever the remotest possibility of danger threatened her safety. Just then, Anna's thoughts were interrupted when she saw Malcolm recover from his brief, sad reverie.

"We're so fortunate to be able to live in such wonderful surroundings," he said as he looked at Anna and returned to the warmth of the moment. "As you know, my mom and dad're still living in Alabama and like the slower pace of retired life down there, but it's ideal for Anna and me to live here with our work being relatively close by. Of course, we don't have your impressive entrance and fortress-like buildings, but we're very pleased to be living here."

"Malcolm, you're far too modest. This appears to be one of the most regal estates in this magnificent area. And as you both know, my great entrance gate is imposing for only one reason: security. But I've enjoyed living there despite it being as much a fortress as a home."

"So," continued Malcolm, "while I was attempting to manage the normal mayhem at Tilner and Associates, how did you both do with Dr. Franzen?"

"He was very informative," began Anna, who went on to relate their conversation with the retired Princeton University professor. After the three had discussed the meeting and its possible implications together with what else Anna and Sal had learned, Malcolm noticed that Sal's glass was almost empty.

"It appears you like the French 75, Sal. May I fix you another?"

"By all means, but only one more until dinner. That was delightful."

Malcolm rose and walked over to the bar just as he heard the faint sound of the phone ringing in the adjacent study. He knew the butler would answer the call and continued to prepare Sal's drink. As he finished and rounded the sofa to deliver the champagne cocktail, the butler arrived and quietly requested to speak to Malcolm alone.

As the two men went into the next room, Anna turned to Sal. "That's odd. Whenever there's a call, our butler just takes a message or alerts us to anything that needs our immediate attention. He's never asked for one of us to speak privately with him before. Strange. Well, anyway, I'm looking forward to meeting your mafia friends."

"They appear to be quite eager to meet you also, Anna. Before I left, they assured me that it wouldn't take long for them to get here once we gave them the word. I've told them about some of our exploits together, and I believe they've concluded that you're certainly someone special. I also told them…" Sal stopped in mid-sentence as he saw Malcolm slowly entering the room, looking as if he had just had the blood sucked out of him. Anna and Sal immediately rose and went over to him.

"What on earth's the matter, Honey?! You look stricken," she said as she took one of his hands in hers.

"Let me sit down first," Malcolm replied as he returned unsteadily to his favorite chair.

"Who was on the phone?" asked Anna while she and Sal stood looking down on Malcolm as he wrestled with what to say.

"I'm afraid I don't know who it was," he said, his eyes darting back and forth wildly as he struggled to make sense of what he had just heard. "He wouldn't identify himself, but his message was quite clear. He mentioned you by name, Anna."

"Hmm," she responded, as she and Sal sat down.

"He told me that powerful people are well aware of the inquiries that you've been making recently and that you should stop if you value your life."

"Now this is fascinating," responded Anna as Malcolm looked shocked at her response to this mortal threat.

"I don't find it fascinating at all, Anna! How can you be so cavalier?!" he responded.

"I apologize, Honey. Please forgive me. Did he say anything else?"

"Yes, he did. He told me—he even referred to me by name," continued Malcolm, "that if I cared anything about our relationship, I would make sure that you stopped your efforts immediately. Then he hung up. Can you make any sense of this, Anna?"

"It makes abundant sense, although I'm surprised that it took this long for a reaction to surface."

"A reaction to what? You expected this?!" said Sal.

"I wouldn't say expected, but I suspected that it could happen."

"Who do you think this was?" asked Malcolm.

"I'm confident that it was a public servant or someone directed by one."

"A public servant?! What in the hell does that mean?" said Malcolm as his eyebrows seemed to cross and uncross.

"It means that my conversation with Assistant Attorney General Gorman is showing results. He's identified for us at least one reason why the federal government is appearing to be so reluctant to perform its most important security function to protect us all."

"What on earth are you talking about, Anna?! You're not making any sense," said an agitated Malcolm as Sal's head swiveled back and forth as if he were watching a tennis match.

"With all of its power and might, our government appears to be running scared, and what it's most afraid of, I believe, is not just overseas. It's right here in our midst. Sal, you must persuade your friends to get here without delay. We've just lost the luxury of time to look into all this at our convenience. The stakes've just been raised, and it appears that we could be standing in between two immense forces that are squaring off for an apocalyptic battle. I think that at present, our insignificance is our greatest weapon, and it's just been made clear that there's no time to be lost if we're to take advantage of it!"

Just then, the Tilner's butler entered the room once again.

"Mrs. Tilner, there's a Dr. Franzen on the line for you. Excuse me for saying so, ma'am, but he sounds quite ill." Everyone had been so preoccupied with the last call that the muffled ring of another one had gone unnoticed.

"I hope Eric's all right," declared Anna to no one in particular as she rose from the sofa. "At least when we left him, he was in perfect health. I'll be right there, Austin."

"Yes, ma'am," said the butler as he left the room with the door open.

"What could Eric be calling about? We left him only a few hours ago," she said to herself as she walked towards the end of the room and then disappeared through the door.

"That Anna of yours is a fascinating person, Malcolm," said Sal, barely shaking his head back and forth. "I have to confess that I've never met anyone quite like her."

"That makes two of us, Sal. Sometimes I find it difficult to come to grips with living with this…well, I think she's remarkable also. But as much as I adore my unflappable wife, it gives me ulcers when she seems compelled to dive into whatever dangerous adventure presents itself. Unlike the two of you, I'm not built that way and simply can't fathom rushing headlong into what could be a disaster."

"In truth, Malcolm, I've always enjoyed the thrill of risk and uncertainty, but Anna's different—she's always ahead of the curve. Unfailingly, she seems to know before anyone what she's getting into, is completely fearless and is always several steps ahead of everyone else. If I didn't know better, I'd say…"

Anna slowly entered the room staring at the floor before looking up and addressing Sal.

"Sal, we'd better get some sleep. We're meeting Dr. Franzen again tomorrow morning as early as we can get to his house."

"Why in the hell didn't he tell us about whatever this is while we were there?!" said Sal.

"He just learned of it this evening and said that whatever it is simply can't wait."

"He gave you no idea why we should retrace our steps and spend most of our day in a car two days in a row?!"

"He wouldn't say over the phone. He insisted we talk to him in person. He's very distraught. You know, I was also with him on the first month's anniversary of his wife's suicide and his horrifying description of everything that preceded it. I don't remember ever seeing a person so devastated and inconsolable."

"I'm sure he was, Anna, but what bearing does any of that have on what he now needs to tell us, and why's it so damned urgent?" asked Sal.

"In that tortured conversation about his wife, he sounded very different than he did just now. Then, he was openly struggling with a still-open wound. The man I just finished speaking with was another person altogether. He sounded utterly terrified. So frightened that we hadn't made it through the conversation before he suddenly dropped the phone mid-sentence. With the line still open, I heard his footsteps take off and suddenly stop. Then I heard the unmistakable sound of him vomiting."

29

"Come in, please come in," said Eric Franzen soberly after he opened his front door for Anna and Sal. "I can't tell you how relieved I am to see you both. I've been a nervous wreck ever since I got the news. I haven't slept a wink."

"The news? What is this news, Eric?" Anna shot back as they all moved into the living room. This time there were no refreshments.

"What am I saying?! Of course you don't know. That's why you're here. My God, I feel as if I'm losing my mind."

"Please just calm down and tell us what's happened. Start at the beginning," said Anna in a vain attempt to enable Eric to organize his thoughts.

"Yes. Yes. That's what to do," said Eric as he took a deep breath and paused briefly before going on. "I've told you about my scientific friends and colleagues who live around here. Of course, you'll remember that they're the ones who told me about the trucks and the Eugenics Record Office."

Anna and Sal nodded their understanding while becoming impatient to learn what had upset Eric so seriously.

"Yes, go on," said Anna.

"I have another academic friend with whom I'm very close who called me last night. Well, he's both a colleague and a lifelong friend, actually. While we don't get together socially very often, he and I..."

"Please, Eric, we're very anxious to hear what's made you so agitated," said Sal.

"Yes, yes. Of course, yes. Well, anyway, he's also a close friend of Princeton's most famous resident, Dr. Einstein. They both work at Princeton's Institute for Advanced Study in the recently completed Fuld Hall. Several hours after you left yesterday, he called and insisted on seeing me right then. As soon as he arrived, he told me that over a month ago, in very early August, Einstein had been asked by a couple of his closest colleagues to sign a letter to FDR. From what I understand, this letter outlines how recent research shows that uranium can create what's called a nuclear chain reaction. The result is the instantaneous generation of vast amounts of power and energy."

"This's all very interesting, Eric, but so what?" demanded Sal.

"This release of large amounts of energy could be used to develop a completely new type of superweapon that could destroy an entire city!"

"Then, if we had such a weapon, it could be used to counter Germany's aggression and perhaps end the current bloodshed in Europe sooner," asserted Sal.

"No, not exactly. My understanding is that, unlike the creation of a nuclear chain reaction, the actual development of such a weapon is far more complex and speculative than what's known so far. It will take years of research and testing. However, this is exactly what Einstein's letter encouraged the president to commence in light of the fear that Nazi Germany could already be ahead of us."

"I see," said Sal soberly.

"What's more, he says that Einstein indicated that it'll take large amounts of uranium to achieve this."

"Surely the United States has such immense mineral deposits that this wouldn't be a serious challenge for us," suggested Sal.

"Not so, according to my friend. The US possesses only poor uranium ores and in only moderate quantities. On the other hand, the right kind of uranium exists in Canada and Czechoslovakia."

"We're lucky, then, that Canada's so close, right?" persisted Sal.

"Not really. In the quantities required, my friend tells me that the only feasible source is the Belgian Congo."

"Does your friend know if our government intends to make any effort to secure these resources?"

"He doesn't know."

Sal then looked at Anna quizzically. "Anna, you've been unusually quiet," he said, "What do you think about all this?"

"I'm gravely concerned, Sal," she said before turning to Eric. "There's more to this letter, isn't there, Eric? Did your friend say if there was anything else regarding Czechoslovakia's uranium?"

"Well, he said that Einstein indicated that he was aware that Germany has already ceased the sale of uranium from its Czech mines to other countries."

"Then, this is ominous. Germany's already controls Czechoslovakia, and if it repeats its behavior during the Great War, it'll invade Belgium before very long and thereby control its colonies. This would then give the Nazis direct control of this valuable uranium in both Czechoslovakia and the big prize, the Belgian Congo. If your friend suspects that Germany may already be working on this horrific weapon and develops it first while preventing the US from accessing enough raw materials to make one of our own, the consequences for all of us would be unthinkable.... Eric, I can see from your expression that this same fear is what drove you to call me last night. Is that right?"

Looking down at the floor, Eric replied, "Regrettably, yes, Anna. I'm afraid you're correct. That's exactly why I called. I didn't know what else to do."

30

It was an exceptionally muggy day, even for September, Boston's steamiest month. Sal and Anna found the air-conditioned hotel lobby a relief from the oppressive humidity as they waited for their guests to arrive. As Sal had expected, his contact, David Gottlieb, had been true to his word, and a couple of the Jewish Mafia would soon be arriving to check in.

As the two sat watching people come and go—some appeared to be hiding their faces with oversized hats—they remarked to one another how ostentatious the place was. The formally-attired service people were obtrusively attentive and overeager to help. The front desk was adorned with large carved cherubs everywhere and seemed to have been created out of one massive piece of dark mahogany. Rising from the lobby floor were several heavily-gilt Corinthian monoliths overlooking the garish furniture and several oversized chandeliers. Sitting near the entrance, Sal was sure his two arrivals would not enter unnoticed.

"As I said earlier, there're going to be only two men coming, Anna, because more could be a problem for everyone. According to David, Morris Stein and Abe Groveman are among the most reliable people he could find."

"That's good to hear, Sal. We certainly don't need any dependability problems."

"Truthfully, Anna, it goes far beyond that. I don't know how much you know about the Kosher Nostra, as some call it, but, by and large, it's an extremely rough crowd and would as likely cut you to pieces as lose a dime on a prostitute's trick. Most of the Jewish community resent them and wish they didn't exist because they tend to fire up anti-Semitism and hatred of immigrants in general. It makes life for the law-abiding Jews a lot tougher all the way around.

So when I spoke with David about whether he knew some good people who might be willing to help us, he didn't give me their names until he had a chance to check them out. If you can believe it, even some of the Sicilians I knew were pretty suspicious of the Jewish Mafia and went out of their way to make sure they didn't cross 'em. These're really tough people."

"Then I'm doubly grateful to David. The last thing we need is to be worried about being stabbed in the back by one of our own!"

"Here they are, Anna," said Sal as he rose out of his chair and walked up to the two men entering the hotel ahead of an entourage of young men schlepping a small mountain of luggage. Despite having been carefully selected, to Anna, both men looked almost like caricatures of the mobsters they were. Both wore hats and, in spite of the oppressive heat, jackets without ties. They walked with swaggers meant to advertise their extreme confidence in all circumstances. The smaller man, apparently wanting to maintain a fresh, dapper appearance, was patting his face and forehead with a handkerchief before putting it back in his pants pocket.

"Hi. My name's Sal Puma, and this here's my partner Anna Tilner," said Sal as he swung his arm wide to introduce Anna.

"Abe Groveman," said the much larger of the two men. He wore a gray newsboy's cap and held out a meaty hand to Sal while ignoring Anna. She found it difficult to take her eyes off his fleshy, pouty lips, and dark, bushy eyebrows. She also felt that the coarse folds of his hat suited the rest of the man well.

"Mo Stein," said the other, who wore a Fedora and whose face had thin, chiseled features giving him a taught, merciless appearance. This impression softened when he regarded Anna with a smile and offered an unexpected, "How do you do?" Doffing his hat, he extended his hand to her.

"I'm fine, thank you," replied Anna as she looked at both men and thought, "These are the carefully selected, first picks? The runners-up must have been real prizes."

"Why don't you check in and we can meet you in your room when you're ready," said Sal.

Abe grunted unintelligibly while Mo turned to Sal and said, "Give us twenty. We'll be in the presidential suite." Both men then made their way to the front desk, followed by their porters straining to juggle their bags while Sal and Anna returned to their seats.

"I predict," said Anna quietly as the two sat down, "that if Mr. Groveman has any expectation of a career as a social graces instructor, he's doomed."

"He's quite a crude hunk, all right," said Sal. "I must say, I was put off when he ignored you. But then again, when I first met you, I had no idea who or what you were besides a pretty face, so I guess I'll have to cut him some slack."

"How confident are you in David Gottlieb being a good judge of character?"

"I've worked with him long enough to know that he's always been cogent and spot-on with his assessments, so I'm confident these two'll be what we need, Anna."

"I'm depending on it, Sal. At least they certainly seem to be prepared to handle themselves."

"And exactly how would you know that after all of thirty seconds of an introduction?"

"Groveman is too large to successfully hide the revolver strapped to the side of his chest. While the gun was invisible, his shirt was pulled askew by the pistol strap that I'm sure he finds uncomfortably tight against his oversized torso."

"OK, Mrs. Know-it-all, where did Mo Stein hide his?"

"He didn't have one."

"So how can you say that he's prepared to handle himself?"

"He uses a knife."

"And how did you come by this fascinating conclusion?"

"When he offered me his right hand to shake, he had a noticeable callus at the base of his index finger, a common trait for heavy knife users."

"Oh? And exactly how do you know that?"

"If you really must know, when I was one of the few women in the Marine Corps Reserve, I persuaded some of the men who were highly trained in hand-to-hand combat to let me spar with them. When it came to the knife training, I saw that the best ones had calluses like Mo's, and before long, I had developed one also. They told me it was a common characteristic of knife fighters."

"Good God, Anna! So then why do you presume he always uses his right and not his left hand when he's wielding his knife?"

"He probably uses both hands for knifing, but when we first saw him, he used his right hand with his handkerchief, then replaced it into his right rear pocket, and then took off his hat with it. It's a reasonable assumption that he favors his right hand."

"All I can say to all this is that you must be hell to live with, Anna," said Sal smiling.

"I'm not sure, but I do know that Malcolm sometimes says he gets frustrated with me."

"Now, there's a shocker!"

After giving their new acquaintances an extra few minutes, Anna and Sal went up to the suite, knocked, and waited in front of the double doors to the suite. Mo, the less imposing of the two men, opened the door and welcomed the pair into the expansive living room. Abe was seated in a comfortable chair at one end of the room and made no effort to get up and greet his guests. As the other three approached the remaining chairs and sofa, Anna walked up to Abe and extended her hand.

"It seems that you were unaware that I was standing right next to Mr. Puma in the lobby. Let me introduce myself. My name is Anna Tilner, and you're here because of me."

The man was taken aback at such an aggressive move by the diminutive woman. Slowly making an ungainly effort to lift his bulk out of the chair, he extended his hand while struggling to locate a vague memory of what would have to pass as a civil introduction. Anna found herself mildly enjoying the man's obvious discomfort.

"Yeah, I guess I just didn't notice. Sorry, but I ain't used t'spendin' much time with uppity dames, so why don't ya just have a seat."

"Probably wasn't asked to sign many dance cards at cotillion," thought Anna as she sat next to Sal.

"So whaddya got," asked Abe, now taking care to look at Anna.

"We're doing an important investigation," began Anna, "We'll be looking into a project that we believe may interest you. It could be dangerous, and, if we fulfill our objectives, you could be responsible for saving the health, if not the lives, of a good many people."

"What people?" asked Abe.

"People like yourselves, Mr. Groveman," responded Anna. "Jewish people. You could also be responsible for saving others as well, but that remains to be seen. And that, gentlemen, is what we're here to uncover. Exactly who's involved in this project and who's at risk."

"And who's runnin' the show?"

"I'll be calling the shots, Mr. Groveman," replied Anna.

"You?! You?! But yore a broad for Chrissakes!"

"Ah, Mr. Groveman, and here you said you didn't notice."

31

Attending the German Nuclear Weapons Program meeting had been a painful experience for Aldus Stromberg but less so for his colleague and friend, Georg Loh. Aldus was barely able to control himself as the two physicists ducked into an unoccupied sitting room after making a rapid exit from where a small collection of scientists and Reich military officers were still milling around. The meeting that made Aldus so angry had been organized to discuss how to advance nuclear fission and chain reactions with several Wehrmacht officials who were now officially in charge. It soon became apparent to both men that all of their efforts would ultimately be in vain, and any progress would be stillborn.

"That meeting was an outrage—a grotesque mockery of science, us, and Germany!" declared Aldus after slamming the door and throwing his papers on a nearby sofa. "What's the name of this supposed effort, Georg?! German Nuclear Weapons Program?! Ha! Will it yield anything useful? Only if we intend to talk our enemies to death!"

"Please relax, Aldus. We must hold out some hope that we can somehow enable this effort to help us win the war," replied Georg, Aldus's closest associate in the program.

Pacing the floor like a caged animal, when Aldus heard this, he suddenly stopped, gave his friend a withering look, and launched into another tirade. "Then you'll please explain to me how there's a subatomic chance of developing anything now that this lunatic Hitler is in charge! He has publicly rejected science as being real, has banned any Jewish scientist from being able to do anything productive, and then has scared them out of the country! As if all that isn't enough, he then sends the ones who're left to the front lines or concentration camps! This is utter madness, Georg! It confirms my original idea that the more distance there is between us and this mockery of a scientific initiative, the better!

"I also can't stomach the fact we now have to answer to the German Army Weapons Agency! These boneheads have intellects that are exceeded by that sofa over there! They know less than it does about science. What's worse, they don't care, not in the least! For all of them, winning the war requires nothing more than a bigger mortar, a more powerful tank, bigger conventional bombs, and faster airplanes. How on earth was this Neanderthal Hitler able to grab power and then populate all of the government agencies with nothing but thugs, low-life criminals, and reprobates who know nothing about the responsibilities he handed them?! Far from making Germany great again, Hitler's turning the country into a giant serfdom where there's no law but his whim, and his impulses are nothing if not morally bankrupt! We're the culture that gave the world Beethoven, Goethe, Bach, Gutenberg, Kant, and yes, Einstein. We have utterly debased ourselves! How did we ever sink so low?!"

Georg had decided that with the limitations forced on Aldus's small group of scientists, it was best to let him rant and release frustrations that had been growing for months. He remembered how his friend had even destroyed a grandfather clock out of sheer frustration when he learned that some of his stellar scientific associates had been drafted into the army as foot soldiers several months before Germany's invasion of Poland.

"What infuriates me the most, Georg," he said as his voice began returning to normal, "is that I've seen what the Americans are doing, and they seem to be serious about making a fission device. While what I saw in Chicago this past summer was preliminary to any large-scale effort to build one, I saw no sign of the anti-science, anti-intellectual, anti-Jew idiocy that's everywhere in this country.

"I wouldn't say this to anyone else, but my biggest fear is not that America will build one first. That would be devastating enough for Germany, but there is something else that I believe is considerably more dangerous to our future."

"Are you referring to America's ability to build an unstoppable conventional war machine if she enters the war?" asked Georg.

"No, I'm not. I think our greatest enemy isn't America. The menace's within our borders, right in our capital—it's the maniac who's running our country. He's demonstrated his determination to dominate Poland and other countries to the east under the absurd cover of Lebensraum! As if we needed vast amounts of other peoples' land to accommodate our German population when he intends to get rid of so many of us he calls undesirables! He'll stop at nothing to turn Germany into a terrible weapon resulting in the deaths of God knows how many people, Germans and non-Germans alike.

"Then there's the fact that he's appointed such criminal fanatics as Himmler, Goebbels, and Göring to carry out his plans. I fear that this Lebensraum nonsense is only the prologue to what could be his grand megalomaniacal plan to control Europe, then Britain, perhaps Asia, and ultimately North America. Mark my words, Georg, every success he's had since taking over the Rhineland, Austria, Czechoslovakia, and now Poland, feeds his perverted idea of the legitimacy of his absolute dictatorship until it will likely end in one, immense cataclysm for Germany. I believe that if this horror comes to pass, he'll justify our massive destruction by blaming the Germans for being too weak and undeserving since we were unable to fulfill his grotesque grand design!"

"Aldus, you need to calm down. Let's go some quiet place, have a beer, and discuss something more pleasant. I must believe that what you just described is something that can't happen. The German people are too rational and wouldn't allow it! No, I don't believe it's possible! How could they conceivably tolerate the deliberate execution of a national plan that is nothing less than suicide—a domestic genocide?"

"Just wait and see, Georg. I'm warning you here and now: remember this conversation!"

32

"Come in, Hahn. Come in. I'm glad you're here," said Maximilian Graff seemingly indulgently as he motioned for his guest to enter while his butler walked out of the study and silently closed the door. Hahn instantly found such convivial behavior from his boss entirely out of character, making him suspicious and apprehensive.

"Thank you, Herr Graff. I must admit I was quite surprised when you asked me to meet you in your grand home. It is truly magnificent."

"Thank you, Hahn. Would you like something to drink before we get into why I called you here?"

"I'm just fine, Herr Graff," said Oscar as Maximilian motioned for him to be seated while he poured himself a small glass of amber-colored spirits. Oscar kept his eyes fixed on his host as the man hobbled over to a comfortable chair next to him, sat down, and put his glass down very gently on the nearby rococo occasional table.

"You've done very well for me, Hahn."

"Thank you very much, Herr Graff," said a stunned Oscar who had rarely heard a compliment pass Maximilian's lips, amplifying his apprehensions.

"I've asked you here because I'm assigning you a special, secret mission that only you and I, and whomever you believe is appropriate to discharge these tasks, will know anything about. This secrecy is critical. Is this absolutely clear?"

"Am I to understand that Karl knows nothing about this?"

"Stampf, in particular, is not to be aware of this. Is that clear?" he declared with a sudden edge to his voice.

"I understand completely, Herr Graff."

"Good. Now then, I'm entrusting you with a series of tasks of the utmost importance that I've had in mind for some time. All but one involves the project near Oyster Bay that you've been overseeing. The facility, which I've decided to call 'Eingang,' is finally ready to enter a new phase. There is already some equipment that was recently delivered to the lab complex. There is a person I want you to contact to oversee getting it set up without delay. The rest of Eingang will involve a longer-term initiative, and I will brief you on this when the time's right."

"What's the other task you mentioned?"

"I'll discuss that with you when we're closer to the time of its execution. Until then, you'll not mention any of this to anyone, not a single person. Am I clear?"

"Yes, sir, completely clear."

"Now then, do you have any questions about what I've told you so far?"

"I have no questions, but I must admit that I'm eager to see what you have in mind for the...you're now calling it Eingang?"

"Yes. Considering what you first told me about your convictions and your dedication to the Bund—which is not long for this world, by the way—I know you'll be pleased with what I'll be asking you to do. We're on the verge of a new world, Hahn, and it is one that will be vastly superior to the old one. You'll be playing an important role in this."

"This is very exciting, Herr Graff. Now the person you wish me to contact regarding getting the lab set up, who is it?"

"He is a great scientific thought leader and has been the executive director of the Eugenics Record Office for years. It is my understanding that this man's work has guided significant initiatives in Germany for years, directed by Adolf Hitler himself."

Suddenly, Hahn reflexively shot up out of his seat, gave the Nazi salute, and looked into the distance with an erupted, "Heil Hitler."

"Yes, Hahn, I thought you would find all this appealing," he said as Oscar sat down again.

"It's all exhilarating, Herr Graff. Now this person, the one running the Eugenics Record Office, will he be spending the majority of his time with the Record Office or with us?"

"That's my concern, Hahn, but he tells me that he has lost his enthusiasm for running the ERO, as he calls it. Too much political interference. He'll soon be with us on a full-time basis."

"Excellent. Then what is the man's name, Herr Graff, and will he be expecting my call?"

"Yes. He knows your name and is waiting to hear from you. His name is Laughlin. Dr. Harry Laughlin."

"I'm deeply honored that you have placed this trust in me, Herr Graff. I won't disappoint you."

"Of course you won't, Hahn. You wouldn't be here now if I weren't convinced that you would properly discharge your duty. In any event, any failure on your part would be the last thing you ever do. Have I made myself clear?"

33

"I have no idea what you'll find once you're in there," said Anna to Sal, Abe Groveman, and Mo Stein as she pointed to a large map of Long Island spread out on the hotel room's dining table. "According to the two local residents who it seems are the only ones who know anything at all, this project's been under construction for several months, but its purpose is shrouded in total secrecy. They started becoming curious when heavy grading equipment kept traveling past their homes, and they eventually traced it to this site. Very quickly, a giant berm was erected around the entire area, no doubt to keep out unwanted guests and prying eyes. Then building materials started arriving and, according to our informants, the construction crews seem to have finished their work in record time. All of this is going on in the middle of nowhere. It's so far off the beaten path that our friend Dr. Franzen was surprised when his neighbors were even aware that anything was going on."

"What's up with this place anyhow, and why d'ya think we should give a damn?" asked Abe.

"The possible significance of this place comes from the person I just mentioned, a friend of Sal's and mine, Dr. Eric Franzen, a retired university professor who lives on Long Island. He's very familiar with some genetics work he finds troubling that's been underway for years at a place called the Eugenics Record Office, or ERO, in Cold Spring Harbor, a small town on Long Island. He tells us that it's rumored that this work is about to be shut down, apparently because its source of funds has become suspicious of its true nature. University friends of Dr. Franzen's living near Cold Spring Harbor began noticing trucks entering and leaving the Eugenics Record Office but only in the small hours of the morning. They took whatever their cargo was and headed down the one road that goes to this desolate area along Oyster Bay, which is not very far away from Cold Spring Harbor. These secret nighttime shipments and their transport to this desolate area that's now the site of this mysterious facility, combined with ERO's disturbing 'research,' if you can call it that, lead me to suspect that something dangerous could be going on at this Oyster Bay location. In fact…"

"Come on! Why in the hell do I give a shit about any o' this, Tilner?" an impatient Abe butted in.

"Here's why. The ERO's research's been involved with defining and creating a superior race by selectively eliminating 'less desirable' people. Unfortunately, the 'undesirables' include Jews, blacks, and others condemned as unfit by these researchers and by Nazi sympathizers. I'm concerned that the Oyster Bay compound may be somehow carrying on this awful business or maybe even something worse."

"I'm sorry, Mrs. Tilner, but I still don't understand why you've chosen us to do this," said Mo skeptically. "Isn't this the business of some government agency?"

"Under ordinary circumstances, you'd be correct, Mr. Stein. It would likely be the US Department of Justice and its FBI. The reason we turned to you is that there's also something peculiar going on within our government that may be making it reluctant to take steps to monitor or, if warranted, stop whatever's going on here. Your job's to investigate this compound and see if we can determine what its function is and if it's dangerous in any way. To accomplish that, Sal will work with you both to map out a surveillance plan. Once you've been able to see what's going on there, we'll be able to plan our next steps. Meanwhile, I have some tasks of my own to attend to."

"And those would be…?" queried Sal.

"I'll be working to unearth what's behind our government's reluctance to do its job."

"That sounds like one tall order, Anna," answered Sal.

"It is, but I have a long-shot idea of how I might find out."

"So what else'll you be working on, Anna?"

"I'll let you know when I have something more to go on."

Sal's arched eyebrows assured Anna that he had no idea what she was talking about, and, at least for the moment, that's exactly where she needed him to be.

34

Anna and Sal had no sooner arrived at her home from their meeting with Abe and Mo when she left Sal and entered her study. After quietly closing the door, she sat at her desk and took a long look at her telephone before picking it up.

That evening, Malcolm came home from work and gave Anna a big hug, greeted Sal, and asked how their meeting with Sal's friends went.

"Well, Sal can tell you that we both saw the two men as colorful people. Isn't that right, Sal?"

"I guess that's as good a word as any. These guys are hardly candidates for Tilner and Associates—Killer and Associates, perhaps, but not your firm. Anna's right, they're very…well, colorful."

"Then I think we should have a colorful cocktail to show gratitude for their willingness to help and to assert my wholehearted expectation that they will stand between you two and any dangerous consequences."

"Honey, if there ever were people who it's impossible to imagine shrinking from danger, these two are certainly in that category," declared Anna.

"Well, then, that would make four of you, wouldn't it?" said Malcolm mordantly as he went to the bar to mix some drinks.

Over dinner and into the evening, the three kept coming back to the mysterious facility along Oyster Bay and speculating what its ultimate purpose could be. Each idea kept returning them to the same point of frustration— not having seen the place.

Turning to Sal, Anna said, "After you and your cohorts've finished your surveillance, we should have considerably more productive conversations," offered Anna. "We're all eager to get a firsthand account of what's there."

As the threesome broke up to retire to their bedrooms for the night, Anna asked Malcolm to go ahead, telling him she would be along directly. After he left, Anna turned to Sal.

"I just wanted you to know that I'll be leaving very early tomorrow morning to meet someone who might be able to be of some help to us, and I didn't want you to be concerned with my absence. I probably won't be able to return until tomorrow evening."

"Ok, Anna. I get it. I won't ask where you're going. Anyway, I'll have my own hands full with Frick and Frack tomorrow. We should have completed our surveillance planning by the time you get back."

"Excellent. Now I have to attempt to reassure my husband that I won't be in any mortal danger. As you well know, he has a tough time with my exploits. My biggest concern is worrying about him worrying about me."

"Someday, you might think about listening to him, Anna. After all, you don't need to be doing all this."

"I promise that I'll be the second one to follow your advice, Sal, immediately after you decide to do the same."

"Touché, Anna. I guess I deserved that. With that, I'm going to turn in. Good night."

To arrive on time for her lunch appointment, Anna was on the road long before the sun rose. As she traveled along the dark, sparsely traveled highway, she thought of Malcolm's profound discomfort with her behavior and the regret she felt for putting him through such turmoil. She recalled how his mother had first told her of the death of his first wife and their first child in childbirth and how shattered he had been for years. Even now, twenty-three years later, she could see his pain instantly resurface whenever he sensed her being in the slightest danger. She saw it again the night before when she had told him her plans for the following day. On several occasions, she longed to have him experience the comfort she felt from confidence in virtually every circumstance. She also knew it could never be. It was the only persistent source of friction in their otherwise happy relationship.

Hours later, she was ensnared in Washington D.C. traffic and began reflecting on the meeting ahead. She hoped that she had made enough of a connection with the person she was about to see that he might help enlighten her about what she did not yet understand. Filled with anticipation, she pulled up to a small, fashionable Georgetown restaurant. She was early and took a table in a discrete nook in the dining room where she could see everyone who entered. Twenty minutes passed before her guest arrived.

"Richard, it's such a pleasure to see you again," said Anna standing to shake the hand of the young man approaching her.

"Anna, I feel the same way," replied young Richard Cohen as he shook her hand and then pulled out his chair.

"Thanks so much for agreeing to meet me on such short notice. I trust you'll have some lunch?" asked Anna.

"Thank you. I'd be delighted. The Justice Department's been particularly busy, so I had to start early this morning. I'm quite hungry. What's good here?"

"Everything's excellent, but the crab cakes are particularly delicious. That's what I'm having."

"Then I'll do the same."

"Excellent choice," said Anna before signaling the tuxedoed waiter and giving him their order.

As the server turned to leave, Richard continued to study the elegant menu. "This is certainly a lovely restaurant, Anna. I don't ordinarily dine in such elegance. This isn't the usual beltway eatery I'm familiar with. How'd you ever find it?"

"I was introduced to this delightful little place by my husband and my father-in-law. They came here whenever they were in the Capital, which was fairly frequently. Despite its elegance, it's not known as a power vortex by many of the usual celebrity players, so you can usually enjoy a quiet meal without the usual fuss."

"Well, thank you for introducing me to it. Before we begin, I must tell you something, Anna. After our last discussion, I felt dreadful about laying such a heavy personal experience on a total stranger."

"You needn't worry, Richard. My reaction was what I told you at the time. I was quite moved that you felt comfortable enough to tell me what you did, thereby elevating my status from stranger to friend. I'm grateful we had the exchange, which was part of my motivation for wanting to see you today."

"However I may be of help, it would be my pleasure, Anna."

Over the next thirty minutes, Anna shared with the young man Fess Tilner's concern over the apparent close-mouthed attitude of senior federal government officials regarding the growing undercurrents of racial hatred and the people and organizations stirring them up. She then focused on his body language as she turned to the topic of her conversation with the assistant attorney general the month before.

"I had a brief but interesting conversation with your boss. Did he mention it to you?"

"Actually, after his big buildup of you, I found it curious that I never heard another word about your meeting."

"Thanks very much for telling me this, Richard, although I'm afraid that's what I was expecting."

"If you don't mind me asking, what happened?"

"I don't want to put you in any possible compromising situation with your boss, so let me just say that I was testing what I had heard from my father-in-law."

"And what did you learn?"

"After what you just told me, I'm prepared to say that what I heard reinforced my confidence in my father-in-law's view. For your sake, I'd better leave it there. There are powerful people involved in all this, and I wouldn't want anything I've told you to get you into trouble." She had decided before they met that the death threat she had received through Malcolm would best remain unsaid.

35

Anna returned home just in time to join Malcolm and Sal for dinner. Afterward, they sat in the living room where Sal concluded his description of what he and his cohorts had spent the day planning. He indicated that they had set the following night for their reconnaissance mission. Since Eric's Long Island neighbors saw that construction had apparently just been completed, they expected that the place would not yet be operational, making it less likely that anyone else would be there. He concluded with an admission that Malcolm found intriguing and disturbing.

"In the end, I guess I was surprised how sophisticated Abe and Mo were with surveillance techniques."

"I wouldn't have thought this'd be part of their skill set," said Malcolm. "It always seemed to me that mobsters are more about brute force than precision planning."

"Ordinarily, I'd have to agree with you, but these guys are skilled assassins and have to be careful and cagey if they're going to survive. They said their longevity came from years of planning complex 'whacks,' as they called them, of powerful, well-guarded mobsters. A single mistake, and they'd be as good as dead. I'm glad I wasn't involved with that end of the business."

"Did they show any remorse or regrets over how they've spent their lives?" asked Malcolm.

"Regrets? I'm sorry, Malcolm, but these people occupy a different universe than the rest of us. To them, assassination's just a business, a cold-blooded, highly methodical one and, given their high-profile targets, they're well paid. I think that if they had such feelings, it wouldn't be long before they'd lose their ability to fog a mirror."

"Incredible. It's just unbelievable to me that such people exist," responded Malcolm as he let out a deep breath before turning to Anna. "So what horrible things did you learn today, Honey?"

"My appointment was very different, Dear—it was benign. You'll remember I met briefly with the assistant attorney general, Eric Gorman, a little over a month ago. Before sitting down with him, I had the unexpected opportunity to meet and speak briefly with Richard Cohen, his senior aide. He told me of the torture and death of his Jewish grandparents in Germany a year ago, something that's left him having to cope with anguish that'll probably be alive as long as he is."

"At this point, how long had you known Richard?" asked Malcolm.

"I had just met him."

"And you were able to elicit this horrifying personal experience from a total stranger the first time that you both met?" asked Sal before Malcolm could ask the same question.

"Fortunately, we had some good connection points that made him feel at ease enough to share this with me, so yes is the answer."

"So, what made you want to see him again today?"

"I'm hoping that he'll enable me to see behind this mysterious federal veil and understand why on earth the federal government's behaving as it is."

"So, did that happen today?"

"No. Today was only step one where his responses enabled me to broach the topic of his boss's peculiar behavior and the government's apparent stonewalling. He told me that his boss hadn't even mentioned our meeting, which confirmed my suspicion that Assistant Attorney General Gorman is part of this conspiracy. The next step should tell me what I need to know."

"Couldn't you have wrapped this up all at once?" asked Sal.

"Very unlikely. This's fairly tricky for Richard. You may not know this, but all federal employees must take an oath to support and defend the Constitution before they can be employed. In particular, the oath requires them to defend against all enemies, foreign and domestic."

"So how does that put him in a tricky position?"

"He'd immediately be conflicted after he heard why I was there. You see, while he's required to uphold the Constitution against foreign and domestic enemies, his job wouldn't be protected if he refused to follow any of his boss's orders that conflicted with his pledge unless it were strictly illegal."

"Wait just a minute, Anna! I don't understand. How does any of this apply to your conversation with him?"

"It's a little technical, Sal. Although I don't yet understand the reasons why this should be the case, I have a suspicion that the source of this strange stonewalling by the federal government might just start with FDR himself. If so, any challenge made by Richard, or any other federal employee, to this unwritten policy could result in his immediate dismissal, even if the policy appears to shield domestic enemies. Unfortunately, even for people determined to fulfill their oaths to support and defend the Constitution, they're not afforded any protection at all. On the contrary, doing and saying nothing would be Richard's safest course. While that would eliminate him being of any help to us, now that I've told him what I have, I'm banking on his being too upset to keep still. This's the quandary Richard now faces."

"When'll we know if he decides to make a move?" asked Malcolm.

"If he does, I don't think it'll be very long."

As if on cue, the telephone rang in the next room. "Maybe that's Richard now," she said as she heard the muffled sound of the butler answering the call before coming into the living room.

"It's for you, Mrs. Tilner. The caller's name is Michael Rudman."

"Michael Rudman? Thank you, Austin. I'll be right there," she said as she rose to go into the next room, followed by a curious Sal and Malcolm.

"This is Mrs. Tilner," said Anna, ignoring the quizzical looks of the others.

"Hello, Mrs. Tilner. My name is Michael Rudman. You don't know me, but we have a mutual friend in Dr. Eric Franzen, someone I've known for many years. I live only a few miles from him on Long Island, and he's been talking to me about you and what you're looking into. I'm one of the people he mentioned to you who first tipped him off that there was some curious activity at the facility not far from him. I am very much hoping we can speak in person."

"It's nice to meet you over the phone, Mr. Rudman," said Anna as her two listeners looked at one another, shrugging their shoulders.

"Actually, it's Dr. Rudman, I was a professor and a chemist at one time, although many years ago. I'd prefer it if you called me Michael if you don't mind."

"I see, Michael. Please call me Anna. You no doubt know from Eric that I'm in Boston, so you must believe this can't be handled over the phone?"

"Yes, I do. I'm aware it's a distance. However, I can no longer travel, and I'm confident you'll find the trip worthwhile."

"Is there nothing you can tell me at present?"

"I feel safe enough to say that it involves who's behind what you're investigating."

"Can you give me his name?"

"I'm sorry, but no. That must wait until we meet in person."

"I see. Where and when would you like this to happen?"

"At my home. I would like to ask Eric to join us, as well as another person whom I've known for several months who'll be able to be of considerable value to the conversation."

After working out the timing and directions and knowing the call was coming to a close, Anna's curiosity got the better of her.

"Of course, I'd be very grateful for anything you can tell me. I understand that this may be delicate, but are you sure there's nothing else you can say before we get together?"

"I'm sorry, but I'm afraid there isn't anything I'm in a position to reveal at the moment," said Rudman before pausing and then adding. "Well, perhaps I could leave you with one thought, Anna."

"Thank you, Michael. Whatever you can say would be greatly appreciated."

"Very well, then. We'll be meeting for us to give you some idea of what you've stumbled into. Think of it as a warning."

36

Looking in his rearview mirror at the back seat of the car, Sal thought that Mo seemed to have enjoyed the six-hour journey from Boston while Abe Groveman had the demeanor of someone with bad constipation stuck in a cold outhouse impatient for relief. Once they had left Queens and entered Long Island, they passed smaller and smaller clusters of modest houses as well as secluded mansions along the way. As they closed in on their destination, the sun was setting, although it had seemed darker for some time due to the dense forest canopy that loomed over the small road that seemed to stretch on endlessly. Turning north and passing through Cold Spring Harbor, Sal wondered how far Michael Rudman lived from where they were now driving. He then thought about Anna's meeting that would be taking place there by the time he and his two cohorts had returned to Boston.

Once the immense berm described by Eric Franzen came into the path of the car's headlights, Sal pulled to the side of the road and turned off the car and its lights. The three men stayed in the car and used a flashlight to examine a smaller copy of the map Anna had used to outline the remote location of the facility they were about to investigate. Unfamiliar with the area's layout and who might be protecting it, the three had decided to stick together, use their flashlights as little as possible, and survey the berm perimeter before entering the interior of the site. After getting out of the car with a knapsack he had taken in case they found anything worth keeping, Sal looked up and gave a silent thanks for a clear sky and a bright first quarter moon that would afford them enough light to avoid any number of unknowns.

After trudging up the berm, they were relieved that there were no signs of guards or lights, something Sal found peculiar. He wrote off his concern to the remoteness of the place, and its not yet being operational. It took them another three hours to trudge along the berm to map the entire site's layout and note the relative positions of the various clusters of buildings.

The berm consisted almost entirely of sand, which made the perimeter-mapping phase of their reconnaissance very arduous, especially for Abe. Sitting down to take a brief rest, the three men discussed their next moves. After a few minutes and faced with Sal's and Mo's impatience to get going, Abe firmly insisted on resting a little longer before descending into the areas where the buildings stood. "This ain't what I'm designed for, so let's just hang on for just another couple o' minutes so I can catch my breath. Okay?" Then he added under his breath, "Schmucks."

The route the three had settled on would take them first into the largest cluster of buildings. "C'mon hulk, let's get a move on," urged Sal. "We only have until dawn to get this done." Sal's urging was met by Abe with a barely audible, "Schmuck," as he struggled to get his great bulk up out of the sand and prepare himself for the descent into the complex.

The first group of dark buildings appeared to have structures that were all the same size and configuration. After jimmying the main door of the nearest structure, they entered what seemed to be a barracks. Again, Sal gave silent thanks for the moonlight that streamed through the windows. The vast room was filled with bunks without mattresses abutting a large shared bath facility at the end of the building.

Examining the other buildings in the first group, they counted twenty-five identical structures. Still shocked by their size, Mo was the first to speak. "These are huge! Who in the hell d'you suppose these quarters were built to house? Each building must be able to handle several hundred people."

As the men slowly made their way to the next part of the compound, they came upon another series of buildings that appeared to have a different function. Jimmying the door of the first one, Sal was the first to speak.

"These look as if they're made for vehicles of some kind—lots and lots of vehicles. Is there anything in the workbenches along the side walls?"

Opening several drawers, Abe looked back at Sal and replied, "Nope. Nothin' here."

After returning outside, Sal made quick drawings and notes of the buildings, their sizes, configurations, furnishings, and their approximate physical relation to one another in the facility. As he did so, Abe and Mo kept gazing over the entire facility, periodically shaking their heads in silent disbelief.

"So," said Sal, "What're we missing? What else's here?"

"I thought I saw something over there by the last vehicle building, or whatever it is," said Mo. "It wasn't a building, just some sort o' wide road. You can just see a part of it from here. See, over there," he said as he extended his arm and pointed.

"Let's go," said Sal as he took off briskly in the direction Mo had pointed to as the others followed.

Arriving at the beginning of the road, they were able to see that it consisted of two broad, adjacent lanes. One was covered in decomposed granite, while the other had a clay-like covering that had been imported to cover the mostly sandy terrain.

"And where the hell does this go?" asked Abe.

"Let's find out," said Sal as he started walking down the road that turned in a wide arch, went straight, and then turned again about a quarter-mile away before seeming to head toward the beach.

"Now what the hell's this all about?" asked Abe, catching up to the other two. They had stopped when they had a clear line of vision to the shore.

"Who knows?" offered Mo.

"Curious, this place," said Sal. "It's so big and secret, I'm guessing the military constructed it. It's about the size to hold a small division of troops. I just don't get why they're no guards anywhere—that's odd. Maybe this place's supposed to be protection against an invasion or maybe its a sheltered departure point for our troops going to Europe. Sure looks like they're convinced we're in for a war, doesn't it?" The other two nodded their assent.

"Well, we've seen what we came for, whaddya say we head back?"

"Thank God," said Abe, expending no effort to hide his impatience to leave.

Looking for where they had entered, the three were walking on the far side of the complex next to a large, dense grove of trees when Sal looked into the wooded area and something caught his eye.

"What's that, over there through the trees?"

Sal took out his binoculars and aimed them at a dim light that was peeking through the forest. After a few seconds, he turned to the other two who had also been trying to figure out what they were seeing.

"Can you make out what it is? It's not clear to me."

"No idea, Sal," said Mo while Abe continued to stare through his glasses without responding.

"Let's take a look," said Sal. "It looks like nobody's around, but keep your eyes peeled just in case," he warned as he turned to enter the dense woods with the others again following him.

After a couple of minutes, the three came into a clearing where they saw a half-dozen smaller buildings carved into the ground, several feet below the level of the forest. The light was coming from something inside the nearest building. As the three approached it, Sal thought out loud, "Now what the hell is this?"

Unlike the barracks, a thick forest surrounded this area. Focusing their flashlights on the front door lock of the first building they came to, they pried the door open and entered the building. The first thing they saw was a room containing stacks of cardboard boxes lining the walls and piled up to the ceiling. After moving his flashlight back and forth across the boxes, Sal focused it on the writing on one of the boxes.

"This stack says 'ERO-Immigration.' The one next to it is labeled 'ERO-Eugenics-Scientific Basis.' Look at all these boxes. Here's another one that says 'ERO-Societal Basis.' It looks as if they're all sealed. Let's take a look in one of 'em."

After ensuring that they would be able to unseal the box with a minimum of damage, the three men spread out the contents of the 'ERO-Eugenics-Scientific' container.

"Would you look at all this shit!" exclaimed Sal.

"It looks like unending charts, graphs, and profiles of thousands of people," observed Mo. "Here's a stack of some forms called 'Field-Workers Monthly Report.'...Look! Here's a graph showing various races and their characteristics with a whole bunch of photos of people.... Looks like most of them are black or—this one has pictures of a large number of people with the letter 'J' under them. Here's a chart called Racial Pedigrees that has little boxes connecting family members, I guess. It seems like it's trying to show what happens when different races intermarry.... If the rest of all these boxes are like this, there must be maybe hundreds of thousands of documents, books, and pictures here just in this one building. My God, what are these people doing? What in the hell's all this stuff, and what's it all doing here?"

"I'll take a few samples of this for Anna to see," said Sal. "There's so much of it that there's no way anyone'd notice. Maybe she'll have some ideas," he said as he stuffed some items in his knapsack before the rest of the articles were put back in their box, and the trio headed into the next room.

It was here where Sal thought he had first seen the dim light, and it was immediately apparent to all three that this room was entirely different. There were no piles of boxes against the walls, and there were far fewer windows that were all elevated above eye level. The walls were lined with metal cabinets while the middle of the room had several large rectangular tables made of what looked like stainless steel. Overhead swiveling lights were cantilevered whose curved shells were made of the same material.

As Sal examined the lights, he said, "The shells of these lights must have reflected the moonlight that I saw. The windows in these buildings are too high for the moonlight to have reflected off these tables."

"And what are these tables for?" asked Mo.

"They're each about seven by three feet, I'd say," said Sal.

"Yeah, but whatta they for?!" asked Abe impatiently.

"Beats me," said Sal and Mo, almost in unison.

Sal went over to one of the cabinets, opened it, and focused his flashlight on it. "There's nothing in these cabinets either, so there're no clues as to what this's all about. Pretty strange if you ask me."

"This whole place gives me the creeps!" said Abe to no one in particular, causing the other two to stare at him briefly.

After examining the next five buildings, they saw that all had been outfitted identically and had tall stacks of similar boxes with various labels lined up against the walls. The mysterious rooms with stainless steel fixtures were also the same. Unaware of anything else to see, Sal made some rough drawings of the last buildings to wrap up his final task before they began heading back to the car.

As the three walked back to the berm where they first entered, Abe was the first to break what had been a long period of silence. "I'm hopin' we ain't never comin' back here again. This's 'bout all I'm willin' to take." Once again, silence enveloped the three men as they started trudging up the large berm before descending on the other side and getting back in their car to return to Boston.

37

As the headlights periodically flashed across her face, Anna was sure Sal and his comrades had been in one of those cars as they returned from their reconnaissance mission on Long Island while she made her way to the same vicinity. She also spent a good deal of time imagining Michael Rudman and the dark nature of what he had to reveal. It was late morning by the time she came to the end of the longest part of her journey and made the last turn onto the small country road that passed by the Franzen home with its flowering trees and bushes. After arriving and getting out of the car, she paused to take a deep breath before going up the brick walk to get Eric for their brief ride to meet Michael.

The front door opened as Eric smiled and said, "It's great to see you again, Anna."

"It's also a pleasure to see you twice in little over a week," she replied.

As they walked to the car and eased themselves into their seats, he added, "Thank you for agreeing to pick me up. This'll be an interesting meeting for all of us, I daresay. I'm sure it'll be disturbing but interesting. Michael lives just up the road. It's not very far."

"Of course, I'm happy to give you a ride, especially since you know where we're going. I just hope there comes a day when we can enjoy one another's company under happier circumstances," she said as Eric nodded his assent. "On the phone, Michael sounded as if he's in ill health. Is he all right?"

"I'm afraid his health is quite frail, but then he's eighty-eight years old. Sometimes I feel old at sixty-nine, and then I think of Michael, who was born a decade before the Civil War started."

"He's certainly seen some history. How'd you meet him?" asked Anna while Eric directed her where to drive.

"I've known him for nearly twenty years. I met him when we were both teaching in the chemistry department at Princeton. As he probably told you, he's one of the neighbors I was referring to who's been following the progress of this facility along Oyster Bay. He's frail but as inquisitive as ever. He's also very wealthy. He'd have plenty of staff to keep an eye on whatever's going on there for him."

"He made our meeting sound foreboding over the phone. Is that how you see this?"

"I'm afraid I very much do, Anna. He has a significant history with the person who's behind this strange facility, and he doesn't paint a pretty picture of the man."

"Who's this mystery person?"

"He's an extremely wealthy industrialist by the name of Maximilian Graff. Are you familiar with that name or his firm, Graff Industries?"

"No, I'm afraid not. What is Michael's relationship with Graff?

"Sixty or seventy years ago now—I think it was in the early 1870s—Michael was the young chemist who was largely responsible for getting the first chemical business off the ground for Maximilian's father. It was then called Graff Chemical and became very successful in designing and producing pesticides. Over the years, it made both men very wealthy. I don't know the details, but somewhere in the early 1890s, Michael and Graff had a terrible falling out."

"That's when he left Graff to teach chemistry at Princeton?"

"Yes. He makes it very clear that it was one of his best decisions."

"Michael said that we'd be meeting another person. Do you know who that is?"

"Yes. Karl Stampf. He's Maximilian's current executive director. Maximilian hired him when he took over the company after his father, Fritz, had a bad stroke about the time that the Great War began. Then, it was still Graff Chemical."

"So Michael used to work for Fritz Graff while Karl's much younger and is still working for Fritz's son, Maximilian. It sounds to me as if whatever prompted Michael to leave Graff in the first place was so troubling that it continues to plague him."

"Yes, you're quite correct. It's all a fascinating but alarming story. Here, turn left on this street. It's not far up this road."

Anna and Eric drove up a road canopied by dense trees that shut out much of the mid-day sunlight. After making a sweeping turn, they came upon an imposing gate with a guardhouse to one side. Past the entrance, Anna could see the road disappear into rolling, manicured lawns bordered by heavily wooded forest.

"I certainly wouldn't argue that Graff Chemical made Michael a very wealthy man, Eric."

"Yes, it did."

After the car stopped, Anna rolled down her window to give her and Eric's name to the guard.

"Mr. Rudman is expecting you both," he said pleasantly. After he pressed a button, the gate opened at a glacial speed.

After a couple of minutes, the car came upon a large but inviting home. Quite apart from what she had heard about the imposing granite structures of the Vanderbilts and DuPonts, Anna found Michael Rudman's Victorian mansion, with its turrets, sculptured railings, and fine brick and woodwork, attractive and inviting. Michael's butler was already near the entrance to welcome the guests and accompany them inside.

Once they entered the rather modestly-sized foyer, their host met them, and everyone quickly dispensed with the formalities that accompany a first meeting. Anna was sensitive to Michael's sad eyes that his ready smile was unable to obscure. Hunched over, he was still tall and fastidiously groomed. "I'm so glad to meet you, Anna," he said warmly. "I've heard such wonderful things about you that I'm eager to get to know you better. And you, Eric, it's always good to see you again. Please come in."

"Your home is very charming, Michael," volunteered Anna as the old man led them into a bright and airy living room that put Anna in mind of an older version of Eric's cheerful home.

"It's the right place for me to spend my remaining years, I believe. Please sit down and make yourselves comfortable while we're waiting for our last guest, Karl Stampf. I just learned that he had an unavoidable, last-minute meeting but should be here within the next half hour or so. We'll have lunch as soon as he arrives. Would you care for something to tide you over?" Anna and Eric both opted to wait for lunch.

"Eric, you're responsible for getting us all together, do you think that there's anything we should discuss before Karl arrives?" Michael inquired.

"First thing, I think it would be helpful for Anna to hear about your relationship with Maximilian's father, Fritz, and how it ended."

"Oh, very well. Unfortunately, this raises memories that are still quite painful for me," said Michael as he turned towards Anna. "I was very young, living in Chicago, and impatient to make my mark as a newly-degreed chemist. I was approached by a neighbor, Fritz Graff, to become his business partner in a new venture. Even though he was younger than I, before approaching me, he had earned a fair amount of money from running his own local transport business. He had prospered literally from the ashes of the Great Chicago fire and was an extremely ambitious, restless young man. He was eager to use my technical knowledge and his profits to start a chemical company. We decided to begin with pesticides."

"It wasn't too long after we started Graff Chemical that I witnessed Fritz's volcanic, violent temper that immediately made me wonder how long I'd be able to work with him. In the beginning, our business prospects looked bright, and I couldn't afford to turn down the share of the company he had offered me in a long-term purchase agreement. As time went by, however, we went through the first of several major and minor business downturns. Fortunately, we had built a broad enough customer base that we were always able to remain afloat. As it turned out, I was wise enough to stay until I had earned my full share and had already become wealthy.

"It turned out to be a deal with the devil, however. After we'd been in business for over twenty years, we ran up against the horrible Panic of 1893. Fortunately, both Fritz and I had salted away our personal earnings, which were substantial. But the finances of Graff Chemical itself were handled entirely by Fritz, and he'd decided to put most of the company's assets in high-yield bonds that the Panic wiped out. This precipitated our final conversation. He made the unbelievable assertion that, despite his insistence on always being totally in charge of the business side of our relationship, it had somehow been my fault that he'd been investing the company's profits in bonds that the Panic almost entirely obliterated."

At this point, Michael paused and took a long drink from a large water glass he had next to his chair. Both Anna and Eric could see plainly that, despite the age of these memories, the wounds that accompanied them were still raw. Having had her own successful business at one time, Anna understood the realities of commercial challenges. However, as was the case with Eric's story about his wife, she suspected there was something more important to come.

"I'm sure this's very difficult to relive," said Anna. "I suspect that Graff still had more to say, which is why you decided you couldn't stay with him any longer. Is that true?"

"I'm afraid you're right. After considering him a partner for decades and putting up with so much of his bile for all that time, I found that his disgusting words rocked me to my core. In fact, I think they were the proverbial straw that broke the camel's back. They still haunt my mind! He…he called me a worthless…a worthless kike and that I should burn in Hell!… What's more, he blamed…my God…he blamed me for not using my…my huge Jew brain to protect our money since that's what Jews are supposed to be so good at! I was so shocked and hurt by his vile insults that I knew…I knew then and there that I could never have anything more to do with such a monster. Unless you're Jewish and have been the lifelong target of terrifying anti-Semitism, you couldn't possibly know how shattering and life-altering this experience was for me."

At this point, pain washed over Michael's face as he shut his eyes and dropped his head slowly, gently shaking it from side to side. Not having heard these details before, Eric was deeply moved by his friend's obvious distress. Anna was also touched. That was not her only emotion, however. Her anger was aroused by Maximilian's father, Fritz, someone so weak and self-centered as to be wholly unable to accept responsibility for a disaster of his own making. Worse, he was able to bolster himself only by savagely attacking his close and long-standing partner, the one person who had protected him from himself for so long. It was apparent to Anna that Fritz's outrageously cutting racial abuse had been deliberately designed to gut him with a mortal wound.

After a brief attempt to comfort Michael, Eric and Anna saw him begin to recover when his butler entered the room. "Mr. Rudman,

Mr. Stampf is approaching the house." Hearing this, Michael perked up and recovered some of his pleasant demeanor.

"Yes, Charles, ahem. Please see him in. He'll be joining us here, and then we'll all have some lunch." As the butler left, Michael turned to the others. "I'm so very sorry to have given my raw emotions free rein, but I haven't spoken of these things since they happened, and I haven't yet been able to cope with them fully. As you'll see, Karl seems to've weathered his relationship with Maximilian Graff better than I could with his father."

"How did you meet Karl?" inquired Anna.

"I've known him only for a few months. In his endless conversations with Maximilian, he'd heard of me and looked me up just before this Oyster Bay facility got underway."

"Was his contacting you in any way related to Oyster Bay?" asked Anna.

"Oh my, yes. You see…"

Just then, the butler entered the room with a trim and handsome but weathered middle-aged man whose cheeks were slightly warped into the sides of his face. His hair was dirty blond, and his eyes were a soft, dark blue that gave him a tender appearance that Anna suspected belied a hard-baked nature underneath.

"Hello, Karl," said Michael warmly.

"Michael," he replied with the same warmth as the two extended their hands.

"I'd like to introduce you to my guests, Dr. Eric Franzen and Mrs. Anna Tilner."

After the greetings were exchanged and the formality of titles and last names was abandoned, Michael looked at everyone and said, "Well then, let's go into the dining room and have a bit of lunch before we hear Karl's part of the story, shall we?"

38

A heartwarming getting-to-know-you conversation accompanied the exquisite blue crab salad served on Michael Rudman's antique English porcelain. The camaraderie, food, service, and splendor of a beautifully appointed dining room gave no hint of the dire topics that were to follow the meal. Sitting between Karl and Michael, Anna was quickly struck by the depth of their love of and devotion to America.

Their dedication to Maximilian Graff seemed to her to be quite another matter. Karl's view of his boss was far more superficial and opportunistic than how Michael had earlier described his relationship with Maximilian's father. Karl shared with her that he considered the wealth he had accumulated to be no more than equitable compensation for his having saved Graff Chemical and then Graff Industries from jeopardy and Maximilian from himself on innumerable occasions. The sense of loyalty he had initially felt to Maximilian had died. The endless, acrid, verbal abuse he felt forced to endure had killed it. As a consequence, Karl was convinced that he had more than earned his wealth and, if anything, had been Maximilian's benefactor. He was more than square with the House of Graff.

"There," said Michael to his small assembly of guests now seated in his living room. "I trust the lunch was to your satisfaction." After a warm murmur of agreement, he began the discussion.

"You've all heard my history with Fritz Graff, and now Karl'll be able to share the next chapter. He hasn't told me everything, but what I've heard so far I find extremely unsettling, which is, of course, why we're all here. Karl?"

"That was a wonderful meal, Michael, and thank you for bringing us all together. As you no doubt know by now, Michael and I've shared an experience that, while it's made us both wealthy, I wouldn't wish on anyone. Michael knew Fritz Graff when they were both young, and Graff Chemical was just starting out. He quickly and frequently suffered from Fritz's outrageous verbal assaults. Still, it was nearly twenty-one years later that he decided to take a different path and became a chemistry professor at Princeton. For him, it was a wise and fruitful choice.

"Then, there's me. I grew up in a family of German-Americans, and, unfortunately, my father never had what we commonly refer to as the Midas touch. We were always poor, but I refused to believe that in this great land of ours, I couldn't make something of myself. I worked hard for years and became a vice president of operations for a large chemical products company when along came Maximilian. Impressed with what I'd done up until then, he lured me away to run Graff Chemical. At twenty-eight years old, this was a great opportunity. It wasn't long, however, before I began experiencing what had driven Michael out of Fritz Graff's world so many years before. However, based on a few of Michael's descriptions of Fritz Graff's behavior, I believe that Maximilian started getting even worse than his father. He is much darker.

"The day after we lost an important contract to the Magnum Corporation in 1935, Maximilian descended into a level of hatred and menace that I'd not seen before. He aimed his fanatical hatred at the people he saw who conspired to make him fail—all the world's Jews. I still see him rocking back and forth as if he were about to explode, pledging to use everything at his disposal to rid the earth of the Jewish 'vermin,' as he called them, once and for all. From that moment on, I ceased to know, much less understand, the man I still work for." Karl then paused for a few seconds, staring above everyone's heads, seemingly far away from the living room and its occupants.

"Well, anyway," he resumed. "Eric has already told you about this project that's been underway for months now along Oyster Bay. I'm convinced that Maximilian's behind it, and it has something to do with the horrific pledge he made to me four years ago."

"I'm sorry," Anna interjected. "You're 'convinced' that your boss's behind this? How's it possible that Maximilian's senior executive officer is no more than 'convinced' his boss's involved? How can you not know?"

"Well, you see, I've been deliberately excluded by Maximilian from knowing anything about this project. From the beginning, it's been overseen by another Graff executive, Oscar Hahn."

"And who's Oscar Hahn?" asked Michael.

"Until he came to work for Maximilian, he was a gauleiter, or regional leader, in the German American Bund, a corrupt American Nazi organization that I believe is now in its early death throes. We got to know one another fairly well, and, apart from his ridiculous Nazi racial ideas, I find him quite pleasant to be around.

"Then this past summer, something important happened that's still a mystery to me. Oscar told me that Maximilian had declared that I was to have nothing to do with a secret project that Oscar was to be responsible for. Furthermore, I was to know nothing about it. This secrecy, together with Oscar's strong pro-Hitler sympathies, is part of why I'm so suspicious of this project."

"What about Graff Industries? Is it still operating?" asked Anna, who now assumed the role of lead interrogator.

"Oh my, yes. It's doing quite well with its pesticides and related agricultural chemical business."

"And you're running this for Graff?"

"Yes, that's correct."

"Is there anything else you're doing for him?"

"I'm afraid so."

"And whatever this is, makes you suspicious of the Oyster Bay project?"

"You should understand that this summer, just before Oscar revealed to me the existence of this mysterious project, Maximilian made me sign a strict secrecy agreement with Graff Industries."

"Weren't you required to sign some confidentiality agreement when you joined Graff originally?"

"No. Maximilian trusted me implicitly, and I guess the idea had never occurred to him."

"So, what changed?"

"The Oyster Bay project. Oscar let slip to me that Maximilian refers to it as 'Eingang.'"

"Is that just a pet name that has some special significance to him, or does the word mean anything?"

"I'm afraid I have no idea."

"So, getting back to your confidentiality agreement, do you intend to abide by it?"

"I've always been a loyal executive wherever I've worked, but having to sign that agreement together with some things I've seen recently makes me very disturbed about what Maximilian is secretly trying to do at Oyster Bay. I'm so concerned about it that this meeting we're having is, in fact, a breach of my confidentiality agreement."

"What have you seen that's concerned you so?"

"I review all of Graff Industries material expenditures, and over the past several months, I've noticed peculiar expenses recorded in such a way as to hide their purpose."

"Can you give us an example?"

"Of course. The most recent instance occurred two months ago when I questioned a sizable payment for what was described on the bill as 'Scientific Equipment.'"

"And why did you find this odd?"

"At first glance, I didn't, Anna. We buy scientific equipment all the time in our development of more effective pesticides, but always from the same trusted vendors. If I hadn't been paying attention, I might not have seen anything unusual. However, in this case, the vendor was Stehlinz, a medical equipment manufacturer, and the shipment was to go to the Eingang Group at Oyster Bay."

"Medical equipment?"

"Yes. This was very strange. The Graff Industries I know would never need medical equipment. Other companies we know and trust perform all of our human and animal toxicity testing. Besides, we'd never done business with this Stehlinz outfit."

"And what did you make of this?"

"Since I was prohibited from knowing anything about Eingang, Oscar felt bound not to discuss it. So I looked into it myself. I found the bill of lading that itemized what was purchased. I was horrified! It listed such things as surgical tables, operating instruments, and surgical equipment. At the time, I wondered why in the hell we were buying such things?"

"Do you now have any idea what this's all for?"

"By itself, it's a mystery. However, when put together with several other things that occurred earlier, it makes me shudder to think what's about to be going on at Eingang!"

"What are these missing pieces of the puzzle, Karl?"

"I can't believe I didn't see all this long before now. Towards the end of last year, Oscar was very proud to inform me that Maximilian had been invited to Berlin to attend a Nazi dinner honoring Charles Lindbergh, of all people. At the time, I was curious why Maximilian had said nothing about this to me. Anyway, at the dinner, Lindbergh was awarded the highest Nazi medal, the Service Cross of the German Eagle, which is the greatest distinction the Nazis give a foreigner. The award was given by no less than Hermann Göring himself. Can you believe it?!"

"Do you know how Maximilian received an invitation to this exclusive event?"

"It was money, of course. For Maximilian, everything's always about money and power. I uncovered the fact that he'd given a check for twenty-five thousand dollars to the Nazis and listed it as a foreign relations contribution."

"What else's worried you about what you've seen?"

"About the same time that I learned about Maximilian's Berlin trip, a note crossed my desk from our head chemist saying that he had been instructed—he didn't say by whom—to order a sizable shipment of a certain pesticide for one of our customers. We didn't manufacture this particular formulation, so I didn't think anything of it."

"How long has this head chemist been working for Graff Industries?"

"A little over a year or so."

"Were you responsible for hiring him?"

"This was odd, Anna. Maximilian introduced me to him and ordered me to hire him as our head chemist. Ordinarily, I was responsible for hiring decisions, let alone someone so senior in the organization."

"Do you know how Graff met him?"

"This is also quite unbelievable. Maximilian said something about having met him at some German American Bund function at Camp Siegfried in Yaphank. He was a Nazi chemist in charge of a laboratory there that I understand Hitler himself was keenly interested in. Shortly after Maximilian returned from visiting this place, he introduced me to him and informed me of his new position with Graff Industries."

"Getting back to the pesticide that this person was responsible for ordering, what is it about this that now concerns you?"

"I discovered the truth about the so-called scientific equipment purchase only a couple of months ago. However, we received the bill of lading for this pesticide nearly a year after I'd first heard about it—it had just arrived."

"Why wasn't it ordered for such a long time? Wouldn't your customer be wondering where it was?" asked Michael.

"Ah, we finally come to the heart of the matter. Who was the customer? None other than the Eingang Group! And what was the chemical that was delivered? A hydrogen-cyanide based pesticide. And who shipped it to us? IG Farben, the immense German chemical conglomerate that is one of the largest financial supporters of the Nazi party."

"But Graff's always been in the pesticide business, Karl. What's so unusual about this?" asked Michael.

"Good question, and one I had to research to answer. This product consists of prussic acid, as well as an eye irritant, and one of several adsorbents such as diatomaceous earth."

"For those of us who aren't chemists, what's the practical significance of what you just described?" asked Anna.

"Well, you see, a variant of this concoction was originally used to fumigate such things as orchards, trains, and to delouse clothing. This more recent version has a particularly disturbing history."

"What's that?"

"Its forerunner was extremely quick and lethal for humans and was first used as a poison gas weapon by the Germans in The Great War. After that, it was banned as a weapon, but its descendant is available as a pesticide. It's been used under the trade name Cyclone."

"Has anyone else heard of this chemical?" asked Anna as the others shook their heads.

"It's unlikely this name would be familiar to you. Since IG Farben manufactures it, it's far more widely known by its German name."

"And what's that?"

"Zyklon B."

39

The day after returning to Boston from the meeting at Michael Rudman's home, Anna visited her office for the first time in nearly two weeks to pick up her messages and check in with her staff. As she walked through the firm's impressive lobby, she was struck by how the quiet stateliness of Tilner and Associates contrasted with the steaming cauldrons of conflict and controversy that permeated her extra-curricular investigative work. It seemed ironic to her that she should feel this way knowing that her firm was usually at the very epicenter of resolving human warfare, whether it had been physically violent or ruthlessly commercial. Somehow the sedateness of the office environment seemed to her to belie the firm's central role in resolving serious conflict.

Immediately after Anna sat down at her desk, her young assistant walked quickly into the office and handed her a small note. "I was told that this message was important, Mrs. Tilner. He called yesterday and requested a return call the minute you returned."

"Who's the caller?"

"His name's Richard Cohen."

Two minutes later, Anna's aide was surprised when her boss rushed out of her office, saying over her shoulder, "I don't know when I'll be back." The young lady stared at her desk and wondered what Anna could have learned that caused such an urgent response.

Half a mile away, Richard was waiting for Anna on a park bench in a secluded part of Boston Common near Brewer Fountain. "What on earth are you doing in Boston, Richard?" panted Anna after racing from her office.

The young man stayed seated, staring straight ahead. He responded with a question that Anna found foreboding.

"Did you know that the very first mustering of colonial militia to fight the British troops, which had been injected like a pestilence into our colonies, occurred in this very park?"

Before she could answer, he turned and smiled weakly at her before saying, "Please have a seat, Anna. I've been waiting for you. I've been in town since yesterday, so I'm glad you returned today." As Anna sat down next to him, she was concerned by the dour, almost dejected appearance of the young man who had been so effervescent barely two days earlier.

"Why didn't you call me first, so you didn't have to sit around waiting for me?"

"What I need to tell you…well, when you hear what it is, you'll understand why I couldn't wait to meet you face-to-face."

"You have my full attention."

"When we left one another the other day, I found myself dwelling on what you'd said about our government's aggressive silence concerning some of these rabidly racist, extremist groups. I hadn't been aware of how strongly I'd been repressing this, but when I told you what happened to my grandparents in Germany, this and your concerns got me all stirred up, and I couldn't help talking to my boss about it."

"How did you approach it with him, Richard?" asked Anna apprehensively.

"I made the presumption that you and your father-in-law were correct in your assessment. If my boss were either overtly or subtly being manipulated into suppressing information, I'd have to be very careful."

"Wise," said Anna with relief.

"I ignored your meeting with him and said that I'd received a confidential alert from several sources who'd made it appear that somehow our government could be being held hostage by certain extremist groups."

"Did he ask who this information was coming from?"

"Of course, so I had to lie. I told him that this had come to me rather obliquely from family members in Germany who, for obvious reasons, were unwilling to say where they'd heard it."

"Did he accept this?"

"He appeared to, but then he said something that astonished me. He told me that if I valued my job, I'd remain silent on this whole issue and not delve into it any further. Not expecting this response, which flies in the face of the oath I took to uphold the Constitution, I said that this was clearly at odds with the rules I swore to follow and asked what could be behind such a command and what should I do? He hesitated for a few seconds and then said that he wasn't privy to all the details, but it had been made clear to him that there were vast forces at work that, if disturbed, could be detrimental to America's ability to wage war, should the need arise. Then he reiterated that I was not to get involved with anyone who raised the issue, let alone someone inquiring specifically who or what was behind it."

"Which is, of course, exactly what you're doing at this very minute."

"Yes, of course it is, but his open confirmation of your suspicion, and that somehow our ability to wage war is what's behind this peculiar governmental silence shocked me. I don't understand it, but this scares me. It's what compelled me to see you."

"Then I need to warn you about something. People are aware of my meeting with your boss, and I received a call discouraging me from pursuing my questions any further. Of course, this could apply to you if you do anything similar, so you must be very careful. So far, I think you've handled this the best way possible. However, in light of this potential threat, what's driving your sudden decision to drive all the way up here to secretly meet with me and do precisely what your boss just dictated you shouldn't?"

"It's very personal, Anna....When I told you about my grandparents, of course raising the memories of them and their violent deaths disturbed me, but there were other reasons why I simply couldn't sit back and do nothing."

"Can you share any of this with me, Richard?"

"Yes, and it's part of the reason I'm here. You see, not long before the Nazis murdered my grandmother and grandfather, she warned me about what they'd been experiencing in Germany in case it ever started happening in this country. Apparently, despite Hitler's constant railing against the Jews, communists, gypsies, and a whole host of other 'undesirables,' the German government has been silent on the violent Nazi groups that've been quietly arresting, roughing up, and even murdering these people. Her warning was eerily similar to the concern you voiced concerning our government's silence about certain militant racist groups here, something I found deeply troubling."

"I don't know that I would characterize this as only being personal. It's also about being concerned for this country, Richard."

"I'd agree, except that when you said you were also a Yale law grad and that we shared being denied entry into Skull and Bones for discriminatory reasons, we had a closer bond than I'd expected. Then, what you later told me at the restaurant that so closely echoed my own grandmother's distressed warning further reinforced this personal link with you."

"I certainly agree that we've had several interesting common experiences."

"Well, there's more."

"And what's that?"

"The minute I laid eyes on you, I was instantly transported back to my grandparents' home in Berlin. They always had the usual family pictures all over their dressers and cabinets and on the walls. You see, you remind me of my grandmother when she was young. She was a beautiful woman, and I always felt intensely proud of how other people reacted to her and the wise counsel she gave me. You very much put me in mind of her."

"Thank you, Richard. Of course, I'm very flattered to hear this. If she's any indication of what your parents were like, I'd say they all have produced a most remarkable and engaging young man."

"That's very kind of you. There's just one more thing."

"And that is?"

"As unbelievable as this may sound, my grandmother's name was also Anna, Anna Cohen."

"Good heavens! It's no wonder why all of this enabled us to establish a bond so quickly," responded Anna before pausing and looking up to the sky.

"Richard, since we're together, there's a favor I need to ask of you, but you're completely free to refuse. Now that you know that others may be watching what you're doing, this request could be dangerous. However, if you can find anything out, it could dwarf the significance of everything we've been discussing."

"God Almighty, Anna! What could that possibly be?! Is our government doing something even worse?"

"This time, it's not our government, Richard. It's about what the Germans might be up to."

After Anna finished her explanation five minutes later, Richard stood suddenly and, in a strained voice, said, "Sorry, Anna, but I've got to return to Washington right now." Struck by the urgency of his demeanor, Anna bid her now-close friend a quick goodbye, this time with a hug. As he abruptly turned to walk back to his hotel, he worried that he might not be able to make it before having to throw up.

40

As she walked the half mile back to her office, Anna knew her decision had been correct to withhold from Richard what she had learned from Sal and his surveillance team. She had put Sal's information together with what she had learned at the Rudman meeting, and what she saw was a terrifying vision of why the Eingang facility was built and what lay ahead. "Richard has more than enough on his plate without having to imagine all this as well," she had decided before meeting him.

After spending the rest of the day into the early evening at her office returning calls and signing several documents, Anna left for home feeling as if the weight of all of humanity's impending disasters were hanging around her neck. Even with the steely nerves that had served her so long and faithfully, she felt them straining under the burden. Shortly after she arrived, Malcolm also returned from the Tilner offices. The minute he came in, he walked up and gave her a long hug and kiss just as Sal walked in and joined them.

"Honey, I must say, you look abnormally at ease considering what you learned at Michael Rudman's yesterday," he said as he left to fix French 75s for the three of them.

"I certainly agree," said Sal.

"Looks can be deceiving, boys," said Anna. "Sal, have you made the arrangements to revisit Eingang as we discussed?"

"Yeah, but I've got to tell you, Anna, Abe was none too pleased to hear that he's going back to that place. It's fascinating that such a brute of a person should react this way, but he thinks it's a really creepy place and I can't say I disagree with him. I still don't understand, though, what else do you think we're going to find there."

"Based on what I learned from Karl Stampf," explained Anna, "I could be wrong, but I fear there's another kind of facility, maybe two, that we haven't discovered."

"Other facilities? What do you think they're for?" asked Malcolm.

"I'd rather not say until we discover their actual purpose, if they exist at all."

"Do you have any idea what we'd be looking for?"

"Not really, but I'll know it if I see it."

"Okay, Anna. I've learned not to quarrel with you," said Sal as Malcolm brought the drinks to the coffee table.

"Good thinking, Sal," said Malcolm. "That makes two of us. Even though we're still several months shy of Christmas, I think it's appropriate for us to toast to at least two wise men," he said, attempting to inject levity into a rapidly darkening conversation.

"I met with Richard Cohen this morning," said Anna abruptly as both Sal's and Malcolm's glasses suddenly stopped inches from their lips.

"Richard Cohen, Assistant Attorney General Eric Gorman's senior aide?! That Richard Cohen?! What the hell's he doing in this neck of the woods, for heaven's sake?!" said Malcolm warily.

"I would've told you about this at the office, but it arose so quickly and unexpectedly, by the time I returned, you were already in court."

"What on earth's up with Mr. Cohen?" asked Sal as he finally took a sip of his drink.

"Perhaps we can get into the details later, but he confirmed Fess's suspicion that there's a wide-ranging cover-up taking place. He said his boss told him that there were 'vast forces at work that, if disturbed, could be detrimental to America's ability to wage war, should the need arise.' Also, in no uncertain terms, he ordered Richard to butt out if he wanted to keep his job."

"I wonder what the hell that all means," said Sal.

"There's one additional piece that he might be able to shed light on that could outweigh everything else."

"Outweigh everything else?!" said Malcolm. "This just keeps getting worse and worse. You're being too mysterious about this Anna, and it's really got me spooked!"

"What exactly is this 'additional piece' you mentioned?" asked Sal.

"As soon as I know I'm not on a wild goose chase, I'll describe it all to you both. In the meantime…"

The ringing telephone interrupted Anna, who then paused while the butler answered it. The second he entered the room and announced that the call was for her, everyone quickly proceeded into the next room.

"Hello?…Oh hello, Richard.…What's wrong?!"

As the one-sided conversation continued, Sal and Malcolm became increasingly unnerved at not being able to know what Anna was hearing at the other end of the line. She appeared to be increasingly unsettled, putting Malcolm even more on edge with each passing second. After a minute of only halting responses that made no sense to either of the two men, Anna finally had a chance to respond to her caller.

"Richard! Please, just calm down now! Take a deep breath! Unfortunately, what I feared, we now know's the case. You've every right to be upset. I want you to pull back and forget that we ever talked about this.… Yes, yes, I know, but this kind of threat comes from some powerful people, and it's simply not worth jeopardizing your safety.… Listen to me! I want you to drop it, drop it once and for all! Please do this if for no other reason than I'm very concerned for you and, in light of this, would never want you to endanger yourself. If anything happened to you…. Of course. I feel very strongly about this, so please do as I say…. Thank you. That makes me very relieved to hear. We'll talk again soon….Yes, of course. Thank you for letting me know. Goodbye, Richard."

By this time, both men were aghast, but Malcolm was unable to control his anxiety.

"Goddamnit, Anna! What in the hell's happening?! I demand that you take your own advice to Richard and drop whatever this is this minute. I'm serious this time, Anna. I mean it!"

Anna knew that whenever Malcolm addressed her by name that he was terrified. Nonetheless, the size of the stakes dictated her response.

"I know how worried you are, Honey, but I'm begging you to trust me. I have no feasible alternative here. For all our sakes, we have to find out what's going on in Germany. Otherwise, we could all be facing an unthinkable threat."

"Would you please stop speaking in riddles?! It's driving me nuts! What's this horrific secret of yours?"

"All right, all right, Malcolm," sighed Anna. "If you must know, then you can suffer the anxiety that knowing'll bring. Is that really what you want?!"

Sal then spoke up. "Malcolm's voicing my concern as well, Anna. The worst thing for both of us is the torture of not knowing. Maybe your iron will can withstand such stress, but I assure you, we can't!"

"You're both wrong! If we're all facing the possibility of Armageddon, and I'm not positive that we are, then knowing in advance about the instrument of our destruction would be of little comfort."

"So you're saying that Germany could be making some horrific weapon that could wipe us all out?!" demanded Malcolm.

"That's the possibility, but still only a possibility, until I can find out more."

"Well how on earth do you expect to find out what's going on four thousand miles away with a super-secret weapon in the middle of the most repressive, secretive, violent government on earth?!"

"There might be a way without actually having to go there."

"Now, hearing that makes me really worried!" said Malcolm pointedly.

"I assure you that you needn't be. Since even Richard's most superficial and innocuous inquiry into what our government knows about this has already raised some ugly red flags, I have an alternative."

"And what's that, pray tell, and why didn't you think of it earlier?" said Malcolm sarcastically.

"Richard was the quickest and potentially the most reliable source of information, but let me get a couple of questions answered before I say anything more. If what I have in mind can be arranged, I'll give you my solution. It's a long shot, but it won't involve any physical risk to anyone. I promise, Honey. Can you bear with me just a little longer?"

"What choice do I have?" said Malcolm, already calmed by the promise of Anna's safety.

"I suspect we both know the answer to that."

Sal stared at each person for a few seconds and slowly shook his head.

41

"I appreciate your responding so quickly to my call, Eric. Have you been able to find anything out?" asked Anna.

"Yes, I have, and your timing's excellent," he replied. "I spoke with my physicist friend who lives close by, and he said that the person you need to meet is a Dr. Georg Loh, spelled L-O-H. He's been working closely with Dr. Aldus Stromberg, the head of the German advanced weapons initiative, since the beginning. He's also been a very close friend of his for years."

"And my timing?"

"Oh, yes. Well, Dr. Loh's also close friends with some of the top physicists in this country and will be coming to Columbia University to visit some of them next week. With my friend's help, I believe we could set up a meeting with Dr. Loh while he's here. I must point out, however, that this may well be fruitless. Since Germany has invaded Poland, and both Britain and France have just declared war on Germany, Dr. Loh will probably be extremely tight-lipped about any knowledge he has of Germany's advanced weapons plans and progress."

"Regardless, that's excellent news, Eric. Thank you ever so much for getting this ball rolling. Please convey to your friend my deepest thanks and set up a meeting as soon as possible."

"I presume a scientist of your own will be accompanying you, or would you like me to recommend someone?"

"No, thank you, Eric. There's a unique person I'd like to accompany me who isn't a scientist. I feel confident she'll be able to be of critical help to us in discovering Germany's advanced weapons intentions."

"Well, I certainly hope so, although, as I said, considering the current environment, I'm not at all optimistic. As I said, I don't expect that he'll be willing to say a word about what he knows even to his closest American colleagues. Of course, my friend, Dr. Joseph Altenau, would want to be present to make the introductions."

"I understand. If Dr. Altenau works at Columbia, does he live in New York City?"

"Just outside the city in White Plains. He's about twenty-five miles away or so."

"Since he's so close, perhaps we could meet with you both beforehand to ensure that the meeting with Dr. Loh has the best chance of success. I'd be delighted if you'd join us, Eric."

"I'll be happy to arrange it. What's the name of your friend, Anna?"

"I still have to get her consent, but her name is Eva Hauser. She lives in Alabama."

"Alabama? Is she part of the faculty at the University of Alabama? Perhaps we know some of the same academics?"

"I'm afraid not, Eric."

"Then, if you don't mind me asking, can you tell me what you believe qualifies her to be a part of what I'm confident will be a very erudite discussion?"

"It's not easy to explain, but let me just say that I've worked with her before, and she has unique talents that, in this case, could be critical for our country."

"I see, a government official then," said Eric with an evident tone of disdain and disappointment.

"No. When we get together, I'll make sure you understand exactly why I'm convinced she may be the only person who can do what we need."

"Very well. I'll take your word for it. I'm intrigued and look forward to meeting this friend of yours. Since Dr. Altenau lives not too far away, perhaps we could all meet at my house with him the day before we meet Dr. Loh at Columbia. You and your friend could spend the night here, and then the three of us would drive into the city where we'd rejoin Dr. Altenau for the meeting with Dr. Loh."

"That would be wonderful, Eric. Thank you for your gracious hospitality. I'll look forward to hearing from you regarding the dates and then I'll arrange to meet Eva at Grand Central Terminal before coming straight to your house. Thank you again for making all this possible. I can't overemphasize how important this meeting could be."

As she hung up, Anna broke into a broad smile imagining Dr. Eric Franzen laying eyes on Eva for the first time. She knew if she had described Eva over the phone, any possibility of this critical meeting would have been dead instantly. At least for the time being, her own credibility with Eric would have to suffice. "Scientist?! Academic?! Faculty?! Government official?!" she said to herself. "Is he in for a shock!"

Later that evening, Sal's and Malcolm's reaction to Anna's announcement regarding Eva was what she expected.

"You've done…WHAT?!" they said in almost perfect unison.

"I've spoken with Eric twice today and it's all set. Eva's arriving by train in New York City the day before we're to meet Dr. Loh at Columbia University. He's a senior Nazi physicist working on Germany's advanced weapons project. It should be quite a meeting."

"Quite a meeting?! Anna, are you out of your mind?!" said Sal with a grimace that Anna had not seen before.

"You've both seen what miracles she's capable of performing, so let me ask you something. Consider the following. The Nazis appear to be hell-bent on taking over the world, and our two major allies have declared war on them. It appears that we're going to be working on our own advanced weapons weapon project, and we're about to meet someone in the center of a secret Nazi weapons project that could determine the outcome of a war that is heading straight for us. Is there any other way to find out what the Germans are doing?"

"Okay, Anna," said Malcolm. "It was just such a shock to think of Eva meeting these elite, high-powered scientists. I admit I just couldn't see beyond what I'm sure'll be their initial, horrified reaction to her."

"Remember what we all thought when we first saw her. Do you, Sal?"

"Of course I remember. How could I forget being told by you that this seemingly feebleminded young black woman could be the unique key to uncovering and dismantling the most vicious criminal conspiracy I certainly've ever heard of? My God, Anna, it's the most extraordinary thing I've ever seen!" said Sal as his eyes showed him retracing his memory. "If I hadn't already witnessed with my own eyes and ears the things this miracle of nature can do, I sure as hell wouldn't have believed it. But will they?"

"I don't need to point out the stakes here're simply too great to not use any resource we can. By the time Eric or Altenau has any thought of turning back, the train will've already left the station. Any reversal by either of them would mean what for them would surely be unthinkable professional humiliation. I'm not concerned about what Dr. Loh thinks, and Dr. Altenau and Eric will be able to better understand Eva once they meet her at Eric's house. Of course, they'll still feel embarrassed, if not betrayed, at having to present her to Dr. Loh, but their sensitivities pale against the importance of what we could learn. This could be our best and only chance to see what's going on behind the Nazi curtain. But, there's no doubt that these'll be meetings to remember. I must confess, I can't wait!"

As Anna was explaining her rationale, Sal was thinking back on his initial reaction to someone who soon became the most miraculous character he had ever encountered. Seeing Eva for the first time, Sal recalled how mystified he had been that Anna, who herself was then still on probation in his eyes, could possibly believe that Eva could be of any use to anyone. This subdued young black woman was someone who spent most of her time staring at the floor, who's speech ability was primitive at best, and who almost always communicated through Anna. He also recalled his shock as he eventually witnessed how the massive crime she and Anna uncovered would have remained invisible to law enforcement, and even the FBI, were it not for Eva.

Sal then shifted his attention to the upcoming meeting that Anna had arranged with Eric Franzen. He found himself chuckling as he imagined the world-renowned scientists, so steeped in the rigorous pursuit of truth that their lofty disciplines demanded, coming face to face with the humble, incomprehensible Eva Hauser.

42

"We're getting close now," said Sal to Anna while Mo and Abe remained silent in the back seat. It was well past two a.m. when the car's headlights swept over the deserted road that was covered over with low-hanging, heavy tree branches. Abe was silently regretting having become involved in this adventure that he found beyond creepy.

"I certainly hope that we find whatever it is that you think's here, Anna," said Sal. "We're just about to reach the giant berm that surrounds the place. Here, we're coming up to where we pulled over the last time."

After the car came to a halt on the side of the road, Sal leaned over to get his knapsack that contained a flashlight and the crude map he had drawn on his last visit. As he put it on the seat next to him, he looked over his shoulder into the back seat, where the moonlight enabled him to see Abe appearing to stare out at the berm. Abe was actually examining a tall chain-link fence with barbed wire on the top, erected at the base of the berm that followed its curves off into the darkness. It had not been there before. He was sure that their prior visit had everything to do with its sudden appearance. He felt queasy.

Pointing his flashlight down on the map sitting on the car seat next to him, Sal went over with Anna what the men had discovered on their previous visit one last time. She had studied his sketch before they left and, with his latest observations, felt she had a good idea of how the facility was laid out.

As Sal, Anna, and Mo prepared to get out of the car, Abe made what everyone thought was an odd declaration masquerading as a request. "I ain't really up for this. Ya mind if I just sit this one out while ya run around lookin' for whatever the hell yer lookin' for?"

"If you're just going to stay in the car, Abe, I'm sorry you came all this way for nothing," said Anna. He gave his customary undecipherable grunt and made no sign whatever of preparing to leave the car.

"Okay. Suit yourself," said Sal as he and the others got out and shut their car doors quietly.

"When the hell'd they put this up?" said Sal as his flashlight caught the fence. Fortunately, he had presumed that there would be some such barrier on his first visit and had gloves for everyone as well as a wire cutter. After making a hole in the fence, the three quickly crawled through to the other side. Getting up the berm was every bit as challenging as before, making the three relieved to stop at the crest and survey the place. Thankful for enough moonlight to help them find their way, Sal thought that it seemed brighter than before. Anna was especially grateful that they could keep their flashlights off while they made their way down the berm into the facility.

Sal then followed the same route that he and the other two men had used before, beginning with the large barracks. This time there were several cars parked outside the first barracks they came to. As the three crept along to avoid making any noise to wake the occupants, Sal waited until they were well out of earshot before reacting.

"Those cars weren't here the last time," whispered Sal to Anna. "No doubt due to our last visit, there must be a small security force in that first barracks. All of these buildings are the same—filled with bunks together with personal storage and bath facilities. Far ahead of us there on the left beyond the last row of barracks is the next series of buildings that we think are garages. They're smaller and tucked away in a heavily wooded area closer to the beach. There's also some sort of road to the beach from there, but there's not much to see. Let's go to the buildings where we found all the boxes."

They approached the dense trees through which Sal had seen the reflected moonlight revealing the final building cluster they had examined. Walking towards the building they had entered the last time, Sal turned to Anna and explained in a low voice, "This's the one we went in that has all those boxes of materials I told you about. The other five buildings are virtually identical, boxes and all, but I'll be damned if we could figure out what their purpose is. I'll go and get the door open."

As he approached the building, he saw that the door he had previously jimmied had been replaced with one that was harder to open, making him wary. "Looks like someone's installed a new door since we were here. Keep your eyes peeled." After struggling with it, he said, "Damn! The first one was a hell of a lot easier to open. Anyway, let's go ahead on in." As Sal and Mo followed Anna into the first building, Sal halted abruptly.

"What the hell?! They're all gone. This's where all those stacks of boxes were, Anna. The photos, drawings, and other things I showed you were from here. There was a ton of boxes lining these walls that were filled with all sorts of stuff. Now they're gone, but why?!"

No sooner had Sal finished his last question when all three heard the muffled sound of people running in the distance. As Sal doused his flashlight, they all rushed to the window and saw several flashlights aimed in their direction bobbing in the darkness. "Someone knows we're here. Sal, lead the way. Is there a back door?" Anna said quietly. Sal was not surprised by Anna's coolness. Many times before, she had demonstrated to him the same presence of mind when confronted with threats. Sal led the three quickly out of the room and towards the other side of the building, where he remembered seeing a back door.

Once outside, the three darted around two of the other buildings and into the forest nearby. Anna then said to the other two, "You go on ahead. I'll meet you at the car. I want to get a closer look at these people."

"That's crazy, Anna! They might be out to kill us," Sal responded.

"Of course, Sal, but I don't want to leave before seeing for myself something I've suspected ever since my conversation with Karl Stampf. Now go, before they see you!" said Anna quietly but urgently.

"Okay, but don't overstay your welcome!"

"How could I mistake this for a welcome? Don't worry, and I won't. Just get back to the car."

Within seconds Sal and Mo had disappeared into the woods while Anna lay down in the grass and took out her binoculars. It was a minute or so later that she saw the group of men with flashlights come into the clearing and arrive at the same building she had just left. They entered and, after a brief delay, bright spotlights flashed on that bathed the entire complex in something approaching daylight. Having searched the building and found it empty with the back door unlocked, the first man out the door to scour the complex for the intruders gave Anna the answer she had been expecting. She rose quietly and ran through the forest to get to the berm.

By now, Sal and Mo were trudging over the top of the berm when they caught sight of the car and instantly fell to the ground. Standing in the bushes on the far side of it were two guards with pistols. There was no sign of Abe. As Sal and Mo whispered to one another about how to handle the situation, they heard Anna coming up the berm from behind. Sal eased back away from Mo and signaled to Anna to be silent as she approached the crest. After alerting her to the presence of the guards, she got down on the ground and crawled forward to see exactly where they were standing.

"Where the hell's Abe?!" whispered Mo to Sal and Anna.

"Wherever he is," said Sal quietly, "these guards are pretty good signs that he didn't go voluntarily."

"Sal, are you still carrying that little Colt subnosed revolver of yours?" asked Anna.

"Always," replied Sal. "I have it in my ankle holster."

"And Mo, you have your knife, right?"

"Yeah, but how'd you know I had a knife?"

"We can talk about that later. How're your throwing skills?"

"I can hold my own."

"Good. I'm hoping you won't need to demonstrate your talents tonight, Mo. Just the same, you need to be ready. Here's what we're going to do," said Anna.

It had been nearly thirty minutes since the two guards standing in the bushes by the car had assisted in an awkward, bloody effort to subdue Abe. He had been so tough to handle that instead of four guards remaining with the car as they had planned, all but two were needed to control him. Now lying in wait in the forest next to the car, one of the guards turned to the other and gave his reaction to the challenge Abe had presented.

"I ain't wantin' to ever mess with such a moose again. Shit, he was one tough sombitch," he said quietly in an effort to relieve his boredom.

"Man, you ain't kiddin'. What a monster machine!"

Just then both of them heard a noise coming from the top of the berm across the street. As they crouched into the bushes behind the car and looked towards where the sound was coming from, in the moonlight they saw what appeared to be a woman trudging down the large sandy barrier and crawling through the hole in the fence. After

Anna walked across the street, she reached for the driver's door just as the two guards came around opposite ends of the car aiming their pistols at her.

"Don't make a move!" said the one near the front end of the car. "Where're the others?!" he demanded.

As Anna raised her hands and turned to face him she said with a scowl, "Others? There were two and now they're dead thanks to your buddies."

"Keep yer hands up where I can see 'em," ordered the guard. "Jess, check her fer weapons," he said to the guard at Anna's back.

The guard came around to her front and put his pistol into his holster to frisk her when, in a single, lightning-fast move, Anna grabbed his wrist, twisted it, forcing him to spin around in front of her as she grabbed his holstered pistol and held it to his head. At the same moment, the guard at the front of the car felt a gun muzzle press against the bone behind his ear.

"Drop it and kick it away!" hissed Sal as he held his pistol tightly against the back of the man's head. The guard instantly complied.

"Mo, take this revolver and cover this guy," said Anna as Mo came around the back of the car, took the revolver and aimed it at the guard.

Anna looked at both guards for a few seconds before saying, "Where's the big guy who was in the back of the car?"

After a few seconds of silence, Anna said sternly, "If you think that you're going to stay silent and also stay healthy, you're mistaken. I'll ask only one more time. Where did you take him?!"

"We dunno...we dunno where they took him," said the one Sal was guarding as his head jerked up and down nervously.

"But he's here, right?!" demanded Sal.

"I dunno fer shore where, but I think they got 'im in the compound somewhere."

"Very well," instructed Anna. "Undo your bootlaces, take off your belts, your boots, and your socks."

It took only a few minutes before the two men were gagged with their own socks and their faces were pressed against the fence with their hands spread high and apart, each wrist tied to the fence with their bootlaces. Their ankles were then lashed together to the fence with their belts. Satisfied that the two men were going nowhere soon, Anna, Sal, and Mo crossed the street where Sal put the two pairs of boots into the trunk before joining the other two in the car. After Anna turned it around to head for Eric's house, they passed the two guards splayed out on the fence.

"Where in the hell did you learn that slick move spinning that guy around and taking his gun, Anna?" asked Mo.

"Women Marine Corps Reserve in hand-to-hand training a long time ago."

After Mo's facial expression grimaced into a question mark, Sal broke into the conversation. "Don't even ask, Mo. She's too full of surprises."

"Well, another thing that surprises me is that they were able to get Abe. It's unbelievable! Abe's one of the toughest people I've ever known. He's as far from a pushover as there is."

As they drove, Anna was well aware of Mo's concern for his friend as she said, "We need to get to Eric's place first and then we'll be right back, Mo. Eric's only a few minutes away."

"That's assuming Abe's even still alive, he protested. "We've been here for nearly three hours!"

"I think they've probably had him for only a little over an hour and we'll need to go through the front entrance with the car this time. We'll need a couple of things from Eric to pull that off," said Anna.

43

The intense lights seemed to burn right through Abe's swollen eyelids. With sweat cascading down his forehead and chest, it was converging with blood coming from countless wounds on his naked body. He was barely conscious. The one thing he was most aware of was that the prolonged torture had stopped. The pain had not. His hands were tied together behind his back with a chain that rose to a large pulley anchored in the ceiling, keeping only his toes touching a large floor drain, his enormous weight causing excruciating pain in his shoulders, neck, and back. His torturer and an assistant had finally left the room after having interrogated him for what seemed to Abe to have been an eternity. Considering the prolonged and relentless abuse they had delivered, both were surprised that he had remained conscious.

Keeping his foot on the gas, Gus was impatient for the half hour to pass before he would arrive at his boss's office. Oscar was desperate to get a progress report as soon as possible and Gus knew that he had spent the night at his office to save time. After driving up to the small building, he went inside and woke Oscar up. Pulling up a chair, Gus wasted no time giving his report.

"We been poundin' on that son'bitch real hard fer quite a while," he declared. "He don't look in great shape, but fer a Jew he's tougher 'n I thought...big 'n real tough. But he told us somethin'. His name's Abe Groveman 'n he'n two other guys was the ones who broke in the other day. He don't seem to know nothin' 'bout why or nothin', 'ceptin' the other two's names are Sal Puma and Mo Stein, another Jew, and—get a load o' this—there's some broad named Anna Tilner. I got their names written down here on a piece o' paper. I ain't too worried 'bout 'em, though, 'cause the broad's callin' the shots."

"I wish I could share your optimism, Gus, but I have to alert Herr Graff that we've captured and are interrogating one of the vandals. You're absolutely sure he doesn't know why they were there?"

"Trust me, he ain't said much, just that they was all takin' a look 'round. They was jus' curious. That's how I took it. But give me a few more hours, and we'll wring 'im out real good."

"All right. Keep at it and see if there's anything else you can get out of him. Let me know immediately if he says anything new. I need to know why they were really there. No one goes all the way out there just for some damn joy ride. That's why Herr Graff chose that area in the first place. We have to find out who's behind this right now, and we have to stop them, you understand?"

"Yessir, Oscar. I'll get back over there and get right on it," said Gus as he exited Oscar's office, motioned for his assistant interrogator to join him, and walked towards his car to return to Eingang.

Left alone, Oscar stared at his phone. He felt uncomfortable after recalling the week before when he was subjected to his boss's withering response after delivering the news that someone had breached his beloved Eingang. Even though he had reported that nothing was damaged or appeared to be missing, Maximilian's shouted responses were still bouncing around in his skull.

"You goddamn well better find out who's done this, Hahn! And right goddamn now! Have I made myself clear enough for you, or do I need to get Erstad in here to give you some stronger motivation that you'll never forget?!"

While Oscar's inescapable aversion to even the threat of violence aimed at him had always tied his stomach in knots, he found having to endure Maximilian's outbursts particularly brutal. He was about to admit that people had again broken into the facility in less than a week. Instantly an intensely unpleasant internal sensation revisited him. At least this time, he was not empty-handed and had contrived an excuse that he hoped against hope would save his neck.

Oscar knew that Maximilian never seemed to sleep and insisted on receiving important news at all hours. He also knew that his boss was particularly volatile in the early morning, just about the time Oscar was placing his call. With every ring at the other end of the phone, Oscar's anxiety jacked up several notches until the other receiver was lifted. The voice seemed to scream through the earpiece.

"Graff! Let's have it!" Maximilian's voice bristled with hostility, which did nothing but instantly siphon off much of what little confidence Oscar had mustered.

"Ah, sir…this is Oscar Hahn, Herr Graff. Well, ah, Herr Graff, it worked just the way I planned it," he said with an unsteady tone that belied the reassuring intent of his words.

"What worked just as planned, for Chrissakes?! What in the hell're you talking about, Hahn?!"

"Well, uh, the trap we laid for the vandals…we caught one of them last night, and we're interrogating him as we speak."

"So, what the hell've you learned?!"

"Give me a little more time, and I'll have a complete report for you, Herr Graff. We've got to wear him down first."

"For your sake, I'd better be satisfied with what you tell me, Hahn. You're not going to like what happens to you if anything jeopardizes Eingang! I've been working on this way too long for some idiot to screw it up. Now get me some goddamned answers or forget worrying about what you're going to fix for your next meal! You got that?! Now get on with it!" Click.

Once again, Oscar's cool exterior had been marginally successful at hiding the sickening turmoil he felt inside. After hanging up the phone, he dashed out of his office and flew into the adjacent bathroom to lose what remained of his dinner.

44

Eric Franzen sat having an earlier-than-usual morning coffee. He appeared to be gazing out of his living room windows across Long Island Sound as the first rays of morning sun spread through the handsomely-decorated room, giving it a warm, muted glow. While his surroundings were sumptuous and he especially enjoyed his first sips of hot coffee, he was unaware of any of this. His mind was far away, preoccupied with what Anna, Sal, and Mo told him after Anna's loud pounding on his door had awakened him.

Realizing that leaving Abe behind for any length of time would be a death sentence, Anna had told Eric that they needed to return to Eingang immediately and find him before his captors tortured him to death. Eric now understood the fierce perils his unexpected guests were facing and offered them his house as a local sanctuary where they could return after rescuing Abe. By the time Eric was absentmindedly pouring his first hot cup of comforting stimulant, they were already long gone.

Driving along the deserted Long Island country road with the first signs of dawn flashing through the trees, Anna, Sal, and Mo worked through their next moves. "How do you propose we find out exactly where Abe is in the compound, Anna?" asked Mo nervously as he hunched forward from the back seat.

"I'll explain my plan when we get inside the compound."

After seeing the last plan work out successfully, Mo replied, "Sounds reasonable to me."

"Believe me, Mo, with her, it always does," said Sal.

"So, if we need the car to get Abe, this time we can't sneak in again. How're we going to get through the gate? We know there'll be a guard there now," queried Mo.

"I have another idea," said Anna.

"See what I mean, Mo? With Anna, there's always another idea," said Sal as Anna pulled the car to the side of the road before reaching the berm.

Turning away from the steering wheel to look at both of her cohorts, she explained, "This time, boys, you won't have to do a thing except hunker down and stay completely silent," she added as Sal looked at Mo, while both arched their eyebrows and shrugged their shoulders.

Minutes later, Anna's car passed the two gagged guards lashed to the fence and continued along the road for a half mile until they came to the facility's main entrance. There was an immense guard dressed in a khaki uniform who emerged immediately from his small guardhouse and held up his hand as Anna brought the car to a stop just in front of the entrance gate.

The man said in an unusually hoarse, high-pitched voice, "Ma'am, you're gonna have to turn around. This here's a private facility and there ain't no trespassin' allowed of any kind," said Gunther Gundshau.

"Thank you, officer, but I'm Mr. Graff's private secretary with an urgent written message from him for Gauleiter Hahn regarding the prisoner who's being interrogated."

"I been workin' for Mr. Graff for a long time 'n I ain't never seen you before!"

"You wouldn't have. My office is in a separate building at the Graff estate, and I see him only twice a day, once before he sees his first appointment in the morning and once after he's finished with the last one. Everything else's done by telephone, and personnel matters are handled at the executive offices, so I'm not surprised we haven't met."

"Well, sorry ma'am, but I ain't lettin' no one in here 'cceptin' Mr. Hahn 'n Mr. Erstad, 'n anyway, they both ain't here now."

"Then, I'll need to see where the prisoner's being interrogated immediately."

"I jus' told ya, ma'am, I ain't lettin' you in here under no circumstances 'n I ain't sure where he's bein' held besides."

"Then you'd better see this," said Anna as she grabbed an envelope sitting in the seat beside her. "As you can see, it says 'URGENT INSTRUCTIONS!' and Mr. Graff himself signed it. I don't need to tell you what happens if he's not obeyed instantly, do I?"

"I dunno, ma'am....Ya know, I ain't come up 'gainst this b'fore."

"Listen to me! This is extremely urgent because the prisoner's being tortured, and if he dies before these instructions are followed, you'll be the next casualty! You can call Mr. Graff's office if you like, but he had these instructions couriered to me and, considering the time that's already been lost, he'll be furious to learn that their delivery has been delayed, even by a minute. I've worked for him for years, and I've seen this before. I can assure you, you don't want to even think about what your final hours'd be like, so please open the gate."

"I can't...I jus' dunno.... Oh God... Okay, ma'am...I guess so... Okay, if you say so."

Once the tall chain-link gate opened, Anna drove into the compound as the first full rays of sun peered over the horizon. After entering the barracks area, she turned a corner and again saw several cars parked at the first building. She was relieved when they had passed it without any lights being turned on inside. Continuing to the far end of the complex, she pulled in behind one of the empty barracks, stopped the car, switched off the headlights, and turned around and leaned over the front seat.

"You can come out, Mo. I'll open the trunk for Sal," she whispered.

"You know, Anna, I've got to hand it to you," said Mo quietly as he sat up from the back seat floor and removed his covering. "I asked Sal at Eric's house, even though it's so close by, why the hell were we all there when it's so urgent that we find and rescue Abe. He told me not to worry, that you never did anything without a good reason. Okay, I thought. Then, I wondered why you asked Eric for an envelope, a pen, and a dark blanket. I remembered Sal's response, so I said nothing. I just thought maybe you were concerned about getting cold."

"Concerned? Yes. Cold? No," said Anna as she got out of the car. Ducking her head back into it, she added, "I'm glad you now understand that I haven't lost my mind. I'm also relieved that the guard hadn't ever seen Maximilian Graff's signature."

After raising the trunk lid, she quietly apologized to Sal. "I'm sorry for this, but Mo was smaller and was more easily concealed under the blanket on the back seat floor of the cab."

"I'm fine," whispered Sal as he strained to unwrap himself, grimaced, and then struggled to get out of the small trunk. Standing a bit stiffly, he dusted off his trousers and said, "I like the way you sweet-talked that guard into opening the gate. From the sound of his squeaky little voice, he sounded like he was about four feet tall and weighed fifty pounds."

"Oh brother. You couldn't be more wrong, he was huge. I don't remember ever seeing anyone who's larger."

Just then, Mo joined them at the back of the car. Anna looked at both and began quietly describing her plan.

"As we know, the first building in this row of barracks must be housing a small contingent of security guards. They appear to be still asleep, so whatever we do, let's keep it that way.

"Now then, thanks to our helpful guard, we know that Abe's here somewhere and that neither Oscar Hahn nor Gus Erstad is. It can't be long before at least one of them returns, so we have to be quick. First, you and Sal should look in the mechanic's garages to see if Abe's there and, if so, get him in the car. If he isn't, check the buildings where the boxes were stacked. Forget the rest of the barracks. They're too exposed and unsuitable for any interrogation. If you don't find him, then return here to the car. I'm going to look for him where we haven't explored yet, so it might take me a little longer. If somebody shows up and you run into trouble, even if you don't have Abe, get back to the car, get out of here, and go back to Eric's. Any questions?"

"One big question. What if you're nowhere to be found, Anna?" asked Sal plaintively.

"Go anyway. I'll find a way to get out of here and communicate with you."

After showing their skepticism but nodding their reluctant agreement to the plan, Sal and Mo headed off in the direction of the garages. Remembering Sal's sketch of the place, Anna focused on one wooded area that had been overlooked. As she started walking in that direction, she prepared herself to find something she hoped did not exist.

Meanwhile, Sal and Mo were approaching the vehicle service buildings—at least, that is what they thought they could be. Peering through the darkened windows, it did not seem to them that there was anyone inside. After jimmying the door, they entered and again saw what resembled many parallel mechanic's bays. After making a cursory examination and seeing nothing had changed since the last time they were there, they left and went to the next building. This time the door needed no prying. It was already ajar.

"This could be a break for us, Mo. There might be something here," said Sal as both men entered the building cautiously. The windows permitted the early morning sun to give the two men enough light to walk through the place easily. Remembering that the rooms and the cabinets lining the walls had all been empty before, Sal's eyes quickly settled on something new—a large cart had been parked against the wall. He then saw a drawer that was still partially opened underneath a large, scattered array of metal devices on the cabinet's counter.

"Would you look at this?!" Sal said as he went over to the carelessly strewn hardware. Opening the large drawer the rest of the way, he saw it contained several chains like the ones he had often used to work on his farm vehicles. The hardware on the counter consisted of various tools and an array of hooks and pulleys. "Somebody's been here very recently and needed something in a hurry, a real hurry."

At the same moment, Anna was walking through the heavily wooded area in a corner of the facility that remained unexplored by her cohorts. By now, the early morning sun was providing ample light as she walked carefully to avoid any branches or fallen tree trunks. The leaves of saplings and bushes scratched her cheeks as if to warn her to go no farther. Then she saw a clearing up ahead and slowed her pace in case anyone was nearby.

Approaching the clearing with a growing concern for what she might find, Anna stopped and concealed herself behind one of the larger trees near the clearing. "This's very odd," she said to herself. She was gazing at a low mound of earth in the rough shape of a large rectangle she estimated to be about sixty or seventy feet wide by about thirty feet across. It was freshly tilled and planted with thick, waist-high bushes, similar to those growing in the wooded areas. She also noticed that the trees at the right end of the clearing had been removed, creating a wide path that appeared to connect the mound with the rest of the facility's large open area where the other buildings were located. At the edge of the clearing up against the trees stood a large caterpillar tractor as if it were a sentry silently guarding a particularly precious plot of land.

Anna then turned and walked slowly among the trees, parallel to the mound, unable to take her eyes off it when something new came into view. It was the top of a wide dirt ramp that began some distance from the opening in the forest and then descended into the base of the mound. By this time, curiosity mixed with dread was consuming her. With no sign of anyone, she walked into the clearing and towards the edge of the wide dirt ramp. As she approached its upper edge and looked toward the mound, she could see that it was the roof of a structure that had been built below ground. At the base of the ramp, two large metal-reinforced wooden doors spanned its entire width. She judged each of them to be about ten feet high by fifteen feet wide.

Her apprehensions rose with each cautious step she took down the slope. When she came to the large entrance, she found one of the doors unlocked. Holding her breath, she carefully pulled on the massive door to peek inside. It had barely cracked open when she immediately recoiled from an overpowering smell of human waste. Seeing no immediate sign of movement inside, she covered her nose and entered before being assaulted by the intensity of an array of bright lights embedded in the ceiling in orderly rows. As her sight adjusted to the glare, she was able to survey the inside of the strange structure. Near the center of the room was a metal table covered with various tools and rods. In the exact center of the room hung the naked, bleeding hulk of a man with his head hanging down and his hands tied behind his back, suspended by a chain hanging from a large pulley. The other end of the chain was secured to a large hook anchored to the wall. The chain was just long enough for the man's toes to barely touch an oversized drain cover in the center of the floor. Instantly recognizing that it was Abe, she dashed to the table, grabbed a tire iron, and rushed over to the hook. After struggling to dislodge the chain taut with Abe's great weight, she was able to pop it out of the hook, releasing Abe's massive body to crash to the ground in a crumpled heap.

Rushing to him and then crouching beside the large man, Anna could see he was alive, but barely conscious. "We've got you now, Abe! I'll get the others and be right back to get you out of here!" Since it was likely that there would be little time before Abe's assailants returned, she dashed out of the structure, through the trees and into the larger complex to find Sal and Mo. Knowing they wouldn't have Abe and would have likely had enough time to canvass both sets of buildings as she had directed, she dashed for the car.

Mo and Sal were standing next to it, whispering to one another when they saw Anna running up to them between two buildings. "I found him! I found him! But he's been badly beaten and in no condition to walk. We have to get him out of here before the brutes who've been working him over return. I actually can't believe they're not here now!"

"We're gonna need some help, Anna," said Sal. "Abe's a real big guy…. Wait a minute! I saw a cart in one of the garages. I think we could manage to get him to the car with that! Get in the car!"

As Anna drove to the garage to drop off Sal, she turned to him and said, "How big's this cart? Can you manage it alone, and can we somehow pull it behind the car on our way to pick up Abe?"

"Yeah, well, it's not designed to carry a massive human being, but it should work, and I'm sure I can handle it. Now that I'm so well acquainted with the trunk, I think I can pull it behind the car from there."

"Where'd you find Abe?" asked Mo, unable to hide the desperation in his voice.

Pointing in the direction of where Abe was lying in his own blood and waste, she said, "He's in an odd underground building over there. Sal, I'll drop you off first and after you get the cart, come back in this direction. In the meantime, Mo, I'll take you to at least comfort Abe that we're here. After I leave you there, I'll drive back this way and get you, Sal, and the cart. It'll be just a couple of minutes."

"Okay, Anna. This's the building with the cart coming up on the right."

After leaving Sal, Anna turned around, drove Mo to attend to Abe, and stopped at the top of the slope. Seeing the mound and the large doors beneath it, one of which was partially open from Anna's hurried exit, Mo was aghast.

"What in the hell's this?!"

As he started to get out of the car, Anna leaned over the back seat and retrieved the blanket he had used as a cover and handed it to him. "He's in there on the floor and, as I said, he's in pretty bad shape. It really smells horrible in there, and the light's extremely bright, so your eyes'll need a few seconds to adjust. Take the blanket and give him whatever comfort you can until I get back with Sal and the cart."

Anna then sped off to pick up Sal while avoiding the barracks with the sleeping guards. On the way she said to herself, "I just hope Abe can last until we get him to a doctor." She turned a corner that would take her towards the garages and saw Sal pulling a cart intended to carry anything but a person, let alone such a large one. Passing him and then turning the car around, she drove ahead of him and stopped.

Getting out of the car and running around to the trunk, Anna exclaimed, "That's all there was?!"

"I'm afraid so, Anna. It's not ideal, but without it, I'm not sure the three of us'd be able to move Abe three feet."

"Then it'll have to do. Are you sure you can drag that thing behind the car?" she said as she unlocked the trunk lid.

"Easy as pie," he responded as he bent down, ducked under the trunk lid, and climbed into the small space. Facing backward with his legs protruding from the back of the car, he grabbed the cart's handle and signaled Anna to go.

Barely a minute later, they arrived at the top of the ramp leading to the subterranean facility's entrance. Once the car had made its way down the slope and stopped just short of the two large doors, Sal got out and shut the trunk before pulling the cart around the back of the car to get his first glimpse of the strange place.

"My God, Anna! Abe's in there?! What's this hellhole supposed to be?!" exclaimed Sal as Anna approached one of the doors to open it wide enough for the cart.

Looking over her shoulder, Anna replied, "I have my suspicions, but they aren't important now. Let's go in and get Abe into the car as fast as we can. You'd better steel yourself, though. Between the light and the stink, it's pretty rough in there! I still can't believe we've been so lucky to avoid being seen, but this can't last much longer! Let's move so we can get the hell out of here!"

The second the door opened, the smell hit Anna and Sal like a putrid wave of sewage. Covering his nose and squinting, Sal was able to move the cart over to where Mo was kneeling by his cohort with tears streaming down his face, the blanket covering Abe's massive body.

"I've never seen this big guy so vulnerable before, and I've seen him in some pretty awful situations. I'm not sure I know how to handle this," said Mo.

"We all might have to face a lot worse if we don't hurry and somehow get him loaded into the car," said Anna as all three picked out their positions to lift their huge load onto the cart. "My God," said Sal. "I just hope that we can even lift him at all. He's really big."

45

"Who??!" a shaking Gus Erstad shouted to the immense Eingang guard. "You let WHO in here??! You dumb shithole! How'd you do such a stupid thing after I told you that there ain't nobody 'xceptin' Gauleiter Hahn and me t'be let in here! No one, not a goddamned soul! What the hell've you done?!"

"She said she was Mr. Graff's personal secretary, 'n even had some letter from him about the prisoner," said the massive man with the high-pitched voice.

"The prisoner?! You ain't tellin' me you said nothin' 'bout the prisoner to her, did ya?! Well, did ya?!"

"She sounded…she sounded like she already knew about him. She really did," he replied.

Gus then grew quiet before speaking in a low growl with a menacing, slow cadence that suddenly accelerated. "Ya ain't sayin' ya told her he was here, did ya? Wait! Don't say a fuckin' word! Now, you ain't gonna say nothin' that's gonna get me real worked up or nothin'! Ain't that right?!"

As the guard looked into Gus's steely dark eyes that were now darting back and forth, an odd thought flashed in his mind, "His little eyes're too close together—way too close together for that big head o' his." Yanking himself back into the present, he made his last confession.

"Well…well, yeah! That's what she said Mr. Graff wanted."

"Holy shit!" said Gus as he stepped on the gas and crashed through the closed chain-link gate, catapulting it yards in the air before it crashed into the guard's car, smashing its front window before mauling the hood and coming to rest against the side of the vehicle.

Moments earlier, Anna, Sal, and Mo had been bracing themselves to lift Abe. They had to lift him out of the cart and onto the back seat of the car. It had been a real task getting him onto the cart in the first place. Then, it had nearly overturned twice on their way to the car. Had that happened, it would have meant lifting Abe off the ground, something none of them ever wanted to do again. After wrestling most of Abe's body into the back seat, they were preparing for the final push when the crash of the main gate made all three suddenly stop, straighten up, and pause as they wondered what the violent break in the silence had been. Instantly, Anna yelled to the other two to finish getting Abe in the car while she ran back inside.

"What the…?" exclaimed Mo as Sal said sternly, "Hurry up! Let's get him in all the way! Our stay of execution's about to end!"

They were unaware that they were about to receive a brief reprieve when Gus dropped his assistant off at the barracks farthest from the garages. His small contingent of Silver Sword guards was there for just such a contingency.

"You get those bastards outta bed," yelled Gus to his assistant. "Bring yer weapons 'n get 'nough of 'em t'meet me at the underground building in sixty seconds. You got that?!"

After a brief silence in the far reaches of the place, Sal and Mo again heard in the distance the rising sound of a car careening towards them as it flailed wildly around several buildings.

At the same time, Anna dashed out of the underground building, leaving the large door ajar. Running up to the driver's side of the car, she was holding a tire iron and two short metal pipes that she handed to Sal and Mo and said, "Here, use these. Are we ready to go?!"

"Not yet! Abe's not completely in the car!" said Sal with considerable frustration. "His foot's still sticking outta the door."

"We can't wait!" said Anna. "That car's nearly on top of us. We're boxed in here. You both get up the ramp and hide in those bushes on the mound until they get down here. I'll hide behind the front of the car until you can distract them so I can hit them from behind. Now go!"

Just as both men got to the top and dropped into the bushes, Gus's vehicle roared into view. After entering the clearing, it turned and came to a screaming halt at the top of the ramp. Gus jumped out and began running down the slope. Grabbing his pistol and aiming it at the still partially open facility door, he skidded to a halt at the rear of Anna's car.

"You've trapped yourself in there. I got a gun and ain't afraid to use it! Now come out real slow! Ya hear?!" he yelled as he hugged the back of Anna's car for cover until his men arrived.

As Gus was riveted on the door waiting for a response, Mo and Sal crept out from the bushes on the mound above him. They then proceeded quietly out of Gus's view along the top of the ridge adjacent to the ramp and stopped before throwing their pipes at him, the long side of one hitting Gus squarely on the back of his head. Momentarily stunned, he twirled around and got off a quick round that whizzed by Sal's arm. As the gun discharged, Anna shot around the front of the car. Only aware at the last second that someone was suddenly behind him, Gus quickly swiveled as Anna's tire iron crashed deeply into his right shoulder, causing him to yelp and fall to the ground.

Anna suddenly heard the sound of more cars approaching in the same reckless, swerving manner as the last one. Not yet visible, they spelled trouble. Anna jumped into her car and had just started it when a furious Gus Erstad seemed to lunge out of nowhere, yanking the door open and preparing to dive into the car to grab her. Before he could, Anna slammed the gearshift into reverse and stomped on the gas. As the car lurched backward, she jammed her tire iron into Gus's huge head, which was halfway into the cab, stunning him before he fell to the ground, spinning until he finally came to rest. The sudden acceleration had also thrown open the rear passenger door that had been left ajar by Abe's protruding foot.

At the top of the ramp, she stopped and yelled to Sal and Mo, "Get in!" Sal jumped in the front seat while Mo quickly crammed himself into the small space between the front and back seats. After struggling briefly to push one of Abe's legs over onto the rear floor, he was able to pull the other foot inside just enough to reach across and slam the door shut. Anna then turned her head to see two other cars roar up side-by-side and stop about twenty feet behind her. Gus's car was off to one side, making all three block most of her exit. She yelled, "Push yourselves into the backs of your seats and hang on! We have to put these guys out of business, or we'll never get out of here alive!"

Slamming her foot on the gas, Anna was able to build up considerable speed before ramming the back of her car into the front of the other two, puncturing their radiators and putting both out of commission. She quickly wheeled her car around while the Silver Sword guards slowly piled out of their immobilized vehicles, only to see the crumpled rear of Anna's car disappearing through a cloud of dust as it took off towards the main entrance.

46

Before Anna's car disappeared from view, Gus's small contingent of Silver Sword guards, stunned by the wreck, began running unsteadily down the ramp to help their boss. The first to arrive pulled Gus over on his back and saw that his face had been badly scraped when he fell from Anna's car.

"You okay, Ortsgruppenleiter?!" asked the guard just as Gus groaned and moved his head slowly from one side to the other before opening his eyes.

"What happened?!" he said as he raised his hand to his head. "Last I r'member, I saw the prisoner in the backseat o' the car.... Whoa!... I got me one helluva headache."

"They got away, Ortsgruppenleiter. They smashed the front o' both our cars and hightailed it outta here. I ain't sure our cars're gonna run now, but we can use yours t'get to a doctor."

"No doctor!" protested Gus. "Jus' help me up and get us back t'the barracks. I gotta get to Gauleiter Hahn right away. He ain't gonna be happy 'bout this, not happy t'all."

After returning to the barracks and slapping some water on his face, Gus drove himself to Oscar's office. As he stepped out of his car, he still felt unsteady on his feet. A little dizzy and having a fierce headache, he rapped on Oscar's door, opened it, and stumbled inside.

"Good God, Gus! What the hell happened to you?! You look terrible!" exclaimed Oscar after taking one look at his right-hand man's badly scraped face and jumping up out of his seat to help him into a chair. "What the hell happened?!" repeated Oscar as the early onset of foreboding made his skin prickle.

"They got the bastard, Oscar."

"What?! Who's got what bastard?!"

"Same one's that some o' my men chased when me and some others took the big guy hostage. Now he's gone."

"Oh, my God, Gus! What the hell am I going to say to Herr Graff? You know how violent he can be, and I promised I'd give him a full report after we finished interrogating the prisoner. Now what?!"

"I ain't feelin' so great, but if'n ya need me, I'll go with ya and tell 'im what happened."

"Thanks, Gus, but I don't think that's going to help me with Herr Graff. He's as likely to kill me as anything else. Oh my God, what the hell am I going to do?!"

"Look, Oscar. That big bear din't give us much to go on after beatin' 'im up pretty hard. I still ain't sure he even knew nothin', so why don't ya jus' tell Graff that we couldn't get him to say nothin' more and that's that? I'll back ya up. How's he gonna know the difference? It sure as hell'll be better than tellin' 'im he got away."

"That may be my only way out, Gus. But what if he wants to question the bastard himself?"

"Jus' tell him he ain't alive no more. We pressed real hard 'n he just din't make it, 'n we already got rid of 'im. Sounds real good t'me."

"Then that's what I'll say, and yeah, I want you along with me. Okay?"

"Sure, Oscar. Ya always been real good t'me. I ain't gonna pull out now."

"Then, we'll go see him late in the day. Maybe he won't be as angry as he is in the morning. Be here at three, and we'll drive over together."

As soon as Gus shuffled out the door, Oscar walked over to his safe, bent down, and dialed the combination. After fishing through a small pile of documents, he pulled out a telegram he had been holding for months.

"Thank God for Gus. But just in case, I may need some insurance," he whispered to himself.

47

After pulling up to Eric's house, Sal ran up to the front door, opened it, and went into the foyer, and shouted, "Eric?! Eric?! Please call a doctor!" As Eric rushed into the entry, Sal added, "I need something to haul Abe in here with!" Eric told Sal to follow him to his landscaping shed. After locating a large garden cart, Eric dashed inside to call a doctor. Once Sal and Mo had stumbled through Eric's front door with Abe hanging over every edge of the large cart, Anna followed and knew that she could not let more time pass before making a critical telephone call.

"No, no, I'm just fine, Honey," she said to Malcolm. "Please stop worrying. One of Sal's friends got badly roughed up, but I'm sure he'll recover and be just fine," she said as she mouthed the words "I hope!" to Sal, who rolled his eyes. "That's right. We'll be at Eric's until we can have a doctor take a look at Abe, and then Sal and I'll be coming directly home. I know how you worry about me, but please believe me when I say I'm perfectly all right.... Good. I'll give you a call when we're about to leave here.... I love you, too. See you soon, Honey. Bye."

"He had every right to be concerned, Anna," said Sal the second she hung up the phone. "What we just did was very dangerous. Very dangerous, indeed. And we both know that it could've turned out much worse."

"I'm well aware of the danger, Sal, but whatever the real threat is, Malcolm would only amplify it until he became a nervous wreck, and I can't let that happen. I hope you can understand."

"Well, it's your business, and I suppose I shouldn't stick my nose in where it doesn't belong, but I certainly have sympathy for what your husband has to go through with you."

"So do I, and I wish there were something I could do to ease his anxiety."

"Of course, there's one thing you could do."

"I already agreed that I'd stop being myself the second you do the same."

"Okay, okay. I just had to say my piece, whether I should've or not. Now back to Abe. Do you know when the doctor's supposed to be here?"

"Eric told me he'd be here in about fifteen minutes. Let's go and see how the big guy's doing."

As Sal and Anna quietly entered Abe's temporary bedroom, they were both moved as they saw Mo and Eric leaning forward from their chairs next to Abe's bed. Mo's constant attention to his friend and Eric's endless patience, generosity, and kindness made them both think that Abe was fortunate to have such good people around him. Anna was also well aware that had it not been for her, none of this selfless attention would be necessary.

"How's our man doing?" whispered Sal. As they rose from their bedside chairs, Eric motioned for all of them to go into the hall.

After easing the door closed, Eric turned to the other three and whispered, "Of course, I'm not a doctor, but whoever worked this poor man over did one hell of a job. I'm surprised he's even here at all. At least, he finally seems to be resting peacefully since I gave him some pain medication. I must hand it to you all, wrestling this giant into the car and then into my house all by yourselves was quite an undertaking. Perhaps some of you also need some medicine?"

After everyone thanked him for his kind offer but declined, Sal quietly suggested, "While we're waiting for the doctor, why don't we give Abe some peace and go into the living room. We can discuss what we've learned about this strange place. Anna, what did you say Karl Stampf called it again?"

"Eingang."

"Yes. That's it. Eingang," reiterated Sal as all four walked down the hall towards the living room.

After everyone was seated, Sal opened the conversation.

"Originally, I thought that the military was constructing Eingang for our entry into the European war. But Anna and Eric've learned something different. Eric, could you tell Mo and me what you know?"

"Actually," began Eric, "Anna's heard everything from Michael Rudman and Karl Stampf that I have, and she's seen the place, which I haven't. I'd be curious what, if any conclusions, she's come to. What do you think, Anna?" Eric, Mo, and Sal then looked over at her.

"I've been going over everything we've seen and heard, and I have a few thoughts."

"Only a few? Not possible," thought Sal.

"Now that we know that an individual's behind Eingang and not the military, if we're going to understand its purpose, we need to know his motives for creating it. Karl Stampf, Graff's senior executive, believes that Graff revealed his plans in a menacing pledge he made to him in 1935 to do everything in his power to get rid of the world's Jews. Graff increasingly made it evident that he held the Jews responsible for his adversities. Then later discoveries made by Karl, whose racial views couldn't be more opposed to Graff's, show what horrific madness's behind this Eingang place. Karl was excluded from having anything to do with Eingang, no doubt because of his racial convictions. Graff turned its development over to Oscar Hahn, an ardent American Nazi. Now it appears that Graff's madness has driven him to use Eingang to do away with the people he hates, which includes at least Jews and blacks, if not other people he finds undesirable."

"How do you think he intends to murder so many people?" asked Sal.

"My theory is that he intends to use that strange facility where Abe was tortured to murder them using Zyklon B poison gas. This is the same gas that Karl uncovered when he looked into a shipment of the chemical to something called the Eingang Group, bypassing Graff Industries completely. It came from IG Farben, the German chemical conglomerate, a substantial financial supporter of the Nazis."

"How on earth did they come to choose this…what is it again? Oh yes, Zyklon B," queried Eric.

"I believe this goes back to a peculiar hiring situation that Karl described. A little over a year ago, Graff visited a German American Bund facility called Camp Siegfried in Yaphank, not that far from here. Shortly after returning from the visit, he presented Karl with a new hire—the new head chemist for Graff Industries. The man was a former Nazi chemist who headed a special facility at Camp Siegfried that was being eyed closely by Hitler himself because of his interest in America's eugenics progress. Eric informed me that among the chemistry community, it was common knowledge that the activities at Cold Spring Harbor and Camp Siegfried were tightly tied to one another. I'm speculating here, but I suspect that the common denominator is this person who Graff ordered Karl to hire as Graff Industries' head chemist. As a former Nazi chemist, he would have been very aware of the use of the first version of Zyklon in The Great War. He knew of its effectiveness in killing people, and would likely have sold Graff on any experience he had with its use. Interestingly, this was the same visit where Graff was introduced to Oscar Hahn, who was then the regional leader, or gauleiter, for the Bund at Camp Siegfried. He would later head the development of Graff's Eingang along Oyster Bay. When the Bund started to fall apart and Camp Siegfried along with it, Graff hired away Hahn, Erstad, and the Nazi doctor to take advantage of his deadly knowledge at Eingang."

"Does Graff really think he can get rid of great numbers of people?"

"It's all madness, Sal. It's inconceivable that he could get his murderous plan off the ground before law enforcement would discover it and shut it down."

"And those barracks, why would he pay to house so many people when he just intended to kill them?" queried Sal.

"That brings up another subject. I believe there's more to Eingang, but I'd rather hold off until I get some clearer evidence to confirm my suspicions."

Just then, the doorbell rang, and Eric got up to go to the front door. "That must be the doctor I called." After letting him in, Eric turned to his guests. "Who would like to accompany the doctor to answer any questions he may have about Abe?"

"I'll volunteer," said Anna.

Nearly thirty minutes went by as the doctor made his evaluation and came into the living room with Anna. After they exchanged introductions, everyone sat to hear his diagnosis.

"I must admit I've never seen someone so physically abused as your friend. Why didn't you take him straight to a hospital?"

"We didn't have access to a phone," explained Anna, "and we're unfamiliar with this area. Rather than use up critical time trying to find a medical facility, we thought it best to bring Abe straight here to Eric's house where at least he could rest comfortably until a doctor arrived."

"I see. Well, fortunately, even miraculously, it appears from my preliminary examination that, apart from multiple severe lacerations and contusions, he has no permanent or internal damage or broken bones. I'd like him to remain here and rest until tomorrow morning. Then, I'd like him to check into Huntington Hospital, where I'm registered and can observe him for several days. I'll order some x-rays taken just to make sure I haven't missed something. I can also make the arrangements for an ambulance to pick him up if you'd like."

"That would be best," volunteered Eric.

"Now then, if you have no questions, I must be off."

After thanking the doctor and seeing him out, everyone felt relieved and surprised that Abe's prognosis was so benign considering how badly damaged he appeared.

"All of us can certainly use a break," said Anna. "Mo, will you please stay with Abe after he's dropped off at the hospital in the morning?"

"I'll be happy to stay with him until he's well enough to be released," he replied.

"I know where Huntington Hospital is. It's just a few minutes from here," explained Eric. "You can stay here until he's well enough to travel if you find that suitable."

"That's very kind of you, Eric," acknowledged Mo. "I've been Abe's partner for years, and I very much appreciate you offering us your home so I can watch over him while he recovers."

"That settles things, then," declared Anna. "So Sal, you and I are on our way back to Boston first thing tomorrow morning. The following day, we'll drive back down to Grand Central Terminal to pick up Eva. Then we'll bring her straight here to meet Eric and Dr. Altenau. That will give us plenty of time to prepare for our meeting with Dr. Loh at Columbia the following day."

"Sounds like a plan," agreed Sal.

48

Ever since Oscar and Gus had met on the Long Island Express going to Yaphank over four years earlier, they had developed an unusually strong bond despite how different they were. Oscar's desperate need for Gus's fearless appetite for violence had enabled Gus to realize his dream of running his own elite paramilitary Silver Sword guards. As a lifetime loner, Gus had initially resisted getting close to Oscar, but he had taken increasing pleasure in having the gregarious and charismatic Oscar as his friend. Since Gus was a young boy, he had always shied away from such a relationship, always fearing an inevitable rejection. The early codependency of the two unlikely comrades had developed into a true friendship in which both had complete confidence.

As the two drove the ninety minutes to Maximilian's estate to deliver the bad news about their hostage, Oscar became increasingly edgy with every mile. Eventually, he found himself unable to contain his misgivings.

"This meeting really has me on edge, Gus. You know what a monster this guy is, and I'm glad you were willing to come along. I know he fears you."

"Thanks, Oscar, but I r'member a few months back when we first met at his office. There was that big goon, Gunther Gundshau, in the back o' the room and he'll prob'ly be there again. If he is, 'n anything goes south, I'll take him out. You okay with that?"

"Let's just hope it doesn't get to that, but to answer your question, yeah, I'd be better with that than the alternative."

As the car arrived at the estate, Oscar's preoccupation with what was coming made him fidget and unable to concentrate. A large man came out of his guardhouse, and before Oscar could roll down his window, Gus whispered, "What d'ya know? So Gundshau also guards Graff's mansion."

"Gauleiter Hahn and Ortsgruppenleiter Erstad here to see Mr. Graff," said Oscar unsteadily.

"Go on in. He's waitin' in his office," said the large man who peered inside the car as he spoke.

By the time the car finally came to rest in front of the mansion, Oscar was in a mild panic. Getting out of the car, he felt wooden and as if his mouth were filled with cotton. As he walked, the distance to Maximilian's office made his legs feel as if they were turning into rubber by the time the butler delivered them to the office door. Unable to collect his thoughts, he just stood at the door until finally, Gus knocked on it.

"Get in here!" thundered the voice through the closed door.

Gus opened the door and signaled Oscar to enter the room ahead of him.

"This doesn't look good for you, Hahn. I see you've brought your strong arm. So, what do you have to tell me? You'd better make it worth my while!" said Maximilian, ignoring Gus's facial wounds.

After a few seconds of silence, it was apparent to Gus that Oscar was paralyzed with fear and unable to speak. Finally, Gus took it upon himself to give the dreaded report.

"Mr. Graff, he din't give us nothin' new."

"What?! You still don't know who's behind all this?! You both'd better get back there and don't come back here until you have something for me."

"It won't do no good, Mr. Graff. He's dead," responded Gus.

"He's DEAD?! DEAD?! My God! I have morons, nothing but morons working for me! Not only did you allow someone to break into Eingang not once, but TWO times, now you're telling me you've killed the only lead we had!! This incompetence must come to an end! As for you, Hahn, you and I'll have a final reckoning! You can depend on it! Now get out! Both of you get out!!"

Both men quickly filed out of the office as Oscar hoped they could get out of earshot before Maximilian shouted at them again. As they hurried outside, Gus saw Oscar moving even more robotically than when they had arrived. As the two came to the car, Oscar stopped abruptly. Turning to face Gus, he looked as if he were about to say something. Then, without uttering a word, he turned slowly and continued to the driver's door and got in.

For the first time in a long time, Gus was rattled. As he got into the passenger side, he couldn't fathom what he had just seen. The one person he held in the highest esteem, a former gauleiter of the German American Bund, this sophisticated and impressive leader, and his only real friend in the world, had been standing facing him, completely unaware of the growing wet circle on the front of his khaki slacks.

49

"I know you have to leave again for New York tomorrow to pick up Eva and then return to Eric's place," said Malcolm. "All I can say is, I'm glad you're here safe and sound, both of you, at least for the moment," he concluded as the three of them sat enjoying an after-dinner brandy in the Tilner's living room. "You can take my car. I'm still not quite sure how yours even made it back here. The entire back end's a wreck."

"You know how happy I am to be back here with you also, Honey, especially since I'm in considerably better shape than my car," replied Anna.

"I'll be happy if I never have to go back to that place again," volunteered Sal.

The rest of the evening was spent recounting to Malcolm what had happened at Eingang while sanitizing the most violent parts of the experience. In response, Malcolm seemed almost embarrassed to share his workaday experiences at Tilner and Associates, where the gravest physical threat anyone faced regularly was a paper cut. Before retiring for the evening, they returned to the topic of Eva.

Turning to Anna, Sal could no longer contain his curiosity, "How do you hope to ever explain Eva even to Eric, let alone to this Dr. Loh, a total stranger?"

"You're right, Sal. There's no way to explain her to anyone. You remember how skeptical you were when you first met her. Nothing I could've said would've convinced you of her gifts. You had to see them for yourself to understand. Since she and I first met, we've spent enough time together where I believe I generally understand how she's likely to respond to different situations. Eric is a perfect person for Eva to demonstrate what she can do, and I'm sure she'll impress him just as she's made believers out of us all."

"I hope for all your sakes, especially Eva's, that your right," said Malcolm. "This could be devastating for her if it all goes south."

"It's important to understand something," observed Anna, "What Eva does, she does naturally and effortlessly, so I'm confident this'll go well. Considering the stakes, it has to. Now then, I don't know about the two of you, but I'm ready to turn in. Sal, I hope you get a good night's sleep. We have to take off early tomorrow," she added as the relaxing evening came to an end.

Although only six weeks had gone by, so much had happened since she walked through the Boston train station to meet Sal that it seemed to Anna to have been more like six months. This time, as she and Sal walked together through New York's Grand Central Terminal, she felt a warm sense of comfort and excitement, knowing that she would be working with Eva and Sal again despite the ominous circumstances that were bringing them together. As they waited for the train to enter the station, Sal also felt a slightly giddy sense of anticipation at seeing Eva again.

Once the train stopped, they walked onto the platform and waited as the exhaust steam billowed out of the train's engine. The excitement of all the people rushing around them heightened their eagerness to see their unusual friend. After a significant number of the passengers had disembarked, they began to wonder if she had missed the train. In the middle of expressing misgivings to one another, they saw a middle-aged, black Pullman porter come through the steam holding Eva's arm. The twenty-three-year-old woman was dressed neatly and walked carefully. Continually looking at the ground, she seemed to be oblivious to everything around her.

Approaching them, Anna looked at Eva and said, "Hello, my dear Eva. I can't tell you how I've been looking forward to seeing you again."

Anna then turned to the porter. "Hello. I'm Mrs. Anna Tilner, and this is Mr. Sal Puma. I made the arrangements for her to be looked after on her trip here. Thank you very much for doing this. She's a very special young woman."

"My name's George, ma'am. Just doin' my job, 'n I like helpin' out these poor folks when I can. This one's real quiet, though. She ain't said nothin' the whole trip. Seems to be a little…well, ya know…. Anyway, she been no trouble t'all and I'm glad I was able to help."

"Thank you again, George. I'm glad you were able to make sure she got here safely," said Anna as she took Eva by the arm. The second Anna's hand touched her, Eva looked up and into Anna's eyes.

"Now ain't that somethin'," said George. "She ain't looked up since I met her. You gotta have the magic touch or somethin', ma'am."

"Oh no, George. I know it may be hard to believe, but this young woman is the one with the magic touch. Anyway, thanks again for watching over her for us. It's much appreciated." After Anna thanked him with some money, he tipped his hat, turned, and made his way back to the train.

Moving slowly back into the main terminal, Eva stopped abruptly. In response, Anna and Sal also came to a halt as Anna turned to her and asked, "Are you all right, Eva? Do you feel okay?" Just then, Eva turned and gently put her arms around Anna and held her close to her with her eyes peering over Anna's shoulder. "Yes, yes, Eva," said Anna as she hugged her back, "I've missed you, too. Sal and I are very, very happy to see you again."

With that, Sal held out his hand and gently put it on Eva's shoulder. While Anna couldn't see it, he then witnessed something that surprised him. Despite having a facial expression that offered no inkling of what the young woman was feeling, Eva's eyes had released a few small tears that were slowly trickling down her cheeks. In the entire time he had spent with her, even in the most harrowing of circumstances, he had never seen Eva cry.

50

"Well, please come in, come in. Dr. Altenau's already arrived," said Eric with his natural, welcoming smile as Anna and Sal came through the doorway. Still focused on them as they walked into the house, he added, "Mo's away at the hospital and won't be back for several…" He suddenly froze as he caught sight of Eva who was standing still, staring down at the front door threshold, seemingly unaware of his presence. Eric was dumbfounded, appearing to all the world like a block of granite.

"Eric, it gives me great pleasure to introduce you to Eva Hauser," said Anna as she turned around and looked at Eva. At the same time, both she and Sal struggled to repress their amusement at seeing a distinguished Princeton professor suddenly stripped of all aplomb. While Eric, Anna, and Sal stood just inside the front door, Eva was still outside. "She indicated to me," added Anna, "that she's been looking forward to meeting you. Would you like to come in, Eva?" she prompted. It was another awkward few seconds before Eric had recovered sufficiently to assume at least a semblance of his typically gracious manner.

"I'm so sorry. Where on earth are my manners for heaven's sake? Please come in, Eva. My name is Dr. Franzen. Let's go into the living room and meet Dr. Altenau, shall we?" he said in a strained voice that again tested Anna's and Sal's ability to contain themselves. It was not lost on either that Eva was the only one who Eric had failed to extend his hand to in greeting.

As the new arrivals came into the living room, Dr. Joseph Altenau was also stunned by Eva's presence and remembered to stand only after Anna and Eva were almost on top of him. "Hello, Dr. Altenau. It's a pleasure to meet you. My name is Mrs. Anna Tilner, this is Mr. Sal Puma, and our special guest is Miss Eva Hauser."

"Yes, yes, of course, yes.... It's...yes, it's, of course, a pleasure to meet you...you all also."

After his guests were seated, Eric looked at them and said, "I've prepared some refreshments for us all. Anna, perhaps you could help me in the kitchen for a minute?"

"Of course, Eric," said Anna, readying herself for a muffled storm of protest.

As they entered the kitchen, Eric closed the door and abruptly turned to Anna while unleashing the flustered man who had done his best to be a civil, if not a gracious host. "This is an outrage, Anna! I don't understand it! I don't understand it at all! Who is this person, and how did you expect me to bring her before Dr. Altenau, let alone Dr. Loh?!"

"Please calm down, Eric. Eva is not someone whose reasons for being here I'll be able to explain to either you or Dr. Altenau. They defy explanation. Instead, you must see for yourself someone who is one of God's true miracles and is probably the only one who can help us get to the bottom of the true nature of this threat."

"What in the hell are you talking about, Anna? This is the most unexpected behavior on your part." Eric's use of a curse in her presence assured Anna that she had his undivided attention.

"Please forget the refreshments, Eric. Unless I've made a miscalculation, if you think my behavior is unusual, I'd like to show you what unique behavior truly is. Now let's go back in the living room," she said as she turned to open the door, being careful to ensure that her befuddled host was right behind her.

Once back in the living room and before he sat down, Eric turned to Joseph Altenau and was unable to avoid making a disclaimer. "Joseph, I must say that this is all as shocking to me as it is to you. Miss Hauser's presence was not what I was expecting, and I hope you'll be able to forgive me if you're offended in any way."

"Now, now," Joseph said comfortingly. "Based on what you've told me about Mrs. Tilner, I'm sure there's a good reason we're all together so please relax and sit down."

"Thank you, Dr. Altenau," said Anna. "I'm confident that Miss Hauser's presence and her importance to our task will become clear shortly."

"If you can indulge me, we're not at the university, so why don't we dispense with the formality of titles. My name is Joseph Altenau."

"Thank you, Joseph. I believe that'll facilitate the progress we'll all have to make in a very short time. My name is Anna, this is Sal, and our dear friend is Eva."

"Excellent," he replied.

Anna then sat in between Eva and Eric while Sal and Joseph sat on either end. Just then, Eva turned her head and stared at Eric with an intensity that immediately made him very uncomfortable.

"Eric, please offer Eva your hand."

"You want me to do what?!" exclaimed Eric.

"Please, Eric, just offer her your hand."

Looking completely mystified and apprehensive, Eric was also becoming intrigued. He first turned and looked at Joseph before lifting his hand and hesitating before finally holding it out and turning to face Eva.

"Now, Eva, please hold his hand." Reaching out and touching his hand, Eva suddenly began trembling before making a low, moaning sound while looking straight ahead and remaining expressionless. Eric reflexively pulled his hand away. The second he did, Eva stopped shuddering, sat perfectly still, and again looked down at the floor.

"There. Now Eva, why don't you and I go in the kitchen?" said Anna as she rose while gently taking Eva by the arm as she also stood up. The two then left the room.

"This's preposterous, Sal. What's Anna up to? I'm going to cancel our appointment with Dr. Loh immediately," said the badly flustered professor as he rose to use the telephone.

"Eric, please don't do any such thing," advised Sal as he held out his arm to restrain Eric. "I promise that you'll not regret having a little more patience. I felt the same way you are now feeling and had to see for myself what a true miracle this unassuming young black lady is. I wouldn't attempt to predict or describe what I believe you're about to witness, but Anna'll be better at explaining what she knows about Eva."

"This all sounds like poppycock, Sal! Just lunacy! Don't you think so, Joseph? I can't believe this's happening. My God, how naïve I was to believe that Anna was my friend. I simply can't understand how she could embarrass me so profoundly in front of a colleague, of all people. This is something I will simply not be able to forgive.... I don't know what I'm going to do. I now profoundly regret having made any efforts on Anna's behalf to set up this meeting tomorrow. Do you have any idea how prominent Dr. Loh is? My God, he works directly with Dr. Stromberg, one of the most preeminent physicists in the world. And now, I'm about to introduce him to this...this...this common black woman. Oh my God, what've I done? What on earth have I done?"

Sal was impressed with Joseph's calm demeanor that was in stunning contrast to Eric's blathering. Knowing that nothing he could say would calm him down, let alone satisfy him, he just allowed Eric to continue his rant. After several more minutes, the kitchen door opened, and Eric finally fell quiet as Anna brought Eva back into the living room before they both sat down.

Sitting between Eva and Eric, Anna looked at Eric and began, "First, I must say that Eva's very distressed, Eric."

"She thinks she's distressed, well, what about me?!" he blurted out before turning to see Joseph's response, which was sphinxlike.

"I'm sure all of this is very difficult for you, Eric, and I do regret any discomfort you're feeling at the moment. I can assure you that it won't be in vain.

"Now then," she continued as she looked at Eva and patted her arm before looking back at Eric, "you should understand that Eva uses a combination of her own sign language and basic words to convey her thoughts...."

"This isn't helping, Anna! It's not helping one bit!" Eric interjected as he put his face in his hands, displaying his deepening sense of foreboding.

"Eric," said Joseph, "please settle down. All this fretting can't be good for you."

"I agree," added Anna. "I was about to say that she and I've developed a means of exchange where she feels comfortable sharing what she sees with me so that I can communicate it to others."

"Now I'm even afraid to hear what it is you're going to say that she's seen!" said Eric, still unable to control his self-pity.

"Eric, I hope that you can trust me enough to do what I'm about to ask you."

"I'm afraid that the nature of your request will determine that, Anna. I hope you can understand that my confidence in all this is very shaky indeed."

"Yes, I understand. I need your indulgence by going with me into another room where the two of us can have some privacy for a few minutes."

"Hmm. If that will help bring this entire dreadful episode to a conclusion, then I know just the room," said Eric as he stood and motioned for Anna to follow while Sal and Joseph rose out of courtesy. The two walked silently down the long hallway to Eric's study. The minute Anna entered the room, she knew it had been his sanctuary for many years. Books were crammed into every available sliver of the abundant shelf space. Tall stacks of manuscripts and technical magazines covered the floor and crowded the sides of an oversized fireplace in one corner of the wood-paneled room. The well-worn, comfortable chair and love seat made it apparent that he spent many hours here. The minute Eric sat down in his easy chair, a calm seemed to settle over him and appeared to relieve him of some of the stress and anxiety that had been causing his invective. Anna saw this as the perfect place for him to endure what she was about to say.

"I requested that we be alone because of what Eva has shared with me, which I realize will be very difficult for you to hear. Since it's still uppermost in your mind, Eric, she's seen Sarah, before and at the point of her suicide. She's also briefly endured Sarah's suffering over the loss of her brothers that led her to take her own life."

This remark instantly aroused Eric's fury as he began to shout, "Goddamnit, Anna, how unforgivable of you! She knew all this only because I'd already told you! This proves nothing! I can't believe you decided to put me through this torture all over again!"

Ignoring his outburst, Anna forged on calmly, "I've told her nothing about you, Sarah, or her death, Eric. Please let me continue. Unfortunately, in addition to Sarah's deep depression preceding her death, Eva also saw something else. She saw the profound pain that both you and Sarah endured long ago when she had her first miscarriage just after you were married, and the second one that was so devastating that it made you both move away to Princeton."

As Anna spoke, Eric froze as he struggled to reconcile the rage that had him in its grip with the total bewilderment he was suddenly experiencing. He knew that these most private and tragic losses had never been shared with anyone outside the doctors, himself, and Sarah. Anna's words were the first reference to these tragedies that Eric had heard uttered in decades, and he found himself paralyzed by lightning bolts of explosive, conflicting emotions.

Remaining completely silent, Eric could not conceal his profound perplexity as he stared down at the floor and then slowly up to the ceiling. Finally, he turned to face Anna, who looked deeply into his eyes. She saw a change. His severe inner turmoil was gradually dissolving into sheer wonder.

"I…I…I'm simply…I'm completely speechless. I don't…don't have any idea what to say. I am bowled over," said Eric as he fell back into his chair and stared straight ahead.

"Having had a similar emotional reaction to what you're now experiencing," said Anna, "I hope this helps to demonstrate why I find Eva to be a unique resource for the menacing challenge before us."

It was a full thirty seconds before Eric was able to respond.

After blinking several times in rapid succession, he turned to Anna. "I'm so profoundly embarrassed that I've treated you so terribly. I should have kept in mind what your father-in-law told me about you rather than giving in so quickly and completely to my own fears of being professionally mortified. I am deeply sorry for the way I've behaved."

"Don't give this another thought, Eric. Please comfort yourself with knowing that everyone I've seen who has witnessed Eva's gifts has felt the same confusion and perplexity. I've witnessed it on several occasions."

Anna spent a while comforting Eric that his response was natural and, especially considering the unthinkable experiences he had recently endured, that his emotional reactions were quite understandable. He took considerable solace from their discussion, enough so that Anna was comfortable suggesting that it could be time to return to the living room.

"I don't know if you feel recovered enough to join the others, but they must be feeling considerable suspense."

"I suppose I'm ready to return, but now I'm so ashamed of myself that it'll be difficult to face them, especially Eva. She fell victim to some of my lifelong prejudices and a withering, completely undeserved dismissal. How can I ever explain myself to her?"

"You won't need to, Eric. She'll already know."

"Yes. Yes, of course she will. How miraculous this all is—how miraculous she is. Yes, let's go back to be with Eva and the others, shall we?"

Everyone instantly saw a very different Eric Franzen from the man who had left the room. As Anna sat down next to Eva, Eric seated himself on Eva's other side and, without saying a word, gently patted her arm. Anna wondered if he noticed Eva's barely perceptible nod. After profuse apologies by Eric for his behavior, he did something that surprised everyone and evidenced a remarkable transformation—he discussed his devastating experiences with his wife.

"You have no idea how difficult this was," he said. "My desperate attempts to reassure Sarah that her miscarriages were not her fault were sheer agony for both of us. Still, she was emotionally desolate and utterly inconsolable on both occasions. For her, the second miscarriage was all she could take. It made her conclude once and for all that she was, and would always be, a maternal failure. The emotional toll of all this was so great that we decided we'd give up trying to have another child and that we'd never speak of it again."

Anna was thrilled that Eric's shocking, harrowing experience with Eva had enabled him to confront his and Sarah's dark secret and then be able to share it with others. As he explained his tragic experience, Anna hoped that he might also feel liberated from having to silently bear the oppressive horror of his wife's suicide alone.

"I'm so deeply moved by your and Sarah's terrible loss, Eric," said Joseph. "I can't say how sorry I am to hear this."

Eric then looked at everyone before saying, "I must admit that I have a humbling confession to make. In the last few minutes, I've been forced to come face-to-face with a terrible injustice that I've inflicted on another person in this room, perhaps the most innocent of us all. I owe you a profound apology, Eva." Once again, he smiled, nodded, and put his hand on Eva's arm.

"I must also confess that going through this personal tragedy again is indeed profoundly distressing. The fact that it's so excruciating and, as a result, is so near the core of my feelings, if Eva's gift were unable to perceive it, I would have had to question her capabilities. As it is, she's raised something that at various times in my life I've struggled with, but because it stayed bottled up, I couldn't escape it. With her bringing it into the light with Anna, I must say I feel the lifting of a terrible weight that I've had to bear for many, many years."

"Considering how quite unbelievable all this sounds," inquired Joseph, "I hesitate to ask, but is it in any way possible that Eva could've learned of this somewhere else?"

"Absolutely not. Our solemn vow to never raise any of this again to one another or anyone else was absolute. Until just now, that pledge had remained unbroken for over forty years."

"Please understand, Eric," said Anna, "We're all well aware of how hurtful these things are to relive. They're obviously profoundly meaningful to you, and it appears that these are the feelings and experiences that Eva is most sensitive to and are the first to impact her. However, please be aware that she isn't just a passive reporter of what she sees. It was explained to me by an expert in these matters that as she's sensing them, she feels them as deeply as the person who's conveying them. It comes at a considerable emotional cost to her."

Anna had just said something that instantly piqued Eric's interest. "What kind of expert, Anna?"

"Are you familiar with Dr. Leo Kanner, an associate professor of psychiatry at Johns Hopkins University?

"I'm afraid that's too far afield. I don't believe I've heard of him."

"I have," volunteered Joseph. "My son's a psychiatrist, and he's mentioned Dr. Kanner to me several times in different contexts. I understand he's quite a pioneer in his field."

"That's correct, Joseph," replied Anna. "He's a leading authority in a new field of study he's calling infantile autism. Come to think of it, you both might recall hearing of him in a widely-reported exposé a couple of months ago that was prominent in many major newspapers. He uncovered a group of judges and attorneys who had arranged to have 166 institutionalized people farmed out to wealthy families in the Baltimore area to provide free domestic help. Unfortunately, by the time Kanner had tracked down these victims, they had been afflicted with all sorts of issues such as tuberculosis, prostitution, imprisonment, sexually transmitted diseases, and even death."

"Yes, I seem to remember that scandal," said Eric, "but what does this have to do with Eva?"

"Kanner was also very active in rescuing hundreds of Jewish physicians in Germany from the Nazis and finding work for them in this country. One of those people, Dr. Carl Roster, worked directly with Dr. Kanner and interviewed Eva."

"What did he say about her?"

Turning to Eva, Anna asked her, "Is it all right if I tell them about your meeting with Dr. Roster and what he said about you?"

After a second, Eva made an almost unnoticeable nod as she opened up her hands with her palms facing towards the ceiling.

Looking at her with a warm smile, Anna replied, "Thank you, Eva."

"She's okay with my telling you. On our first visit, when Dr. Roster said to me that he would evaluate her and then explain his conclusions, he came out of his office with Eva an hour or so later in a highly agitated state. He said he couldn't tell me anything until he had the opportunity to speak with Dr. Kanner, who was ill and at home. He then left us abruptly without saying another word and rushed back into his office. I found his response perplexing, but we arranged to return the following day.

"When he and I finally did sit down together, he said that he'd been practicing psychiatry for twelve years, but nothing had prepared him for his experience with Eva—she possessed attributes that were beyond the present understanding of psychiatry. However, he and Dr. Kanner diagnosed her as having high-functioning infantile autism, which he was careful to distinguish from mental retardation or feeblemindedness."

"What are these distinctions?" asked Eric.

"He told us that, among other symptoms, people with autism have limited language skills and an impaired ability to interact with other people. He also said that Eva shows signs of what he termed "gifted" aspects of intelligence. According to him, there's already some evidence to suggest a connection between autism and elevated intelligence levels in specific areas. Eva's characteristics appeared to fit."

Eric then looked directly at Eva, who turned slowly to face him. "When you looked at me before I held out my hand, I felt you...how should I say this...I felt as if you were somehow boring into the depths of my soul. I was unnerved, but at the same time, I wasn't the least bit afraid. I've just never had such an experience like that in my life."

Looking back at Anna, he added, "Did Dr. Roster say anything about this?"

"Yes, he did. Just so you know, Sal and I have both experienced this, so we know what you're talking about. In Dr. Roster's case, I believe that in his first session with her, he had experienced something similar to what you just did regarding your wife, Sarah. In his case, it concerned Eva having sensed what he experienced when he was still working for Dr. Hans Asperger, a pediatrician in Austria. He saw numerous children condemned to death by the Nazis because they were either feebleminded or had other mental problems. Roster is Jewish, and, together with this shocking experience with Dr. Asperger, he made up his mind to leave Austria for America, where he went to work for Dr. Kanner. When Eva felt his deep emotional distress from this horrible memory and then conveyed it sufficiently well for him to understand that she had also felt this, he became quite perplexed and had to put off our meeting.

"He told me that her uncanny ability to see into another person as she does and feel their emotions appeared to him to be some extraordinarily developed version of synesthesia, a rare condition that is not yet well understood. While it's presently believed that there are several versions of this condition, in Eva's case, she evidences a supernormally developed empathy for other people giving her an uncanny sensitivity to their feelings, thoughts, and even sensory experiences. He was careful to point out that he didn't want to say that this was some paranormal mind-reading ability or some other magical capability. On the other hand, he had no way to explain how she could have known his personal experiences except through some form of clairvoyance. He simply had no scientific explanation or understanding of how her unique characteristics work together or separately. The one thing he did say was that aspects of my dear young friend here make her nothing short of a prodigy, a true natural miracle. Finally, he apologized for all this seeming to being very unscientific, but indicated that Dr. Kanner agreed with his conclusions wholeheartedly."

Then Eric turned to Eva before looking back at Anna and said, "So basically, the experts are as baffled about this young lady as we all are. Is that an accurate assessment?"

"I'd have to agree," said Anna.

"In our current situation, Anna, you think that if Eva meets Dr. Loh that she'll be able to see—for lack of a better word— what he knows about the German advanced weapons program?"

"I know this requires a leap of faith, but I'm relying on several things. First, her insights occur without any special effort and are completely natural for her. Second, I have to presume that, as a physicist working with one of the world's leading authorities in this field, the Nazi weapons program is so near and dear to Dr. Loh's heart that it must be top of mind for him. If not, we may strike out, but, considering the stakes involved, we should do everything we can to see what the Nazis are up to. For us, Eva is nothing short of a powerful secret weapon."

"Secret weapon," said Eric under his breath as he turned to Eva, smiled, and added, "Yes, my dear, I believe that's precisely what you are."

51

The day's revelations had been staggering for many at Eric's dining table. Still, the dinner, wine, and camaraderie during the meal helped to lighten the emotions that had beset the group earlier in the day. Anna was pleased to see that this return-to-semi-normal meal indicated how greatly Eric's earlier torment, Joseph's bewilderment from his introduction to Eva, and Sal's concerns about the success of Eva's introductions had eased.

Despite the feeling of mild, escapist reverie that Eric's wine had helped to lubricate, Anna felt a pang as she looked at the person seated next to her. Eva, the center of the day's attention, sat silently, unable to enter into the conversations all around her.

"You can see for yourself, Eva," Anna said quietly as she reached over for Eva's hand, "They're pleased you're here. It's clear that you've made quite an impression on these people, and they're grateful for what you may be able to do for everyone tomorrow. I'm the last one who needs to tell you how extremely proud I am to know you and how grateful I am that you're here." Anna's face crumpled as she felt Eva's response in the form of a gentle squeeze of her hand.

As the evening drew to a close and everyone appeared to be in good spirits, the phone rang. Eric rose from the table to answer it and turned to his guests and said, "Now, just keep enjoying yourselves. I won't be a minute." The conversations resumed, and people's conviviality immediately returned as if the phone had never interrupted them.

A couple of minutes later, Eric returned with a solemn expression. Motioning to Anna, he said, "Could I please speak with you for a moment?"

As Anna entered the next room with Eric, she saw the phone on a table with its handset lying on its side.

"Is something wrong, Eric?"

"I don't know. Karl Stampf's on the line and needs to speak with you."

Anna went to the table and picked up the handset. Her expression betrayed some misgivings. "Hello, Karl. It's good to hear from you again, but I'm concerned about the reason for your call."

After several moments of listening, Anna responded, "Do you have any idea what he wants and why he needs to speak with me?... Do you know how urgent this is?" Eric's facial expression revealed pure puzzlement.

"I see. Hang on one second," Anna said before putting her hand over the mouthpiece and turning to Eric.

"Karl says there's a very urgent situation that's arisen that requires I meet with him tonight. May I invite him to come here?"

"Of course, if it's so urgent."

Uncovering the phone, she continued, "Karl, I trust you know the directions?... Good. We'll look forward to seeing you in about a half hour or so." Putting the phone back on its cradle slowly, Anna was deep in thought. She then turned to Eric.

"It seems that Karl needs to discuss something with me that he was unwilling to get into over the phone. It concerns the person who's been in charge of Eingang, Oscar Hahn. I'm curious as to what he thinks I could do, much less want to do for that Nazi. We'd better get back to the others and wind up the evening before Karl gets here. With everything that Joseph has heard today, he probably doesn't need to be burdened with suspicions that this could raise. Besides, he has a bit of a drive back to White Plains. We're seeing him at Columbia tomorrow before we go into the meeting with Dr. Loh, correct?"

"Yes, Anna, that's what Joseph and I discussed. I agree that we should end the evening promptly to avoid unnecessary suspicions. This's a small community, and rumors about this Eingang project already have people on edge. We don't need to introduce any more drama by having anyone learn that the senior executive for the person who's behind it all is paying us a visit," replied Eric as Anna nodded and the two began walking back to the dining room.

After the gathering broke up, Sal and Eva went to their bedrooms. Joseph Altenau had left only ten minutes earlier when Karl drove into Eric's driveway. After greeting him, Eric showed him into his library, where Anna was waiting for him.

"I'll leave the two of you alone, then," said Eric before Karl thanked him, and the door closed quietly.

"I greatly appreciate your seeing me at this late hour and on such short notice, Anna," he said as he sat in Eric's easy chair. "I didn't think that this could wait."

"So, what are your concerns about Oscar Hahn?"

"Please understand that he's not a close friend, but he is a friend, and I have great sympathy for anyone who has to face Maximilian daily as he does. My concern is for Oscar's safety."

"His safety? Did he tell you that one of us was captured, severely tortured, and would've died if we hadn't been able to extract him from Eingang, the place that Oscar Hahn runs?

"Yes. Eric informed me of this."

"So, he was responsible for my friend's torture, our being assaulted and shot at by his henchman before we were able to escape."

"Yes. That'd be correct."

"Then, considering that only hours ago I was one of those he was trying to capture and kill, why would he believe that I'd ever want to see the man?"

"He understands this but says he doesn't have anywhere else to turn. He desperately needs your help. He's terrified that he is about to be murdered."

52

The next day, as Anna drove with Eva sitting next to her in the front seat and Eric in the back, he advised her that they were not far from Columbia College's Faculty House. An austere building in New York City, Faculty House was where Eric and Joseph had decided to get together before meeting with Dr. Loh. The three of them would first meet Joseph in the second-floor lounge where they would wait for the arrival of his illustrious colleague. After confirming all this, Eric suddenly chuckled.

"What have you found so amusing?" asked Anna.

"This is highly irreverent, I know, but I just recalled something I find quite ironic about the Faculty House. Think of it: we're about to meet someone who's in the upper echelons of an effort by the leader of Germany to help him conquer the world. At least that's what I think the lunatic is expecting to do."

"I'm afraid I don't see what you find so humorous," confessed Anna.

"Well, I was just getting to the funny part. Although the original Faculty Club moved in the early twenties to its current location, before that, it sat on the site of the Bloomingdale Insane Asylum." Hearing it aloud made Eric chuckle once again as Anna enjoyed a moment of levity that was bizarrely incongruous with the gravity of their mission. "Ha! What an irony! Oh yes, here we are, Anna," said Eric as he indicated where to park.

After coming up the stairs, they walked into the spacious, sparsely-furnished lounge where distinguished scholars and their guests visited. Eric led Eva and Anna towards a relatively discrete conversation area with sofas and occasional chairs at the far end of the room. He then advised them, "When Dr. Loh arrives, we'll all move into the reception room across the hall where we'll enjoy a private luncheon."

The three people then sat down just as Joseph Altenau entered through the main door. Eric jumped up and walked down the length of the large room to welcome him while Eva and Anna remained seated.

"Thank you again for arranging this, Joseph," said Eric warmly as both men extended their hands to one another. "What a striking contrast from yesterday's introductions," thought Anna.

After walking to where his two female guests were seated, Joseph appeared to be genuinely happy to see them both. "Hello, Anna. It's wonderful to see you again," he said as she returned the warm sentiment. He then turned to Eva, who was looking at the floor.

"And you, Eva. I'm most pleased to see you here," as he extended his hand. Eva then looked up, grasped it slowly, and stared into Joseph's eyes. Joseph instantly halted any further greeting and looked intently into Eva's penetrating gaze. After a few seconds, they released one another's hands, and Eva once again stared at the floor.

"My God!" exclaimed Joseph looking at Eric and Anna. "Now I understand what you were all talking about yesterday. I've just been most benignly invaded," he said before pausing, looking off into the distance, and then turning once again to Eva as he reached out his hand to gently touch her arm. "I'm very moved by what you just did, Eva. It was extraordinary. I've never had such an experience in my entire life. Somehow, I felt completely safe with your inspection of who I am and just hope you feel the same way about me." A subtle smile came over Eva's face as she nodded almost imperceptibly. As Joseph continued to look at Eva, there was a brief pause before Eric heard him say under his breath, "That was incredible, truly incredible."

After sitting down and briefly sharing their similar experiences with Eva's benevolent scrutiny, the small group moved to the matter at hand. Anna once again covered the logistics for the meeting that had been discussed at Eric's house to ensure that everyone was on the same page.

"I must say, Sal was certainly good-natured about staying behind and accepting my assertion that the fewer people involved in this meeting, the better. And you, Eric, have certainly created a reasonable justification for including the two of us. Eva, as we discussed, Joseph'll introduce you and me as Eric's gifted friends who he felt would benefit significantly from being able to attend an informal meeting with such a prominent physicist. He'll also say that we've agreed to remain quiet during the meeting so that he, Eric, Dr. Loh, and their friends can enjoy one another's company. When Joseph introduces you, please look Dr. Loh in the eye and extend your hand in greeting. Whatever you see, please don't do anything beyond giving him a smile and a nod. We'll discuss it when we're alone. Are you okay with all this?"

While Anna was speaking, Eric stared at Eva, who was again looking at the floor and not appearing to be aware of her surroundings. When Anna finished her explanation, Eric was not entirely convinced that Eva understood what Anna had said. After she looked up, a single, slight nod from Eva convinced him that he was wrong, prompting him to remind himself once again about being too quick to judge a book by its cover.

The conversation then turned to how Anna had come to meet Eva and how they had worked together before. Both of the academics were taken aback by the horrifying experiences they had shared and were eager to know more. Just then, there was a minor commotion outside the main door to the lounge at the other end of the room.

In came a small group of men all struggling to keep up with and paying close attention to a short, balding man with a wispy ring of white hair on the sides and back of his head. Appearing to Anna to be in his early sixties, he had an engaging smile that looked out over a slight paunch that gave the little man a benevolent appearance. Surrounded by his friends, he kept walking sprightly and speaking animatedly while the small circle of colleagues followed him into the room.

When Joseph saw Dr. Loh, he immediately rose and walked over to the group. Instantly, Georg Loh broke off his thought and headed toward him with an outstretched hand. "Dr. Altenau. Dear Joseph. What a pleasure it is to see you again. It's been a long time. You look very well, very well, indeed. I'm eager to meet these special friends of yours."

Careful not to ignore the other men surrounding Georg, Joseph turned to the entire group and said with a smile, "It's so nice to see all my friends here just to see me! Georg, you must let the younger men keep up. They almost look winded," he said with a wide grin and a chortle as he grabbed Georg's hand and clasped his arm with the other.

"No, Joseph, it is I who have to keep up with them," replied Georg. "I'm enjoying exercising my legs and my English so I can keep up with your German and feel…now, how d'you say…oh yes, feel on top of the world!"

"Unsinn, mein Deutsch ist nicht so gut wie dein Englisch! Please forgive me, all of you," said Joseph as he turned to the others surrounding Georg. "I would greatly appreciate being able to steal away our distinguished friend just for a few moments, if I may," he said as he smiled, thanked the others, and shepherded Georg away from his coterie of admirers.

As they walked together to the other end of the expansive room, Joseph turned to Georg. "Except for Dr. Franzen, the two people I'm about to introduce you to will not be participating in our discussions but are here instead to listen to the exchange. Nonetheless, they are very special to me and are both exceptionally gifted."

"I see. Well, as I said, I'm very interested in meeting them," replied Georg as they approached the area where Eric, Eva, and Anna were sitting.

As Eric stood to greet the other two men, Joseph said, "This is my long-time friend, Dr. Eric Franzen. While his field is not physics but chemistry, I've told him about our history together, and he's been quite keen to meet you." The two men then shook hands and exchanged some short pleasantries.

Anna was the first woman to approach the short professor, as Joseph said, "This is my good friend Mrs. Anna Tilner who comes to us from the very powerful and highly regarded law firm of Tilner and Associates in Boston." After expressing their mutual pleasure at meeting, Joseph turned to introduce Eva, who was standing behind Anna.

"And this is an extraordinary guest of mine," said Joseph as Eva came into Georg's view for the first time. "Miss Eva Hauser, one of Dr. Franzen's most gifted students, is also here to observe."

Georg suddenly stiffened when Eva extended her hand. Standing perfectly still, he made no move to reciprocate. Seeing the awkward pause resulting in Eva's withdrawal of her hand, Joseph faced his friend and said, "Georg, remember we're in America, at Columbia College. We respect all people and their views here. Were Columbia College admitting women, I can assure you this person would be at the head of the class. I vouch for her absolute superiority."

"Aber sie ist ein Mohr!" protested Georg.

"Sie ist ein Wunderkind, das ich zutiefst schätze! Ich bin verblüfft, dass du mich in meiner Heimat so beschämen kannst!" responded Joseph with an intensity that surprised everyone, including Eric.

After another pause, the edge of Georg's mouth twitched before he finally reached out his hand slowly, and Eva grasped it gently while looking into his eyes. At that moment, Georg suddenly appeared to be paralyzed, unable to move, look away, or remove his hand. While only a few seconds transpired before he was able to pull his hand away, it seemed like minutes to everyone else.

Aghast, nearly everyone focused on the short, portly scientist who was now clearly struggling to recover his demeanor that had been so much on display just seconds before. Only one person was looking elsewhere. Anna stared at Eva, who was rocking slightly forward and backward and, to Anna's eye, appeared to be reeling inside. She sensed that behind the relatively passive look on Eva's face, there was a seething mass of emotions that she was struggling to control. It was everything Eva could do to follow Anna's instructions to reveal nothing of what she saw until the two of them could be alone.

"I must return to the others!" blurted Georg in an oddly robotic way. He then turned abruptly and hurried away to rejoin his fellow physicists still assembled at the other end of the room. Anna, seeing that Eva was losing her struggle to keep her equilibrium, took her by the arm and sat her down on the sofa. Once seated, Eva continued to rock slightly forward and back, which Eric and Joseph noticed, alarming both of them.

"Eric, it may appear to be rude, but I believe we need to get Eva back to Eric's house," said Anna as Eric nodded his assent. "Joseph, if you'd be so kind as to tell Dr. Loh that Eva is not feeling well, and it'd be better if she were able to go home."

"Of course, Anna, but of course," said Joseph as he turned to Eva and smiled while slowly shaking his head. "My little prodigy, what did you see that has disturbed you so? What a burden your gifts must be to have such sensitivity to the misery all around you. I just wish it were in my power to comfort you."

After putting her arm around Eva, Anna looked at the others and said, "When I learn what Eva saw, I'll tell you right away. However, before we go, Joseph, what was your exchange in German with Dr. Loh?"

"Oh yes," said Joseph, now suddenly looking a little unsettled himself. "I haven't seen Georg in several years, and I'm afraid that during that time, Nazi Germany has changed the man I knew. He was taken aback by Eva's black skin and was protesting having to shake her hand. When I reminded him that we were in America and not Germany, he tossed my advice aside and said, 'But she's black.' I found this rejection of his deeply offending to all of us and especially to Eva, so I reacted by insisting that she was a prodigy whom I deeply admired. I didn't find saying this satisfying enough, however, so I added that I couldn't believe that he would shame me so in my own homeland. Then I felt better.

"You know," Joseph continued, "Eva doesn't feel so well, and after that exchange with Georg, neither do I. They can all enjoy their lunch without me." He then turned and looked at Eva and said, "I apologize again for this man's insulting behavior and Eva, I hope you can understand how important this was and that you can forgive me for having made you endure such an introduction."

All eyes fell on Eva, who then stood up a little unevenly and quietly took Joseph's hand and squeezed it. This expression of a newfound relationship between two such vastly different people moved everyone. It was a bond that would have been inconceivable barely twenty-four hours earlier.

53

"Considering Abe's appalling appearance when he checked in to the hospital, I'm as stunned as Anna that he'll be released tomorrow. Are you sure that's what Mo said, Eric?" inquired Sal.

"Quite sure," he replied. "He was very relieved to have the doctor's original assessment confirmed. I agree with you, though, Abe looked as if he were near death. Despite that, it sounds as if there were no serious or permanent injuries, only terrible surface abrasions that must've been unthinkably painful and will, no doubt, leave some unsightly scars. Mo's with him now and won't be back until late this evening."

After a brief pause, Sal again turned to Eric. "Eva and Anna've been in your study for quite a while now. From what you told me, it sounds like this meeting with Dr. Loh was quite explosive. I'm very concerned that Eva wasn't able to learn anything."

"I'm not sure that's the case," said Eric. "However, we'll have an answer of some kind shortly. You're right about how the meeting was so surprising, though. It was all we could talk about all the way home. Poor Eva. Although she's not very expressive, she was quite upset. The drive seemed to calm her down, but I can't wait to learn what she saw in those few seconds when she held Loh's hand." Just then, Anna joined the two men in the living room.

"Where's Eva?" asked Eric.

"She's had quite a day and decided to rest for a while," replied Anna.

"I can certainly understand that. She's been through quite an ordeal today. What did she tell you?" asked Sal, unable to bridle his impatience.

"A good deal. The best news is that it sounds as if, for all the Nazi's bluster about being a master race and everyone else being inferior, they are oddly unenthusiastic about taking a gamble on a new and untested weapon technology. It seems that Hitler doesn't have much respect for scientists or science. In short, what I got from Eva's depiction of Loh's experiences with Stromberg is that it doesn't sound as if Hitler is at all serious about pursuing this speculative weapon."

"Don't you think our government would want to know about this?" asked Eric.

"No, I don't," said Anna.

"Why on earth not?!" asked Eric.

"To begin with, despite my father-in-law's connections, there's no chance our government would even listen to us about something so monumental, let alone take what we have to say seriously. If, miraculously, they were somehow intrigued, then we'd have to reveal how we came by this information, which could cause unending problems for Eva as well as the rest of us. Even then, if our government had any confidence at all in the validity of this information, the possible absence of a Nazi competitor could only reduce its appetite for spending the time and money this could require. With the Japanese being as belligerent and aggressive as they've already shown they can be, they might take on the challenge, or maybe Russia would. In any event, we need to remember what Eric told us about Einstein's letter to FDR warning of someone else creating one of these things. If this is a course America decides to pursue, we'd be far better off having the first one. On top of that, suppose we did nothing and someone assassinated Hitler. What if a new leader felt differently and wanted to take on the challenge? No, in all respects, at least for the foreseeable future, we're better off with our government being spurred on by the threat that Germany's working on this superweapon."

"If you thought all of this would ultimately be just an exercise anyway, why did we put Eva and the rest of us through all this?" asked Eric.

"If Eva had seen that Germany was actually developing such a weapon and they'd made significant progress, that's something we'd have had to take to the government, especially if Eva were able to have any idea of how far along they were. I'm relieved that this isn't the case. Thank heaven for the German skeptics and their Luddite Führer. This was indeed good news."

"Did Eva say anything else?" asked Sal.

"Unfortunately, yes, I regret to say that she did. I was so concerned with what she could tell us about Germany's efforts to make a superweapon that, initially, I wasn't aware that she'd seen a great deal more than that. When she appeared to be so upset at meeting Dr. Loh but then revealed to me that Germany was probably not going to pursue this superweapon, I was puzzled by her extremely negative reaction. Regrettably, now I'm not."

"Are you saying that there's some other horrible weapon that the Nazis are devising?"

"Not exactly, but effectively, yes. Of course, since this is reality through the eyes of Dr. Loh, we must rely on what he's seen. The picture Eva paints is dark indeed. Ever since Hitler took over in early 1933, the Nazis have imposed a steadily tightening noose around the necks of mostly Jews, blacks, gypsies, mentally ill or deficient people, and anyone else not fitting the very narrow definition of being acceptable to the regime. They've declared such people ineligible for legal rights and government jobs. They've stolen their homes, businesses, and possessions, and disqualified them from attending German schools. They're even murdering sick and disabled people. It's being reported that this is happening all over Germany and now Poland."

"Eva told you all this? Does she understand what a Jew is? I can't imagine she's ever experienced anti-Semitism where she grew up in Alabama," queried Eric.

"Much of this I've read on my own, but nearly all of the current information comes from her. Sometimes it's difficult to make out precisely what she's getting at, but thanks to what I already know, I'm able to piece it together.

"Regarding being Jewish, she appears to understand this concept all too well. I have no doubt you're correct that she wouldn't have encountered Jews growing up or understand why some people hate them, but she did have one powerful experience on this score that I'm aware of. When Dr. Roster, who's Jewish, examined her, she was able to see and feel his reactions to helpless Jewish children being condemned to death and taken away in front of him. It seems that Eva sensed his awareness of himself and these children as Jewish, however she interprets that, and therefore different. Of course, it's regrettable that she doesn't need to be Jewish to have a profound understanding of racial hatred and brutality. The color of her skin has taken care of that. As a consequence, she's been able to apply these concepts to what she saw in Dr. Loh's experience."

"All this sounds like a terrible nightmare," said Eric as he struggled to comprehend such unbridled, widespread evil.

"There's something worse," added Anna.

"Worse?! How could living in such a grisly hellhole be any worse?!" asked Eric as he raised his eyebrows.

"This is only partly due to what Eva shared with me." Looking at Eric, she then said, "After you asked me if I'd read Hitler's Mein Kampf, I read both volumes, and if he continues to be faithful to the plans he's outlined, as Eva's account indicates he is, Germany is headed straight for a very dark place indeed."

"I've read only a portion of the book, but based on what you know, what do you foresee?" asked Eric.

"If we're to believe Hitler's manifesto, all this increasingly horrific oppression that Eva's described is only the tiniest step into a grim future that he feels destined to create. I fear that what we're aware of and, far more significantly, what we aren't, is only a preface to the main event. I believe that before this's all over the Nazis will have perfected a grotesquely efficient machine that will have committed mass murder on an unprecedented scale by a government driven by ruthless, racist criminals."

"We can only hope you're wrong, Anna. I don't know about you, but I find myself feeling completely exhausted just thinking about all of this. It sounds like something out of the Apocalypse."

"I'm afraid that's exactly where this madman's manifesto leads me. Speaking of the Apocalypse," Anna observed, "Oscar Hahn should be arriving shortly."

54

It was apparent to Anna that Eric was emotionally depleted from both the meeting with Dr. Loh earlier in the day and Eva's horrifying revelations. He was in no mood to listen to anything that Oscar Hahn had to say and bid Anna and Sal goodnight before leaving for his bedroom at the far end of the house. Despite the immense emotional loads that had been lifted from him the day before, as he walked away, he appeared to Anna to be a broken man.

It was only a few minutes later that the gauleiter showed up and was reluctantly shown into Eric's study by Sal and Anna. Seated in the love seat facing them, he was surrounded by Eric's books and magazines. Faced with his Nazi uniform, together with Eva's harrowing description of what it represented fresh in their minds, Anna and Sal found it particularly difficult to be sitting in the same room with him. After a few awkward seconds, Oscar began to speak.

"You must understand that this is very difficult for me, Mr. Puma and Mrs. Tilner."

"Oh, I'm quite sure it is," replied Anna. "It was barely seventy-two hours ago that your henchmen were trying to kill Sal, me, and our partners after already brutally torturing one of us. And now you sit on a love seat, of all things, across from us. No, I have no doubt this's difficult for you. But let me be clear. The only reason you're here is that we're doing a favor for Karl Stampf, who sympathizes with your situation. In light of our recent history, I, for one, don't share his sentiment."

"Neither do I," asserted Sal.

"Of course you don't," replied Oscar, "and I wouldn't either if our positions were reversed. What happened to you wasn't my choice, however. I was following orders from someone I've always thought could be a dangerous person."

"If you have always thought that he was a dangerous person, why did you continue to work for him?"

"There are ideas he embraces that are consistent with my own beliefs, so for a long time I turned a blind eye to his darker side. Now I can no longer afford to do that."

"What you really mean is that you can no longer afford to look the other way now that his violent nature has been aimed at you," declared Anna sharply. This brutal confrontation with the truth stifled any response Oscar could make without looking foolish. Looking down, he remained silent.

"So what do you want and why do you think we'd have any interest in helping you?" demanded Anna.

"I'm sure that Karl's given you a fairly complete picture of Maximilian Graff," he began as Anna and Sal both nodded. "You've seen the Oyster Bay facility…"

"You mean Eingang?" said Sal.

"Yes, Eingang. Now that you've been there, do you know what its purpose is?"

"That's been puzzling us," said Sal while Anna stayed perfectly still.

"I don't know all the details, but I'd be willing to tell you what I know in exchange for protection from Graff."

"Why don't you just use your head goon to protect you?" prodded Anna. "I'm speaking of the one who appeared to be in charge the other day and did his level best to tear me out of my car before I managed to give him what I'm sure was a serious headache."

"You're speaking of Gus, Gus Erstad. Yes, he's very physical."

"I'm not sure I'd be so generous, but it's one way to describe him," added Sal.

"Gus is very loyal to me, and, as a result, so are his men. They would take any order I gave them."

"Are you saying you'd be willing to sabotage Eingang?" asked Anna.

"Yes, I am. I've heard that when the facility is completed, Graff intends to lay everyone off anyway, so no one would be jeopardizing his job if we destroyed the place and then disappeared."

"But what about you? Why're you willing to do this?"

"As you've no doubt guessed by now, I'm a staunch supporter of Herr Hitler."

At this ludicrously conspicuous disclosure, both Anna and Sal had to stifle what would have been a sarcastic guffaw.

Unfazed, Oscar continued. "While I've been in the service of the German American Bund and have upheld its support of Nazi Germany, I'm also a loyal American who deeply loves this country. So, having said all this, can we make a deal?"

"Give us a minute," said Anna as she motioned for Sal to join her in the next room.

They entered an adjacent bedroom and shut the door. "Would you be willing to put him up at your compound in Montgomery, Sal, at least until we've dealt with Graff?"

"A Nazi in my house?! Anna, you can't be serious!"

"If he's willing to give us some meaningful information about this Eingang facility, enough to charge Graff with a serious crime, I believe it's worth giving him the protection he wants. On the other hand, if there's not enough evidence, he's also willing to use his men to destroy the place. Giving him what he wants could be the most patriotic thing you've done since you were a government informer. Besides, your estate's so large you could go for months without even knowing he was there. What d'you say, Sal?"

"Damn it! I can't believe I'm agreeing to this, Anna. You know, you just might make a good lawyer someday," he said with a wink and a shrug as he bowed and swept his arm towards the door.

Once back in Eric's study, the two again sat across from Oscar. "We've come to a determination, Mr. Hahn," indicated Anna. "However, for you to receive the protection you want, there are several conditions."

"And what might those be?"

"As some form of restitution for the horrible injury you inflicted on Abe Groveman, you'll agree to work with both him and Morris Stein to gather strong evidence about Eingang's illegal purpose before we decide it should be destroyed. That means there must be enough clear proof for us to make a convincing legal indictment. If we decide there isn't a strong enough legal case, then you would destroy the entire facility. Is this clear to you, and do you accept these terms?"

"Yes, I understand. You must know how much I hate working with Jews, but I'll go along. Are there any other conditions?"

"Yes, there's one final requirement. I'll call this insurance that you're telling us everything that you know."

"What?! How on earth are you going to do that? I'm not agreeing to be tortured or anything like that!"

"No, no. We're not barbaric like your Gus Erstad. I assure you that it'll be completely painless. First, tell us what you know about Eingang and how you came to know Maximilian Graff."

Visibly rattled at the thought of physical abuse, Oscar gradually relaxed as he settled into explaining his relationship with Gus Erstad and Maximilian Graff. He told them about his meeting Gus on the Long Island train to Yaphank, his introduction to Maximilian at Camp Siegfried, his subsequent employment, and his secret assignment to oversee the creation of Eingang.

"I suppose you're unaware of the meaning of Eingang in German."

"Actually, I do know what it means," responded Anna.

"You do?" exclaimed Sal as he turned to her.

"I asked Joseph before he left," she replied.

"Well, I don't know a word of German. So what does it mean?" asked Sal.

"It means 'Entrance,'" responded Anna.

"And what's the significance of Graff's choice of this word?" asked Sal.

"It was only recently," began Oscar, "I learned that he designed it to be Germany's beachhead when it would ultimately invade the United States."

"Invade the United States?!" exclaimed Anna.

"Yes. Of course, you wouldn't be aware of this, but Graff says the Führer is developing a superweapon that he believes will enable Germany to defeat America in the coming war. As a first step, Germany would need a secluded area to land a preliminary reconnaissance force, its vehicles, weapons, and ammunition. Eingang is ideal for such a purpose."

"So, you believe America's entry into the war in Europe is inevitable?" asked Anna.

"I believe that, yes."

"And you claim to be an American patriot?!" said Sal, brimming with sarcasm.

"Bear in mind that what I've just told you are Graff's objectives. Mine are different. As I said, I love this country. It's given me the freedom to combine my love for my mother country with that of my adopted one. If I didn't love America, why would I be here telling you all this?"

"So how do your beliefs differ from Graff's?" asked Anna.

"I don't believe that with or without some superweapon, Germany has any realistic chance of defeating the United States. True, I believe that the Führer will continue to force all of Europe and perhaps Asia under his control. However, I believe he's wise enough to see that were he to attack the United States, it'd mean the end of the Reich. Instead, I'd like to see the two powers in a more collaborative, cooperative relationship. In fact, as evidence of my good faith, I'm prepared to give you this." Oscar then reached into his shirt pocket, removed a small, neatly folded piece of paper, and handed it to Sal.

"What's this?" he asked as he unfolded what appeared to be a telegram.

"It's evidence of what Eingang's true purpose is."

"But it's in German," said Sal scanning the piece of paper.

"Yes, but I can translate it for you," said Oscar as he retrieved the telegram. "It says: 'Dear Mister Graff: The Führer sends his congratulations on your commencement of Eingang to help facilitate Germany's landing along America's northeastern shore once Germany has conquered Europe and is prepared to march on the United States. This is of great significance to the Reich, and we look forward to the day when our armed forces can use it to establish a beachhead in America in our continued conquest of Lebensraum. You are a true and honored member of the German Reich. Heil Hitler, Hermann Göring, Successor to the Führer'"

"What are the circumstances surrounding the origin of this document, and how did you come to possess it, Mr. Hahn?" asked Anna.

"When Graff attended the celebration of Herr Lindbergh in Berlin a year ago in October 1938, Herr Göring made the award to the famous American aviator. Afterward, Graff spoke with Herr Göring about his idea to create Eingang. He told me that Herr Göring was very impressed and promised to tell the Führer about it. When Graff put me in charge of developing Eingang, he gave it to me to inspire me in my work."

"Well, thank you for the explanation," said Anna as Oscar returned the document to Sal. She then asked, "There are several buildings that appear to be outfitted for medical purposes. What exactly are they designed to do?"

"Dr. Harry Laughlin was selected by Graff to be the executive director of this part of Eingang, where he would conduct medical experiments and sterilizations."

"Experiments?! Sterilizations?!" asked Sal.

"Yes. We believe in purifying the Aryan race by ensuring that inferior races are not permitted to continue to breed."

"Of course you do," said Anna calmly as Sal shook his head.

"And the subterranean sealed chamber, what's that designed to do?" she asked.

"Here, I agree with Graff. We need to eliminate the people who degrade our culture, who make it weaker. This facility would have been used as a beginning to eliminate such undesirables."

"And exactly how would this be done?"

"We have a large supply of Zyklon, Zyklon B actually, a pesticide that would be used to gas these people so they would no longer represent a threat to our race."

"And who do you consider to be these people who represent a threat to your race?"

"The Jews, of course, as well as the blacks, criminals, mentally ill and retarded, and homosexuals, to begin with."

"You see nothing terribly wrong with this?" asked Sal.

"Certainly not. Eugenics research has shown us how destructive such people are to our race if they're allowed to breed at will."

"Then, who exactly do you consider to be your race?"

"Isn't that quite obvious? The northern European Aryan race."

"How well do you know our Constitution?" asked Anna.

"Very well. I find it to be an outstanding document."

"If so, how do you square your racial beliefs with the Constitutional declaration that it is 'self-evident that all men are created equal, that they are endowed by their Creator with certain unalienable rights, that among these are life, liberty and the pursuit of happiness'?" asked Anna.

"Mrs. Tilner, I'm shocked that you're so naïve and hypocritical. Where was this concept when the American Indians were decimated and then subjugated? Even today, your misguided claim of equality in the Constitution rings hollow. To your credit, however, the Führer finds America's treatment of its blacks to be enlightened and in line with his own views. These beings are obviously inferior and should be oppressed and prevented from diluting the white race. It's readily apparent that this was the original intent of America's Founders because nowhere in the Constitution does it say that these inferior races are to be considered equal. In fact, if I remember correctly, in the mid-1850s, no less an icon than the chief justice of the Supreme Court declared that the Founders' Constitution regarded blacks 'so far inferior that they had no rights which the white man was bound to respect.' Now I ask you, does that sound like a nation that really believes that 'all men are created equal'?"

"I see," said Anna quietly as she turned to Sal. "Sal, could you please keep Mr. Hahn company while I retrieve our special partner." Turning back to Oscar, she added, "As I indicated to you earlier, there is one last requirement. To fulfill this, I will be introducing you to someone who'll enable us to conclude our investigation." Anna then rose and left the room.

Sal had always admired Anna's self-control and the many instances he had seen where she was able to remain eerily calm. What he had just witnessed added another chapter to this chronicle. Seething inside, Sal had taken Anna's lead and did everything in his control to maintain an outward appearance of calm. Now, forced to sit alone briefly with someone whose worldview he loathed, he was impatient to see how this person, so infused with pseudo-scientific, perverted, and barbaric racial ideas, would handle the final part of his interview. While they were waiting, he returned to a topic he found infinitely less repulsive.

"You must be very afraid of Graff to be willing to turn on him like this," said Sal.

"Yes, in fact, I do fear him, but I also fear that his encouragement of Germany's invasion of the United States could lead to the destruction of Germany. Over time, this has become very clear to me. After giving it a great deal of thought, I realized I couldn't live any longer with his mortal threats or the danger I see him being to both the Fatherland and to my adopted homeland. I would never..."

Stopping briefly to acknowledge Anna entering the room, Oscar suddenly froze as the person following her came into view. "Mr. Hahn, I would like you to meet Miss Eva Hauser."

55

Shooting out of his seat, Oscar shouted, "This is an outrage! An outrage! What's this…this person doing here, and why am I forced to be in this room with her?!"

"If you're interested in our help, you'll need to meet our final requirement of meeting with Miss Hauser," declared Anna while Eva stood looking at the floor.

"I don't understand this at all! Why is she here?!"

"You can begin by shaking hands, Mr. Hahn," said Anna.

"What?! I've never touched a…a…a Negro in my life and I will not submit to having to do so now!"

"It seems you have a shorter memory than I thought," Anna responded evenly. "You are here because of Maximilian Graff's apparent death threat if anything happened to Eingang. Not ten minutes ago, you agreed to destroy it to spite him and remove this peril to America. I'm sure he'd be interested in hearing that the person he entrusted with building his precious Nazi entrance has admitted to agreeing to wipe it off the face of the earth. He'd also be curious to know why you provided to an attorney written evidence of something that would look and sound very much like sedition, if not treason. This proof would enable people who have the means to make him face harsh justice. Have you forgotten all this, Mr. Hahn? Surely, you just needed a reminder. If I were you, I would shake the young lady's hand and sit down."

Anna and Sal could see the turmoil in Oscar's face as he struggled to weigh the violence he would face from his satanic boss against having to touch the hand of a black person. Both Anna and Sal were dumbfounded how Oscar's hatred of someone he had never met could be so profound that choosing his own violent end could be remotely preferable to merely shaking her hand.

Eva was still looking at the floor in front of her. She then looked up and walked over to Oscar and put out her hand. In response, Oscar seemed to go into a daze and fell back into a stack of magazines before scrambling to his feet.

"Please just relax and sit down, Mr. Hahn," advised Anna.

Still seemingly in a trance, Oscar slowly stumbled forward before turning around and falling into the love seat. Breathing deeply and looking straight ahead, he now seemed paralyzed as Eva sat next to him.

The thought occurred to Anna, "How tragic it is that these two people can sit on either end of this small sofa while also being at opposite ends of the universe."

"Now, this is something you don't see every day," thought Sal as he looked at Oscar in his starched, khaki gauleiter uniform, stubbornly avoiding the existence of the young black woman sitting next to him.

"Now remember what I said about your having to meet this last condition, Mr. Hahn," advised Anna. "This will be your last opportunity if you expect us to provide you any protection from someone who will hunt you down until you're caught and killed, if not from destroying his property, then from running out on him. If protection is what you want, then just remain calm and don't move. Don't move now. Eva, please put your hand on the man's hand."

Eva slowly reached out and touched Oscar. Sal readied himself to take Oscar down if he showed any sign of moving to hurt her. After a quick twitch by Oscar when the two touched, Eva leaned forward and continued to stare at him as he looked straight ahead. Finally, wincing before pivoting his head and looking into her eyes, Oscar stiffened as everyone remained deathly quiet. As the two locked stares, he was transfixed until he began to shudder.

Suddenly he jumped up from the small sofa and spun around, keeping his eyes fixed on Eva, who had fallen back into the love seat. Then he began screaming, "Out! Out! Get out! Get out!" As he continued shouting, he turned, lurched forward, and fell headlong into a pile of magazines. Frantically struggling to get up as his shoes skidded on the slick covers, he finally stood and stopped screaming while remaining riveted on Eva. Slowly, he began backing away from her until he clumsily made his way around another magazine stack and backed up against the wall, his arms outstretched in front of him with his palms out. His head drooped onto his chest before he let out a low growl as his eyes looked up, giving him a demonic appearance.

Just then, Anna got up and walked over to the man, slapped him, and declared, "That'll be enough! Settle down!"

Oscar shook his head as if he were coming out of a daze, put his arms down to his sides, and then looked around in disorientation before seeing Anna. "What…what just happened?! Was I in a trance?!"

"No, Mr. Hahn," said Anna. "You were not in a trance. Miss Hauser was inspecting you. Please sit down while I have a private conversation with her about what she saw."

"What she saw?! What d'you mean what she saw?! What is this thing, anyway?! A black witch?!"

"Nothing of the sort, Mr. Hahn. She has a miraculous gift, and I imagine now knows almost as much about you as you do, perhaps more. Before we confirm our offer of protection and let you go, I'll need to speak with her. Now, just sit down. We'll be a few minutes."

"This is preposterous! I'm not…"

"Mr. Hahn! Get ahold of yourself before you say something that could eventually doom you. We'll be back shortly. Now, sit down!"

ordered Anna, as Oscar, unprepared for Anna's forceful demand, silently walked to an empty chair and sat down.

Turning to Eva, Anna smiled and said, "Eva, you look exhausted. I know this's been difficult for you. Let's go to another room." Eva then stood and walked over to Anna, who gently took her arm before both women left the room.

Sal was curious about what was running through Oscar's mind, but his profound distaste for the man made him unwilling to speak first. After the study door closed, Oscar looked over at Sal with fear covering his face. "My God, I'm afraid to know what she saw."

"You should be, Mr. Hahn. You really should be," Sal responded before the two fell into a prolonged silence.

56

"It's late, Mr. Hahn," said Anna as she returned to Eric's study without Eva. "We're now confirming our commitment to protect you under the following conditions. First, you provide what, in our sole determination, is strong enough legal evidence against Maximilian Graff to charge him with a felony. This includes your commitment to testify against him. Second, at our direction, you physically destroy Eingang. If I were you, I'd get my men organized without delay."

"Well, what did she say?! What in the hell did the black witch see?!" pleaded Oscar.

"As Anna's already told you," declared Sal as he rose to show Oscar the way to the door, "all you need to know is that you've been straight with us and we'll be straight with you. Get some rest. You've got a lot of work ahead of you." After protesting briefly, Oscar finally relented and left the house.

As soon as the door closed, Sal turned to Anna and said, "Is Eva all right?"

"She's fine but feeling very drained and she wanted to be alone. In addition to her giving me his vision of a completed Eingang, at least to the extent Oscar'd been informed of it by Graff, she saw Hahn's hatred of Jews, people like her, and many others. She saw images of things he'd seen in German newspapers and magazines that were horrifying for her. She also saw Hahn's impressions of conversations he had with Dr. Harry Laughlin, the racist eugenics expert, concerning sterilization and euthanasia procedures that were profoundly distressing. While these things are difficult enough for us to think about, I know it's far worse for Eva since she's faced such violent hatred growing up in Alabama. I'm relieved that she just wants to be left alone for a while. Imagine what it would've been like for her if she'd returned. I would've described to Hahn what she'd seen only to have him get back on his Nazi high horse and viciously attack the dangerous inferiorities of people like her. He would be merciless after his terrifying experience with her. Even if Eva weren't too exhausted to come and hear what Hahn had to say, after seeing what a toll this has taken on all of us, I was certainly in no mood to listen to any more Nazi racial garbage."

"Of course you're right," said Sal. "Eva's and our welfare is infinitely more important than satisfying that ridiculous Nazi's curiosity," he added, as he slowly nodded his concurrence.

"There was something else, however," said Anna.

"That's no surprise," said Sal. "This guy's probably got a whole bunch of bizarre ideas about how his master race's going to conquer the world."

"No doubt, he has many perverse ideas," replied Anna, "but this concerns Eva and is something I haven't seen before."

"Something to do with Eva?" asked Sal. "What d'you mean?"

"I've seen Eva have many different reactions to what she's seen. She's exhibited reactions of sadness, horror, disbelief, affection, tenderness, and joy. Until tonight, however, I hadn't seen any sign of rage, but now I have."

"That's odd, I didn't see any anger in her tonight," said Sal.

"I didn't either, but then it wasn't directed at us. Instead, Hahn was the target, and after I understood what she'd done, I could see why he was so panic-stricken. Apparently, she can go beyond just sensing what others feel and have witnessed. If angered enough, Eva can also project her feelings onto them. In this case—please don't ask me to explain this—what she saw in Hahn enraged her so that she was able to vividly convey to him a lifetime of her and her family's senseless suffering and brutality at the hands of whites. I can only speculate, but I'd imagine for a racist like Hahn, this could make him intensely uncomfortable, if not completely terrorized. I don't think we saw anything less than that with him tonight."

"Incredible!" Sal exclaimed quietly. "Our dear little innocent Eva can defend herself! Thank God."

57

"What d'you mean you haven't seen him?! Where in the hell's he gone?!" roared Maximilian Graff into the phone to Oscar Hahn's long-time adjutant, Fredrick Stengle.

"Uh…I'm sorry, Herr Graff, but, ah, the gauleiter hasn't been around here in a couple o' days."

"You'd better fucking find him and get him here to me before I hang up the phone! Did you get that?!"

"Yessir. I'll do everything I can and…" With only crackling coming from the other end of the phone line, Fredrick realized that he had just missed his deadline. "My God, what'm I supposed to do now, for Chrissake?!" he said out loud, desperation flooding his body as sweat suddenly formed on his forehead and around his neck, dampening the top of his starched brown shirt collar. After rushing out the door, Fredrick ran to his car to drive to Eingang, desperately hoping that his boss would be there.

Pulling up to the Eingang front gate, he frantically rolled down his window and started shouting before the guard could say anything. "Have you seen Gauleiter Hahn?! Is he here?!"

"I'm sorry, Herr Stengle. I haven't seen him for several days."

"Open the gate!"

As the just-repaired gate swung wide, he jammed his foot down on the gas pedal, the car spraying dirt behind it as he took off for the barracks where Gus Erstad and his men were housed. His car was still rolling when he jumped out and ran into the barracks.

"Ortsgruppenleiter Erstad?! Ortsgruppenleiter Erstad?!" he yelled as he rushed inside, slamming the door into the wall. The rest of the men in the barracks shot around to see the source of the commotion. Barely stopping at the first man he came to, between pants he repeated the question.

"He's in his office, Herr Stengle," the man replied.

While he was running to the end of the building, he yelled once again, "Ortsgruppenleiter Erstad?! I need to see you immediately!"

"Yeah, yeah! I heard ya all the way down here!" said Gus as he opened the door. Seeing the terrified expression on Oscar's petrified adjutant, he said, "What the hell's goin' on?"

"I just got off the phone with Herr Graff and he needs to see Gauleiter Hahn immediately!"

"You're his goddamn adjutant! You ain't tellin' me you dunno where he is?"

"I haven't seen him in a couple o' days! Have you?!"

"Hell no! I was thinkin' he was at his office with you! Ain't nobody heard from him?"

"Not that I know of?!"

"I'll go and check his house 'n then get back t'you," said Gus, jumping up to leave.

As he rushed past his office door to search for his friend Oscar, he suddenly remembered the striking vision of his hero in a funk, unaware that his pants were soaked with urine, following the threatening meeting with Maximilian three days earlier. Hopping into his car, Gus wondered if that last encounter and Maximilian's threat of reprisal had pushed Oscar over the edge. He was worried if he would still be at his house and if he would ever see his friend again.

While these thoughts were preoccupying Gus as he shot off in his car, at the very same time, Karl Stampf was arriving at Maximilian's mansion. Maximilian had summoned him but Karl was unaware of why.

"He's waiting for you, Mr. Stampf. Please go on in," said the secretary. No sooner had his shoe passed over the door's threshold when he heard the acrid voice of his boss, a sound that he was surprised to find was beginning to exhaust his tolerance of his boss's behavior.

"Stampf! What the hell are you doing about this?!"

"I'm afraid I don't have any idea what you're talking about, Mr. Graff!" he said as he approached the desk and sat down.

"I'm talking about Hahn, of course!"

"What about Oscar?"

"What's wrong with you, Stampf?! Don't you know he's disappeared?!"

"This's the first I've heard of it," he replied calmly.

"I've ordered his flunky...oh, what's his name..."

"You mean Fredrick Stengle?"

"Yes, that little shit! I've ordered him to find Hahn and bring him straight to me!"

"What would you like me to do?"

"Stampf, are you completely worthless or what? Haven't you heard a word I've been saying?! Find Hahn and bring him to me and do it right goddamn now!"

To Karl, this should have been just another demeaning order, the latest in an endless litany of abuse that he had long ago accepted as being part of his job. But not this time. In a flash, he recalled the week before when his predecessor, Michael Rudman, had recounted his disgust with similar affronts, and how he had come to the point where enough was enough. Now, as Karl walked out of the mansion, he felt his anger erupting from a cauldron of too many outrageous experiences. Maximilian's decades of relentless verbal abuse, his insulting demand for a secrecy agreement after so many years of Karl's loyal service, his betrayal of Karl when he hired Oscar Hahn to oversee Eingang, was all capped by Maximilian's latest orders that he was to learn nothing about Eingang. "And what was the objective of all this secrecy?" he thought. "To hide the horror of a plan that had been festering in Maximilian's obsessed mind for years." In seconds, years of suppressed fury were welling up inside him.

Then he thought of his advice to Oscar to seek help from Anna, who might know of a way to escape. This act of defiance of Maximilian suddenly tempered his rage and made him decide to hold his tongue—but only until the time was right for him to settle scores once and for all. He could feel it coming.

58

"What in the hell're you doing in my house?" demanded Oscar as he came through the front door.

"And where the hell you been, Oscar?!" asked Gus as he got up from Oscar's living room easy chair after setting down his beer on a side table.

"You ain't been 'round for days, and Graff's been all over people to get you t'his office pronto."

"Did he say what he wanted?"

"Hell, Oscar. You ain't no dummy. You heard him the last time we was in his office. He was real hot 'bout Eingang bein' invaded!"

"Yeah, yeah. I know, but I have a way out. Anyway, listen close, Gus. There's been a change of plans," he said as both men sat down on adjacent chairs.

Oscar then revealed that he had heard a rumor that Maximilian planned to fire him, Gus, and the rest of the Silver Swords now that construction of Eingang was completed.

"Then who the hell's he gonna get to run 'n guard the goddamn place if he lets us go?!"

"That I don't know, Gus. He must have people lined up. I guess since I fell out of favor, he doesn't trust anyone associated with me, and that would be you and the other Silver Swords."

After a pause, Gus responded, "Why that sombitch! That ungrateful sombitch! After all we done for him!"

Now no longer blinded by any residual loyalty to Maximilian, Oscar shared with Gus his disgust with his soon-to-be ex-boss.

"I recently became aware that Eingang's true purpose is to help Germany invade America. As unlikely as that may be, it can't be allowed to happen. I've agreed to gather enough evidence of all this to hang Graff legally or, failing that, to destroy the entire facility."

He then outlined how he would be pulling documents and plans together and how Gus and his men were to destroy Eingang if and when he gave the green light. He stressed speed and complete secrecy so that by the time Maximilian knew anything, it would be too late.

"What about Gundshau?" asked Gus. At the mention of this name, Oscar's mind flashed back to his first image of the enormous enforcer from the first meeting he and Gus had had at Maximilian's office. Gunther Gundshau had stood at the back of the room ensuring that whatever Maximilian wanted his guests to do, they would comply. Ever since the main gate for Eingang had been installed, Gunther had manned it periodically, and both Oscar and Gus had been waved through by him many times. Oscar knew that, unlike Gus and his men, Gunther would always be loyal only to Maximilian.

"You'll have to take care of him before any of this demolition work starts. If Graff learns anything before we're finished and gone, we're dead."

"Got it."

"You'd better go alert the Swords to what we're doing and then get some sleep. Tomorrow's going to be a busy day," advised Oscar. Gus nodded before standing with a grunt and leaving his empty beer bottle on the table.

Gus was long gone, and Oscar had been asleep for almost two hours when the phone in his bedroom rang. Still more asleep than awake, he fumbled with the phone and was barely able to croak into it.

"Ahem…Hello?"

"Hello Oscar, this is Karl. Thank God I finally got you!"

"Karl? Ah…Karl who?" said Oscar, still in a stupor.

"Karl Stampf. I'm sorry for calling so late, but there's something you need to know right now!"

After struggling to pull his thoughts together, Oscar finally recognized Karl as Maximilian's senior executive officer with whom he had developed something of a friendship.

"Yes, Karl. I apologize, but I was deeply asleep, but I'm with you now. What is it?"

"I just got home from a Graff Industries security staff party, and most everyone had quite a bit to drink. I had enough, too, until I heard something that sobered me up on the spot."

"Security staff party?! What security staff?!"

"Yes, I thought you knew we have a security unit for Graff Industries that's overseen by Gunther."

"No. I had no idea there was any security besides Gus and the Silver Swords! Well, anyway, what did you hear?"

"Maximilian wasn't there—he rarely attends these things—but I was with a group of Graff Industry security officers, and I overheard something alarming. They've been ordered to say nothing about this to anyone, or they could face dire consequences. I'm not sure what that means, but when you hear what one of the others said—his tongue was quite loose by this time—you'll have some idea."

"Karl, please get on with this. You're making me very nervous."

"Well, you should be. You know how paranoid Graff is about Eingang and anything getting out about it. Well, now that it's virtually done, apparently he's given an order to Gundshau to clean the slate!"

"I already heard this. He intends to lay off all of us, doesn't he?"

"Lay you off?! Oscar, you don't understand!"

"What the hell do you mean, I don't understand?!"

"The order means that Maximilian wants you, Gus Erstad, your assistant, Fredrick Stengle, and the rest of the Silver Swords who have any knowledge of the facility to vanish."

"You don't mean…surely you don't mean he intends to murder us all?!" said Oscar hoarsely as his worst fear was being resurrected and confirmed, undercutting the relief his agreement with Anna and Sal had given him.

"Could it mean anything else?! The old man's finally gone nuts, I'm afraid that…Hello?! Oscar?!…"

59

Gus Erstad had just come through his friend's front door when Oscar picked up where his desperate summons on the phone had left off. Until he spoke, Gus was puzzled why he had been called at such an early hour in the morning.

"Did you alert the rest of the men what the plan is?"

"Yeah. They're ready to go when we give the word. But tell me I ain't here 'cause ya wanted t'make sure I talked to 'em?"

"It's far worse than we thought, Gus."

"What's worse?!"

"Graff intends to kill us all!"

"What?! Who told ya that?!"

"Karl Stampf. He runs Graff Industries for Maximilian, and he overheard it at a security staff party earlier tonight!"

"Who in the hell's he gonna get t'do this? He ain't got no other armed men like us, right?"

"Karl just told me that Graff has a separate security outfit for Graff Industries, and it's headed by Gunther Gundshau!"

"Well, I'll be damned."

"I don't know anything about these people, even where they're headquartered. The only one I'd recognize is Gundshau. I don't even know what they have in the way of weapons, but knowing Graff, they're probably well armed."

"We can't wait to make a move tomorrow, Oscar…"

Suddenly, the front door burst inward off its hinges as several armed men charged in and grabbed Oscar and Gus, holding them both at gunpoint. Then the mountainous Gunther Gundshau entered the room.

After taking a long look at both men, he began giving orders to his men. "Take 'em both to Eingang. Ya know where. Keep it quiet.

We ain't wantin' the guards there to know nothin'. I'll follow on. Now go!" The small group shoved both men out the front door before they were thrown into the back of a van, and the door was slammed shut and locked.

Still inside the house, Gunther went to Oscar's office and began rifling through his papers, most of which concerned Eingang's construction. After wading through several piles, he came across one small note that had been put aside and appeared to have nothing to do with Eingang. It contained a name, a phone number, and an address that were new to him. He grabbed the note and stomped out the front door to join his men.

As the van made its way in the early morning darkness through Eingang's front gate, Oscar was paralyzed with fear while Gus's face showed no sign of anxiety. Oscar found no comfort in his friend's composure. Finally, the van came to a halt, propelling Oscar's stress into panic. The van door opened, and pistols were waving at the two men to get out and follow the other men down a long ramp.

One of the armed men opened one of the two large doors. As light streamed out from the interior, the guards shoved their prisoners into the large room. Gus knew the room well from his torturing of Abe. Except for someone having cleaned up the human waste that accompanied Abe's interrogation, it looked all too familiar. The place was barren except for two chairs, a chain hanging from the ceiling, and a table that was covered with various tools.

Having overseen its odd construction, Oscar was aware that the underground facility was intended to gas "undesirables" to death. Now facing a similar fate, he felt his hands and legs go numb. Gus's face was granite-like in its passive expression, revealing no emotion of any kind.

After the two men were shoved into chairs with their hands tied behind them, the four other men's pistols were trained on them. Oscar's feeling of being bound with his hands tied painfully behind him prompted the fleeting feeling of being trapped that he had experienced only once before in his life. It was the helpless, captured sensation that Eva had projected onto him less than two days before that began his momentary, horrific journey through the world in which she had grown up.

After a few more minutes, Gunther entered the room and walked right up to Oscar.

"What the hell's this?!" he shouted as he brandished the note he had retrieved from Oscar's house in front of his face.

At this confrontation, Oscar became so unhinged that he was unable to utter a sound.

"I'm gonna give ya one more chance, Hahn. What's this address, and who's Anna Tilner?! Ya better start talkin', or ya ain't gonna be able to after I get done with ya," said Gunther as he picked up a steel rod and tapped Oscar lightly on the cheek.

Oscar felt terrified at the prospect of giving up the identity of the one person offering him sanctuary, but his chances of surviving long enough to take advantage of her offer had just vanished. Desperate to survive the immediate threat, he was finally able to spit out some words.

"Okay…Okay…She's…She's the one who led the break-ins and…and that address…that's where she's staying!" As he revealed this information, he suddenly pictured Eric Franzen's study and his profoundly troubling experience with Eva. With the menace now facing Oscar, Eva's repulsive invasion of his soul jolted him into figuring how he could avenge himself while lessening his immediate jeopardy. A sudden inspiration gave him the strength to find the words he now felt could offer him a reprieve. As he spoke, he discovered increased conviction with every word he uttered.

"There's someone else....Yeah, she's bad news. It's a nigger who's played some role in all this. I've forgotten her name, but she's staying at that address with the Tilner woman. She's an evil bitch! And that note you have's about a plot to destroy Eingang! We were about to capture them both when you guys busted into my house. We have to protect Herr Graff and Eingang!"

Momentarily taken aback by the flustered vehemence of Oscar's revelations, Gunther thought for a few seconds before he spoke. Turning to his crew, he issued his commands.

"All right. The boss's gonna be here soon, but there's enough time t'get the two broads. You two come with me. You two watch the prisoners till I get back," he said as he motioned for the other two men to follow him out to the van. As he approached the massive door, he stopped and turned to the people left behind. "We ain't gonna be long. Get two more chairs and some more handcuff cord," he ordered before turning and going out the door.

60

Eric Franzen's large picture windows were glowing with the faintest hint of dawn, making Long Island Sound flicker with soft sparkles while a jellyfish on the sand shimmered with a muted radiance. A fox moved silently along the shore. Anyone sitting in this living room looking at this view would have a sense that somehow all was right with the world, and that the coming day was filled with promise.

Not this morning, however—no one in Eric's house was appreciating this peaceful panorama. Everyone had gone to bed late and was still asleep when Gunther's van rolled to a silent stop at the entrance to the semicircular driveway. He and his two henchmen got out of the vehicle before Gunther surveyed the house and gave them final instructions. The three men then slowly approached the front door in the dim morning light. Through the windows they could see that the inside of the house was dark, lit only by the first signs of dawn, reassuring Gunther that this would be a walk in the park.

After Gunther quietly jimmied the front door open, he turned to his men and motioned for them to go inside. Silently passing them in the entryway, Gunther glanced into the living room before turning to look down the long hallway and seeing several closed doors behind which he figured his quarry must be sleeping. Going to the first door with his men close behind, he turned the knob slowly, opened the door a crack, and peered inside to see a small bathroom. Closing the door carefully, they silently passed to the next door, opened it, and saw the shape of two people asleep in twin beds that protruded from the side wall. Motioning to one of his men to stay by the door and the other to go to the nearer bed, he approached the farther one. Both men took out their pistols and, on Gunther's signal, put the muzzles hard against the temples of the two people while clutching their mouths tightly. Muffled screams came from both, prompting the man by the door to poke his head out in the hall to see if anyone had been alerted. The hallway was still quiet, with only a dim light coming from the windows in the living room at the end of the hall.

Gunther again pressed his pistol hard against the head of the woman he was holding who had instantly stopped struggling and was silent. After turning on the light at the side of the bed and looking at her, he brought his mouth right up to her ear and whispered, "So, if it ain't Mr. Graff's personal secretary. You got some other piece o' paper fer me to see?" Accompanying the man's warm, foul breath, Anna found his strange hoarse, high-pitched voice to be far more menacing when he whispered.

Again he brought his mouth to Anna's ear and whispered, "No screamin', or it'll be the last thing ya do," he said as he released his hand from her face. "What's her name?" he demanded, nodding at the young black woman.

"You don't want her. She's too…"

"Her name or she's dead," whispered Gunther sharply.

After a moment, Anna relented, "Eva Hauser."

Everything suddenly went black for both women before the two assistants pulled their unconscious prey over their shoulders and quietly sneaked out of the room, down the hall, and out the front door. Walking as quietly as they could on the gravel driveway, they got to their van, loaded both women into the back, and silently locked the door. Giving the place one last look, Gunther saw that Eric's house remained still and dark, as if nothing had been disturbed, and everyone was still comfortably asleep in their beds.

Starting the engine and letting it idle, he eased out the clutch as the vehicle stealthily proceeded forward before a bend in the road made it vanish from view.

61

Oscar felt his stomach tighten as he looked over to the door and saw Anna and Eva in their bare feet and pajamas being dragged into the big room, still groggy from having been hit over the head. As they shuffled along, Anna instantly understood how and why they had been kidnapped—Oscar had led their captors to Eric's house and, no doubt, still resented how Eva had assaulted his mind. She knew this was to be a final reckoning to reveal who was leading the attempts to uncover what secrets Eingang held. She hoped that her sex would make it unlikely for their captors to believe that it was she who was heading the entire effort.

After the two new arrivals were thrown into their chairs with their hands tied behind them, Gunther cleared enough tools aside to sit on the table, and then stared at the four captives for a few seconds before speaking.

"Nothin' ain't happenin' to any o' ya till the boss gets here. He wants to find out what ya know 'bout this place. I ain't gonna lie to ya. If ya talk and ya make sense, it'll be quick. If ya ain't gonna talk, then it ain't gonna be quick and we gonna make it real slow and drawn out. So ya better talk or yer gonna wish ya was dead already. Ya can yell all ya want, but this place ain't lettin' no sound outta here. Got that?"

Anna glanced at Oscar and Gus and thought fleetingly that there could not be two more different people on earth. Gus was sitting perfectly still without any discernible facial expression. Next to him, Oscar's face was badly contorted, his lips partially closed but stretched wide, exposing a number of his teeth, as he rocked back and forth in his chair moaning.

About a half hour elapsed—an eternity for the victims—before the lock on one of the doors clicked, and the massive portal started to move. Gunther jumped off the table where the tools were sitting, ran over and pulled it open wide enough for the visitor to enter.

This was the first time that Anna had seen the profoundly twisted man behind Eingang. After all she had heard about him, he appeared taller and older than she had pictured him. Although he hobbled, she noticed he was able to drag his badly deformed right foot and walk with remarkable dexterity. His slicked-back salt and pepper hair matched his large, carefully-trimmed, uniformly-colored mustache except for a completely white patch at one end of it. This odd feature seemed to accentuate a periodic twitch from the same corner of his mouth. He was dressed impeccably, wearing a long camel beige coat, holding a pair of gray suede gloves, and, for some unapparent reason, he carried a riding crop in his left hand that he kept flicking up and down.

"So, Gundshau, you called, and now I'm here. What's the meaning of this, and what am I looking at?" growled the man.

"These two broads is part o' of the group that's broke into Eingang, Mr. Graff."

"Is that so?" said Maximilian with a hard edge to his voice and a slow speaking cadence. Turning to Anna, he used the same voice to ask, "And who might you be?"

"Mrs. Anna Tilner."

"Why would you say you're here, *Mrs.* Anna Tilner?" he asked mockingly.

"This facility has been raising eyebrows in the local neighborhood for some time now. I'm part of a team seeing if there's anything here that should be concerning to anyone."

"And what have you discovered, *Mrs.* Anna Tilner?"

"What this place is intended to be is extremely troubling, mysterious, and destructive."

"Destructive. Destructive? Interesting."

Then Maximilian slowly turned his head towards the young black woman bound in the chair next to Anna. As was her custom, Eva had her head down looking at the floor.

"And what, pray tell, have we here?"

After a prolonged silence, Maximilian looked over at Gunther and asked, "Does it speak?"

It was at this moment that Oscar was surprised to find his revulsion at Eva being rivaled by his disgust for Maximilian. He was now eager to see if the black woman would psychically assault this person for whom he now felt nothing but contempt.

Anna saw Maximilian looking down at Eva as a cat eyes its first captive mouse. Taking the riding crop and pressing it gently against Eva's cheek, she flinched slightly. Unable to rouse more of a response from her, he put his riding crop in the hand with his gloves before slowly reaching for her chin to force her to look at him. As he grasped her chin, Oscar was amazed when Maximilian showed no apparent reaction. Then he lifted Eva's chin and stared at her as she slowly raised her eyes and fixed on his. Oscar was holding his breath and waiting for a profound reaction, but the two just stared at one another for a few seconds.

Suddenly, Maximilian stumbled backward as he yanked his hand away from Eva, yelling in a voice utterly foreign to Oscar, "Ach! Was zur Hölle?! Geh aus mir raus!! Get out!! Get out of me!!" Still stumbling backward, Maximilian then fell onto the floor with his gaze fixed on Eva. As he lay on the ground, Maximilian's face hardened before he yelled again in the same strange voice, "You're a witch!! You're a goddamned black witch!! What in the hell've you done to me?! You've soiled me, soiled me, you filthy bitch!" At this point, Gunther rushed over to his boss as the rest of his men remained transfixed with their mouths agape.

As Gunther bent his considerable bulk down to help his boss stand, Maximilian's fury erupted as he shouted to his security chief, "Kill them all! All of them! I want to be rid of them! Now! And I want you to use the new procedure, understand?!"

"Yes, sir. I'll take care of it, but ya gotta leave first," responded Gunther as he motioned to his men to abandon the room.

Maximilian hobbled out first, still protesting loudly at the assault Eva had just delivered. Once the rest of his men were outside, Gunther ordered them to head up the slope on the opposite side from where the limousine was parked, as he sealed the large door shut. Once they were all at the top, a still agitated Maximilian shouted a final instruction to Gunther.

"Just make goddamn sure it's done properly, and the bodies are disposed of as you did before, Gundshau! I'll wait in my car. You have your orders. Now don't dare fail me!" As he signaled his understanding, Gunther motioned for his four men to follow him to the mound. He had done this several times before, although this was his men's first experience with the odd facility. After walking into the low bushes near the center of the mound, Gunther pointed a short distance away and said to one of his men, "You, you go over there to that little clearing in the bushes. There's a bin that's got a bunch o' canisters, masks, and gloves. Bring me one o' the cans and five sets o' gloves 'n masks." After the man returned with the materials, Gunther began briefing his crew.

"Ya gotta be careful with this stuff. It's real strong. Ya gotta put on these masks and gloves before ya open the can. They got real strong pellets in 'em, so be real careful. Now, ya see this little metal chute comin' outta the ground here, yer gonna take turns unlockin' 'n liftin' up the lid and pourin' some pellets into it. Then they fall inta the room below us that we just left. So, that's what yer gonna do. Got it?"

One of the men eyed the can with its skull and bones emblazoned on the center of the label and the large, orange lettering. As he was about to put on his mask, he turned to Gunther. "What's this do anyway…what's it called? Looks like…Giftgas? What the hell's that mean? And this other name. What's Zy…Zyklon B?"

62

Sal had been a light sleeper for as long as he could remember. Not long after Prohibition became law in 1920, this had been valuable for him as a bootlegger and especially so after he became an informer for the federal government.

His habit had been just as critical then as it was now. It enabled him to have a front-row seat the minute he heard Gunther Gundshau's van approaching and then coming to a halt at the end of Eric's driveway. Getting out of bed and peering out of one corner of the window, he saw it douse its lights. His bedroom was at the far end of the house from everyone else's, putting him closest to the driveway entrance. The voice he heard when Gunther was giving instructions to his men was faint but unmistakably the same as the Eingang front gate guard he had heard but was unable to see from inside the trunk of Anna's car, the man he had imagined being so tiny. Now he saw that Anna had been right—he was huge.

"We ain't gonna be here long," Sal heard Gunther say to the other two men in a lowered voice. "We ain't got much time 'n I ain't real comfortable leavin' Hahn and Erstad alone with my men. That Erstad's a tough sonofabitch. We gotta make this quick!"

"My God, they've already got Hahn and Erstad!" Sal said under his breath. Seeing the large guard and his two henchman approach the house, Sal knew it would be impossible to resist whatever it was they were up to, so he kept an eye on them from his window. As they quietly entered the house, Sal silently walked over to his bedroom door and opened it just enough to watch them as they walked away from him down the darkened hallway, checked the first room, and then entered the second. After a couple of minutes, he saw the two guards with Anna and Eva pitched over their shoulders quickly exit the house. "Shit!" he muttered.

No sooner had he seen the men throw the two unconscious women into their van and quietly depart than he ran down the hall and rousted Mo and Abe out of bed. Abe's skin was still badly damaged from his earlier abuse, but he had regained his ability to move with what Sal regarded as remarkable agility for a man his size. After waking Eric, he told him what had happened and that he and his two partners would be leaving immediately to rescue Anna and Eva. Having seen and heard Eingang's big guard with the high-pitched voice directing his men, Sal knew where they were going. It was only a few minutes later that he and his two comrades piled into the car, pulled out of Eric's driveway, and headed for the place they had all hoped they would never have to see again.

Approaching Eingang's main gate, Sal was relieved to see that his hunch had been correct—the monstrous guard was busy elsewhere with his captives. No one was in the guardhouse. Recognizing the need for more men and the risk that he faced in recruiting them, Sal opened the main gate and headed toward the barracks area just as the first full splash of sun peered over the complex. He turned a corner and came up to the first building where there were several vehicles parked just as they had been on their trip to rescue Abe. As Sal drove slowly past the cars, he saw in his rearview mirror what appeared to be a limousine crossing his path far behind him. Judging from its distance and speed, Sal was confident they had remained unnoticed by whoever was in the large car.

Pulling up to the barracks, he braced himself for what was coming. After he, Mo, and Abe exited the car and quietly hurried up to the front door, Sal gave a silent prayer and expelled a deep breath as he pondered his chances of unifying two sets of mortal enemies. He took another deep breath and then opened the door. As the three entered silently, the loud snoring assured Sal that he was in the right place. Turning on the lights, Sal took charge gruffly.

"Everybody up! Get up! Get up now!"

It took several seconds for the twenty or so stunned Silver Swords to realize that there was a stranger in their midst who was yelling out commands that demanded their obedience. Struck by the authoritative tone of the man's announcement, all eyes were soon on him.

"Listen up, everyone! My name is Sal Puma, and I know your boss, Oscar Hahn. Earlier this morning, I learned that he and Gus Erstad were both captured by Graff Industries guards, and as I stand here, they're being held captive on the other side of this camp. This's being done on the orders of Maximilian Graff. You all know who he is. This is a warning, gentlemen! They and two other people, who are friends of mine, are about to be murdered, and so are all of you unless you help us rescue these people. We can't do this alone, and we have to move right now! Any questions?"

"We ain't seen you before! How d'we know this ain't some kind o' trick 'n yur really just out t'get us?!" yelled one of the men.

"If that's what you think, then answer me this," said Sal. "If I had the men and arms to get rid of you and intended to do that, why would I have awakened you and exposed myself and these two men to all of you instead of just killing you all as you slept?"

"Then what about the demolition work we was s'pposed to be gettin' ready for this mornin'?" asked another one.

"That was part of an agreement that my associates and I have with Mr. Hahn. Now that he's been taken prisoner, our first priority is to rescue him, Mr. Erstad, and my two associates. Is all this clear to everyone?" He looked out over the small group to see most of their heads nodding in agreement.

After quickly answering a few more questions from the still bleary-eyed group, Sal was surprised to see that they appeared to be coming around. After it looked as if most of them had agreed, he gave them his plan to rescue the captives while being careful to alert them to the risks involved and pointing out that they would be working with Mo and Abe. After his explanation, Sal once again demanded that they affirm their dedication to his plan. He was relieved when, after a couple of holdouts finally gave in, the response was unanimous. The guards threw on their clothes, collected their arms, loaded themselves into their cars, and followed Sal and his two compatriots toward the subterranean facility where Abe had been tortured, the likeliest location to find Anna, Eva, Oscar, and Gus.

The small caravan traveled cautiously beyond the open area containing the barracks and garages before heading into the stretch of cleared forest leading to their destination. Seeing the area just ahead, they all came to a halt before reaching the clearing. Between them and the ramp were the two cars Anna had immobilized during Abe's rescue. Just beyond them, at the top corner of the slope facing the facility's two large doors, sat the limousine Sal had seen earlier in his rearview mirror. From where he sat, Sal was just able to make out the back of the driver's head.

Sal then motioned to the others to quietly leave their cars and follow him stealthily through the forest next to them. Suddenly Sal signaled everyone to stop and fall to the ground. He saw one of the large doors on the subterranean facility open slowly before a well-dressed man having a deformed foot emerge and begin an agitated, awkward trek up the slope towards the limousine. At the same time, he saw four guards making their way up the other side of the ramp followed by Gunther who was the last one to the top. The well-dressed man shouted a final order to Gunther before getting into his limousine. Sal then watched as the other five men walked towards the mound covered in thick, waist-high shrubs.

Sliding on his stomach over to Abe, who was closest to him, he whispered his marching orders. "Neutralize that driver in the big car and the man in the back seat, who must be Maximilian Graff. Use those two disabled cars to get close to the limousine without being detected then wait for my signal. When you hear my order, make your move on the car. Got it?" Abe nodded as Sal quietly made his way over to Mo and the other men.

"Here's what we're gonna do," said Sal quietly. "Pass this along to anyone who can't hear my voice." After hearing Sal's directions, the men nodded before several briefed the others who had been out of earshot. When everyone was ready, Sal motioned the group to prepare for their assault by lining up along the edge of the forest. Everything was ready when Sal saw that the five men on the mound were putting on what appeared to be gas masks. Then two of them bent over below the tops of the shrubs covering the mound. While he was unable to make out what the men were doing, he had been able to hear the final orders Maximilian shouted to Gunther about the disposing of bodies. To Sal, this, together with the appearance of the gas masks and the men's standing over the subterranean room, spelled certain death for everyone trapped below. Seeing that Abe had positioned himself behind the derelict car nearest the limousine, he yelled, "Go!"

Instantly, Abe jumped up, drew his pistol, ran up to the driver's door and yanked it open. As the driver struggled to grab his pistol, Abe put the gun to the man's temple and shouted, "Don't do nothin'!" Then he saw Maximilian reach for a pistol in his shoulder holster. Abe immediately shot the driver in the head and, as Maximilian swung out his arm to aim his pistol, Abe shot him in the shoulder, causing him to misfire and graze Abe's temple before yelling and slumping down on the seat in pain. Abe, bleeding profusely from his shallow head wound, threw open the rear door, grabbed Maximilian's pistol and held him at gunpoint. "You ain't doin' nothin' or goin' nowhere!"

At the same time that Abe was subduing Maximilian and his driver, Sal, Mo, and the Silver Swords had drawn their pistols and were rushing the men standing among the shrubs. Caught off guard and struggling to remove their face masks, Gunther and his men were slightly delayed pulling out their weapons and aiming them at the onrushing insurgents. In a burst of gunfire, both sides shot at one another wildly, with Sal, Mo, and the Silver Swords bringing down Gunther and all of his men while losing one of their own.

As silence and smoke filled the void left by the gunfire, Sal was the first to reach Gunther and his men. Still aiming his pistol at the men on the ground as he approached, he kicked their weapons away and knelt to determine who had survived. It quickly became apparent that the men who had been shot were all dead, while Abe signaled that Maximilian's car was secured.

Just then, Sal was hit by fumes emanating from the opened canister's contents that he suddenly realized surrounded him—the pellets had been strewn all over the ground when the man holding the open can had been hit. The gas was rapidly scorching his skin, eyes, nose, and throat as he began to hyperventilate. He immediately grabbed the gas mask sitting on the ground next to the nearest corpse and pulled it over his face. Yelling for his men to run from the area, he grabbed two more gas masks next to the bodies closest to him, dashed over to the ramp, and ran down to the entrance.

As he broke open one of the doors, he desperately hoped he wasn't too late for Anna and Eva. Once inside, he saw a small pile of the pellets on the floor near the center of the room. Bound to their seats about ten feet away, Oscar and Gus were already yelling that the gas was burning them. While Anna and Eva were farther away from the pellets, Sal knew it would be a matter of seconds before they were afflicted. He dashed over to the two women, put masks on them, and undid their bonds. He then ran over to the other two who were now writhing in pain and released their hands, enabling them to follow Anna and Eva, who had already rushed outside. As soon as Oscar and Gus passed through the partially opened door, they fell to the ground, gasping for air. The last one through the door, Sal pushed it closed to prevent any more of the fatal gas from escaping.

Once Anna and Eva removed their masks, Anna comforted Sal that they both were unharmed. Satisfied that the two women were all right, Sal turned to one of the Silver Swords and shouted, "Call for ambulances and the police!" The man immediately left to summon help as Sal went over to Oscar and Gus, who were both face up and breathing very heavily. Sal knew that if he'd spent the time to locate two more masks, they would probably not be breathing at all.

By this time, Anna and Eva were walking up the ramp when Anna saw Abe standing in the limousine's open driver's door, still aiming his pistol at the person who had collapsed on the back seat. Holding the side of his forehead with his other hand, blood was streaming between his fingers, down his shoulder, and onto his chest. Running over to him, she reached into the cab, grabbed Maximilian's suede gloves, gently pulled Abe's hand away, and pressed them hard against the big man's head.

"Here, Abe. Hold these tightly. They'll help stanch the blood flow. Do you feel dizzy or light-headed?"

"I'm good," he replied.

"Considering that you're still conscious and able to hold Graff at bay, that wound must be superficial. Just hold those gloves firmly until the ambulances arrive and you should be fine." Anna was about to return to Eva when she heard something she did not expect from Abe.

"Thanks, Mizz Tilner. I ain't been helped by no woman b'fore. Never. Now, don't ya worry, I'll just keep this bastard pinned til the cops get here."

"You're very welcome, Abe. I have to hand it to you, considering the hell you've been through the last few days, I'm surprised you're up and around, let alone getting the best of Graff and his driver. You're a very strong man. We're all grateful for what you and Mo've done here. I'll never forget the two of you."

After she noticed a grin form on Abe's face, she turned to walk away when she heard something she had come to know, Abe's barely audible grunt. "That's also something I'll remember you by," she thought as she walked toward Eva.

Anna knew that Eva had been terrorized by the experience. As she reached over to take Eva's hand gently, she immediately felt Eva's entire body trembling, prompting her to remember that Eva's particular synesthesia would physically impact her whenever she witnessed violence. Anna had a difficult time imagining what torture Eva must have experienced over the past hour. She felt her eyes filling with tears that such an innocent soul should have to endure the torture caused by the malevolent acts of others who were so far from being innocent.

It was over an hour before several ambulances and the local police arrived, and by that time, Maximilian had lost consciousness. He, Abe, Oscar, Gus, and the dead men were all then loaded into ambulances with Mo accompanying Abe. As the ambulances drove away, the police continued to interview those remaining at the site. Waiting for his turn, Sal looked at Anna and Eva and shuddered to think that only his quick reactions had stood between them and their certain deaths. Anna, on the other hand, was disturbed that of all the casualties, three of the survivors were the men most directly responsible for the existence of this nightmare called Eingang.

As the police cordoned off the entire area as a crime scene, Anna and Sal took the lead in explaining to two detectives what had happened. Astonished by what they were hearing, the detectives knew that the area would soon be crawling with federal officers. They consumed another hour interviewing all the witnesses while some of the police donned gas masks and investigated the interior of the subterranean facility. When the detectives approached Eva, Anna told them that she had been traumatized so severely that she would be an unreliable witness until she had been able to recover.

Anna then explained her association with the legendary Tilner and Associates law firm and informed the senior officer that she would be informing the Department of Justice of the existence of the facility so they could take the appropriate actions. After radioing the police dispatch office and confirming Anna's credentials, the lead detective left to wrap up his initial investigation.

Before calling the DOJ, however, Anna knew there was someone else who needed to have his mind put at ease that she had come through unscathed. Her husband would be beside himself when he learned what had happened, but she knew this would ultimately surrender to the relief of knowing that his wife and her friends were unharmed and that the threat was finally over. Since telephones had not yet been installed at Eingang, this conversation would have to wait until they returned to Eric's house, only a short drive away.

After helping Eva into the car to return to Eric's house with Sal, Anna pulled Sal aside and asked him to call Malcolm to tell him that she and Eva were fine.

"Aren't you going to call him?!"

"I will when I join you and Eva at Eric's place."

"What?! Why aren't you coming with us?!"

"Don't worry. There's something I need to look into. I'll be there very shortly. I'll get a ride with one of Gus's men."

"What the hell'm I going to say to Malcolm?"

"Why don't you tell him that now that Maximilian and his creatures have been taken into custody, I'm looking for something that'll help ensure that nothing like this ever happens in America again. Just reassure him that I'll call the second I get to Eric's."

"That's it?! That's what you want me to tell him?"

"There's still something out here that I don't want disappearing before I can confirm its existence."

"Why all the mystery, Anna? Why can't I tell him what you're after?"

"After what you will've just told him, it'd worry him to death." This did not make Sal feel any better about the conversation he would be having with Malcolm.

It was sometime later before the police cars and ambulances finally left the site. After one of the Silver Swords agreed to return Anna to Eric's house, he joined the rest of his crew who were returning to their barracks to wrestle with what to do next.

Anna was finally alone and scanned the area surrounding the subterranean facility. She was dreading the very thing she was searching for, almost hoping she would never find it but now certain that she would. As she looked over at the clearing in the woods separating the subterranean facility area from the rest of the compound, she saw the lone caterpillar tractor that had been left behind after the land had been graded.

After walking over to it, she went up to the front blade and treads to inspect them. Several minutes later, she began following the tractor's tracks into the far woods where a narrow path the width of the tractor had been cleared. She judged she had been walking about one hundred feet along the path before she came to another smaller clearing in the woods. Walking to the middle of it, she stopped and looked down as her eyes widened. After taking in a deep breath, she slowly released it, billowing her cheeks as the hot breath brushed over her lips. It was time to return to Eric's house. Her darkest suspicion had been confirmed.

63

In his silent trip back to Eric's with Eva, Sal had worked himself into a lather. He had become infuriated with the senseless violence that Maximilian had brought down on all of them. He was particularly upset as he tried to comprehend what a terrorizing experience that morning must have been for Eva. The more he thought about it, the angrier he became that such malevolence could be visited on such an innocent person.

Pulling up and stopping in front of Eric's house, Sal walked around the car to open Eva's door. As he helped her out of the car, he held both her hands, and said, "I can't imagine what you've been going through, Eva. This morning your gifts were nothing but a curse for you. I don't know how you deal with it."

As Eva looked into his eyes, she gave his hands a gentle squeeze. Taken aback, Sal paused before saying softly, "I can't believe this! After all the trauma you've gone through over the past few hours! You're the innocent one who felt everyone's pain in a way the rest of us can only try to imagine, and here you are trying to comfort me?!" After several seconds, Sal added, "Eva, I've never said this to anyone before, but to me, you're...you're as close to an angel as I can imagine. If there were more people like you, this world would be a much better place." After a few more seconds, they both turned and silently walked into Eric's home.

A half hour later, one of Gus's men dropped off Anna at Eric's and she went inside. She was not looking forward to the call she was about to make to Malcolm and knew it would, if anything, be more difficult for the person at the other end of the line. She went into Eric's study and quietly shut the door.

After the twenty minute conversation, she was barely aware of sitting in the study as she slowly put the telephone back on its cradle.

Malcolm had made it clear how disturbed he had been until he heard from Sal, and she felt consumed by a mixture of sadness and regret. She resolved that in the future, she would resist getting involved in any more dangerous adventures. It was simply too emotionally difficult for her husband and their happiness together.

For the moment, however, her personal needs were eclipsed by a larger one. She needed to eliminate once and for all the evil that had nearly ended her and Eva's lives while threatening untold numbers of others. Despite the rabid curiosity of Malcolm, Sal, and Eric, her next move was to check in on Eva to see how she was doing. Before she could even walk the short distance to Eva's room, however, the phone rang, and Eric found her to say that the call was urgent and for her. It was Richard Cohen, the young aide for the assistant attorney general she had last met at Boston Common near her office.

"Why, Richard, what a shock! I was going to give you a call later today," said Anna before she launched into describing what had just taken place at Eingang. At several points during her explanation, it was clear from the shallow gasps coming from the other end of the line that Richard was horrified at what had been transpiring on Long Island. He was also curious how a person who just a few hours before had been bound and facing a grim execution could sound so remarkably calm. Anna finished her story by giving him directions to Eingang.

"Now that you're aware of this and where it is, please alert the right people at your office so that the justice department can immediately begin an in-depth investigation of this Eingang facility. To facilitate this, once the brief's completed, my firm will send a copy to the Department of Justice to assist in its preparation of filing federal actions against Maximilian Graff. He'll be leaving the hospital in chains. Now then, you called me, Richard."

He thought Anna's story was a perfect segue for the news he had called to give her.

"My, that's one hell of an ordeal you and your friends've been through, Anna. It sounds as if you headed off an unthinkable nightmare. As soon as we hang up, I'll get the ball rolling at my end. But before I do, let me get to the reason for my call. Remember how I told you that a couple of my family members were well connected and responsible for getting me my job as an aide to Assistant Attorney General Gorman?"

"Yes, I recall," she replied.

"Well, one of them has just been added to the group designing the newly created Executive Office of the President for FDR. After I received that threatening phone call that made you ask me to drop any inquiries I was making, I was so angry with the anonymous threat that I decided not to take your advice."

"Oh, really?"

"Yes. I went to my uncle and asked him if he could quietly determine why our government was being so reluctant to crack down on certain domestic fascist, Nazi, and white supremacy organizations. What he told me was terrifying and disheartening. The bottom line is that a sizable group of powerful American and German industrialists've banded together in a variety of relationships to protect and enhance the dominance of their industries. They have done so to assure their enhanced profitability if we enter the war, apparently something FDR privately believes is increasingly likely."

"Do you have any idea who these people are who can pull such weight?"

"In some cases, yes. My uncle told me about people either heading or acting at senior levels within JP Morgan, the DuPont Corporation, which controls GM, Andrew Mellon, the Rockefellers, and Ford, to name a few. Together they either control or have significant influence over many of the world's largest vehicle manufacturers, banks, and oil, rubber, and chemical corporations. Also, some've acquired foreign companies, such as GM buying Adam Opel, Germany's largest car manufacturer, to profit from the war they know is coming. They've also created American subsidiaries of large German companies and formed cartels with them, such as GM and Standard Oil with IG Farben. They're doing all this to maintain control of the major resources necessary to wage war. As an example, he told me that GM and Standard Oil created a joint subsidiary with Farben to use American expertise to create a special synthetic fuel without which the mechanized Nazi war machine would barely be able to function at all."

"So how do all of these powerful, entangled alliances relate to our domestic Nazi and white supremacy groups?"

"Well, it turns out that the most powerful of these domestic extremist organizations have obtained their funding from the very same people who, eyeing the profits that come with war, have created these ties with one another and huge German industries."

"I see," said Anna. "So, what you're saying is that it's not enough for these people to generate immense profits from selling to both sides enough equipment and arms to decimate one another, thereby assuring that they end up on the winning side regardless of who is victorious. In addition, since they largely control our country's ability to wage war, they are holding this over the head of the federal government to serve other purposes—namely, forcing the feds to look the other way when it comes to clamping down on their pet Nazi-sympathizing and racially-violent organizations—basic extortion. Is that about it?"

"One other thing. It seems that some of these same industrialists support such violent organizations so that they can use them to bust up labor unions or discourage their many thousands of workers from joining them. It's all pretty ruthless, Machiavellian actually, if you ask me."

"That would certainly explain why the feds hound some of these radical organizations while others are left alone."

"Correct."

"This is very disturbing and could spell real trouble if and when we go to war."

"Yes, it could."

"All I can say is that I'm grateful that you've been able to uncover this information and that you've shared it with me. I'm not convinced there's anything to be done about this at present, but it certainly shows how politics and industry facing potentially profitable and catastrophic war can create dangerous bedfellows. Thanks again, Richard. I very much appreciate all your help."

As soon as she hung up the phone, Anna shook her head and then continued her walk to Eva's room to see how she was feeling. After gently knocking on the door, she entered to see Eva sitting in a chair looking out a window. As soon as she entered the room, Eva turned to see her, stood, and walked up and hugged her. Anna was gratified at this unusual expression of affection but was not surprised that their harrowing experience earlier in the day could have inspired such strong feelings in the young woman.

"My dear Eva. How are you feeling now? Are you calm enough to tell me what you saw inside Maximilian Graff?"

Eva sat down and reached out to Anna to sit in the adjacent chair, which she did. What ensued Anna found to be devastating.

64

"This suspense is unbearable!" admitted Sal as he and Eric sat in the living room waiting for Anna and Eva to join them. "And what on earth could Anna've seen at Eingang after we left that she found so disturbing? It'd be very unlike her, but I just hope she's not overly dramatizing all this. It's bad enough as it is. I simply can't..." He stopped mid-sentence the second he caught sight of Eva as she entered the room ahead of Anna and sat on the sofa next to Eric. To Sal, Anna appeared to be somewhere else as she walked stiffly into the room and sat down next to Eva. She seemed to be still wrestling with what Eva had just told her.

" I'm sorry for leaving you all hanging for so long, but before I met with Eva, there were several missing pieces to this puzzle. I was hoping she could complete it for me before I sat down to give you my conclusions about what we just endured and what it all means. As expected, she's been invaluable—nothing short of brilliant.

"As you may remember, about a year ago Maximilian Graff was able to buy his way into a dinner honoring Charles Lindberg that the Nazis held in Berlin. Lindberg was receiving a medal from them for his services to world aviation that was awarded by Hermann Göring, the second most powerful man in Germany.

"At this dinner, Graff had a conversation with Göring that convinced him that it would be to his benefit to help the Germans. Göring told him that Germany was making great progress toward the development of a super bomb, something that Eva enabled us to understand is false. To Graff, this meant that Germany was virtually certain to win the war that he sees as inevitable. Accordingly, he needed to assure himself of a position in the Third Reich in America to safeguard his wealth and social position.

"This appears to be similar to a deadly game some other powerful American industrialists are playing to assure the security of their industrial dominance and enhance their wealth. A short while ago, I learned from Richard Cohen, the senior aide to Assistant US Attorney General Eric Gorman, that this's been going on for some time.

"Now back to Graff. To impress the Nazis with his dedication and support for their upcoming victory, he created Eingang. He designed this hellish place to achieve several objectives. Sal, you told me that when you first saw Eingang, it looked as if it were something the US military might build. Well, it wasn't our military that built it, but it was indeed intended for a military purpose. You remember all those barracks and vehicle garages and the road leading to the beach?" Sal nodded. "Those things were exactly what you thought they were except for one thing. Graff designed Eingang to house and support an initial Nazi reconnaissance force, hence its German name. As you'll remember, Eingang means 'entrance' or 'gateway.'

"Then there were the mysterious buildings filled with what looked like medical equipment. Well, that wasn't exactly their purpose. Instead, this was to be where Jews, blacks, criminals of the state, mentally-retarded people, and any person deemed undesirable in the Nazi mind, would be experimented upon, sterilized, or murdered in the interests of creating the Nazi super race."

At this point, Eric became visibly upset as he thought of his wife, Sarah, whose fears of the Nazi capture and annihilation of her siblings led to her suicide. Unable to contain himself, he interrupted Anna's explanation. "That simply can't happen here! It just can't be allowed to happen here!" he said imploringly.

"I'm sorry, Eric. I realize how horrible it is for you to hear this, but it has already happened here."

"What?!" exclaimed both Sal and Eric.

"Sal, after you left me behind at Eingang, I walked over to the tractor that was left behind despite the entire site having been developed. On its blade, I saw evidence of something I had feared from the beginning."

"And that was?" queried Sal.

"Lye. I followed the tracks of the tractor to another clearing in the forest not far from the underground facility where, without you Sal, Eva's and my life would have ended horribly. In this other clearing, there was a pit dug out by the tractor. It was to hold the dead bodies of people who Maximilian intended to murder in that gas chamber."

"But surely that never happened!" said Eric feebly.

"Tragically, Eva enabled me to understand that Graff had already begun testing his deadly machine. He rounded up several dozen blacks and Jews from the poorest neighborhoods in New York City and gassed them before throwing their bodies into a large pit and covering them with lye. It seems that he planned to repeat this until the layered bodies filled the pit. Then, as the bodies began to pile up, I suppose he'd dig additional pits using the tractor."

"My God!" exclaimed Sal. "This is all horrific! How did Graff get away with kidnapping all those people?"

"Eva's perception was that he had ordered Gunther Gundshau to offer work to people in the poorest neighborhoods who remain largely invisible to the rest of the city. By the time any of these poor wretches knew any better, if they were even able to figure it out at all, they were in the gas chamber, and it was too late."

"But all this is so ghoulish and so elaborate. Why the Zyklon B, the gas chamber, the tractor, the pit, and so on?! Why didn't Graff just shoot the poor bastards?! Wouldn't it've been quicker and easier than going through all this other rigmarole?"

"Eva didn't see anything about that, but I expect that the sound of guns going off all the time would sooner or later alert authorities that this wasn't just pheasant or deer hunting, especially with the large berm surrounding the mysterious place. Besides, Graff knew pesticides intimately and had to've been aware that this particular one, Zyklon, had been used in the Great War as a weapon to kill people. This later version, Zyklon B, is more advanced, if I can even use that word, to murder people more efficiently."

"This is all too painful for me. It's simply beyond my comprehension," lamented Eric.

"I couldn't agree more!" said Sal. "This Maximilian Graff is a grotesque monster! This plan of his was evil. Now that he's caught, I'm sure our justice system won't be forgiving."

"As hard as it may be to believe, Graff's plan was even worse," added Anna.

"Worse?!" exclaimed Sal. "How could it possibly be any worse than grabbing innocent people off the street, gassing them to death, and then throwing them in a pit while creating a convenient little entrance and barracks for the Nazis to invade America?!"

Anna continued. "Eva was able to see that part of Graff's plan was to assassinate the president, which would assist the Nazi's invasion by throwing the government into chaos."

"You're not serious!" exclaimed Sal as Eric lowered and shook his head.

"I'm afraid I am," responded Anna.

"And who in the hell was he going to trust to do that? He sure couldn't have done it himself," said Sal angrily.

"He was trusting Gunther Gundshau to do that."

"Who is this Gundshau character, anyway?" asked Sal. "Didn't Graff trust Oscar and Gus to do his dirty work?"

"Eva saw that Oscar, Gus, and the Silver Swords were intended only to oversee and assist the development of Eingang and when it was finished, they were always going to be quietly murdered and disposed of there. In Graff's mind, this would ensure that whatever they knew about Eingang would be buried with them."

"So what makes Gunther Gundshau the anointed one?"

"Because Gundshau is Maximilian Graff's son.

"What?! His son!? My God!" exclaimed Eric.

"Illegitimate apparently, but his son nonetheless. Graff must have rejected his hulking son much as his father had rejected him, even depriving him of a proper education. Only when Graff needed someone whom he could trust absolutely to keep Eingang's darkest secrets was he forced to give his bastard son a chance to be useful. It's indicative of the man's delusional sense of domination that he felt he could trust someone so completely whom he'd abused for so long."

"Did Eva see this, too?!" asked Eric.

"Yes, I'm afraid she did. Without her, we wouldn't know most of this."

"Don't tell me she saw anything more, Anna. This is all simply too horrific to believe!" said Eric with a profound sadness weighing down his voice.

"It pains me to say this, but, unfortunately, there's one more thing."

"Graff is secretly a German!" blurted Sal.

"No, Sal, no. He's an American, all right. However, he's also Jewish."

"What the hell?! You can't be serious!" exclaimed Eric, his curse signaling the depth of his horror. Sal was speechless.

"Eva was able to once again look to her background as a black woman in the South together with her prior experience with Dr. Roster, the Jewish psychiatrist who first evaluated her, and then with Dr. Loh. She was able to use these concepts to understand what being Jewish means, which enabled her to see that Maximilian's father was partly Jewish. It seems that he had learned this as a child from his mother before Maximilian's father inadvertently killed her."

"My God," said Eric with profound sadness. "Then why on earth would he support the Nazis who've already been so unthinkably cruel to the Jews?"

"Piecing this together from what Eva gave me, it appears that Graff's hatred for Jews, despite his being partly Jewish himself, was deeply ingrained in his family. It was all made worse by his father's complete rejection of him, and the father's belief in a conspiracy that Jews had always been responsible for his family's financial failures. Michael Rudman's sudden departure and the Graffs' ensuing decline were simply more evidence of this plot to ruin him. Worst of all, this hatred seems to have spiked the day his father unintentionally killed his mother, someone Graff had always loved deeply. I'm speculating, but perhaps over time, every aspect of his father became a generalized object of hatred that continues to fester in Graff's soul."

Once Anna finished sharing what Eva had seen together with her own thoughts, the room fell silent. The listeners were mulling over the events of the prior twenty-four hours in light of what they had just heard. Several minutes went by before anyone said anything. Eric was the first to break the silence.

"Think of all these various groups of poisonous people we've been discussing—they're all rich, powerful, fascistic, unthinkably cruel, selfish people who're all kneeling at their altars to worship their particular gods of hatred and greed. Now, I'm struck by a stunning irony."

"What's that, Eric?" asked Sal.

"Here we are, we've just witnessed firsthand the elaborate, obsessed creation of a powerful, deranged person. He was not only hell-bent on using his awful might to create a torturous killing machine, but he was also determined to catalyze a potential national catastrophe. In so doing, he sought to feed his deepest hatreds by killing countless thousands, and yet, in a matter of hours, it's all been destroyed. And what colossal force was it that was able to accomplish this remarkable feat?"

Eric then stared at Anna and Eva. "I'm so ashamed to admit that when we first met, I was so inclined to underestimate both of you so profoundly. Now having lived with your gifts and courage over the past weeks, I'm in awe of you both. Lacking any of the elaborate machinery and resources of power wielded by Maximilian Graff, together, you were able to cause his downfall. To me, this's nothing short of a miracle for which this country will always be in your debt."

"I'd make one clarification," added Anna. Turning to Eva and smiling warmly, she said, "Without this young woman's miraculous ability to see what the rest of us can't, this would never've occurred. I'm humbled that such brilliance is in the soul of someone so utterly innocent and benevolent. All of us are indebted to you, Eva. For her selfless, heroic, and indispensable help, I'm working with our other Tilner partners to set up a generous fund to assist her and her family."

At this point, everyone but Eva was wondering the same thing. Was this seemingly simple miracle of nature, always having lived in the humblest of circumstances and deprived of any formal education, truly comprehending the profound admiration and support that Anna and Eric had intended to convey to her?

As it usually happened with Eva, the answer came quietly. She turned first to Anna, then Eric and Sal, while extending her hands to each, giving them a gentle squeeze. Having seen it before, Anna wondered if Eric had been able to notice Eva's endearing way of indicating that she understood—her almost imperceptible smile.

# # # #

About Renney Senn

Renney's first experience with writing outside a classroom began when he founded and edited what is today the official university newspaper for the University of California at San Diego. After a rewarding career as an entrepreneur in a variety of manufacturing and technology industries, he wrote a manuscript (unpublished for the present) about the outrageous, true story of one of his startups. Encouraged by the result, he has now completed his third historical novel, *Cathedrals of Venom*, in the Mystery and Thriller genre. His first novel, *The Turncoat*, and his second, *Hidden Insight*, are available in both eBook and paperback editions.

Connect with Renney Senn

Thank you for reading *Cathedrals of Venom*. I am grateful for your entering its world and trust you feel the time was well-spent. If so, I would greatly appreciate your writing a brief review on Amazon. Here is the link to do so:

https://www.amazon.com/Cathedrals-Venom-Renney-Senn/dp/B088T7TCR3#customerReviews

Thank you for helping other people to determine if this would be a worthwhile read for them.

Should you wish to reach me, my Facebook page for *Cathedrals of Venom* is:

Renneysenn3

Made in the USA
Coppell, TX
30 June 2020